MISTLETOE AND MAGNOLIA

A MAGNOLIA BLOOM NOVEL BOOK 2

PAULA ADLER

DRAGON DREAMS PRESS, LLC

Mistletoe and Magnolia, a Magnolia Bloom Novel Book 2

Copyright © 2020 by Dragon Dreams Press, LLC

All Rights Reserved

This book is a work of fiction. Any names, characters, companies, organizations, places, events, locales, and incidents are either used in a fictitious manner or are fictional. Any resemblance to actual persons, living or dead, actual companies or organizations, is purely coincidental. No part of this publication may be reproduced, stored in or introduced into a retrieval system, or transmitted, in any form, or by any means. For permission, contact the author at Paula@PaulaAdler.com

ISBN – 9781951282042 (e-book)

ISBN – 9781951282127 (paperback)

ISBN – 9781951282080 (audio)

ISBN – 9781951282134 (hardback)

ISBN – 9781951282226 (large print)

LCCN – pending

Cover Design by Hang Le

Copyedit by Joyce Lamb

MAGNOLIA BLOOM, in order
Springtime in Magnolia Bloom (Coming March 2021)
Mistletoe and Magnolia (Book 2)
Return to Magnolia Bloom (Book 1)
Welcome to Magnolia Bloom (Origin novella)

I hope you enjoy MISTLETOE AND MAGNOLIA, Book 2 in the Magnolia Bloom series. If you missed Paige's story in
RETURN TO MAGNOLIA BLOOM, please visit Amazon.com

I'd be honored if you'd consider leaving a review on your favorite sites (Amazon, Goodreads, BookBub). It's the most amazing thing you can do to help other people find my books.

Please sign up for my newsletter at PaulaAdler.com or email me at Paula@PaulaAdler.com to receive my next free novella, updates, and information on all future releases.

To Tracie—
The most amazing partner in writing crime anyone could dream of! I can't imagine doing this without you.

Praise for *MAGNOLIA BLOOM*

I can't recommend this entire series enough. By the end, you'll be wanting to visit Magnolia Bloom and rub Penny the Dragon's nose and cuddle with the adorable sheep, Lulu. ~ Penny, Amazon Review

Hallmark Holidays at the Castle, Halloween through Christmas. I would love for PBS to make a mini-series of this series so I could binge watch it! The overall story arc brings many generations together, many secrets become exposed and pain gets soothed and healed. This is an awesome series. ~ GranJan, Amazon review

Strong women and community; struggling together when necessary. Groundbreaking, unhindered my race, gender or religious affiliation. A strong and proud testimony to the human spirit. ~ Molly, Amazon review

Wonderful writing. I couldn't put it down. Highly recommend. ~ Bestselling author Dee Davis

"Deeply emotional and richly imagined, the world of Magnolia Bloom is a universe that captured me and wouldn't let go, long after I turned the final page." ~ New York Times and USA Today Bestselling author Jean Brashear

Paula Adler gifts us with a multi-generational family saga that combines romance, heartbreak, an honest-to-goodness Texas castle, travels to exotic locales and a cast of characters who'll grab your heart and not let go. The love gluing the MacInnes family together shines through on every page, even when they're dealing with the pain all families experience. So pour a cup or a glass, snuggle into your favorite chair and prepare to become an instant member of the clan! ~ Bestselling author Merline Lovelace

I wanna read more! ~ ElizrdbthSpeaks, Amazon review

Checks many boxes, contemporary, romance, historical, family saga, southern Literature, and women's fiction. ALL OF MY favorites I will seek out Paula Adler from here on out. ~ Natalie F., Amazon review

Get nice and comfortable, (you) won't want to put the book down. ~ Sofe, Amazon Review

Can't wait [to] continue the saga. ~ Lisa G., Amazon review

It pulls you in and keeps you wanting more. ~ Sasha, Goodreads review

CONTENTS

1. Kiki — 1
2. Fina — 11
3. Kiki — 19
4. Juliette — 29
5. Kiki — 38
6. Fina — 46
7. Kiki — 53
8. Juliette — 63
9. Kiki — 76
10. Fina — 84
11. Kiki — 93
12. Juliette — 106
13. Kiki — 113
14. Fina — 125
15. Kiki — 130
16. Juliette — 136
17. Kiki — 145
18. Fina — 151
19. Kiki — 163
20. Juliette — 171
21. Kiki — 178
22. Fina — 184
23. Kiki — 190
24. Juliette — 199
25. Kiki — 206
26. Fina — 213
27. Kiki — 218
28. Juliette — 223
29. Kiki — 230
30. Fina — 240
31. Kiki — 244
32. Juliette — 248

33. Fina	255
34. Kiki	259
35. Juliette	268
36. Kiki	275
37. Kiki	281
About the Author	289

1
KIKI

For the record, I followed the directions to addiction recovery with GPS perfection. *Just go straight to hell and make a U-turn.* While the mushroom cloud has cleared from my field of vision, I can still see flames in my rearview mirror.

And I have one person to blame for my monumentally messed-up life.

Me.

Well, me and my charming frenemy, vodka. In the not-too-recent past, I could have changed my middle name to Tito's. Grey Goose would have been more accurate, and I might have passed it off as a cool call sign if I'd been an aviator instead of a public affairs officer. Turns out, the United States Air Force doesn't play games with DUIs, and they're not called career killers for nothing.

If there's one good thing about said event happening with my superior officer in the car, it's when said officer is related to a very powerful family who made sure the DUI turned into running a red light. I neither asked for nor deserved the reprieve from my bad decision-making, but the family's intervention had nothing to do with helping me and everything to do with protecting their handsome, future politician. His image in DC is informed by his current officer trajectory, so to no one's surprise, I was... invited to separate from the only career I've ever had or wanted.

While the events in question aren't late-night monologue-worthy, I, Major Rebecca "Kiki" MacInnes, was the disposable one in this scenario.

Which is the short version of the long story of why I'm on a balcony spanning the North and East Turrets of Castle MacInnes outside of Magnolia Bloom, Texas.

The sound of the double doors to my left opening interrupts my stroll down memory lane, and I still have to blink to remind myself I'm truly living here now. At the moment, my coffee and I are waiting for the sun to rise and beat up the currently pleasant temperature of sixty-four degrees. The low sixties might not qualify as fall in most places, but in East Texas, October temperatures were often a Yahtzee throw whether it would be sweaters or flip-flops... or both. We had many Halloweens either sweating behind our plastic masks or vying for a Michelin Man ad in puffy coats.

"Hey, Traycee. Have a seat." With a wave of my hand, I invite my new friend and ally to join me. The beautiful wrought-iron table between us has borne witness to many sunrise breakfasts and heart-felt conversations over the decades. If roughly twenty-five years is used to calculate a generation, this table has hosted six since it was brought from Galveston when my ancestors Evajean and Alisdair MacInnes established Magnolia Bloom. I'm sure it's heard more salacious dialogue than will be provided this morning, but maybe the castle ghosts will forgive me for preferring boring-but-sober over titillating these days.

"I couldn't resist the invite, even if this is crazy-early."

I check my watch to see it's already seven, as sunshine is not an accurate indicator of time in Alaska, my most recent, and final, duty station. I haven't reacclimated to my home state yet, either in time or temperature.

I give my head a wobble. "Early's relative, but my relationship with mornings is best described as 'there appears to have been a struggle.'"

"I hear you." She settles in and puts down her travel mug bearing the stylized MBE logo of her store, the Magnolia Bloom Emporium. She looks effortlessly comfortable in black leggings and a T-shirt positing the question "Surely Not Everyone Was Kung Fu Fighting?"

I rest against the high back of the rocker. "For the last fifteen years, I've either crawled out of bed at an ungodly hour, or didn't go in until the middle of the afternoon but stayed up all night. Add in my last assignment, and the Alaskan sun cycle adds a whole 'nother level of why 'daylight hours' is a debatable term."

Traycee's nose-wrinkle eloquently expresses her feelings about the subarctic. "I could handle neither the cold nor the endless-day-and-night thing. The only ice this girl wants is in her tea."

"When I got there in February two years ago, I wondered what fresh hell I'd fallen into. There's a lot of beauty in Alaska, but not, in my opinion, in the dead of winter. Still, I've been away from Texas so long I've forgotten when autumn actually begins in our beloved Lone Star State."

"I guess you've erased all those Halloweens and Thanksgivings in shorts, then. Weather Channel says we're going to have another week of low eighties before we finally stay in the seventies for a while."

"Which is as awful as seeing Christmas displays already going up."

"Eighty-one shopping days left."

It's my turn to grimace. "Of course you know."

"I do. Halloween gets a little more shine, then it and fall-slash-Thanksgiving are relegated to the edges. From here on out, it's all Santa, all the time. The fat guy in the red suit gets all the love in retail."

"I've always been on the purchasing side of this fence until now, so Fina's got her hands full teaching me retail and event calendars. Paige left the office in great shape, but with Mina's wedding on top of everything else, it's a little hectic."

"From what I've heard, it sounds like it's been an entire season of a soap opera around here."

"Not quite, but keeping all the moving parts straight takes a pen and paper sometimes. Aunt Violet was the matriarch of the clan for a long time, and my sister, Paige, felt overwhelmed trying to step in earlier this year, especially if you add in she thought her marriage was over. Mina and Fina aren't blood, but they were Violet's rocks, so they might as well be on our family tree. They were angels to Paige, and now me. Then, add the bonus material of finding out Violet gave up twins for adoption when she was still a teenager, and… whew!"

"You need to write a book about all this someday."

"No literary tomes in my future, thanks, but I'll take you down to meet Juliette soon. She's really sweet. But to wrap up, I don't think we're so different from any other family—"

"With a Scottish castle in East Texas."

"Point to you, but really, is there such a thing as a normal family?"

"Not around here." Her expression's amused with a hint of sadness lagging behind. "All joking aside, I'm really happy for Mina and CT. I've known him for years through our merchant association and think he's a super-nice man, but I didn't see it coming."

"I don't think anyone did, least of all Mina. But he's a doll, and Fina's delighted for her twin, but so much has happened so fast. Losing Violet, finding out she gave her girls Juliette and Noelle up for adoption, Mina getting engaged, end-of-year holidays… I think Fina's only got one nerve left, and it's stretched thin. Which is why I'm determined to get up to speed in record time."

"If there's anything I can do, all you have to do is ask."

"I'll take you up on your offer when I know what to ask for. Now, let's go down to the kennels, since you're really here for puppies and not me."

She laughs, as expected, but wags a finger at me. "Don't count yourself short. I'm here for you *and* puppies."

She stands and slides her oversized sunglasses onto her nose against the already blazing sun. We take our travel mugs with us, and I lead the way through the turret and down the narrow steps depositing us onto the east lawn. The manicured grass extends for some fifty yards down to one of the estate's three docks, places I have hardly had time to visit. If I don't soon, the water will be too cold, and my only choice will be our local hot spring, which isn't a horrible second option.

"Love the hair, by the way." I manage to keep the envy out of my voice at my new friend's style. Today, the not-shaved side of her head is woven in an intricate profusion of cornrow braids, each a surprising variety of colors.

"Spent all day at the shop yesterday. Have the migraine to prove it."

"Worth it, though."

"I'll admit it when the ibuprofen kicks in. Tara can do miracles for you, too, if you give her a chance."

"Soon."

I don't doubt Traycee's sister's talent behind the salon chair. When I'm ready, I'll happily trust her to work her magic on my wavy mess, but I'm still guilty of wearing reg hair. Becoming a regulation breaker doesn't happen in mere months of civilian life, as my color-coordinated closet and hospital-cornered bed will attest. My combined years of ROTC and active duty have me hardwired to French-braid my mop into submission.

If I have to be honest, feeling tucked and together provides the illusion I'll be okay. Someday. Dealing with my separation from the Air Force still brings nightmares, and has been, bar none, the most painful thing I've ever done... sober. Even though I'd been on the wagon for a while, by the time the actual day came to execute the papers, it was a test of my ability to keep from coming unglued and driving straight to the package store before the ink was dry on the last signature.

Traycee scans the quiet scene as we walk, our destination a series of barns and sheds still hidden by a dense copse of pecan trees. "I could get used to this."

"It does seem like a fairy tale, but you know better than anyone the business side of running something this massive takes away a little of the patina."

"I'd hardly call the Emporium massive, but it's like the folks who tell me they want to be their own boss so they can take time off whenever they want."

I cut her a side glance. "Do you bother to tell them how idiotic they sound?"

"Nah, they wouldn't believe I haven't had a vacation day in three years, or how glamorous it is to unload and tag stock."

I've been in a business position for only a few weeks, but I already know to roll my eyes. "Oh, yeah, all that free time when you're self-employed."

A quietness settles over Traycee, but I don't interrupt the moment. I'm happy to be outside in the sunshine and know the peace invites the mind to wander. I was a little shocked the first time she walked into an AA meeting over in Atlanta. I mean, I know there addicts in Magnolia Bloom, but I didn't peg Traycee as one of us in the few times I met her. We've become fast friends and traveling buddies since Atlanta and Texarkana are the closest places for us to attend in-person meetings.

Her steps slow to a halt, and she turns to look at the castle. Our beautiful Scottish anachronism looks straight out of a postcard with the morning sun striking the bluish-green schist stone Evajean MacInnes had shipped from both her and her husband's ancestral homeland to complete her project. It took years, of course, but Evajean and Alisdair created something magical here. Something allowing a determined woman to soar at a time no one believed a female could be an amazing architect. Evajean and the groves also healed Alisdair's lonely and wounded soul, so the magic is hardly one-sided.

The first generation of American MacInneses began a legacy, establishing the mind-set that it doesn't matter what's happened in the past, you can make your future anything you wish it to be.

"I hope so."

"You hope what?"

I didn't realize I whispered my prayer aloud and feel the blood rush to my Scottish-white cheeks. "That I can live up to the MacInnes legacy. I'm not so sure most days."

She hooks her arm around mine and starts us walking again, the dry grass crunching under our shoes. "You gonna be fine, girlfriend, if you keep showing up."

"So they tell us."

"Paige believes in you. Fina and Mina." She stops again and takes her arm back, but puts a hand on my sleeve. "Me."

I cover her fingers, then break the contact. Her gregarious nature and generosity are sweet, but still hard for me sometimes. I'm not used to it. Not Traycee in particular. I'm not used to anyone looking at me with such kind concern, and it makes me itch to get back to my project car waiting in the extra stall in the mechanical garage. It's where I usually head for solitude, letting the 1962 Ford Fairlane I bought at an auction keep me absorbed and out of trouble. It's going to take a lot of TLC to get her in shape again, but that's what project cars are for. It's a far cry from the Porsche 911 I'm driving now. She took me nearly three years to restore.

Sensing my tension, Traycee changes the subject. "I miss Violet so much. She'd ask me over to pick up her latest quilts for the shop, but I know it was an excuse to give me a break from town. This is the first time I've been here without her."

Pain squeezes my heart. I now occupy the suite Violet lived in for almost fifty years. My older-by-a-decade sister occupied it for a few short months while she was negotiating what she'd thought was the end of her marriage. Now I'm the next MacInnes in residence to hold the keys to the castle, even though I feel guilty taking over Fam One. Occupying the apartment reserved for a direct MacInnes descendant feels like a duty I'm not fit for.

I'm qualified in the genealogical sense, but my years in the military mean I can actually count the number of days I've spent here. It adds to the intensity of my impostor syndrome every time I sit in V's office. But while I'm here trying to put my life back in order, I'll accept the mantle of temporary chatelaine of this incredible estate. I'm determined to be of service to my family and my program.

And I'm terrified. While my résumé shows an impressive history of dedication and determination, recent events give lie to my current facade. I'm grateful I have a chance to reinvent myself, but I constantly fight the certainty I'm going to fail so much more than myself. I hold an entire family legacy, with hundreds of lives dependent on our estate, in my still-shaky hands. Luckily, I'm not swimming in the deep end alone. I have Fina—and Mina, when we can pull her out of the clouds.

I steer my thoughts from the path of fear and doubt to pick up my conversation with Traycee.

"I loved V, too, but the truth is, you were closer to her than I was. I was hardly ever here. And of course, no one was closer to her than my sister."

"I only talked with Paige a few times while she was here, but she's a doll."

"She is, and I'm really excited we're getting closer these days. We're ten years apart, so it wasn't until recently we've connected as adults, and I have my fingers crossed I might get the chance to get to know my brothers, too."

"Brothers?"

"Twins in the middle. Paige was already out of the house before I was old enough to grasp my family's dysfunction, and the boys only ever needed each other, so in a lot of ways, I was an only child."

"Ooof, that's some classic birth order shit right there."

I wish I could say my nod is merely agreement and not a bitter acknowledgement of the truth. "We're such a ridiculous stereotype, we could be the poster child for several sections of the DSM."

"When you find out the shrinks have an entire manual laying out our crap, it kinda punches a hole in our belief we're terminally unique. Still, having the Goose out of the way has to be a big help."

I give a dry chuckle. "No doubt, but since my big sis is traipsing across Europe with her newly reconciled hubster, I appreciate you filling the void of friendly ears."

I'm utterly sincere. Having Traycee around makes me feel like I'm not trying to climb out of the addiction trench alone, and I hope I provide her with similar solace.

We pass the giant rolling doors to the kennels, eventually reaching the normal-sized entry, and I lead the way inside. We've barely made it five feet before a tall figure steps into the breezeway.

"Good morning, Miss Kiki, Miss Traycee."

"Hi, Brian. Traycee's here to pick up her puppy."

Brian Steele has been a fixture at this estate for as long as I can recall. When I learned he and Violet were friends and lovers for most of their lives, I felt a little volcano of *Hell yeah! You go, V!* bubble up inside me. It turns out Aunt Violet had a lot of secrets and semisecrets in her life none of us expected, but I'm glad for this one. She deserved whatever happiness she found with stoic Brian.

I don't know him well, another casualty of not being on the property much, but sadness hollows his eyes. My heart constricts for him, and I hope it's only the newness of grief making him appear less than healthy. Regardless, it's not my place to ask, so I keep my worries to myself. I'll ask Fina later if he's okay.

"Y'all come this way."

Traycee winks at me as we do as we're told, but it's easy to follow the yips and barks to our destination.

Moments later, we're standing in a small room with *Fancy* written on the erasable board attached to the wall. The area looks like someone from doggy day care heaven designed it. Fancy is resting on a long cushion, watching her five pups decide between numerous toys and balls to attack. We sink to the ground, and three boys and two girls swarm us, all with fat puppy bellies and lolling tongues.

Brian looks at the whole group with amused indulgence. "Your girl's ready, Miss Traycee. You all set up?"

"I am, and I got everything on your list. Plus, I have all the appointments made with Doc."

Her assurances have Brian giving his seal of approval. His reputation for his love of the MacInnes border collies is known far and wide, as well as the knowledge you'd better obey every single one of his instructions. Failure to do so has had him reclaiming puppies before, and he'd make sure every breeder in the state of Texas knows your name if you get on his bad side.

"Good enough, then. You two have fun, and I'll come back in a bit."

It's impossible not to obey with a pack of pure happiness demanding our attention. Not more than five minutes passes before it's clear one little girl has already claimed Traycee, and not the other way around.

"I think you've been chosen." I don't stop playing tug-of-war with the little boy who appears to be the alpha of the brood.

"I think you're right." She strokes the fur of the beauty with perfect markings climbing into her lap and putting her head on Traycee's arm. Apparently, she got all the calm genes, and my boy got all the rambunctious ones.

"You going to take one?" Traycee's dreamy voice confirms she's already in love with her little fluffy bundle.

Though tempting, I know better. I'll stick with Penny, our fountain dragon. Always patient, waiting for me to visit and stroke her beautiful nose. Willing to listen to all my woes. Never has to be walked. No vet bills. Stone mason invoices, maybe…

"Not right now. I'm lucky enough I can do this every single day if I want to."

I can't speak for Traycee, but I've had exactly as much sitting still as I can manage, even with a determined black and white floof trying to keep me entertained. With every meeting we attend together and every lunch shared, I'm getting closer to my quirky new friend, but I'm hell and gone from being comfortable with myself yet and don't have the extra mental space for the responsibility of a pet. Besides, I move too much to take one on.

"You finish up here and meet me at the castle."

Traycee is too busy falling in love to do more than wave goodbye and assure me she'll see me in a bit. I leave her and Brian to work out puppy details and return to my office with determined steps.

Time to distract my fear gremlin. Deflect the little bastard into getting some work done.

Do anything to stay on my path.

2

FINA

I LOVE MY SISTER, and not simply because she's my twin. Fraternal, but the distinction is irrelevant. Circumstances, some wonderful, some tragic, have kept us physically close all our lives. At the moment, I'm watching both UPS and FedEx trucks pull up, and I lose count of the trips the two drivers make in and out of Mina's side of our duplex.

Considering there's only fifteen feet between our front doors, I step inside on the heels of the departing man in a brown delivery uniform.

"What in the Sam Hill is going on?"

As she reads labels, Mina looks up from the boxes she's arranging into some kind of system I'm not privy to.

"I'm deciding on the lingerie for my trousseau."

I cast a pointed look at the piles of boxes. "How many nightgowns do you need?"

She sniffs and lifts her chin. "As many as I want."

I can't contain my delight. "Good answer. Do you want some help?"

Her attempt at bravura slips and hints of old fears, doubts, and wounds take a bit of the shine from her eyes. "I'm being foolish. It seemed like a good idea at midnight the other night when I was shopping online. Maybe I should go to the mall in Atlanta. I can send all these back."

No and hell no. Not one thing is going to take a nanosecond of happiness from my sister, even if there are days I want to duct-tape her mouth to make her stop talking. I'm both the oldest and her twin, so I have rights and privileges, and I'm determined the past will not haunt Mina's future.

"Stop being silly. They're here, we're here. Let's get to opening."

And like I snapped my fingers, her smile—the real one—returns. I understand her bliss, in a general sense. She'll marry an amazing man a mere month before our sixtieth birthday. We have myriad reasons to celebrate, and I'm thrilled she's on cloud two hundred and nine. She deserves every fluffy one.

Freed from her momentary indecision, she hands me a pair of scissors, and we start slicing through sealing tape. We're soon surrounded by a sea of white, pink, and aqua creations of satin and chiffon. I pick up an almost transparent teddy and hold it out with one finger.

Mina snatches it from me and turns an adorable shade of strawberry. "I don't know what I was thinking. I'll send it ba—"

"Don't you dare. You don't have to try it on for me, but you do have to for CT. You hear me?"

I take the nightie weighing as much as a breath and add it to the growing pile on the back of the chair she reupholstered in a gray Italian tweed. My sister channeled all her artistic skill into creating a mini Sicilian villa on her side of the duplex. My side is pretty and neat, but nothing compared to hers.

Her hand trembles before she clenches it into a fist. After she takes a deep breath and lets it out, she reaches over to smooth the delicate lace. "Yes, sister. I hear you."

I pull her in for a short, tight hug, and to my surprise, she nearly squeezes the stuffing out of me… which only serves to makes tears escape and slip down my cheeks. She no longer hesitates to touch and be touched, a miracle I didn't believe possible in my lifetime.

We separate, sniff, and wipe our noses, then get back to unboxing. And then… She. Starts. Talking.

"So, I've been thinking. What about petits fours instead of a groom's cake, because everyone says the groom's cake is a waste of money and petits fours are the new thing, and we could top them with mints, because they're nigh onto the whole reason we got together, and CT doesn't care, he said to do what makes me happy, but then I thought we could do a chocolate fountain, but it's kind of overdone, but CT loves chocolate, and I love Andes—"

I startle. Hard. Anders? Why is she bringing up Anders after all these decades?

"—but not everyone likes mint, so I'm worried…"

Oh, thank God. Andes. *Andes* mints.

She continues, but it's obvious my response isn't necessary, only my presence. As long as she thinks I'm listening, she's happy.

So. Much. Talking.

I desperately need a diversion from Anders Jensen, but the mere thought of his name has brought icy reminders crackling to life. My memory of seventeen-year-old Anders is frozen in time, inviting and delicious like homemade custard. Those kisses and hot hands in his tent. Sitting with my back to his chest, his arms wrapped under my breasts as we listened to the drummers or singers around the campfire. Secret glances shared across the banquet table during the feast. Giving him my token before he armored up for his turn at the joust. All the moments we played lord and lady at any of the Society for Creative Anachronism events we attended.

Any memories of our brief time together in the SCA have remained frosty and dormant because I can't bear to thaw or throw them out. A suitable substitute hasn't come, either, so they continue to take up space in the side-by-side Frigidaire of my life.

I'm not the same Serafina Greene from forty-plus years ago, so I'm not so foolish as to believe he'd be the same Anders Jensen. But I do wonder how much he's changed. His Nordic-blond hair probably conceals any gray. He's probably still six-four, because I can't imagine him stoop-shouldered. I'm certain his devilish grin and roguish accent could still talk me into anything. Time likely hasn't touched those traits, and I shouldn't revisit them.

I pick an easy diversion and send my thoughts toward the bombshell we uncovered after Violet's death. Her diaries led us to the twin girls she gave up for adoption just after she graduated from college. We're all still reeling from the revelation. No one—not me, not Mina, not Paige—knew this secret. To be truthful, there's some pain involved in the processing, a wound we all know Violet didn't mean to cause, but she had to know would be inevitable. I imagine she left the news in her diaries for this reason. Still, I've never had to make such a heart-breaking decision, so I mustn't judge her.

Sophie and René had refused to have the records sealed and V had left France knowing if her girls wanted to find her, they could. She made her peace knowing they were healthy and happy and loved.

"Fina, you aren't paying attention."

I take a deep breath, hold it. Release it.

"I'm sorry." I recover, scrambling for the last item she rattled off on her twenty-page list. "Petits fours are a great idea, especially with your mints."

"I changed my mind and decided on three separate cakes five minutes ago."

My face heats and mortification hangs heavy. I've upset my sister when she should have nothing but champagne bubbles for the next fifty-plus days and every one thereafter. If our family longevity holds, she has at least thirty years left with CT, and I don't want to be the cause for a single one of them being marred by a moment of doubt.

"I apologize. I'm all caught up in my musings."

"No, sister, it's me. I've done nothing but run my mouth. Come have some tea and tell me what's got you shut down."

As we move to her small kitchen, identical to mine but containing almost every serving piece from the Amalfi collection from Modigliani, her favorite online store. The pattern is too busy for my taste, but my preferences aren't the point. It took years for her to finally buy and use what she likes and to blue blazes with what anyone else thinks.

I decide to respond openly about everything… except Anders. "Violet's heavy on my heart. Juliette and Noelle, too. Not because Juliette's down in the big barn as we speak, but because there's so much we'll never know now."

Mina's expression tightens, and I can see she's struggling. "I hope you'll not think badly of me, but I'm pretty mad at Violet."

I've never thought poorly about her and am not about to start. "I'm right there with you. I don't understand why she didn't tell us, even at the last."

"She always had a sad place, but she truly never slipped, never once told any of us about David Broder or the past. We knew about her and Brian's secret-not-secret relationship, but we respected the way they wanted to be a couple. In the end, we can't imagine having to make such a momentous decision. I just wish she could have trusted us. Paige, too."

I give Mina's hand a squeeze. "From what Paige shared before Juliette got here, she and Noelle grew up happy and loved. Sophie and René are wonderful parents."

"I know. And V did what she thought best for those girls. Magnolia Bloom was a different place back then, and she believed the small minds in a small town wouldn't have given her girls their best lives."

As always with matters of the heart and our town's history, Mina's right. I can't judge Violet. I didn't have to consider being a single mother in the early seventies in East Texas.

Mina pulls her hand from mine and toys with the loveliest engagement ring in all of the Lone Star State.

"Today, if it were Paige or Kiki, the story would be, could be, different. I have to be honest, though. I'm glad I didn't know about David until now. The high road wouldn't have been an option for me on the many occasions the MacInneses and Broders have interacted. I realize David was young, but I can't abide how he treated our V."

As Mina's thoughtful expression spoils, I have to smile. My sister may be the sweet to my sour, but even the good Lord cuts a heavenly side-eye at my twin when her feathers ruffle. I've read the diaries, too, and understand why Mina's clearly pitched her tent in Camp Violet, but it's not the old battles worrying me.

It's the new ones.

"My overriding concern is what's going to happen when Juliette meets him. The resemblance, her mannerisms. The fine folks of Magnolia Bloom will easily connect the relationship dots."

"Our Juliette doesn't seem overly interested in stepping foot outside of the big barn, so it's not unbelievable she can avoid him. Still, what's set in motion will have to play out." Mina sits back, her tone like a judge who's delivered a verdict. All she needs is a gavel.

My throat threatens to close, and my eyes burn hot at the warrior my sister has unearthed inside her. For too long, she lived under the shadow of bruises long faded from her skin but tinting her soul. Happiness at seeing she's a veritable phoenix, and a passionate one, is the best pre-Christmas present I could ever have asked for.

Mina, apparently, isn't done yet. "Juliette's reading the diaries and has to decide for herself. All we can do is be here for her."

A little laugh escapes me. "When did you become the combined Buddha and General Patton of Magnolia Bloom?"

"Since I stopped being a scaredy-cat and got the biggest gift of my life. And speaking of gifts, I've got to figure out what to buy CT for a wedding present. What do you get for a man who has everything?"

I don't need a mirror to know my expression is a little devilish. "You don't get him anything, sister dear. You *give* him something."

"Serafina Greene!" She blushes so pink I wish I had my camera so we could match the color for her bridal shower dress.

"Did we not open four hundred boxes of sexy nighties? You're not consummating your nuptials?" I shouldn't poke at my sister, but our mother swears we first tussled in the womb, and old habits are sometimes… fun.

"What makes you so sure I'm waiting until November? I've never bought a pair of shoes in my life without trying them on first."

She tries so hard to be prim and proper I snort, but not unkindly. If she's comparing her footwear fetish to sex, CT Nelson is going to be one happy man.

"Well, well, do tell."

"A lady does no such thing." She stands, her nose upturned, but I'm not fooled by her pretend huff. "On your improper note, I'm leaving to have brunch with my beau."

She sashays off, and I'm left to wonder where my twin stashed her friskiness and sass all these years. The woman afraid of her shadow, at least where men are concerned, has disappeared, thank the Lord. I guess I really should be thanking CT, but I'm happy to spread the gratitude.

I'm going to miss her. Even though she'll be living only a few miles across town in his beautiful house and helping him at the store, my heart knows she won't be next door in our duplex ever again. I have a two-second thought of asking Momma to move in, but she's so happy at her little apartment complex with the rest of the Grannies, I couldn't ask it of her. Mina will be more Mrs. Magnolia Market than Wonder Twin at Castle MacInnes in short order, and I'm going to have to deal with jealousy's corrosive acid.

My problem's not CT. He's a lovely man, but in my eyes, he always was and always will be proprietor of the Magnolia Market. I never even had a passing thought about him until he took a shine to Fina.

What he's done, with his tender care of my sister and nourishing the bloom of her joy, is awaken memories of a boy who didn't behave like all the others in our SCA barony.

Anders loved to talk and ride horses and swim in the lake. He was the best dancer in the dance guild and best drummer in the music guild. And Lord help me, the best kisser, although I'm not aware of any guild membership for that particular talent. Even the gentlemen I dated when I was teaching medieval history at SMU never measured up. All nice men. All perfectly respectful. All reasonably adequate lovers.

None raised my blood pressure more than a few degrees. None threatened to send my biological mercury through the roof.

I shoot to my feet and slap my hand on the table.

"Stop it right now, Serafina. You're being ridiculous and have too much to do."

I follow my sister at a determined clip, thankful I have a million things on my list, and one of them is talking to Kiki. My walk across the grounds to the castle reminds me it's a delight having her back, even if the circumstances bringing her home are less than happy. I'm thrilled she's here, surrounded by those of us who love her, instead of thousands of miles away in cold and lonely Alaska.

I can make my way blindfolded to my office in the East Turret, one floor up from Violet's. Being a few steps away from my best friend, next to Mina, was one of the joys of my life. I miss V deeply, but I don't miss her being sick, and I sure don't miss her being in pain. It's the loss of her wicked sense of humor and boundless energy hurting the most.

Still, Violet had Brian Steele, and now Mina has CT. Envy threatens to shred every last thread of my good sense, but I can't deny the two women I love more than life got their happily ever afters.

I'm left with twice the work and half the help.

I force my thoughts to my to-do list and away from my self-absorbed nonsense. There's no point longing for what could have been with Anders Jensen, and it's a waste of valuable time thinking about what can never be.

3
KIKI

By the time Traycee comes to my apartment, I've made coffee in the French press and pulled out V's quilts for her to see. One of her arms cradles a sleeping puppy, but she uses her free hand to stroke an exquisitely rendered mariner's compass.

"These are going to fetch a fortune." She traces the binding and runs her fingertip over a line of stitches so perfect they could have been done by machine. Scratch that. They were far better than any done by a machine.

"This means a lot more meals available at the food pantry." I know Violet directed all the proceeds from her creations to different charities in town. No one was supposed to know about her donations, so of course, everyone in Magnolia Bloom did.

"And the women's shelter in Atlanta."

"I can't believe these are the last." Traycee lifts the corner of each treasure, giving me a quick list. "Broken star, Rose of Sharon, two bargello patterns, and three crazy quilts. A veritable trove, but don't you want to give these to your family or save them for the grandkids?"

I decline, even though there's a little selfish part of me wanting to do exactly as she suggests. "We all have our own pieces she made for us specifically, so while the greedy part of me wants to say yes, I have to abide by V's wishes. I have the ones she made for Juliette and Noelle in the closet."

We resume our positions on the balcony, knowing she has to go soon, but make good use of the comfort of Traycee's mom tending the store. Between her mother and grandmother, she has quite a team supporting her endeavors.

She eventually looks up from fondling her new love's ears. "Is Noelle coming over?"

"I don't know. Juliette hasn't talked about her much, and Paige said they were at odds with Juliette's decision to come to America and meet the family. I don't know any details yet, other than they're from Arbois, and she's something of a rock star in the art restoration world. Noelle runs the business side of their endeavors."

"They have rock stars in art restoration?"

"I admit it's a niche, but yeah. In her world, she's a badass."

"I thought you said she was super quiet."

I frown. "I mean she's got a reputation like she's some kind of savant when it comes to repairing paintings and things. I didn't say I understand it. Long story short, Juliette is here for a couple of months, and I'm enjoying getting to know her."

"Still, it's kinda sad about Violet. I wouldn't have guessed in a thousand years she had such a big secret in her past."

"It was a different time, and you know progress comes slowly here. Lord knows we can understand V believing her girls' life would be marred by the stigma of being bastards."

Her expression tinges with disgust. "Such an ugly word. Does anyone even use it anymore?"

"Not our generation so much, but that's the point, sadly."

Traycee is a business genius, but she had her share of fighting entrenched minds when she bought the Emporium and turned it from a white-doily kind of vibe into an eclectic, vibrant, and modern shopping destination. She won the town over, but she had her share of frustration along the way.

"I forgot to tell you the lamp you ordered came in. I meant to bring it, but my brain wasn't functioning when I left the house this morning."

"Fantastic. It's an assignment from my sponsor to pick one simple thing to make the apartment feel like home."

Home.

That's probably not an accurate term. I love Magnolia Bloom, but right now it's more precisely a haven. A hideout. A last chance, since I honestly don't have anywhere else to go. Castle MacInnes is at least familiar and full of love. I'm lucky to have a safe zone where I can concentrate on the important things right now—being of service to my bio family and my found family and staying sober. Not quite two years is a good start, but in some ways, I'm still a babe in the woods.

Traycee blows on hot coffee and takes an appreciative sip. My friend and I have this love in common.

Knowing we need to pivot to a lighter subject, I tip my mug toward her.

"I'm fairly certain learning to drink cold coffee is a requirement to be an officer." I knock back a swig and nearly moan in pleasure. "I wonder if 'you may commence drinking hot coffee' is somewhere in my discharge docs."

"I don't know any military people besides you, so I'll take your word for it."

"You know Uncle T."

She smiles at the mention of my favorite uncle. "True, but I forget sometimes he was a military hero until it's Armed Forces Day at church, and he shows up with all those medals and ribbons on his chest."

She's not wrong. My uncle was a career Air Force officer and served three tours in Vietnam as a young man and saw active duty in Afghanistan and Iraq. He doesn't talk about it much, even to me, but I know he carries scars, as well as pride, from his long years of service. I only wave from a distance when I see him and his partner, Monroe, around the property. I make a vow to address my cowardice as soon as I can. It's odd, but I'm more afraid of seeing disappointment in Uncle T's eyes than I was with Paige.

I may have been at this for a while, but I'm far from done facing demons. Not that Uncle T is a demon…

The promise of the program, though hard to believe in the early days without a small smirk of *yeah, sure*, is addressing the past brightens the future. At first, the journey appears a barefoot marathon over the coals of hell. Sprinting back to the bottle seems a lot less painful than staring down the damage we've done and listing who we've hurt. Who wants to do that? We can find endless reasons why all this get-healthy, do-gooder babble is pointless.

The old-timers don't argue. They leave us to rattle around in our self-made cages until we stop fighting. Ourselves, not them. They've done the work and know no amount of logic, pleading, begging, or bribing is going to change anyone until they're ready. They know we'll either get ourselves into enough trouble, or get tired of hurting and finally shut up and listen. Or thirdly, we'll keep doing what we're doing until we're dead or spend the rest of our lives pretending to be alive.

We sip in silence, the sun now well over the tops of the East Texas hardwoods surrounding Lake Maggie, or, more officially, Lake Magnolia Bloom. The pecans are dropping, so yay on being home in time for one of nature's most amazing gifts. The profusion of oaks and magnolias are green and will stay so, even if our namesake tree is long past blooming for the year.

My mental musings are a form of meditation, odd as it may seem. Having spent so many years in an emotional cyclone, being able to sit quietly and watch the wind rustle tree limbs or water lap at the lakeshore is nothing short of miraculous.

"As much fun as this has been, I've got to get to the shop. You going to Atlanta for a meeting today?"

"Yep. Wanna come?"

"Yep. Mom's at the store, but Gram's coming later. Sundays after church are when the Grannies come to gossip. Sometimes they even buy something."

I've discovered there are three methods of communication in Magnolia Bloom: telegraph, telephone, and Tell-A-Grannie. And the

Grannies far exceed Morse code in breadth and speed of transmission.

"Perfect. Did Gram get Tara engaged yet?"

In Magnolia Bloom, Grannie matchmaking's an art form.

"Lord, I hope not, 'cause then she'll start on me."

"Maybe we should send an email to these online dating sites and tell them they're pikers in the love business compared to the Grannies."

"Girl, toss that idea right now. The only thing keeping the Grannies in line is they haven't figured out the internet yet. As long as they're corralled by notepad, pencil, and in-person shenanigans, we might survive them."

We share a laugh because the truth is, Traycee loves her Gram with a ferocity making a mad honey badger look like a newborn kitten, and I envy her. I have one living grandparent, my grandmother on my mother's side, and she's in a dementia care facility in Oregon, near my parents, who I haven't seen them in... mental calculation commences... three years.

She tips her travel mug at me. "You know, we wouldn't have to drive forty-five minutes to Atlanta if you'd start a meeting here."

Here we go...

"We wouldn't have to drive forty-five minutes to Atlanta if *you'd* start a meeting here."

"You were a reporter, not a comedian, right?"

I don't bother explaining my job. My previous job. I had many over the years, but people assume media means I was an on-air personality or journalist, which is weird. There are thousands of other jobs in public affairs, but I'm too tired to talk about it. Actually, I don't want to. I say what I need to in my shares at meetings, but I try to leave the military and the AA jargon out of my conversations.

Even with Traycee.

She knows ninety-nine percent of my secrets, but the other one percent's a whopper. I've worked the Steps, of course, and I've filled out two whole pages of *The Mindfulness of Self-Compassion*, but I'm still navigating this new life. I will, when I'm ready, but for now, I haven't offered up much about my deepest wound. The rule is to make an amends, or in this case, share something from my past, *except when to do so would injure yourself or others.* Newbies, in a rush to do recovery "right," forget the *yourself* part.

"Speaking of work, I have to put in a few hours before we gallivant off to the thriving metropolis of Atlanta, Texas." I give a chin thrust toward my office door nestled in the turret wall.

Before I can continue the belabored joke, the double doors open, and we both swivel left.

"Hey, Fina." My aunt by love, not by blood, looks harried, and it's barely eight o'clock.

"Hey, sweetie. Hi, Traycee. Your hair looks lovely."

"Thank you, Fina. I can make an appointment for you and Kiki anytime."

She laughs and shakes her head, but not a strand moves in her signature French coil. "Child, I do not have time to maintain the creations your sister comes up with. They're masterpieces, but goodness, I'd fail in the maintenance department."

I take pity on her and do the over-here hand wave. "Do you need something? You seem a little stressed."

She heaves an impressively gusty sigh. "Lord forgive me, but it's questionable if Mina Greene will make it to her Thanksgiving wedding. At the rate she's stretching my last nerve, there may or may not be an unmarked grave on the back forty before the week's end."

Fina's teasing, but I understand her exasperation. Mina and CT's engagement has been the talk of the town, and having been here since July, I've witnessed the bride-to-be's exuberance. The more gregarious of the Greene twins makes my cocaine days look like naps in the park.

"What can I help you with? I don't need to leave for my meeting until noon. Well, eleven thirty to swing by and pick up my hitchhiker here."

Fina rests against the balcony wall, her tall, lean form radiating tension "I don't mean to pile too much on you, but I received an email inquiring about a costume Yule Ball for two hundred people."

"We had five thousand at the games three months ago, and I bet you didn't break a sweat, so what's the problem?"

"I have a year to set up for the games. Who can pull off a costume party of such magnitude with less than ninety days of prep time?" She gives me a signature one-eyebrow arch, and I'm reminded why Fina would have made one hell of a general, or one scary drill instructor…

But one thing I love about Fina? She acknowledges my organizational superpowers.

"Captain Logistics to the rescue. Wait, I shouldn't demote myself. Major Logistics reporting for duty."

What's stressing Fina at the moment is the EW, aka the emergency wedding, sandwiched between all the other notations on the castle wall calendar. An esteemed Dallas councilwoman's daughter lost her venue, and we'll make some desperately needed bank pulling off a dream event for the little bridezilla. We're down to T-minus twelve days, and poor Fina's losing it. All on top of the planning for our pie-sweet but mini-bride-a-saurus rex, the future Mrs. CT Nelson.

Fina drops the teasing, returning to her work-now-play-later personality. Only there's never a later for her.

"If you'll enter the information from their email into a spreadsheet and start on what you already know about the rooms, it'll save me hours. Call our local venues and see if there's a bed to be had at this late date, then move out to Atlanta and Texarkana, and, as a last resort, Dallas. Thank goodness they were smart enough to send the data in a comma-delimited file so you can import everything into the forms."

"Look at you being all tech-jargony." I tease Fina because she's a wiz with a spreadsheet and far and away from ready to join the Grannies. Fifty-nine might technically qualify, but she's got more energy and business savvy than someone half her age.

"Missy, I do not have time for you being a smart-mouth."

"Yes, ma'am." I pretend to be chastised. Those unfamiliar with Fina wouldn't know to take her sharp tongue as charm. "I'm happy to start and finish those tasks for you today. The major will not disappoint."

Not anymore, on anything.

"You're an angel. A bit of a brat like your sister, but I love you anyway."

"I'm trying to be a good stand-in while Paige is gone."

For a millisecond, Fina relaxes, and it's like a little wave of invisible Xanax ripples across the balcony. "I'm so happy for Paige. If you'd told me she'd spend months tearing across Europe like she and Zach are newlyweds, I'd never have believed it. Prayed for it. Didn't think it would happen."

"Me, too. Forward me the email and put it out of your mind."

"Thank you, sweetheart. Traycee, you keep her in line, you hear?" Fina points to me, but Traycee nods gravely.

"Yes, ma'am. It'll take all my strength, though."

I give a Fina-worthy sigh. "Both of you are exhausting. Fina, go. Traycee, I'll walk you out."

Traycee and I walk through the family living room, but I refuse to allow my eyes to stray toward the armory. I still haven't darkened the archway because I can't endure seeing the disappointment in Evajean's and Alisdair's portraits any more than I've been able to face Uncle T.

Yet another line item on my personal spreadsheet I hope is covered in my self-compassion workbook. I'm far from done dealing with my feelings of utter failure as a MacInnes. It's the major player in what kept me a high-functioning alcoholic.

Until I wasn't anymore. The functioning part, anyway. I continued the alcoholic thing in spades for far longer. I'm sure the professionals would have a field day with why my decade's-gone ancestors have such a hold over me. Understanding why my uncle's opinion matters so deeply, with his long and highly decorated military career, isn't hard to figure out. Like my father, he's career Air Force, and everything I hoped I'd be.

And wasn't.

Our route downstairs takes us by the chapel, and I nearly run over a tall, well-built man hurrying through the dark oak doors.

"I'm so sorry, Kiki. Please forgive me." His voice is deep and rich but distracted.

As he steps back, I see he's Harville Crowder, the pastor of our family's church. I haven't gone to church in decades, but Paige told me how he helped her with the loss of Aunt Violet.

"I'm the one who nearly took you out like a Cowboys linebacker at third and ten, Pastor."

I make myself stop talking. The national sport of Texas is another victim in my vodka war. At least for a while. Tailgating's too much of a trigger.

I think I see confusion, but it's only a matter of seconds before his eyes clear and he smiles at me. And damn if his lip doesn't have the sweetest little crooked dip on the left side, and there's a hint of a dimple in his cheek.

"Traycee, always a pleasure."

"Hey, Pastor." Traycee gives him a dose of her thousand-watt personality. "You look pulled nine ways to Sunday. Oh, wait, it is Sunday!"

"What have you got here?" He reaches over to run gentle fingers over the puppy's ears. "What's her name?"

"I'm not sure yet."

"What an odd name for a dog."

We both roll our eyes, even if his lip is clearly twitching.

"Very funny, Pastor. Don't you need to get to the church?"

"Indeed, I do. I'm sorry to rush off."

Other than my poor attempt at an apology, I haven't said a word in all of this exchange. *Tall and well-built* tends to stall my hearing and my common sense. Today, it appears my tongue's decided to tie itself in a knot, and my eyes definitely should not be noticing how his flat-front slacks hug slender hips and long legs and his sky-blue button-down makes his eyes look like the most fought over marble in the bag.

"Ladies, you have a wonderful day." He gives the pup one final pat, then hurries off.

I roll my eyes. At myself.

"What's happening here?" Traycee's gaze volleys between Harville and me.

"One among the many reasons I'm going to hell, apparently, is I've added lusting after a preacher."

Regal and attractive are temptations I won't be led into ever again.

She watches Harville's retreating back, then nails me with a look. "Girl, you know preachers have sex, right? How do you imagine we get little preachers?"

"I don't need a vivid mental picture, thanks, and I'm fairly sure one of his prerequisites is marriage."

"Not necessarily a bad thing."

"Handsome and height are a bad combo for me."

The worst.

"I don't understand how tall and sexy are ever a bad combination, but whatever keeps the cork in the bottle."

"No argument from me."

I send Traycee and her puppy off to her store while I make my way back to the East Turret and Violet's office. After Violet died, Paige took over helping Fina and Mina manage the castle and took care of the lion's share of the backlog of work. For now, I'm temporary chatelaine, the keyword being *temporary*. With Mina whirling in her wedding-planning tornado, I have precisely two jobs. Not screwing up while helping Fina and staying sober.

There's zero room in my life for Handsome Harville, which is to his benefit.

If he's around me too much, he might be collateral damage in a lightning bolt meant for me.

4
JULIETTE

THE QUIET HAS NEVER BOTHERED me.

It is the space I'm the most comfortable in, but the silence between me and Noelle is another matter entirely. In our almost fifty years on this planet, we have never gone a week without talking, no matter how angry we might get. I feel like I've had a limb ripped off. My temperamental sister has always been the touchy one, but she's never been this angry with me.

Then again, I've rarely flown halfway around the world without her before, and never with so much unsaid between us.

The last hour I've spent walking the grounds of Castle MacInnes has been wonderful, if warm. Octobers in East Texas are quite different than northeastern France, at least so far. At the edge of a rippling field of short grass, I find a spot under a towering oak where I plan to read another volume of Violet's journals. The wind carries the contented sounds of a sheep herd, but the noise is so muted I can tell they are some distance off. I add the *baas* and rustles as counter-notes to the perfection of the morning.

My intention to absorb more of the words written by the birth mother I never knew is sabotaged by the approach of the most adorable blacknose lamb.

I can tell instantly my little visitor is a Valais, as my home is hardly a stone's throw from the Swiss border. Their faces are utterly precious, their spiral wool and twisted horns iconic. I've seen these sheep all my life.

I've never had one introduce itself to me.

If I didn't know it was a sheep, I'd be tempted to believe it's a fluffy dog. It bounds right up to me and *baas*, for all the world saying, *Pet me.*

"Bonjour, ma belle. Que fais-tu ici?"

Before my new friend can tell me what he or she is doing here, a beautiful black-eared collie trots up and sits. I translate the look she gives my sweet beauty to be, *You are in so much trouble, mademoiselle.*

Or monsieur.

Apparently, I have an escapee from the herd I can hear but not see.

"Little one, we should return you to your maman, oui?"

The sheep with the sweet black face framed by the softest kinky white wool lifts her front leg, and I swear she wants me to admire the black markings on her knee. I'm not sure why I've decided she's a she, but I'll stick with it.

"Mais oui, tu es belle." I have a feeling she already knows she's beautiful, but a compliment never hurts. The collie cocks her head at me, and I chuckle. "Pardonne-moi. Tu es très belle, aussi."

I'm not sure the dog is mollified to receive her own compliment, but she stands and takes a step toward the tree line, looking back with a distinct follow-me expression.

I retrieve my water bottle and Violet's diary, obeying the gorgeous collie with my too-cute-to-be-real companion bounding beside me. I want to pick her up so badly, but I'm uncertain if I should. Contenting myself with getting her home, I follow the determined pooch and break into the clearing, then risk falling over to stop myself when I go nose to chest with a man holding a shepherd's crook.

It does not take great deductive reasoning to assume I have found the lamb's guardian.

"Lulu, you are now officially more trouble than you're worth. And hello, ma'am."

The man is front-lit by the morning sun, and I wish my Nikon wasn't back at the castle. If I ever wanted an iconic picture of what I imagine a Texas sheepherder would look like, he provides the image. Though not in overalls, he wears denim jeans, and his shirt is red plaid. His boots have borne the brunt of many years of wear, and his cowboy hat, most certainly not for show, covers red hair in need of a barber. The once-beige straw is now sweat- and dirt-stained, and the brim has long lost its original shape.

I am an art restorer, and while I will not deny I have some skill, I'm not a painter in my own right. If I were, he'd be my first portrait. The problem with my silly urge is I believe this gentleman deserves the brush of an American realist to capture his kind eyes but reserved mien. His sun-damaged skin offers another clue he does not play cowboy, but is the authentic item. He needs someone with a true gift to capture the essence eluding me after mere seconds of our awkward meeting.

"Bonjour." I step back and offer my hand. "Juliette Laurant."

"Ah. Miss Violet's girl. I'm Rory Campbell. Pleasure to meet you. Sorry Lulu has interrupted your hike, and I hope Sabrina didn't startle you."

Lulu the precious lamb, Sabrina the gorgeous border collie, and Rory the instantly enigmatic sheepherder. So many introductions so quickly. Which I'll use as an excuse to distract myself from his casual knowledge of my connection to this family.

My family.

"Both Lulu and Sabrina are adorable. Especially this one." I gesture to Lulu, who's determinedly kicking about and returning to butt against my leg.

"She takes advantage of how cute she is, I'm afraid." Rory looks back toward the castle, which is barely discernable in the distance. "You've roamed a bit. I don't normally have walkers so far out."

"I enjoy solitude, and the temperature is lovely this morning. I hope I've not disturbed you?"

"You? No. It's our little escape artist who's the troublemaker."

I reach down to scratch Lulu's muzzle. "Do you name all your lambs?"

Rory bends to smooth Sabrina's still-alert ears. "No, but Lulu is one of those you can't help but want to keep, which is saying a lot since Valais will lamb all year, not like other breeds. Gives me more opportunities to lose my heart."

"I am familiar with them. My family owns a tiny vineyard near Arbois, and I've been to Switzerland many times, as it's so close. I do love their sweet faces."

"Great temperaments, too."

"Indeed. Well, I shall not keep you. Thank you for introducing me to your companions, though I must admit I'd like to take them both back with me to my apartment. Especially this one." I'm unable to help myself and bend again to reward Lulu's continued demand for attention.

"She's just now weaning, so she'd probably be fine with your idea. Would you like to meet the rest of the flock?"

I'm startled by the invitation, although I'm uncertain as to why. I suppose it is because I am most in the company of my paintings, and none of them speaks to me. Not in words, of course, though we have entire conversations in other ways.

"Oui, merci."

He sweeps an arm out and matches his steps to mine. Sabrina takes no excuses from Lulu and urges her along, but the sweet lamb will have none of it. She does a rather impressive bout of dodges and consistently returns to me.

"Looks like you've made a friend." There is amusement in Rory's voice, and I don't try to hide my delight.

Clearly, the place where I was sitting was part of a windbreak between two massive fields. The view unfolding before me is as beautiful as any in Arbois. I don't miss home yet, but the scene is the definition of pastoral. There is a herd of the unmistakable Valais contentedly munching grass and clearing the overgrowth among the trees. Another man is on the far side, a collie identical to Sabrina beside him, both of whom are watching their charges, their postures alert.

Rory gestures in the duo's direction. "He's my boy, Kaden. We were about to move them to a new grazing area when Sabrina took off after Lulu."

"Just the two of you? With so many sheep?"

"I could've done it by myself with Sabrina, but having Kaden and his girl, Sapphire, makes it easier. I'm taking advantage of having Kaden home before he goes back to Tyler to finish up his last year at A&M."

"A and M?"

"Sorry. Silly of me to expect you to know. He's a senior at Texas A&M University over at the Tyler extension not too far from here."

"You sound very proud."

"I am. He's a good boy, and he'll be a good land manager. He's got the noggin for it."

Lulu abandons me and, in a series of runs, hops, and jumps, bounds over to a sheep I assume is her mother. The ewe twists around toward the imp and gives her the cut-it-out look mothers of all species quickly master.

We share a chuckle, and I gesture toward the clearly contented mass of white and black. "They are all so beautiful."

Rory's eyes sweep over the relaxed herd. "When we had an opportunity back in the '80s to acquire some breed stock, it turned out to be the best investment we've ever made. Switzerland has severely restricted export, so the breed-up program is building around the world. This herd, though, is from our original, pure stock. We began crossbreeding them with our Scottish blackface and can call the other herd purebred according to the rules, but these beauties are the real deal."

"Fascinating."

A *hee-haw* captures my attention, and I turn, laughing. "Is that a mule?"

He follows my gaze, and his lip twitches. "Yes. Fiona, our guard donkey."

"A guard donkey?"

"Oh, yes. She was raised with the bunch here and thinks they're all hers. She's vicious in protecting them. Well, from nature's predators.

Man's another issue lately with the rise in poaching. Between her and the dogs, they're as safe as we can make them when they're in the pasture, barring having human tenders."

"I've never heard of such a thing."

"Why would you, if you're not a rancher? I heard you're a painter."

"No, I'm a restorationist, sometimes preservationist."

"There's a distinction?"

"A large one, but it's boring. Nothing so fun as watching these beauties all day."

He scratches behind his ear, knocking his battered hat off-kilter. "They're sweet-natured and quite trainable. Compared to herds we've had in the past, these beauties are a dream. See those two?" He points to the leaders of the pack. "They think I'm their dad. I get them going, and I hardly need the dogs, especially if I have a bucket of feed with me."

The affection in his voice is palpable, and I admit I'm surprised. I haven't given ranchers of any type much thought, and a host of questions spring to mind. "You sound awfully attached."

"Sometimes, which makes it hard to be practical."

"I have a feeling, from our brief conversation, you feel about your sheep as I do about my art. Some paintings break my heart to return to an owner or museum when I'm done, yet I must."

I watch the bunch move around each other, and while, as he guessed, I am no rancher, the long fleece on all of them and a fair number of extended bellies indicate he and Kaden will be busy for quite some time. How such an obscure factoid about shearing came to mind, I have no idea.

I've watched grapevines galore, but not herd animals, and while both scenes are relaxing to the soul, I find the captivating black faces much more interesting. In a matter of minutes, I can make out personalities, and my eye consistently returns to Lulu.

The thing I appreciate most, as I enjoy the breeze playing through my hair and the sun kissing my skin, is Rory's willingness to stand by me. Quietly.

He has not been reticent to talk, but neither does he fill every second with words. Possibly a trait of sheepherders, but I appreciate his stillness regardless of its source. So much so, it startles me when he speaks again.

"Is your sister coming over? Word hasn't reached the gossip mill yet if she has."

"Not yet. And possibly not at all. Noelle can be rather stubborn."

Which only increases my guilt for my feelings of relief to have a break from my twin. As I'm not ready to explore the direction my thoughts are going, I take refuge in an easy excuse to leave.

"I must return to the castle now, as I have so much reading to do." I hold the journal aloft as self-explanatory.

"Learning about your mama?"

"My maman is in Arbois, my home." I know my voice is sharp, but I can't help it. I didn't intend to be rude, but Rory is not the first person to make the mistake. Still, the concern flashing in his green eyes eases the stiffness from my shoulders.

"I'm sorry, I didn't mean to... I meant Miss Violet."

"It is all right. I am sorry for being... pricklish?"

"Good a word as any." If there is merit to the claim a person's invisible energy can be discerned, I sense he harbors no frustration with my reaction.

"Still, I hope you will accept my apology. I am learning so much, and sometimes it's a lot to take in." I stop, wondering where my willingness to share so openly with a stranger comes from.

"I'll accept yours if you'll accept mine. I overstepped. We're not all related by blood around here, but we're all family in the way that matters."

He speaks so sincerely, I have no reluctance to agree. "I do not have a big family. Both my mother and father were only children, and Arbois is not a huge city. I grew up rather provincial. So when our attorney contacted me to say Paige extended an invitation to meet, but only if I wished to do so, I was intrigued. My sister and I have always known we were adopted, but I have never pursued finding out about our birth out of respect to our mother. Also, my sister is rather vehement in not wanting to know."

I hide the pain piercing through me at the memory of our long and loud row when I stood firm in my determination to accept Paige's invitation. All my life, I have tried to accommodate my twin—identical in looks, opposite in nature. This time, I stood firm.

"Bet you weren't expecting a castle."

"Certainly not one in Texas."

Rory's chuckle is nice. Light. Inviting. His energy is peaceful. I have to admit my preconceived notion of Texas men didn't include that particular adjective.

"I bet you're reading a lot about Miss Gavina, too, what with the paintings and all."

"Mais non, unfortunately. I am having a more difficult time finding out about her."

"You need to talk to my grannie, then. Her momma was good friends with Gavina."

I brighten, delighted at this unexpected source of information about the woman who painted her soul onto a series of canvases and never picked up a brush again.

"How wonderful, Rory. Merci."

"I'll get with you later this week, if it's okay. We start shearing tomorrow, so I'm a little busy for a few days, but then I'd be happy to carry you over to Atlanta, well, about halfway between here and Atlanta, to meet her."

Carry me? I assume this is not literal, but another colloquialism I must incorporate into my lexicon.

"Of course, I understand. At your convenience, I would be most delighted."

"Have a nice walk back, and we'll talk soon."

He tips his hat to me, an action I find I like. Rory Campbell is a man comfortable in his own skin, and I am drawn to his quietude and certainty.

"À bientôt. See you soon."

I turn away and walk in the direction of the turret tip peeking over the trees. When I reach the break, I look back.

Valais sheep. In East Texas. On the grounds of a castle. Built by an American woman and her Scottish husband.

I look down at the book in my hands. "Violet, I believe I would've liked to have known you."

The instant clench I feel in my stomach reminds me I have more questions than answers, a warning I should not presume all is as bucolic as the scene behind me suggests. And a shiver strikes through me as I wonder if finding out these answers will be worth the estrangement from my twin.

5
KIKI

"Girl, I can't believe I'm riding in a Porsche. I feel like a movie star."

I pat the steering wheel. "This baby saved my sanity. I bought her at an auction while I was in Germany and spent darn near the whole time I was there putting her back together. I burned through my whole moving allowance getting her back to the States."

Traycee shows me her newly painted nails. "These hands weren't meant for motor oil. Almond or coconut, sure, but anyway, if I can find one of these around here, you gonna do me a solid?"

My laugh is as much cough as humor. "We'll have to negotiate."

"How'd you become a car nut, anyway? Not usually a chick thing."

"It is when you're the youngest of four and desperate to get your dad's attention. I started handing him tools while he worked on a car or whatever needed fixing in the house. He gradually started letting me help, and then I found out I really enjoyed it. Being surrounded by mostly dudes in the Air Force, it just continued."

"Fair enough. So tell me more about your cousin." Traycee adjusts the vent on her side to get maximum AC airflow. The projected cold front won't hit until tonight, so for now we're still in shorts. "Fina, as much as I love her, interrupted before you could give me any good details."

I hold off on my response as I check the GPS so I won't miss the exit to Atlanta. I haven't been there enough times to make the trip by rote, but with my determination to attend a weekly meeting, I will soon.

"Juliette's super nice, but man, is she quiet. She's been here two weeks, and I bet I've talked with her five times. We set her up in the big barn where we have a little studio apartment and workroom. The minute she saw the space, she insisted on staying there instead of in the castle."

"Doesn't she have, like, crazy money?"

Traycee turns the bag so I can snag a handful of chips and drop them into the waiting napkin in my lap.

"She's rich, but not *Forbes* 100 rich. What I know is, she and Noelle have made a small fortune in their business. Juliette's a big deal in the art restoration world, which I know thanks to Google. Her twin runs a store for the things Juliette restores outside of her commissions."

"What did she say about your aunt Gavina's paintings? It's cool as all get-out you found an honest-to-goodness secret treasure."

Nothing stays buried long in a small town, or on Air Force bases. I was intrigued as anyone about the secret room with our aunt's paintings hidden inside. The discovery was made three months ago, but it already seems like a lifetime.

"Juliette says they're museum-worthy. They're in decent shape because they were kept in the dark, but still, the canvases and frames need work. She's going to either restore them or find someone to do it. She's not sure she's staying, but I know from the little we've talked, she has a reputation for spotlighting women artists and bringing them overdue attention. She's determined to give Gavina that chance."

"Seriously cool."

"Seriously."

I munch on my nacho cheese triangles, wiping my hands on the twenty other napkins between the seats. By the time we finish the road rations, we've drained our Dr Peppers and are crunching breath mints as we move into the Second Avenue Baptist Church meeting room. The circle of chairs makes the tension in my throat ease. When the seats are in rows, meaning the group will be bigger, I have to gird myself to stay present. Traycee shines in a crowd. I want to find the exit and run away.

After months of meetings, I should be used to them. Or at least not have a gut full of anxiety, but here I am, faking it until I make it one more time. In between drives to Atlanta or Texarkana, I distract myself, but it works for only a second. Not even toiling away on Fina's data most of the afternoon had diminished the image of the flash of pain behind Harville's kind blue eyes, the sadness in his slightly wonky smile. I haven't been able to avoid the gossip about his divorce, which is almost final, and I do my best to avoid the salacious tittering, but sometimes I'm trapped.

Oddly, my brain's tendency to veer into Harville's lane has me worried, despite my best efforts to get back in mine. I've tried everything. A short, determined meditation. Singing the soundtrack from *Hamilton*. Triple-checking the spreadsheet for typos.

Quadruple-checking.

Yet he's remained planted at the top of my thoughts.

I will not let my imagination stray to tall, handsome, and definitely off-limits—even if he merits his own Pinterest board.

I will not screw this up and let my thoughts dwell on any man, much less the least likely candidate on the face of the Earth for a romantic interest in my life.

The members trickle in, all gravitating to the strong coffee and plates of doughnuts on the small table. I take coffee, refrain from the crullers, and force myself to stay in the room no matter how badly I want to give my attention permission to flee outside and run away on the ribbons of bright sunshine.

"... so thanks, everyone, for being here."

I automatically join the chorus of, "Thanks, Steve."

So much for staying in the room...

I determinedly do better for the rest of the hour. When it's clear one woman thinks she's reached her lowest low but remains comfortable hanging out there, sorrow swirls in my rock-bottom well. I know her journey. The routes she's taken. The lefts she's made when she should gone right.

You're only halfway to hell, sweetie.

Another attendee has transferred his addiction from Jim Beam to meetings, but this one will let him live longer, and hopefully save him from killing someone else.

All that matters is they're in the room. There's no timetable for getting sober and no expiration date on staying there.

Traycee's brutally honest about her roller coaster. She can rile people up, but it's good to have a range of stories to serve both those who need a gentler handhold and those who can use her put-on-your-big-girl-panties-and-get-over-yourself style. She'll temper, with time. I'm hardly the most seasoned veteran in the room, but I'm not the rawest, either. Today, though, I keep my peace. I'm learning to listen to my inner voice when it tells me to sit on something awhile longer before giving it voice. I have to remind myself being here is service enough.

I'm not lying when I echo, "It works if you work it," as we end the meeting. I fold my chair, and a mere minute passes before the room's policed and Traycee and I are moving down the hallway toward the Plexiglas and aluminum doors ubiquitous in any of a thousand American churches.

Sometimes, it feels like I've been in the meeting room or basement of every one of them.

"Hey, you want to tell me what's up?"

Traycee's voice pulls me out of my distraction, and I realize I haven't started the car. "I'm sorry. I'm all up in my head today."

"I hadn't noticed."

I give her a half eye roll, saving a full one for more deserving repartee. "Ever since I got my year chip, I've been feeling off. Shouldn't I be all *yippee* about it?"

"How would I know? I can't claim mine until Thanksgiving. Ironic, huh?"

"I don't mean to be a downer." I grimace. "Sorry again. Poor choice of words."

"Hey, I was an uppers girl, and chill, a'ight? Ain't nothing to stress over. And before you climb back into your big brain, remember the three most dangerous words for an addict..."

We quote together, "I've been thinking."

I point us back to the Bloom, with a stop at a gas station for munchies and cold DPs, letting the satellite radio serenade us until the city limit sign's almost in sight.

"You need to give more consideration to talking to the sexy pastor."

I start so hard I nearly send us into the other lane, which is thankfully empty. "What the... Are you high?"

Her brow furrows in confusion, and then she barks a laugh. "I meant talking to him about starting a meeting at the church, but where your mind went's more interesting."

I know I'm defensive, but I can't stop my back from going stiff. "Don't pretend your phrasing wasn't deliberate."

She fights a grin, which ruins her pretend remorse. "My intention was setting up a meeting, but maybe I did poke a little. Since the door's open, let's chase this rabbit for a second. You've obeyed the rules. No major decisions or relationships for the first year. You're well into year two, so you're in the clear."

"So I go chasing men now?"

"Not any man, or woman for that matter, but it sure seems you could use a quiet place to lay your head. That man's chest sure seems to fit your bill."

I can't tell Traycee yet the extent to which Handsome Harville isn't allowed to fit my bill. On another day and at another time, he'd check all my boxes.

Who am I kidding? He checks them all now. Which is the problem, exacerbated by the part about him being religious.

But I mentally reaffirm my intention to abstain from tall and sexy with more determination than withstanding a gallon of Mexican martinis.

Traycee mistakes my silence for an invitation to continue. "I'm saying recovery is lonely enough, and if the opportunity presents itself, you might consider it."

"I can't imagine a worse idea than the pastor adding me to his burdens list. He's still reeling from his wife leaving him."

"So maybe you can give him a chest to rest upon in return."

I haul in a deep sigh. "You're incorrigible."

"Guilty. I'm worried about you."

I reach across and put my hand on her arm. "You, my friend, are incredibly sweet, but trust me. I don't need a man on the rebound as much as he doesn't need the giant mess currently described as me. And the pastor thing is a problem on a whole other level."

"I have a feeling." She wipes sour-cream-and-onion dust from nails painted a vivid purple. "We'll see."

No, we won't see. "So now you're a witch on top of a wiseacre?"

"Gram says I have the touch."

"You misheard. Your Gram said you *are* touched."

We tussle and tease for the rest of the drive home, mostly with me explaining, again, why I'm not ready to be responsible for a meeting.

By the time I pull around to the rear of the Magnolia Bloom Emporium, I'm feeling both lighter and wrapped tighter. My thoughts are filled with my duty to serve recovery, yet running into a handsome, kind, erudite—

Stop it. Stop borrowing trouble. You don't have to call Harville, no matter how much Traycee is interfering.

I know she's well-intended. Her boyfriend has been her biggest supporter, and she thinks everyone deserves a Vernon. Maybe everyone does, but not everyone gets a Vern or Vernette, and I keep my mouth shut about early support waning fast. Divorce and breakup are nigh onto ubiquitous as someone gets sober. Sometimes you fight family harder than the bottle. Dysfunction abhors peace, so an unhealthy support system will do all it can to pull an addict back into the whirlwind.

We walk through the Emporium's employee entrance, and the chorus of cackles coming from the tearoom makes some of the tension melt from my shoulders. I know exactly who's chatting and gossiping, and the happiness flowing from the room is a little reminder the world is still a good place, that there are still good people in it, even when the news would have me believe everything is on fire.

Traycee has transformed her storefront into the most inviting gift shop on the square. It's a mind-boggling mix of eclectic and homey, and her reputation is growing to the point she needs to expand, and soon. The tourists can't get enough of the embellished clothing, leatherwork, pottery, and jewelry. The locals buy her out of honey, coffee, tea blends, and candy.

For now, we join the Grannies in the small room with three tables and mismatched chairs bought during any number of Traycee's scouting trips around the state. The narrow counter holds homemade treats, and a coffeepot is always hot with whatever exotic blend she's brewing in an insatiable quest to find the perfect bean.

"Hey, Mom, Gram." Traycee tosses her purse behind the counter and gives me the want-a-cup? look.

I decline, moving to take the hands outstretched to me, but speak to Traycee's mom first. "Hey, Ranelle, how're you?"

"Doing fine. Glad to see you."

I turn to Gram next. "Mrs. Everson. How are you feeling?"

The elder Everson gives me a stink eye. "Child, when are you going to start calling me Gram or, at the least, Emma?"

I kiss her weathered cheek. "Right now. Would you like more coffee?" I tap a nail on her empty cup.

"Lord, no. As it is, I'm going to be up half the night. I forgot to dilute my girl's mess, and I'm going to pay for it."

"Don't listen to her," Ranelle chimes in as Traycee puts a mug down and takes a seat between the two women who are her biggest champions. "She drinks hundred octane until midnight, then sleeps like a baby."

I leave them arguing with love-filled voices and make the rounds to speak to the other Grannies. The only one I know well is Emma because I see her the most, despite my reluctance to be informal with her. Gram is delighted with her position as the senior Grannie.

Mrs. Greene, Mina and Fina's mother, sits across the table, holding sway as second-in-command. I've trying to get comfortable calling her Eunice, but it's not easy. The twinkle in her bright eyes makes it no secret where Mina and Fina inherited their spunk.

I give polite excuses to leave as soon as I can. Even though my spirits are lighter, thanks to my effervescent friend, it's not coffee making my stomach roil. It's the blood seeping from under a scab she doesn't know she dislodged.

Maybe my real fear is, even though she likes me now, she won't forever. Her needling about Harville is an aside, but it has a barb. Traycee thinks I'm pretty cool… marginally cool… and she wants everyone to be happy. Heaven knows I understand battling a people-pleasing gene.

The crux of my dilemma is I'm not ready to let her know the real me, and I'm not ready to lose her.

I put on a good show, but this getting-healthy stuff ain't for the faint of heart.

And right now, I still have a little faint hanging on…

6
FINA

When I realize I'm not getting anything accomplished and the morning is getting away from me, I follow Mina's go-to routine and head to town. I can't fetch groceries, not that I usually do the shopping, but the Magnolia Market is her domain and always has been. Instead, I aim for the Emporium Traycee bought some years back and has turned into an amazing gift shop now quite the tourist destination for our little town.

No doubt Castle MacInnes is the biggest draw to Magnolia Bloom, but Traycee and the other retailers are doing a darn fine job of turning us into a weekend getaway, and I hope we'll surpass Fredericksburg as a sought-after locale before long.

I open the door, and the old-fashioned brass bell tinkles. The mixed scents from the candles and potpourri on the shelves make the space smell heavenly, and the air conditioner is working overtime. It might be the first week of October, but Texas weather doesn't seem to have gotten the memo it's fall.

I let the door shut, and I'm surprised to find Traycee's mother, my friend, at the helm.

"Hey, Ranelle, what're you doing manning the till this time of the morning? Is there a meeting of the Grannies today?"

"Lord, I don't know. I think my momma's social calendar is busier than mine. She normally watches the store for Traycee these days, but she's off to Texarkana, I think. Book club or something. The part-time girl should be here shortly."

"Lucky for me, you're subbing in. I haven't seen you in ages."

"It's good to see you. I'll walk here barefoot over a box of Legos if it means Traycee can make a meeting with your darlin' Kiki. I'm so grateful that girl came back to town. She's been a blessing."

"She has, indeed, and she feels the same way about Traycee, I assure you. How's Quinton?"

"Depends on if you ask me or him. Damn fool decided he could get up in the trees to trim the branches instead of letting the boys do it. He now has a broken wrist."

"You should be glad he can still climb trees."

"I am, but it means I have to do more work at playtime since he can't support himself on that arm."

I feel my cheeks heat. I'm no shrinking violet, but Ranelle's confident sexuality has always flummoxed me a bit. When we were in school, she and Joy Baker set the bar for being comfortable in their own skin. I can say I'm on the train, just not in the lead car. As for Ranelle, she's not about to let herself be put on a list for Shady Pines. In fact, she might be married with five kids and three grands, but you'd never know it on an average Friday night when she and Quinton are in a dance-off with Joy and whoever she has her sights on down at Tidy's club.

We all grew up together. Like most Bloomians, we went through all our grades together, diverging only after graduation. I went on to college, but Ranelle stayed in town, marrying Quinton, raising their kids, and helping him run the best butcher shop in town, until he had a heart attack at fifty-five. Which turned both their lives around.

Quinton found Jesus, CrossFit, and nutritional macros, in that order, and now has a body at sixty-two the envy of men half his age. Ranelle has no problem with his focus on healthy fats, protein, and carbs… and various forms of cardio keeping her smiling.

Truth is, I'm a little jealous.

"I have every confidence you're finding a work-around." I make sure my tone is droll.

"What're you up to? Don't normally see you downtown this time of day."

"I needed a break from my sister."

"Ah, the blushing bride climbing your last nerve?"

"A bit."

"Come on back to the tearoom and catch me up on the news. The bell will let us know if anyone comes in."

I settle into an empty chair while Ranelle putters to make us each a mug of Traycee's coffee of the day. A look around shows she's redone the chair cushions in a vibrant orange, green, and black tribal theme, and she's put up a shelves of books by a range of authors in a wild swing of genres. It's perfectly in tune with her rule of there-are-no-rules in the shop. You're as likely to be listening to a recording of spoken-word poetry as you are to hear Wynton Marsalis. And racks of dresses from the women she provides microloans to across the world sit next to distressed jeans Traycee has blinged herself with Swarovski crystals.

It's only a matter of minutes before Ranelle settles in across from me.

"So, tell me what's up? I haven't seen Mina's feet touch the ground in months."

"And you aren't going to, either."

"She deserves it."

I sigh. "And more. But if she doesn't stop talking, I might superglue her mouth shut, and then I'll feel even guiltier than I do right now."

Ranelle squints at me like she's forgotten her glasses. "What do you have to feel guilty about?"

"I feel like a heel saying it aloud, but in so many ways, Mina and I never needed anyone but each other, and now she's got CT and is starting a whole new life. I guess I'm feeling…"

"Left out?"

I play with the handle of my mug, stalling by taking a long sip. "Yes, if I have to be honest."

"If you ask me, what you're feeling is replaced. You've always needed Mina to need you."

I have to force myself to take a breath and sit back. The words are a bit bald, but that's Ranelle's nature.

"I suppose you're right, but I sure sound like a sad sack."

Ranelle reaches across the table and puts a comforting hand on my wrist. "Honey, I don't mean it that way. It's just that you two have been more than sisters your whole lives. I've got three of my own, and I'm not near as close to a single one of them. You're gonna have to say goodbye to a big part of you and do it in the midst of the busy season."

"Is that better or worse? I've got so much going on, I can't see right from left. Mina's wedding, a Yule Ball, Christmas Eve dinner at the castle, New Year's. And then we have this emergency wedding we're putting together for a Dallas councilwoman's daughter who lost her venue."

"I've met the little bridezilla. She came in with her diamond-crusted mama and honored us with a look around. I hope you're charging them an arm, a leg, a shoulder, and some teeth for all the trouble."

"And a spleen and a liver, I promise. But all the gold in Midas's treasury won't make the days longer."

"I guess you'd better learn to delegate."

"Which brings in more guilt that I'm putting too much on Kiki. She doesn't know the castle like we do. She's never been an event planner, and I can't overload her."

I don't expand on my worries about our prodigal daughter. Although Ranelle is well aware of what Kiki's going though, since she and Traycee have become such good friends and companions on their journeys, Kiki's business is her own.

Ranelle clicks a nail against the table, breaking the long silence. "She and Traycee are going to be fine. But tell me more about Violet's girl."

"The biggest thing is one look confirms she's David Broder's daughter."

"Get out."

"Yes, ma'am." I take the next few minutes catching her up on Violet's giving her girls up for adoption once David Broder made it clear he wasn't going to marry her after the accidental pregnancy. One decision, although no small one, set a lifetime of things in motion. "The chickens have come home to roost, as it were. Or at least, one chicken has." I try for humor, but my mood doesn't lift.

"I always thought David Broder and his family were nice people. Don't see them much, except at big town shindigs."

"I don't judge the whole family by the events hardly uncommon even today, but I'm having a hard time finding compassion for him in particular right now. I'll get there, because I do see his point about how things were in Magnolia Bloom in the '70s."

"Considering the Klan ran my grandmother out of this town when she fell in love with a white man in 1940, and she didn't come back until he passed, I can see his point, too, but that doesn't make it right. Gram came back when Momma had me in the '60s, but let's say it wasn't a good time to be anything but white in this town back then, and there were plenty of people trying to keep it that way."

"I know, and it's shameful. You and I are the same age, and we know Magnolia Bloom must deal with its history. It horrifies me we still have men like Clifford Saxon and his ilk around here, determined to keep hate alive."

"There will always be Clifford Saxons in this world, and his son is just like him. They're a cancer, and we can't seem to quite get rid of them."

"Sadly, their oily sludge still leaks from under the rocks every now and then."

"And we have to stay vigilant against them. It gets tiresome, though. I have enough Caucasian in my genes so I'm light-skinned enough to pass, but my momma wouldn't hear of it, even when I was a girl. It made it harder in some ways, but made me prouder in others. And it gave my Traycee those amazing hazel eyes."

"I understand recessive genes, so it wasn't hard to figure out even if I don't know your family genealogy, but I've never given it a lick of thought other than thinking her nine kinds of beautiful, inside and out."

"You and yours never were the kind we had to worry about."

"The fact your statement includes a *we* makes me madder than mentioning the Saxon boys."

"Things are getting better, but they aren't solved. Since we aren't going to fix the racial problems of the world today, let's table them, shall we?"

"Sounds fantastic. To tell you the truth, I don't think I have enough ink in my pen to put one more thing on my list, much less solving racial issues in the South."

A rustle at the employee entrance makes us both turn to the entryway as the part-timer returns.

"Hi, Miss Fina."

"Hello yourself, Suzanne. I didn't know you were working here." It's not like I can keep up with every single resident of Magnolia Bloom, but Suzanne is Brian Steele's great-niece, and he thinks the world of her, so of course, I do, too.

"Traycee hired me a month ago. I love it."

"That's wonderful. You feeling all right?"

"I'm fine. A little low on iron, is all." Her cheeks flush bright red, and she hurries forward with her left hand out. "I went to lunch with Little Joe, and right there in Vivann's, he went down on one knee and asked me to marry him."

She's beaming so brightly she practically raises the temperature in the room ten degrees. I "ooh" over her finger like she's wearing the Hope diamond. My heart goes out to Little Joe, because I know the box store ring is all he can manage on his salary from the paper mill. In my mind, his love makes the stone worth a hundred carats at least. These two will know some tough times, but they're starting out on a lovely note.

"I wish we could afford a wedding at the castle, but it's all right."

I force myself out of my wanderings and process what she's said. "Pishposh, Suzanne, of course you'll have your wedding at the castle. Your uncle Brian has been with Castle MacInnes as long as me, and since you might be the last wedding he gets to come to, you don't even think about anyplace else."

I listen to my mouth running ninety miles an hour and wonder if a person can kick themselves in the backside. I've got the emergency wedding, Mina, Thanksgiving, the Yule Ball, and Christmas Eve dinner, and I put another wedding on my plate?

I've lost my ever-loving mind.

Suzanne throws herself at me, and I barely have time to catch her as she gives me a hug, knocking the breath out of me. "Do you mean it, Miss Fina? We can't afford much. I mean, Momma and Daddy will try to help, but—"

"Stop, now. We'll work it all out when the time comes."

Ranelle steps in and gives Suzanne's shoulder a pat. "Go on, now. Let Miss Fina breathe. You go start making your lists since the store's quiet while I finish this cup of coffee with Miss Fina."

Suzanne gives an equally effervescent hug to Ranelle before floating out of the room.

I think I need to send my diplomas back to the University of Texas and SMU, because I'm foolishly saying yes to everything like an overzealous teenager. Not only have I added to a workload about to wreck me, I've added another wedding where I'll have to glow like Suzanne's my own. She's a doll and all, and I'm truly happy for her.

I'm just not sure I'm that good an actor.

7
KIKI

ANOTHER WEEK HAS PASSED, and I sit in my comfy chair on a bright, perfect, seventy-degree Monday morning. October is almost halfway in the bag, but I spare myself a little pity because I know most of the people in the service industry are in my same boat and don't have the luxury of days off until after the New Year. In my past, all holidays, major and minor, were only excuses to give my distillery of choice a hefty portion of my paycheck.

I look around and wonder if I'm supposed to call this room Violet's office or Paige's. Regardless, I've come to love the iconic space. It doesn't feel like mine, but how many people get to say they have a desk in an honest-to-goodness turret in an honest-to-goodness castle?

Castle MacInnes pays homage to the famous Inveraray Castle on Loch Fyne because my great-great-grandmother has family in the Argyll clan and because she stayed there during the Civil War when her father wanted her safely out of Galveston. Other than the front view causing you to do a kind of double take at the gorgeous schist stone and iconic turrets, if you're familiar with Inveraray, everything about Castle MacInnes diverges from there.

I have no idea what my distant relations in Argyll do with their turrets, but ours—the East Turret at least—provide respite and solace and workspace for a few very lucky people. One of those immensely blessed people is me. No one's happier than I am to see Paige and her rather handsome hubby, Zach, have mended a pretty deep hurt and are... *ahem*... making up in as many countries as they can for the final quarter of the year.

I don't want to cut short her happiness, but I sure wish she'd get back and take over this desk again. Thankfully, being busy makes the hours pass quickly, as the fading sunset attests. Most of all, it's a cocoon where I feel, temporarily at least, safe and secure. And alone.

A rustle at the door turns my attention in Juliette's direction before she can knock.

"Bonjour, Kiki. Ça va?"

"Ça va."

We've now exhausted half of my college French. We have French ancestry on Evajean's mother's side, but the Scottish side pretty much took over once they established Magnolia Bloom and Evajean started building a castle. Juliette has promised to teach me more of her native language, and I've pledged to teach her more slang, although Mina's probably a better source of Texas colloquialisms, even if I am a native.

She waits so quietly I realize I have to nudge her. "Is there something I can do for you?"

"Oui, if you can."

"I'm happy to try." I invite her in with a sweep of my arm to the chair across from me.

"I met a gentleman named Rory on my walk, and he is going to introduce me to his grand-mère, whose maman knew Gavina. I was wondering if you know of anyone else I might speak with? Violet's journals contain fond memories but have little detail of Gavina's life."

I instantly picture Rory's kind, weathered features. He and his family have been the backbone of our animal husbandry, whether horses, sheep, or dogs. I think Alisdair was best friends with Rory's whatever-great-grandfather, and an heir of his family line has been on the property since the first herds and litters were established.

"Makes sense Gavina would know Rory's grandmother. She was

one of the first veterinarians on the estate, and Gavina was involved in everything having to do with the animals around here. I'm glad you met Rory. He's such a nice man, and I love those sheep so much."

"They are adorable. A little one named Lulu decided she likes me, and I want to bring her home quite badly."

"I understand how tempting it would be, but I bet Rory would go into Hulk mode."

"I'm sorry. I do not understand."

"He would be super protective."

"Ah, bien sûr, he is quite the guardian."

The corners of her dark eyes crinkle, and I admit I'm a little intimidated by my cousin, which is rare for me. It's not her beauty, because I refuse to default to such a boring descriptor, even if she is moviestar pretty. It's more if I had to pick one adjective to describe her, I'd choose *intense*.

I ponder a moment to answer her original question. "I'm not nearly as familiar with everyone on the property as Mina and Fina, but my first guess would be Mrs. Greene, their mom. Eunice been the cook here forever."

"Merci, I will speak with her."

"Happy to help. And, Juliette?" I have to say something comforting. I know what it's like to navigate something completely foreign, whether it's sobriety or a new family, and she and I are both in new territory. "I know I'm speaking for the whole family when I say how much we appreciate what you're doing. Gavina was amazing, no doubt. I see the paintings in the armory and the photographs of her in a whole new light. There's bound to be some information on her in the library, too, but it might take some digging."

"I do not mind being a detective. I enjoy a challenge."

My laugh is a little bit of a cough. "Don't be hasty. We lost our master librarian a few years ago, and the family volunteers are all wonderful, but are half a century behind. You might need those Sherlock-level skills."

Juliette tilts her head, her perfectly cut pixie framing a heart-shaped face, the blue-black hair a perfect foil for her luminous eyes so dark it's hard to distinguish her pupils from her irises in this light. I can see a little of Violet in her features, but she looks a thousand times more like her father. She's likely read far enough in the journals to know David Broder is her bio dad, but she hasn't brought him up, so I won't either.

I force my brain back to the subject at hand. "The thing is, I'm afraid you won't find the deeper story of Gavina's life. She wasn't like Violet. She didn't write journals, and from what I know, she was intensely private."

"You mean because she was a lesbienne? C'est d'un ridicule."

"I agree, it's ridiculous."

"One cannot look at the canvases waiting for me and not see the passion she poured onto each one. A single portrait might merely be proof of a talented artist. The series leaves no doubt about the tragedy."

"She lived in a different time."

"I am not the French woman who believes my country is perfect, but in this instance, I find myself angry with yours. I have few avenues to discover a woman who was a master artist. She could have been, still might be, in the Louvre. And she spent her time rescuing horses and playing with dogs. And all because she was gay."

I expect her to go *pfft*, but she stops. I can't help being defensive. "From what I know, she had a good life, so I wouldn't presume the path she chose was so horrible."

"But her talent. Her skill. Wasted."

"Was it? Aren't you working on a barn full of her creations?"

Juliette pulls back, then forces her shoulders to relax. "I'm sorry. I become rather passionate when it comes to art."

I wave my hand and add a twang. "Ain't no thing. Don't you bother your pretty self about it."

She lets the momentary tension go as quickly as I have. "Yes, ma'am."

Her Texas accent is so bad, I groan. "Stick to French, sweetie. I'll need a year to wrangle a proper drawl out of you."

"I will depend on you for my education."

She stands, her posture so perfect I wonder if they teach it in school in France. Or in Germany where she did her graduate work. Either way, I wish I had her regal stillness.

"Again, merci, Kiki. There is not much yet, but come by the barn, and I shall show you the progress I am making on these masterpieces."

I'm pleased at how easily *barn* comes to her, since, like a lot of things around here, it's a misnomer. It's the only climate-controlled place with amazing natural light to suit her needs. Even Evajean's ingenious use of windows couldn't make a castle of schist stone the best work zone for Juliette. As a bonus, the barn serves as an event space in inclement weather and has the one thing she seems to need most—solitude.

"I can't wait."

Juliette leaves me alone with my spreadsheets, laptop, and Paige's impressive document-management system. I have zero idea how Violet or any of our predecessors managed such a huge estate without modern technology. Fifty square miles, thirty-two thousand acres, the castle, outbuildings, three manor houses and other dwellings, stables for horses, barns for sheep, kennels for dogs, paddocks, fields for grazing, fields for farming. It's incomprehensible when I try to take it all in, so I make myself take smaller, more manageable bites.

My phone chirps, startling me out of my studying. Traycee's picture is on the display.

"Hey, Trace. What's up?"

"I'm at St. Andrew's. Can you come over?"

Her voice is harried, and my nerves go straight to high alert. "St. Andrew's? Why?"

"It's Bethanie. CT's daughter. I need you."

"At the church?"

Traycee takes a sharp breath, and the volume goes down, like she's holding the receiver away from her. "Hang on, okay? Kiki will be here in a minute."

I will?

"Trace, what's going on?"

"Pastor Harville called me. He found Bethanie passed out on the back steps, but she woke up enough to ask him to call me. I'm freaking out. Bethanie won't let me call anyone but you."

"Do you need an ambulance?"

"We only have a volunteer ambulance here, so it's a crap shoot if Allen or Eddie will be available. It would be faster if I drove her to Atlanta, but I don't know if she needs a hospital. Maybe? She's talking."

I forget how small Magnolia Bloom is sometimes. I'm out of my chair, keys in hand, and I pound down the back stairway. I can hear the nervousness rising in Traycee's voice, so I default to my respond-now-panic-later mode.

"If she's talking, it's a good sign. Did she say why she called you?"

"I used to be a frequent flier in the beer and wine aisle at the market. Bethanie noticed when I changed from cases of beer to cases of mineral water. Made a crack one day, and I could tell she was several vodkas in but still behind her register. Anyway, I told her about the meetings and left the seed to fall where it would."

"Keep her awake if you can. Is Harville there?"

"Right here."

"Great. If she starts to vomit, turn her to keep her from aspirating. Call the fire department if she seizes. I know we have some EMTs in the VFD who can respond. If you can't get assistance, have Harville call the emergency number at the clinic and see if someone can meet you there."

I hang up and race down to my car. I'm kicking up gravel and despairing at one of the unfortunate aspects of living in a small town. When minutes count, help's an hour away. The good side is, I barely have time to fret before I'm swinging around behind the church and setting the parking brake.

It's Harville's tall, still form meeting me in the back entryway.

"Thanks so much for coming. Traycee's with Bethanie back here." He gestures toward the end of the long hallway.

"I'm not sure what I can do, but I'm happy to try."

Harville's office is cool and quiet when I walk in. Bethanie is sitting, a trash can between her knees.

Wise.

Traycee is beside Bethanie on the couch, not touching her, but vigilant. I'm proud of her. She starts to rise, but I wave her back and go to my knees on Bethanie's other side.

"Hey, Bethanie. Looks like you've had a bit of a rough ride."

She starts to laugh, but it triggers a heave so she stops. "I need to go home. I'm okay."

"Sweetie, you're not okay. I'd bet a pay grade you need some IV fluids. Can I take you to the urgent care and get you fixed up?"

Our local clinic is somewhere between a doc-in-a-box and a really small ER. They aren't set up to handle true emergencies, but I bet they can do a bag of electrolytes in a pinch. If we can reach a staff member.

"I want to go home."

"Is there anyone who can stay with you?"

"Leave me alone, okay?"

I don't try to touch her, but I inch closer. "I can't, Bethanie. I'll take you home if you don't throw up anymore, but I won't leave you alone. If you pass out again, I will take you to the hospital. Are we clear?"

I use my don't-mess-with-me tone but add a dash of softness.

"Okay, whatever. I want to go to sleep."

"Not yet. We need to get some fluids in you and talk for a little while."

As I stand, Traycee does, too. Harville moves in closer, but I make no attempt to keep Bethanie from hearing me. "Harville, please type her address into my GPS. Traycee, go to the store and buy some bananas and electrolyte solution. If there's none in the aisle where the diarrhea medicine is, there'll be some in the baby aisle. Get some Sprite or 7 Up and some crackers. I'll get her home and cleaned up by the time you get there."

Harville has already done his job by the time I stop speaking.

"Is there anything else I can do? Should I call her father?" He still has my phone in his hand, waiting expectantly.

"No!" Bethanie jerks like she's going to stand up but falls back on the couch. "Don't. I mean it."

I give him a quick headshake. "Thank you, but if nothing happens while I'm driving her home, I'll stay with my plan."

"I can come with you. If you need help?"

His generosity and sincerity in this awkward moment resonate in a bruised part of me. I never had someone to pick me up and not judge me. I never had anyone to pick me up at all. It's by the grace of forces beyond my comprehension I always woke up in a position where I didn't asphyxiate.

It's awkward to feel such kindness now, even if it's not directed at me.

"I appreciate the offer. It would be great if you'd help me get her home. I'm reasonably strong, but a passed-out drunk is pure dead weight."

With our plan mapped out, Harville half carries Bethanie outside and eases her into my passenger seat, makes sure her limbs are clear, and closes the door slowly until it gives a firm click. Every moment is measured. He never loses his shadow of concern.

I listen to the GPS and follow the directions, only to realize our destination is a mere block from the church. Harville stays right behind me as Traycee peels off toward the store. When I realize Bethanie's apartment is on the second floor, I'm beyond grateful I accepted Harville's help. He might be slender, but apparently there's some hefty muscles under his button-down, and if I were the confessing type, I'd admit I'm pleasantly surprised.

I fish the keys from Bethanie's purse and have us inside with little fanfare. It irritates me I'm breathing harder than Harville is after the climb up the stairs, but I distract myself by settling my charge on the couch.

Might need to restart some PT there, Kiki, or join a gym. Didn't think I'd lose my stamina this quickly.

"Should I make coffee?" Harville's voice is so sweet, and it's clear he hasn't dealt with passed-out people very often. Ever?

"Oldest myth in the world. Doesn't sober anyone up. All you get is a wide-awake drunk. Just some tap water until Traycee gets here. It's all about hydration right now."

I rummage in Bethanie's room for a clean T-shirt. Harville steps out while I get her ruined blouse changed, although I'm sure, if I needed his help, he'd be there. I wouldn't have to ask twice.

"I want to go to sleep." Bethanie tries to fall to her side, but I stop her.

"Not yet. Your body needs to process some of whatever you've taken, and time's the only thing fitting the bill."

She hunches forward, her elbows on her knees and her head in her hand. I'll leave her be as soon as I can tell she's not asleep sitting up.

Traycee arrives with a sack from Magnolia Market. I start Bethanie on a banana, then hand her a Sprite mixed with an electrolyte tab fizzing away. She declines the crackers, which is fine. It's about what she can handle to settle her stomach, not the food specifically. The potassium from the banana is the best choice anyway.

With Traycee returned to her calm and dependable self, I go to Harville and walk him to the door.

"Thank you so much for helping. I couldn't have gotten her up those stairs by myself."

"My pleasure. Are you sure you don't want me to stay? Help keep watch?"

I put my hand on his arm and squeeze. It wasn't my intent to do a bicep check, but I got my answer about hidden powers. "She seems okay. I'll stay the night to make sure she doesn't start vomiting again or slip into a coma. It doesn't happen often, but I don't know her, so she might not have been honest about only drinking whiskey." I give him the wry-smile-eyebrow-lift combo. "Spoiler alert. Addicts lie."

"You were amazing."

My heart races. Most people don't go into fight-or-flight mode when receiving a compliment, but I seem to be one of the odd few. Harville's kind words make the agony in my gut go supernova. He hasn't realized why I so easily know what to do, and when he does, his admiration will do an about-face so fast he might get whiplash.

"That's me. Mad skills. Thanks again." I use opening the door to hide the shame flaming my cheeks.

For the rest of the night, Traycee and I take turns playing guardian.

Sometimes talking to each other, sometimes lost in our own memories of when we were the ones ruining other people's evenings.

The morning sun rouses a grouchy, hungover, but out-of-immediate-danger Bethanie. Traycee and I both give her our two cents, which she responds to with *uh-huhs*, the behavior straight out of my former playbook. She's listened but hasn't heard, and it's a sad reminder of why I'm grateful to be as far as I am along my new path.

Traycee pulls me into a fierce hug when we get to our cars. "Thank you so much. I didn't know what to do."

I brush a tear from her beautiful cheek. "Hey, what are these for? You did great."

"I… no…" She bites her lips together and won't meet my eyes for a long moment. When she does, there's a guarded shadow I hate to see. "Thanks."

Something pings my gut-meter, but she doesn't elaborate. I chalk it up to the same emotions churning in me. It's hard to see such stark reminders of our previous behaviors, and Traycee is still so newly sober, I'm sure it hit her even harder.

We wave goodbye, and she rolls down her window as we're about to pull out.

"If I make an extra meeting this week, want to come? I know you're getting super busy at the castle and all."

"Sure. Call me."

She drives away, and I sit for a moment, looking at the church in my line of sight down the street. The damage is done as far as Harville is concerned, so maybe I should give some thought to starting a group here in town. I don't want to. I don't want to be responsible for anything but myself right now. Yet there's clearly a need.

I remind myself I've had a long night, and there's no need to make any decisions without some decent sleep. I'll find the gumption to talk to Harville.

Just not today.

8
JULIETTE

I'm lost in the top right corner of the portrait I've named *Hauntings of Regret* when I hear a familiar noise outside. After slipping off my mask, I go to the door and open it to a sweet black face looking up at me.

Baaaa.

I bend and run my hand over her soft back, clearly fresh from the shearing shed, but I'd recognize my sweet girl anywhere.

"Bonjour to you, too. You look so different with your new haircut."

Another familiar voice comes from behind her. "She's going to be renamed Houdini. Lulu is too sweet for this rascal."

Lulu bounds away from him and behind my legs, clearly thinking I'm going to protect her.

"I take it our escapee did not like her beauty treatment?"

"Interesting thing is, this breed is the easiest of them all to shear. They're so placid, and in this heat, they're quite happy with a trim. This girl, though, is going to drive me to drink."

I trail a fingertip down the front of his shirt. "You do not look as though you have come from the sheep barn to mine."

"Kaden's doing the last of the herd with a gentleman we hire every year. Don't know what I'm going to do when Robert retires, because I don't want to take the mantle back up again."

"Your son does all the shearing? That seems overwhelming."

"He and I used to do it all, but I'm quite content to leave this particular job to him and Rob. Gave me time to give myself a little spit shine before we get on the road to see my grandmother."

He cleans up nicely, as the expression goes. He's dressed as I expected for our sojourn this morning to see his grand-mère—blue jeans worn and washed enough times to have formed to his slender frame, a chambray shirt, brown belt.

The differences, though subtle, are obvious. His boots are dark brown and well polished, the hat in his hand is a finely creased felt the shade of a newborn fawn, and he has somehow found time since our meeting and between his busy days of shearing to have his own hair cut. What was a bit unruly peeking out from his battered work hat now sits neatly trimmed and carefully combed, and a hint of spicy cologne tickles my nose.

"Did you stand in line, too?" I let my eyes stray to the white line above his tanned neck, but make sure the teasing is kind.

He blushes and runs a self-conscious hand down the back of his head. "Not exactly, but I probably should've let Kaden have at me. He's pretty fast with his clippers."

"If it matters, I approve and appreciate your efforts on my behalf."

I don't tell him my biggest surprise is the smallest detail. The lining fabric on his collar stand and the front placket of his shirt, unbuttoned at the top to show a hint of this intriguing side of my personal guide to all things Valais-related, is a kaleidoscopic print of purples, oranges, and greens. The pop of brilliant color is beautiful and completely unexpected.

Apparently, assumptions are unwise with this man who spends his days mostly in solitude, even if his charges are largely adorable.

I wave him inside. Lulu hasn't waited for an invitation and is exploring the edges of the space already a comfortable home to me. A small cramp in my back makes me wince and reminds me I've bent over the table for too long.

"That doesn't look too comfortable." Rory notices my momentary frown and eyes my workbench with the canvas laid flat and the simple tools I have collected arranged to the left.

"It isn't. The tracking on my shipment indicates my easels should arrive today or tomorrow, and my personal tools will be here as well."

"Can I see what you're working on?"

"Bien sûr." Even though the unit is quiet, I turn the filtration fan off, and an even softer silence descends on the room. I wait until he has moved to the side of the table and has had a moment to observe the masterpiece I have chosen first.

"Pretty lady." Rory's observation is quaint.

"I am trying to find out more about her. It is clear she is someone of deep importance to Gavina."

He agrees but is intent on the woman caught in a moment of time. "I had no idea Gavina had ever been this much in love."

I cock my head. "I'm intrigued by your interpretation after such a quick inspection."

He looks at me as if he's confused, his brow furrowing. "What other could there be? This little lady looks like she wants to get off her couch and go make love to whoever she's looking at, and since Gavina painted this, well, kinda makes sense."

I don't say anything as his gaze returns to the portrait as if magnetized. I know how he feels.

He continues before I can offer any rebuttal. "I guess that's not fair, because it could be Gavina was a darned good artist, so I'm probably assuming things 'cause I know about her. Gavina, I mean. I'm sad as heck she was alone her whole life, especially if she really was in love with someone as pretty as this." His hand twitches in a short wave. "I was thirteen when she passed, and teenage boys aren't known to be observant, and certainly not of older women, but I caught things my momma and Mamaw said over the years."

He's so sweet and self-deprecating, and something moves inside me. If I were testing him, which I confess might have been a part of my intent, he would pass with proverbial flying colors.

"This is one of the least-damaged pieces. As I am waiting for my tools, it made the most sense to start here, but I admit I am drawn to it quite strongly."

"What are you doing to it?"

I'm bewildered he seems genuinely interested. Art restoration isn't a sexy vocation, although Noelle does accuse me of being obsessed. I'm not, however, prone to thinking anyone but me, and maybe a few dozen in the entire art world, finds what I do particularly compelling.

"I've begun the surface cleaning so I can then remove the old varnish. Even though the paintings were stored in darkness, which is why the colors are still so vibrant, nothing can stop the aging process. The coatings used in the era tend to yellow."

"And you're doing the whole thing with cotton swabs?" The pile of discarded bits beside the work are the reason for his question.

"Not entirely. There are sections where I can use somewhat larger pieces of fabric, still cotton, but this process cannot be hurried. Every detail must be addressed with extreme care, even with this first stage. The closer I get to the paint itself, the more meticulous I must be."

"Makes sense. I guess I never thought about it."

A laugh floats up from within me, and I take a second to marvel. *Laughter* and *floating* aren't words my sister would ever apply to me. "Did you not chastise me in your field that I would not know details about your flock as I'm not a sheepherder?"

He flushes, which is instantly endearing. "I didn't chastise, exactly."

"And I am not, either. I'm merely applying your logic. There is no sense in you berating yourself about the details of restoring a painting if I'm forgiven my ignorance of sheep."

"Well, there we go, then. We've had our first tussle."

I frown, not out of anger, but because I'm searching for a definition. My English is quite good, but these Texans throw terms around which do not come easily to me… or at all.

"Tussle?"

"Like a not-mad fight."

"Ah, then we've reached a benchmark, it seems."

The slow lift of his lips is like the rest of him. Gentle. Confident. Contained.

I study him as intently as I do any new subject, then force myself to look away. Noelle has told me endlessly that I make people uncomfortable, even when I don't mean to. I simply jaw found no other way to gather the data I need to decide if I can risk myself with a person, even on the most basic social level. I don't have her ability to make every human a friend within seconds of meeting. She has a gift I lack completely.

I try to cover my sudden awkwardness by putting away my supplies. "Let me wash my hands, and we can get going, non?"

"Sure thing. It's no priceless painting, but I ran a hose over the truck to get the worst of the dirt off. Sorry I didn't have time to give it a proper wash, but I'm never going so far as to attack it with Q-tips."

He is clearly having a go at me, and even though I feel the heat rising up my neck, I appreciate his effort. To say I'm astounded would be an understatement. I'm hardly a droll spinster. I laugh. Often. But almost never with someone I hardly know.

Change that to never ever.

I think my cheeks might be hurting when I hurry to the sink and make quick work of tidying up.

"What do we do with this one?" I look down to my new shadow watching me, her black-button eyes shiny and curious.

"We'll drop her off at the barn as we leave. Kaden will take her back out."

Lulu follows like the most-well-trained dog I've ever had as we walk toward a large truck with the MacInnes brand emblazoned on the side. The artist in me appreciates how simply the graphic designer denoted a castle turret, a blacknose sheep, and a border collie, all with simple lines and two-color laminate. It's rather brilliant, actually.

I pause, unsure of propriety, but ask, "Can she go with us?"

"Lulu?" He looks down at the lamb, and she looks back.

Baaaaa.

"Apparently, she likes the idea." He gives a chuckle. "I take lambs to see Mamaw and her sisters, and anyone else jaw-jacking with her, so I'm sure it'll be fine. Especially since she's all shorn and pretty."

I don't say anything to make him second-guess his decision. We all walk the rest of the way to the vehicle in blissful silence, including Lulu. Moreover, it's a comfortable silence I find both easy and strangely welcome.

I have always been the opposite of my twin. Noelle makes friends instantly and doesn't know a stranger. On the other hand, I am paralyzed when first meeting someone, and my behavior is often taken as rudeness when it is merely an inability to connect with another person on any level until I know something about them. To become friends or, in some cases, lovers takes me weeks to months to sometimes years to achieve a level of resonance.

I make a mental note to provide my train of thought more time. These weeks of minimal contact with my twin means I've been more lost in my musings than normal, and it strikes me one reason for our disparate feelings about the discovery of this new side of our family is obvious. Noelle has plenty of outlets and inlets for her emotional needs and has a place she can store her discomfort until she decides to deal with it.

I do not.

Therefore, my desire for this connection is nuanced and complex. For her, there is no hole in her history, no delineated sheet of questions. If she feels any angst, she can quickly call on someone to assuage the itch. I do not have such friends or even the skill to know how to ask.

Rory holds the passenger door for me, then the back door for Lulu. She jumps in, poking her nose over the center console dividing the front seats as if she is accustomed to riding there. He meets my eyes with a wry shrug, and I'm curious if my mouth wonders why we're using our smiling muscles so much in one day.

"Merci, monsieur."

He tips his hat and walks around to the driver's side. He slides in, gives Lulu a pat, removes his hat, places it on the dashboard, clips his seat belt, starts the engine, puts the truck in drive, and starts us moving… all in one smooth series of movements bearing resemblance to an orchestra conductor.

"Does that not get tiresome?" I point to the dash.

"Pardon?"

"The constant management of your hat. On outside, off indoors, on with men, off with ladies, inconvenient in a vehicle."

He pauses, frowns, but then his face clears. "I guess I've never thought about it. I'd be a dang fool to be without one in the Texas sun with this skin, so it's always been a part of my day."

He drives with the same temperament as the rest of his personality. Smooth acceleration and deceleration, courteous use of turn signals, nothing jerky or sudden. He drives as he inhabits space. Quietly.

We chat about other odds and ends. He answers my questions about the Texas weather and if all of October will be as hot as it has begun.

"We're different than Arbois, for certain. You're used to seventies in the daytime by now, and we won't really hit them as an average until the end of the month."

I'm touched he's taken the time from his busy schedule to research my home. "I was prepared for the temperature on an intellectual level, but I confess it has been far warmer than I'm used to."

Our conversation doesn't have the chance to delve deeper into mundanity as we arrive at the Spring Valley Retirement Center on the outskirts of Atlanta, Texas. I am not familiar with the area, although I have come to understand Atlanta is the default destination for Magnolia Bloomians who need something more than their small town can provide but don't want to go west to Dallas or north to Texarkana.

All I know is Rory has made quick work of the trip, talking enough to make the drive comfortable but without incessant chatter. Lulu watches the scenery, looking at me at intervals as if asking if I'm enjoying the view. And before I have time to get anxious, as I am wont to do when forced to be in one place for too long – excluding my workspace – Rory has parked, pulled a leash from his glove compartment, and we're met by several ladies in matching scrubs who look about my age.

Lulu immediately takes all the attention, which is fine by me, and after many stops to talk to people who greet Rory by name, he leads me through the complex with the certainty of someone who has been here many times and introduces me to a trio of women sitting under the shade of a towering oak.

He addresses a woman whose body cannot hide the toll time has taken, but whose eyes are as quick and bright as ever.

"Mamaw, this is Juliette Laurant. She's an art restorer from France, and she's working on Miss Gavina's paintings they found a few months back. Juliette, this is my grandmother, Ida Gail Clemson, and those two beauties beside her are her sisters, Aunt Willie and Aunt Myra. This trio keeps the entire staff on their toes."

All three ladies laugh, but Ida takes control of the conversation. "That's because we're old, not dead. Time for being quiet is when you're six feet under." She holds out her hand, which I take, but with care as her bluster does not change that her fingers are ravaged by arthritis. "Sit, sit. You're going to crick my neck if we have to talk like this all afternoon."

Rory and I take the vacant seats around the small table and accept glasses of soda as we settle. Lulu makes the rounds and, after being sufficiently adored, plops down on the grass beside my feet. I admit it pleases me she chooses me for the honor.

We exchange all the usual pleasantries, and I feel my first moment of discomfort when Ida looks at me for a long time, frowning as she studies me like an art patron at an exhibit.

"Rory said your name is Laurant, but you sure look like a Broder. A little too much for coincidence, by my reckoning."

"Mamaw, she—"

"It's all right, Rory." It is unusual for me to interrupt, but I can feel his discomfort as clearly as if he's wearing a sandwich board listing a menu of his feelings. "I am a Broder, technically. My birth mother was Violet MacInnes, and I found out about my Texas connection a few months ago."

Ida pauses, I assume doing the mental math. "I worked on the estate my entire life, and it's no surprise you can't keep much secret in this town. Thing is, I never saw nor heard about Violet getting pregnant. I'm guessing this all happened while Gavina took her to France after she graduated from UT."

The two aunts nod in unison, and Ida continues. "I was pretty busy those years, as Doc Eckert had passed, so I was the only vet for miles in any direction."

Rory interjects proudly. "My grandmother was the first female veterinarian on the estate."

"Thanks to Gavina, and her folks, of course. I don't remember Alisdair. He died when I was eleven, but Evajean and Gavina were forces of nature, I tell you. They knew I was in love with anything with fur or feathers, and even though I was sixteen when I married Earl, they paid for me to go to Baylor and then veterinary school at Cornell. And in there was World War II and me having Rory's mama, Crystal."

"My goodness, how... amazing."

"Why?" Ida is blunt, and the question is not idle. "Because we're all hicks here in Texas?"

I pull back, needing to process the change in energy. "I did not mean any disparagement at all. I merely meant your story is amazing for anyplace in the world at the time, especially for a woman with dreams beyond marriage and child-rearing. France has its own history of suffrage, so I meant nothing derogatory about Texas in particular."

"Mamaw gets riled sometimes." Rory's discomfort touches a chord in me. It appears we are both unnerved by strife. "Miss Evajean and Miss Gavina were something to behold. You didn't have to be blood to get them fired up about making things happen on this estate, or in this town."

Ida's features smooth. "I apologize for being waspish. I wasn't especially close to Gavina, but she'd come to the barns or the stable and tell me to get my behind to school. Not exactly par for the course in the late '30s. I think she got back from France in 1935. Or '38. I can't recall exactly. Before the war. Anyway, in '42, I married Earl, but Gavina would not hear of me not going to college, and let me tell you, when she wanted something to happen, it did—world war or no world war."

"And Earl did not mind?"

Everyone around the table laughs.

"I think my Earl was some kinda reincarnation of Alisdair MacInnes, even though we're no relation at all. Let's say once he knew I wanted to be a vet, he was beside himself because we were too poor to entertain the notion. But Gavina made it all happen. I don't know what I did to deserve someone like him, but he was daddy to Crystal while I was off finishing classes. Those were hard years, and not because of money or even the war itself, but because travel between here and Waco and then Ithaca wasn't exactly easy. I was gone a lot."

I'm starting to rethink how hard I've believed it was for me to pursue my degrees and internships. I realize what I consider difficulties pales in comparison, as I had modern technology and conveniences, and I also didn't have a young child to consider.

I'm more than happy to let Ida continue.

"Gavina was driven. She had it in her to change the world for women and railed against the strictures of society back then. But she wasn't a loud woman and did her part one person at a time on this very estate. The only thing she asked in return was you paid her largesse forward, which is why you'll find a lot of strong female voices in the heart of East Texas, not exactly known as a bastion of feminism, or liberalism of any sort. Lord knows she's proof of how one person can change a whole lot of lives."

Her words make me feel guilty for my prior conversation with Kiki in which I declared Gavina had wasted her life. Hubris is a bitter pill to swallow.

"I can attest to her amazing skill as an artist, but this information is exactly what I was hoping to find."

"It's a good thing you found me now, because when I'm gone, there's not many left to remember her. You can talk to Eunice Greene. She's Mina and Fina's momma. She was the chief cook and knew the family well, but we're about the last of that generation."

"Rory mentioned her, thank you. I will definitely speak to her." I look to Rory and then back to his grandmother. "I'm told Gavina did not leave any diaries, such as those from Violet."

"Lord, no. That woman was a vault. Even as many years as we worked together, when I came home all full of myself, Gavina would steer me right and take a pin to my bubble when I was too big for my britches. She was never mean, but if you want the definition of a straight shooter, it was Gavina MacInnes. You can probably find some film of her, though, in the veterinary office."

I glance at Rory, and he shrugs. "I'll have a talk with some folks when we get back. I know Violet was on a preservation kick of all the estate records, but I have to confess I've never given it a lot of thought."

"Not your bailiwick." Ida takes a drink from her glass, the ice long melted. "So tell me about yourself, Juliette. I hadn't heard about Violet ever having a child, so this is out of left field."

"It's children, actually. My twin, Noelle, and I were born in France. Violet gave us up for adoption, with the help of Gavina."

All three gray heads bob in agreement. "Of course Gavina was involved."

"According to Violet's diaries, she believed both Noelle and I would be stigmatized in the community here. I'm sure her reasons were far deeper, but in the end, Gavina took her to France to see my grand-mère in Arbois and allowed my maman and papa to adopt us. It was an amazing gift."

"You knew you were adopted?"

"Mais oui, my parents never hid it."

"But you're just now trying to find out about this side of your family?"

"It is a long story, but my sister was fervently against knowing anything about our past. Our parents accepted it was painful for her, and over time, it became taboo. I am the one who needed to know, but I put the desire aside as our lives were busy. Then Paige came to France, and once the ball started rolling, I could not stop it."

"I take it your sister isn't here with you?"

"Noelle is quite angry with me. While we are twins, we are not identical in temperament. It surprised her when I remained firm to come here, to explore a family I knew I had in theory, but not in reality."

"So you've met the Broders."

"Not yet. I'm trying to navigate what I've been told both obliquely and directly. In the meantime, my attention is on Gavina and my… and Violet."

"Gavina and Violet should've been mother and daughter, not great-aunt and niece."

"I think the same thing, after reading the diaries."

Ida is quiet for a long moment. "Violet was a force to behold managing the estate, but she wasn't involved in the animal husbandry side of things. She had so many plates to keep in the air, you could look at the East Turret most any night and her window'd be lit up. You knew she was poring over some report or plan. She was a lot like Gavina. Determined. Fierce."

"'Fierce' seems to be a recurrent word, and I see the same traits in Kiki as well, although I know her even less than I know Mina and Fina so far."

"Speaking of twins, they are a hoot, aren't they?"

I assume *hoot* means *amusing*. "Indeed. Each time I see Mina, I expect to see a stream of rainbow glitter trailing behind her."

The ladies and Rory agree in unison. "A surprise out of nowhere, for sure, but everyone is so happy for her and CT."

Ida tap-taps the table. "Goes to show you all your best-laid plans are out the window when love decides to fly in."

I do not wish to come across as negative, so I hide my thought that sometimes love doesn't fly in at all… or, in Gavina's case, it flies away.

It seems Ida reads my mind, or my expression is not as controlled as I believed. "It was a crying shame Gavina never got to have her love, but I'll tell you something age gives me the gumption to say. She poured all her love into this estate because she was too scared to live the life she wanted."

"Mamaw—"

"You hush, now. I've earned the right to speak my mind, because what's anyone gonna do to me now?"

I fight a grin trying to break free and stay silent.

"Gavina was a fine woman. So was Violet, but she found her way with Brian, and them being a couple was the secret everyone knew. They didn't want to be public, and they allowed no shame, but in the end, there's a piece of sad there, too. As for Gavina, I know what life was like for her back when I was a young girl, and it was twenty times worse at the turn of the century when she and that girl had to give each other up. It's not fair, and it's not right, but Gavina also chose to be alone. She didn't have to be. But there's consequences to every choice. Some good, some bad. You have to live with both."

Noelle immediately springs to my mind, and I stumble mentally at Ida's wisdom.

As if sensing my distress, Lulu rises and bumps against my leg. In a move I can see is becoming automatic, I reach down to stroke her silky cheek and gaze into her midnight eyes.

There will be consequences for my decision to open this box, and I only hope I'm ready for the *some good, some bad* awaiting me.

9
KIKI

WHEN MY PHONE pings and I see a text from CT asking me if I'll meet him at Harville's office at eleven, I about put a cramp in my cheek from smiling. All I can think is, *What is that sweet man thinking up now to surprise Mina?*

I type back, Happy to.

I wasn't present for the buildup to the love affair, but Paige has given me the details, and it doesn't take a split second of asking Mina to tell her story for her to levitate off the floor with happiness.

I have about thirty minutes before I need to leave for town, so I throw on a slice of mascara and a swipe of lip gloss, then dive back into the newest rounds of demands from the various members of the emergency wedding, referred to around the castle as the EW. Since I know Fina won't actually take out her precious sister and bury her on the back forty, I might use the empty plot for the bridezilla from Dallas. I'm beginning to think her other venue didn't have a major shutdown after all. They didn't want to deal with Her Highness of Self-Indulgence, Miss Wynona Emmaline Glassman.

I stare across the turret at Gavina's rendering of a street scene in Paris. I've been there twice, and the painting takes me right back… to the parts not lost to an alcohol haze. Between my atomizer gently wafting the smell of ylang-ylang around the room, the morning light streaming in through the window slits, and the new cushions Mina made me when she heard green was my favorite color, the space is slowly becoming mine. The touches from the past, like Evajean's desk and chair, Gavina's painting, Violet's meticulous attention to detail, and Paige's mind-boggling effort to get everything modernized... It all makes me feel at home.

There's no doubt, though, that Gavina's art holds the soul of the room. Most of her work was portraiture, but in the treasure trove there are a number of still lifes and other non-people canvases. I know exactly zero about art, except what I like, so Juliette has been incredibly patient with my questions and observations.

I like my cousin. I don't know the halves and removeds, and in truth, it doesn't matter exactly how we're related on the double helix. I'd like her even if we didn't share DNA. I make a mental note to stop by the barn when I get done in town, because we haven't done more than wave at each other for the last couple of days. She has to be the quietest person I've ever met, and I thought *I* was the quietest person I've ever met...

It takes will, but I force my mind back to the spreadsheet and the room changes Her Majesty is requesting. We made the mistake of giving in to her demand to see the room setup here in the castle and the bookings we've managed both in town and in Atlanta. Now the little twit thinks she's an event planner and is telling us who will go where. We're being as accommodating as we can... for now.

Or rather, I'm being as molar-grindingly helpful as I can be. I'm trying to take every single thing I can off of Fina's list, because she's gonna lose handfuls of her amazing midnight-dark hair of hers if she doesn't catch a break.

When my timer beeps, I close my draft email to Godzilla's love child with Medusa and walk down the narrow back stairs. The heat slams me as I make it to my car, waving back to Rory as I'm getting inside. I'm growing more and more fond of the quiet sheep guy hopping into the utility Gator with one of the beautiful border collies at his side. I don't know which one from this distance, but I'm in love with all of them, so it doesn't really matter. When I can't sleep or the demons make the darkness untenable, I generally choose between climbing under my current project car or seeking out whatever batch of therapists disguised in fur are in Brian Steele's domain.

Brian's been patient, often checking on me at the oddest times of the night. When he doesn't think I'm looking, I see a desperate sadness in his gaunt face. He's always been a thin man, but I'm worried about him. Grief is an evil creature, and I'm afraid the monstrous hooks in this quiet man are deep at the loss of his Violet.

I whisper a hope to the heavens he finds some peace, then force myself to dictate voice notes during my short drive into town. Check on Brian, now that he's come to my mind. Call Uncle T and go see him. Check in with Fina on the Yule Ball and see if she has any more information for me to input. Find Mina and kiss her cheek, if I can pull her down out of the stratosphere.

I haven't even begun to reach the bottom of my list of don't-forgets when I pull into the church parking lot. The doors open into a reception area, and while there's no one at the small desk, an office door is open, and someone I don't recognize peers around the jamb.

The woman gives me a pinched look. I resist the urge the check to see if my hair has escaped from its braid and make sure my blouse isn't pulled out of the waistband of my jeans.

Speaking as someone who spent most of her adult life in a uniform, I note the thin, thirtyish woman is wearing church-office BDUs. White blouse buttoned up to the throat, pencil skirt—navy, of course, and hemmed below her knees. Simple stud earrings, a strand of pearls, and low, sensible, closed-toe shoes. Blond hair pulled back in what I assume is a twist or chignon. When she's close enough, a hint of perfume. I'm not good at those, so I'm guessing Chanel No. 5.

"Hello. How can I help you?"

The nameplate on the door says Delores Bainbridge, but she doesn't offer her hand.

"I'm here to see the pastor. He's expecting me."

I swear I hear a silent sniff, but I can't prove it. I'm wondering what I've done to displease Ms. Bainbridge, then I see her gaze slide past me and morph into something bordering on glazed. Harville's voice explains the entire exchange, or nonexchange, in an instant.

Don't worry, honey. I'm not in the running to be the next Mrs. Sexy Pastor.

"Kiki, so glad you could make it."

I turn, moving to meet him in the opening of the hallway to the private offices, which I know from my previous visit to his inner sanctum. I offer my hand and find my fingers clasped in a gentle but firm grip.

Thank the stars. I cannot stand a limp handshake. Probably too much time in the military, or maybe a natural aversion to them. I don't need my hand crushed in a show of force, and Harville has the perfect balance.

It's another thing I don't need to notice and catalog in the *yes* column where he's concerned. Add in tall and handsome and put together… and did I mention tall? I have no idea why tall gets my pulse all discombobulated, but combined with lean and cute?

Danger! Danger!

"I'm happy to be here. I can't wait to hear what CT's got cooking."

Harville's expression goes confused, but he doesn't say anything as he ushers me to his office. CT, ever the gentleman, rises from his chair in front of Harville's desk and pulls me close to kiss my cheek.

"Hey there, girl. You look pretty as a rainbow this morning. Thank you for coming."

I pat his arm, and we take seats. "I'm happy to be here. Just on pins and needles wondering what I can do to help."

"You were so amazing the other night, I figured you'd be the perfect third leg on any plan we can come up with to help Bethanie."

My head stops mid-nod. "I'm sorry, did you say Bethanie?"

CT looks as confused as Harville did a moment ago. "Yes, my daughter."

"Oh, I know who Bethanie is. I thought I was here to help you cook up something for Mina."

His expression shifts for a moment into pure happiness before it slips back into concern. "I wish that was why I called, but for the moment, I'm in a quandary about my youngest. After I heard what happened, I felt I had to talk to somebody."

Of course he heard. This is Magnolia Bloom, where gossip spreads faster than syrup down a stack of hot pancakes.

The bubbles in my anticipation soda all pop at once.

Harville leans forward and clasps his hands on his desk, grabbing my attention. "CT called me when word inevitably reached him about our evening with Bethanie. I urged him to add you to our meeting for a variety of reasons, not the least of which is you spent more time with her than I did."

Add in the fact that I'm a drunk, and I'm more perfect for the role than he's yet realized.

"I'm happy to help, if I can." I'm sure it's obvious to both men I'm hedging, but the clench in my stomach won't allow for anything more yet.

CT clears his throat. "I was wondering what we could do. I knew… know she's been drinking a lot, but her passing out like this hasn't happened before."

"CT, I'm sorry if this sounds harsh, but I can assure you it has happened before. No one gets to the state where Bethanie is in a vacuum, and she would be one hell of a special unicorn for this to have been the first time. Maybe it's the first time in public here in Magnolia Bloom."

I clasp his arm in a small and ultimately futile attempt to make my words hurt less. The shadows passing over his eyes prove me right.

"I suppose you make sense." He pats my hand, but I can tell his fingers tremble a bit. "What do I do? What *can* I do? I was asking Harville about one of those interventions."

I look at Harville, sitting there with such patience and kindness in his eyes, and I have to look away. It's easier to focus on CT.

"If you believe her life is in imminent danger, or you think she's a danger to others, then yes. You can try. But a judicial intervention would be a mess, and a family intervention is never pretty. Neither has especially impressive success rates. Short term, maybe, but if an addict isn't ready, no amount of begging, bribing, shaming, or strong-arming will get them there."

"So, you're saying there's no hope?"

"I'm saying everyone's bottom is different. Some people can see things have become unmanageable and will reach out. There's no one way this thing goes. Other people have to utterly destroy their lives before they can start recovery."

Ask me how I know.

"But I want to help."

I hear the raw hurt, a father's pain, as he helplessly watches a child of his heart careen toward a cliff, and he can't put up a road block.

"I know you do. I can't advise you on an intervention, but I can give you some ideas and some contacts. It's a huge decision." His eyes go shiny with tears, and my heart breaks for him. "I wish, more than you know, that I had the magic wand to bop Bethanie with. Sadly, in the eighty-five years since AA was founded and with all the loved ones trying since man discovered fermentation, none of us has found the magic key to unlock an addict's bolted inner doors."

"I'm supposed to let her keep going like this?"

I bite my lip. The question everyone asks only has one answer.

"You're not *letting* her do anything. The fact is, you can't stop her. You can tell her you love her, and I hope you will, even if you're mad as hell at her and disappointed and scared. She won't hear you. She'll deny it. If not out loud, to herself. But you have to say the words and let the seeds fall. You can keep trying. Keep reaching out, every time you can. Keep offering help, as long as it's not money. But in the end, and this tears me apart to say it, CT, what happens to Bethanie is entirely up to her."

"Even if she kills herself?"

I put my hand on his arm, squeezing. "Even if she kills herself."

To my surprise, he gives a small laugh. It's more tears than anything, but his mouth curves in a watery smile. "I guess I wasn't expecting you to be so honest."

"CT, I've sat with people who lost wives, husbands, children, and every single one blames themselves. Thinks they could have done one more thing, tried one more time. No matter how much you're praying I'll say differently, the truth is that's not how this damned disease works." I wince, glancing over the desk. "Sorry, Pastor."

His smile shows just a bit of dimples. "I think I can survive the barrage of obscenities there."

We all manage weak chuckles, but it lifts the strain a notch.

"Honestly, the best thing you can do is go online and find some resources for an Al-Anon group close by. Moreover, and I hope you'll listen to me, investigate an Adult Children of Addiction group, too. You'll see it abbreviated ACA or ACoA. I assume there are some groups in Atlanta or Texarkana, but even if you have to hike over to Dallas to get involved, it would be worth your time. And if you order literature online, I'll be happy to walk you through anything you might have questions about."

"Thank you, sweetie. I appreciate everything."

He stands and draws me into a bear hug, and I melt against the solid warmth of his chest. For a moment, silly as it is to admit, he feels like a dad.

For a moment, I feel safe. Cared for. Valuable.

Then I get myself together and push away the selfish thoughts. This isn't about me in any form. This is about CT.

I hope he can read my deep concern and how much I wish I could make this easier on him. "I'll leave you two to talk. Call me anytime."

"I will."

I bid both men goodbye and exit as quickly as I can without actually running. The reception area is empty when I leave, but I'm grateful for whatever the reason. St. Andrew's staffing issues aren't my problem.

I meant what I didn't say to Delores Bainbridge one short hour ago. I wasn't lining up a slot on this season of *Bachelor Pastor*, but I really wouldn't have minded not having to take Magnolia Bloom's crown for Miss Most Screwed-Up.

Needless to say, this is not at all how I imagined my morning. I was expecting to laugh and tease CT...

Not provide even more proof to Harville what a wreck I am. So much for escaping my past in Alaska. I came four thousand miles, and my past followed me every inch of the way.

10
FINA

Kiki is already back at her desk when I return to the castle. I missed Traycee, which is disappointing. I love that girl and have all my fingers crossed for her as much as I have for Kiki as they fight a battle I wouldn't wish on anyone. I'm trying to read as much about addiction as I can squeeze in, but I don't know nearly enough yet.

Time is not my friend, though. It seems for every precious second I carve out for myself, five more things appear on my to-do list. Maybe I need to take it off the cloud server. Maybe ghosts are up there having fun altering the thing while I'm not looking.

I put my self-pity aside as I wait for Kiki to finish a phone call. From the sound of it, she's talking with the manager of our favorite boutique hotel in town. Hopefully, she's found us some rooms before Bridezilla calls and obliterates the last of my patience about the status of our bookings. We need only six more rooms, and we're golden.

Sometimes six might as well be sixty…

I'm ready as soon as she swipes off her phone. "Tell me something good, sweetheart."

"Since you asked so nicely, I'll tell you I talked with Nina at the Rise and Bloom Inn. She had a huge cancellation, so not only did she have six rooms I could snag, she had eight, so I took them all to give us a cushion. Mina must've been praying extra hard at church."

"Hallelujah. You want to shoot an email to our precious little ball of joy and her momma?"

"Happy to. Now, with this fire out, you want to know about the Yule Ball?"

My gut clenches, and I assume it's because of the reminder of yet one more moving target I haven't locked down. The only choice I'm absolutely content with is opting out of teaching this semester. If I hadn't, I'd already be neck-deep in lessons and homework. Score one for me for thinking ahead and making the right call.

"What's up?"

"Nothing in particular. Just that Jensen Pharmaceuticals wants to come for a site visit."

"Wait, what did you say?"

"About the Yule Ball people wanting a site—"

"No, the company name."

"Jensen Pharmaceuticals?"

No. This isn't possible. Not on top of the six thousand other things.

I force myself to take a calming breath. "Anders Jensen?"

Kiki looks at her computer screen and then back at me. "Yes. How did you know? I mean, they're a big company, but I had to Google them."

"It's a long story."

"Sounds like I need to go make popcorn and settle in."

I'm grateful for the quip, but I pivot. "Big events often get preview site visits. I would if I was going to spend the kind of money it takes to book the entire castle and every room within fifty miles. In the busiest season of the year."

"Speaking of, I got a commitment from the new RV dealership in Dallas to bring fifteen units. We have enough hookups, right?"

"Yes, we have twenty-five. If we get the other ten from Texarkana or Shreveport, we've covered the whole list?"

"Yes, ma'am. We're golden."

How I manage to keep a calm exterior while my insides are going ballistic, I don't know. I do know I can't hold out much longer.

"You are a blessing, my darling Kiki. I'll check the spreadsheet in a little bit. For now, I'm going to go lie down for a quick nap."

She immediately goes on alert. "Are you okay? Are you sick?"

"Not sick, a headache. I need to get these pins out of my hair, and I'll be right as rain in forty-five minutes. Don't you worry."

It's clear she doesn't believe me, but she lets me have my lie. "All right, but you call me if you need anything? I can be at your place lickety-split.

"Thank you, love. And I can't tell you what all your help means. You've saved my bacon."

"I'm proud to do it." She wiggles her fingers at the door. "Go. Nap. I'll talk to you this evening."

I don't have to be asked twice, for once glad my sister is nowhere to be found as I force myself to walk out of the back of the castle and down the path to my duplex. I want to run, even though I'm not prone to that particular activity, but I make it to my front door comforted with knowing anyone who might have observed me saw only the unusual occurrence of me going home in the middle of the afternoon, not racing like a madwoman with panic in her eyes.

I shut the door and press my back against the wood, but closing my eyes only makes it worse.

Anders.

The Anders.

My Anders.

Oh, dear Lord, why? Why now? There's absolutely zero chance this is not the same man. While *Anders Jensen* may not be a completely unique name, companies from Denmark do not plan balls in East Texas on a whim, no matter how hard we try in our marketing to make the castle and Magnolia Bloom a desirable, if out-of-the-way, destination.

I feel like my feet are suction-cupped to the floor, but I make it to my bedroom, and as if drawn by a magnetic force of cosmic proportions, I yank open my closet doors and take down the box from the very back of the top shelf. The one containing my favorite garb, headdress, and slippers from the past. There's a trunk full of the rest in the attic, but this dress…

I sit on the bed before my wobbly legs give out and pull the blue brocade houppelande onto my lap, amazed the fabric is in such good shape after all these years. The embroidery is intricate, every stitch done by Mina while I was off gallivanting with the equestrians. It's a stunning piece of artwork, and I had no real appreciation of it at seventeen, other than knowing the dark color against my fair skin and black hair made people's eyes widen. Especially when Anders was my escort. We were perfect foils for each other.

I catalog my chemise, kirtle, belt. Hennin and veil. My strings of fake pearls. My slippers, also detailed by my sister. It's all here. And the memories attack me as I lay each item out on my bed until I get to the bottom of the box and find it.

The white velvet cape lined in white satin Anders bought me at Pennsic. I wore it to every feast or ball for the next year, hating events where it was too hot to show it off.

My fingers tremble as I trace the ornate frog closure, the tight knot of worked leather a little dry after decades of being unattended. It's still beautiful. Stunning, really, if you think about a seventeen-year-old boy being willing to spend the kind of money this quality of workmanship cost.

I feel like a fool, but I move over to my full-length mirror and swirl the fabric around me, attaching it at my throat and bringing the hood over my hair. I imagined myself the envy of every shire or barony we traveled to, and at the rare event Anders didn't attend with me, I was devastated.

Anders Jensen was very good at unhooking my cloak.

And unlacing my kirtle.

My phone rings, and I'm so startled I knock over the perfume bottles on my dresser. I hurry to the bed, tossing aside stockings and gloves, digging for the blasted thing.

It's Mina.

"Hey, what's up?"

"Are you ready to go? We need to leave if we're going to be there on time."

Leave? Be there? What is she…

Oh, my Lord. I forgot about the private dress shopping we set up to start looking for her wedding gown.

"Fina? Are you all right? You didn't forget, did you?"

My laugh sounds hysterical in my ears. I hope it doesn't to Mina's. "How can you ask such a crazy thing? I had to run over to the duplex to grab a… uh… something. Where are you?"

"I'm chatting with Kiki. She said you have a headache. Do you want me to come get you?"

"No!" I get control of my pitch. She can't come in here and see this mess. "No, I'll drive up to the kitchen door. We can take my car."

"Oh… okay."

I hear the confusion in her voice and mentally scramble, digging a laugh up from somewhere. "You know you're so far in the clouds right now you're a danger on the road. This way, you can tell me every little detail about what's changed in the last few hours, and you won't have to concentrate on driving."

"Very funny, sister. Stop wasting time and come on over."

"Be right there."

I jab the off button, then scramble to get out of the cloak, check my hair, find my keys and purse, and race out of my front door like my heels are on fire.

What in the bald-faced heck is wrong with me? The mention of a boy's name, and I'm all in a dither, acting like a buffoon, playing dress-up in my bedroom like I'm a teenager again?

All I can say is thank the good Lord no one saw me.

I add a prayer my brain will return from the trip it's taken to the moon in time to be present for Mina.

It stunned me to no end when she said she didn't want to make her wedding dress. I'd've bet good money, and lost, that she would have wanted to show off her amazing hand at a sewing machine, but no. She wanted to look and try on and do the whole shopping thing.

So I took complete advantage of our contacts in Texarkana and made a private appointment at our favorite salon, and we're going to spend the next whoever-knows-how-many hours making Mina's dream come true.

It's the least I can do for her.

Even if it tears me up twenty ways to Sunday, I'm going to laugh and make this a memorable day for her. And she'll never know I'm aching for my never-will-have as she gets her well-and-truly-deserved.

Time to find out how good an actress I can be…

I pick Mina up as directed, and as I suspected, she talks nonstop the entire trip. We even pick a new burger place for lunch, and it's impressive how much talking she can still do around a cheeseburger and small fries.

When I finally get a chance, I slip a word in edgewise. "I'm still surprised, you know. But if we don't find exactly what you want today, we'll go to Dallas next."

Mina frowns at me, and I'm not sure what I said incorrectly.

"I don't want to make my dress, but I don't want to spend a fortune in Dallas to get a fancy label."

"Says the woman who only wears Ferragamo shoes."

"That I buy at the thrift stores or at Trader Days, then restore myself." Her huff is indignant.

"I'm teasing you. Don't get prickly."

"I've spent all my life counting pennies, and just this once I don't want to."

My heart breaks to hear the vestiges of fear in her voice. She's conquered so many of her demons, but I guess no one gets all the cobwebs out.

"You listen here. You're going to get the prettiest dress between here and New York City, no matter what it takes. You're going to look so beautiful Harville will have to keep smelling salts in his pocket in case CT faints right there at the altar when he sees you."

She ducks her head, and her cheeks pinken. "You think so?"

"I know so."

With that said, we're in the parking lot of a small boutique with a modest sign inviting us to Celestial Designs. You wouldn't know from the exterior that inside is a selection from fabulous designers, both known and those trying to break into the lucrative bridal market.

Celeste herself meets us as soon as I pull the door open and urge Mina in ahead of me. Hugs and kisses happen all around, and I am about have to add weights to Mina's ankles to keep her in the chair while we're served refreshments and Celeste goes over the information sheet we supplied earlier.

The plan is I'll go first, and we'll choose my matron-of-honor dress, then we'll concentrate completely on Mina. Celeste's assistants bring out an assortment of dresses, but I know instantly which one I want. Of course, it's up to my sister, but the midnight-blue drop shoulder in baronet satin is singing to me from the hanger. I dutifully try on a rose silk with hi-lo hem and the forest-green A-line shantung linen. They're pretty, would require minimal alteration, and are all quite nice.

Even before the helper zips the side of the blue gown, I look in the mirror, and for a moment, I'm seventeen again. Lord above, I don't want to be a girl again, but the surplice bodice, off-the-shoulder band sleeves, and body-skimming skirt flaring into a trumpet hem revealing a flirty hint of silver lining, looks like it was made for me. I've always been the tall and bony one compared to Mina's petite frame and curves I've envied all my life, but this dress makes me look… voluptuous. A word not often used to describe me.

I feel beautiful, and vibrant, and… sexy.

When I come out and step up on the small stage, Mina starts crying.

I rush to her side and put my hand on her arm. "Oh, honey, what's wrong? If you don't like it, I'll take it—"

"Don't you dare." Her voice squeaks before she clears her throat and wipes her eyes carefully so she doesn't smear her mascara. Then she laughs. "On the other hand, maybe I should tell you to take that off right this instant, because this is supposed to be my day, and what am I gonna do if everyone's staring at you?"

I feel the blood in my exposed chest heat. "Now you're being silly."

"I am not, and get back up there so I can see this from all sides."

I do as she asks, feeling awkward now. Then I look in each of the mirrors set so every angle is covered and know I'm buying this dress, even if I can't wear it for Mina's wedding. I'll find somewhere, someday. We have fancy events at the castle all the time, so—

"We'll take it." Mina's voice is firm, and I feel Celeste's delight from across the room.

"You haven't even checked the tag." I have a moment of panic, because I haven't checked, either, but Mina is intractable.

I take a look at the price when I'm back in the dressing room. It's both much more than I want to pay for a dress, and yet much less than I was anticipating the entire walk down the hall.

I'm back in my slacks and tunic in no time, almost giddy knowing the dress is being carefully tended and placed in a specialty dress bag with Celeste's logo on the front. It frees me to give all my attention to Mina as she tries everything from a tiered barrage of lace making her look like a five-foot-two ice cream cone to a tight bandage body-con dress so wrong it leaves me speechless. We both know they were ridiculous choices, but I'm delighted to see this side of my twin, the part of her I've been watching emerge.

In the end, I'm the one in tears, because she chooses a Venetian lace V-neck gown, the simple bodice beaded and enhanced with about a million iridescent seed beads. The high empire waistline is perfect for her shorter stature, and the long line of satin-covered buttons down the back is the perfect touch. She nearly cries at the mini train fulfilling all her wedding dreams.

I join her on the platform and touch her sleeve. "This is the one."

She stares into the mirrors, and tears slowly fall down her cheeks. "I know. Thank you."

I can't help but frown. "For what?"

"For everything. For saving me. For loving me. For being there for me all these years until I finally got my happily ever after."

"I wouldn't change a thing."

I look over at the bag hanging on the hook by the door and wonder if I didn't just spout the biggest lie I've ever told my sister.

Part of it is true. I wouldn't change a thing about saving her from the hell that was the beginning of her adult life. But my confounded brain was thrown into a blender earlier, and the bits of dust from hearing a name I thought I'd assigned to a locked room forever are drifting over my memory. If I had a chance, I might change shutting a beautiful boy from Copenhagen out of my life, because in this crazy, mixed-up moment, I wish he could see me in my new dress. I even have an insane thought about having the white velvet cloak cleaned and the creases steamed out.

But as Momma always said, if wishes were horses, beggars would ride. So it's best not to think about things not meant to be. I made a decision four decades ago, and I've had to live with the consequences ever since. No sense stirring the pot now.

Sorry to mix my metaphors, Momma.

I pull my thoughts back in line and vow to make sure Mina has my undivided attention for the rest of the afternoon.

We finalize our purchases and take our precious dresses, hitting the road to get back to Magnolia Bloom in plenty of time for Mina to go to a late dinner with CT. I go back to my duplex and pick up the mess I made. I fold all the memories carefully, box them away, and restore my past where it belongs. In the closet. In the corner. Out of the way.

Where my dreams need to stay.

11
KIKI

My meeting with CT and Harville seems like a lifetime ago... and yet about thirty minutes. Now it's Friday, and the emergency-wedding preparation is in full swing. I've put the final touches on the chapel, from the bows on the ends of the pews to the satin runner rolled and staged by the doors. The flowers are stunning, which is no surprise, but regardless of the imminent arrival of our PITA bride, I'm thrilled with how everything has turned out.

I hope Wynona Emmaline Glassman agrees.

If she doesn't, I can't be held responsible if I yank out a hank of expensively dyed blond locks.

The last once-over should have eased my tension, just as flipping back the leather cover on my tablet and checking the shared spreadsheet on the cloud server should have settled my gut. Unfortunately, even though the "completed" column has more red checks from Fina, blue from me, and even a surprising number of green from Mina, my nerves are wrecked. I'm not exactly sure when she's been answering emails, but I'm not going to complain.

When I told Fina to stop worrying and get on with their dress shopping, I meant it. What I didn't realize was how much I'd regret it. I've looked at my watch seventeen thousand times, wondering when

Fina is going to get here and take over, and I don't like how much the old voices are trying to convince me one little vodka tonic won't hurt.

The doors of the chapel click shut behind me, and I move toward the front office, the space used to meet with clients. The walls are painted a cool and calming blue, the furniture is overstuffed and comfortable, and the atomizer gives off bursts of a soft lavender scent at regular intervals. Numerous incandescent lamps offset the cold fluorescent lights overhead. I wonder if any of it will trick Bridezilla into behaving.

"Good evening, Kiki."

I don't have to turn around to know exactly who's there. The deep voice flows over me in three words.

"Pastor." I turn and call up my public affairs officer expression. I might not be a PAO anymore, but I learned a lot of tricks over the years, especially in a career where outward displays of emotion were severely frowned upon.

"Please, you have to call me Harville. We've been through enough already to be friends."

I'm saved from answering when I see Fina coming down the hallway, but my gut redlines into fear when she stops and puts a hand against the wall, coming to a dead stop. I race the rest of the distance between us and screech to a halt.

"Fina, what's wrong?"

When she lifts her face, I swear her pallor is moss green. "I don't know, but I suspect it's something we ate. Mina called me and said she thinks she saw last Tuesday's dinner come up."

"You look like you're about to do the same."

"That's what I feel like. Honey, I'm so sorry, but I can't meet with Wynona and her momma tonight. I'm going to have to ask you to do it."

Panic replaces the earlier fear. I'm nearly mowed down by utter, gut-wrenching terror at being dubbed the front person to handle the steamroller known as Councilwoman Gretta Glassman and her Mini-Me. I'm Superwoman, Wonder Woman, and Captain Marvel all rolled into one when I'm doing my duties behind the scenes. Note the keyword *behind*.

"I... I can't. I don't know—"

Fina pivots a hard left and races to the public bathroom. I follow, yanking paper towels from the dispenser and running cold water over them. I wince as the audible evidence of her misery continues for a long minute, feeling a little green myself when she comes out of the stall and takes the proffered towels.

"Thank you. Oh, Lord, I haven't had food poisoning in years, but if Mina's doing the same thing, it means we had some bad food in Texarkana earlier today. We stopped for a burger at a little place we don't normally choose. Seems we made a bad decision."

I help her out of the bathroom, put aside my terror, and concentrate on one thing at a time. Fina's skin feels clammy, and her color has gone from green to see-through. My sole task for the next few minutes is getting her to one of the golf carts parked outside the main kitchen, then it's a quick drive over to her place.

"Let's get you to bed. I'll take care of Bride- and Momzilla, then bring you two some supplies."

"I'm sure between the two of us we've got everything we need."

"Ladies? Is everything all right?" Harville's voice is filled with concern, and I'm a bit surprised at how much relief I feel hearing his soft baritone.

I turn a bit so I can look at him. "Fina's really sick. Can you get her to her place? I can stall the Glassmans until you get back."

I'm shocked my voice sounds so professional and calm. More of my PAO training coming to the rescue.

"Of course."

"Thank you, Harville." Fina's voice is already weaker, and my concern must show, because she puts on a brave face. "I'm fine. Might have a rough night ahead of me, but I'll be right as rain tomorrow. And you'll be fine, Kiki. I'm sorry to leave this on you."

"I won't let you down. I promise."

She reaches over and pats my cheek, her eyes full of love. "I never thought for a second you would."

Harville ushers her away, solicitously holding her arm and putting one hand around her back.

When they round the corner out of my sight, I let a moment of dread sweep over me. Number one, I am not the front person. Never have been. Number two, this is not my area of expertise.

Then I remind myself this is no different than preparing for a meeting of the brass where I was entirely responsible for the event. I'd double- and triple-check my reports and printouts, verify hospitality had prepared the meeting room, quintuple-check the seating chart, because heaven forbid General Meyerson be next to Lt. Colonel Waters. I could do it in my sleep.

This is no different.

Sucking in a deep breath, I click on the notes section for today's event and refresh Fina's list of key points. The chapel is ready, as it's what the Zillas want to verify before the big rehearsal dinner Mrs. Greene is finalizing in the big kitchen. I might be a gnat's hair from doing my own toenail tossing, but I can't blame the Glassmans for wanting to see with their own eyes that everything is in order. I'd want to, if I were in their place.

Still, I wish I wasn't girding my loins to greet the demanding duo.

As if I've conjured them, Wynona and her mother enter the foyer, looking around with sharp gazes until they laser-focus on me. Both women walk at a sharp clip in my direction, and it's all I can do not to turn around and run.

"Where's Fina?" Mama Glassman looks behind me as if Fina is somehow hiding back there.

"Unfortunately, she's taken ill and has had to go home. I'm happy to step in and answer all your questions."

Please let me have answers to their questions.

"This is quite inconvenient. I hope it's not something contagious."

I blink, then bite my tongue not to snap, *I'm so sorry Fina has contracted a stomach bug with the sole intention of putting you out.*

"Not at all. She ate something which sat poorly. She's quite distraught this might upset you."

"Yes, well, we'll have to move on." Mom steps forward, moving like the pointy end of a snowplow, and Wynona moves an instant behind her. I take up the rear, and we form a single-file train down the hallway to the chapel.

Momzilla moves to the doors and pulls the ornate handles, grunting softly when the doors don't budge.

"What is this?" she demands, donning her Dallas councilwoman do-you-know-who-I-am? affront.

I hide the fear barreling up my spine like a race car driver's hit the nitro button. "I'm sure it's stuck. You know how doors get in old buildings."

"Good evening, Mrs. Glassman. Wynona. So good to see you."

My knees almost give out in relief. I didn't think for a minute Harville could get back this fast. I must have been standing in the foyer longer than I thought. No matter how it happened, I'm so grateful for the intervention I could cry.

Mrs. Glassman moves away from the doors and goes into full politician mode, offering her hand and a perfected smile where I got frowns and disapproval. I don't care, so long as her focus is on him and not me.

As her mother and Harville step away, Wynona goes to the doors and repeats her mother's move. While Harville is taking care of Mrs. G, I have no buffer from G, Jr.

"What is going on here?" Her demand is so shrill I wince.

"Nothing's going on, I assure you." I grab a door handle and pull, trying to pretend I'm giving it a little tug when in fact I'm yanking for all I'm worth. My attempts are no more successful than theirs were.

No. No, no, nonononono…

These doors opened with effortless ease for me less than an hour ago. I spent the entire day decorating the place, arranging and rearranging until it was nothing short of spectacular. I was in and out a hundred times.

"I want to know what kind of funny business you're trying to pull." Wynona's hiss would scare an enraged cobra. "I told Stanford we should have the ceremony at his church, as it's so much bigger, but no. He wants this day to be about us, not the congregation and thousands of people. Even though he's sweet, I should have tried to make him change his mind."

Maybe it's stress. Maybe it's blinding fear. Maybe it's worry about Fina. Maybe it's a combination of all of the above, but my muscles go from trembling to rock-solid in the space of a heartbeat. I noticed Fina wasn't a hundred percent all afternoon, but I chalked it up to doing too much. Armed with knowing how sick she was becoming, yet how many hours she plowed through to make sure everything is in place, cold anger freezes my dithering insides.

I'm close enough to get into Wynona's space without it being too obvious. I may be making the worst mistake of my life, but I used to have a pretty damn good gut for making a call in a tense moment. I hope I'm not screwing up, but I don't stop myself.

"Look, a lot of people have been busting their butts to make this wedding happen for you. Fina and Mina both have been dog-sick all day, but they've kept at it. For you. To make your day stunning. I'm sorry I had to come in as the second string, but the least you could do is show a little appreciation. Not to me, but for their sake."

I wait for the monster to jump all over me and storm out, vowing to sue the castle for everything we're worth, but to my utter shock, tears well in the green eyes that are part of the reason she won Miss Teen Dallas a few years back.

"It's... I just want everything to be perfect."

Her shoulders drop, and shock turns to disbelief as compassion rises in place of my previous impatience.

"I promise you everything is exquisite."

"Then why won't the doors open?"

I can hear desperation behind her pretense, and I relent.

"I don't know. I'm sure it's something easily fixable. Let me call our maintenance guy, and we'll have this sorted out in no time."

"I'm sorry I've been such a bi—"

"Bridezilla?"

"Yeah, let's go with that."

I hand her a tissue from the pack Fina told me to always keep in my pocket when any member of a wedding party is involved. *Male or female,* she said. *Daddies tend to get verklempt, too.*

I lead her away from the recalcitrant doors. "Come sit down and talk with Pastor Harville. I'll see what's wrong. It won't take but a minute."

Before I can prepare myself, Wynona yanks me into a hug, and I realize she's shaking. I pat her back, then give her shoulder a squeeze as I set her away. "It's all going to be okay. I give you my word."

She blows her nose rather indelicately, and I stuff down an amused snort.

"I love Stanford so much, you know? And I want this to be the happiest day of our lives."

I know it's not my place. I'm not the counselor in the room, but once again, I let my mouth get ahead of me. "This shouldn't be the happiest day of your life."

She pulls back, shock creasing her features.

I look her in the eye, thinking if I'm in for a penny, I might as well be in for the full pound. "Tomorrow should be a wonderful day. It should be full of love and laughter and dancing and kissing. But it should be the *start* of a lot of happy days, not the culmination."

Wynona stares at me so long my stomach feels like it's turning to concrete.

"That's really beautiful."

I pretend nothing abnormal has happened. There's no way for Wynona to know my offering an opinion so many times in less than five minutes has never happened before. And never when so much is at stake. I can only assume my blood sugar is low, or high, or whatever the opposite of normal is, or some other organ is failing, because I'm not sure exactly who or what's taken over my body. This isn't *normal Kiki*, and I don't have time to examine whether I like her or not. Not until I've finished running this gauntlet.

"You join your mom and the pastor. I'll be back in a moment."

As soon as she steps away, I walk as fast as I can without showing the panic trying to trip me and send me sprawling. As it is, I have to pull up like a pilot going vertical to avoid Mrs. Greene as she's coming out of the kitchen.

"Lord, child, what's chasing you? A bear?"

"It feels like it. I've got to find Brian, or someone else from maintenance."

"Why? What's wrong?"

"I was in the chapel, making sure everything is ready, and now Wynona and her mother are here, and the doors won't open."

Mrs. Greene gives me a sad look. "Oh, dear, that's not good."

I'm about to walk past her and race to find Brian, but I do a slow turn back to her.

"What did you mean by 'oh, dear'?"

"The castle is upset about something."

Fina has told me stories about things breaking or other ways the chapel wouldn't let couples in who weren't right for each other. I passed it off as more MacInnes lore, but…

She nods sagely. "Yes, sir, something's happened, and I'm not sure what."

"I don't mean to sound rude, but you're not asking me to believe the chapel is deliberately keeping the doors shut."

She looks at me like I've grown a second head. "That's exactly what I mean. You don't need Brian. You need to figure out what's got the castle uncertain about whether this wedding is supposed to happen or not."

"*I'm* supposed to figure it out?" I realize my voice is almost at the same shriek decibel as Wynona's a moment ago and get it under control. "How in the world am I supposed to do that?"

"Honey, I don't know. I'm a cook, not a psychologist."

She about-faces and returns to the kitchen, leaving me standing in the hallway with my mouth half open.

Part of me wants to race out the back door and proceed with my original plan. The other part of me checks my watch as I jog to the front of the castle, knowing the groom and the rest of the bridal party will be arriving any minute.

Good Lord, is this what Fina and Mina do all the time? I don't mind helping out, but this insanity isn't what I signed up for.

The doors open as I get closer, and a dark-headed young man comes in, laughing with a shorter, blond guy. A troop of men and women about their same age follow into the gorgeous foyer that has impressed thousands of tourists and guests.

The group acts like being in a showcase castle is no big deal and continues cutting up with each other, even though they've clearly seen me. I suppose, to people raised with tons of money, maybe it is no big deal, or maybe I'm being a little judgmental and need to stow it and get to work.

I peg the taller boy as Stanford. "Good evening. I'm Kiki MacInnes. Let me show you to the chapel."

"Stanford Barrymore." He holds out his hand, which of course I shake.

"Good to meet you. Come this way."

I get the crowd down the hall, and within minutes, the bride is kissing Stanford, Mrs. Glassman starts stage-directing, and I edge toward the chapel doors as innocently as I can. I stop when I bump into someone, and a quick glance shows my compatriot for the evening.

"I'm sorry, Harville."

"Running me over seems to be a thing with you." His eyes twinkle as he teases.

Which makes a blush flame my cheeks. "That does seem to keep happening. I hope you'll forgive me."

"Easy as done."

"How was your chat with Wynona?"

He looks at the young people, especially the intended. She has her arm hooked in Stanford's, and they're gazing at each other like there's no one else in the room.

"I have to be honest and tell you when I first met them, I had some serious reservations. My radar on couples who are going to make it is usually pretty good."

He stops, and for an instant, his eyes are haunted, his expression's strained. I'm no psychic, but it isn't hard to figure out he's thinking about his own marriage, but seconds later, his kind pastor armor overshadows his sadness.

"Anyway, I knew there was no way I was stopping this wedding, but I sure had an itch to." He turns to me, and those dimples pop out, and my pulse jumps in what is clearly now going to be an autonomic response. "Then now, as I was talking with Wynona, pure joy came from her, and my concern melted away. I don't know what happened, but something shifted."

I hear a soft click behind me and feel a puff of cool air. I turn, and there's the barest crack where the two doors have separated. I frown at the wood and then decide I'm being foolish. They were stuck momentarily is all. Nothing mystical about hundred-year-plus doors getting persnickety in the humidity.

After that, there's not a moment to wonder or reflect. Harville does his pastor thing, and we're all in the chapel doing the run-through. Everything comes off effortlessly, and before I can believe it, I'm being pulled into another effusive hug from the T. rex now turned blushing bride.

"Thank you so much. Everything is perfect, like you said."

"You're welcome. Tomorrow is going to be everything you dreamed."

Stanford leads all the young ones out, and Mrs. Glassman has been joined by Mr. Glassman and Stanford's parents without me noticing. The moms and dads watch the retreating youngsters with affection and follow their noses to the banquet room, ready and waiting for Mrs. Greene's feast.

I give Harville a nudge. "Are you going to the dinner?"

He jolts himself out of wherever his thoughts have gone. "While they invited me, as the couples usually do, I declined. As I usually do."

"I don't blame you." My eyes follow the merrymakers as they round the last corner. "So much giddiness gives me the jitters." I hold up a hand before he can tease me. "I mean, I'm happy for them, but I don't think I've ever been so googly-eyed and…"

"Optimistic?"

I see more than compassion in his warm blue eyes. I see understanding.

"As good a word as I can come up with, much as I hate to say. I'm probably not much more than ten years older than them, but I feel ancient by comparison."

He gives a little huff, but it seems like camaraderie. "I turn forty next month, and for the first time in my life, I'm dreading a birthday. And not because I'm afraid of the number."

"Forty's not old."

"Not in calendar years."

"So when's the day?"

"The eleventh."

I tilt my head. "You're teasing me."

His frown tells me he wasn't. "I'm not. Why would I?"

"Because my birthday is November eleventh, too."

"I know you're not supposed to ask a lady—"

"I'll be thirty-six. And since this is a wonderful coincidence, we should celebrate together and start our new friendship off right."

Something flashes across his eyes, and I hope I'm not misinterpreting, but I decide, since I've been on a winning streak, to trust my gut one last time. "Listen, Harville, I'll lay it all out here. The last thing I need in my life is romantic complications, and although I dubbed you Sexy Pastor the other day when I bumped into you with Traycee, I know you're not available, and I'm not looking. So how about we take romance off the table?"

He honest-to-goodness blushes at his new title, and I decide I really like this tall, handsome man. What I need, though, is a friend.

Just a friend.

His mouth does that slow crease, giving me a hint of the dimples I find I wait for with near breathlessness. Yes, he's hella sexy, but it's the sweet man, the kind man, who makes my pulse dance.

Which it shouldn't. And I need to get my limbic system under control, pronto.

"Sounds like a great idea."

"Well, then, SP, I need to get to work, and you probably have pastorly things to do."

He cuts me a side-eye. "Why do I have the feeling I was wrong to think you were shy and quiet?"

"Oh, I am, with people I don't know. I can be a bit of a card with people I do. I have the feeling you get really tired of people treating you like you're some kind of paragon, and I promise I won't treat you like a god if you won't treat me like I'm nothing but broken."

He holds out his hand, and I don't hesitate to put mine in his warm palm. "Deal. So what do we do first?"

"I'm not sure. Tomorrow's going to be a real test for me, with Mina and Fina down for the count. I'll get up early and go running, as I have to get myself back in the habit before I lose it completely, and I'll need the pre-stress-release. Everything's ready for tomorrow night, so the day is pretty clear. Is there anything I can do to help you?"

"You have plenty on your list already, so no, but back to the subject of running. Where do you go?"

"I'm a beginner-level jogger. I keep to tracks or well-maintained trails, so I'll go to the high school until I learn the layout around here better."

"Great, I'll meet you there. What time?"

"Really? You're a runner?"

"I prefer the gym, but I run to get my cardio in."

"There's a gym in Magnolia Bloom?"

"A pretty new one. Traycee's dad is partners with another guy. They converted an old gas station over on First Avenue."

"Huh. Interesting."

"Want to check it out?"

"Absolutely, but next week. Tomorrow is all wedding, all day. Sunday is cleanup and pulling out Christmas decorations. I understand the Fun Run finalizes here at the castle, so Fina says there's tons to do."

"Don't take on tomorrow's sorrows today. And as I'm sure you have some last-minute items to check off your list for the rehearsal, I should go."

"I wish I didn't have to say you're right, but you're right. I need to make sure Mrs. Greene doesn't need anything and hang around until the revelers are out the door. But if you're game, I'll see you at the track at six."

I watch him walk away, having a sense his step is a little lighter. More, I hope it's because of me.

I hurry to check on the servers and thank all the stars I'm wearing flats.

This is going to be a long night, but for the first time all evening, I'm relaxed, despite all I have to do.

I have the feeling Harville needs a friend every bit as much as I do. And maybe one thing is going right in my life after all.

As long as I don't screw it up…

12

JULIETTE

I HAVE SPENT a lot of time wandering around in my thoughts since my trip with Rory to visit his grandmother and aunts. It turned out to be a lovely time all around, even if my brain is reeling from all the information I gleaned from the talkative bunch. Once Ida said her fill, the sisters added more tidbits about Gavina and life on the estate when they were girls. A lovely picture, all in all.

My tools have arrived, and I've settled in nicely, but the peace in my barn is not reaching the corner of my mind where Noelle is stubbornly ignoring me, her arms crossed over her chest and her face turned away. That's how I picture her, anyway. She has sent me a barrage of invoices and purchase orders to approve, but otherwise, there has been no contact between us.

Yet another car passes by my open bay doors, making me wonder how many delivery people are needed for one wedding. I toss down my scalpel in disgust. Not too hard, because I do not mistreat my tools, but with enough force I know it is time to get away before I let my discontent risk marring the canvas. I turn off the fans, cover the frame, hit the button to shut the doors, and make my escape. I'm grateful for the use of an estate truck to explore downtown Magnolia Bloom sooner than I intended, though my plan was to give myself another week before I risked making an appearance. I am well aware how quickly a new person garners attention in a small town.

I understand Magnolia Bloom is making quite a splash as a tourist destination. Fina has mentioned another town remaking itself from near ruin into a craft and wine locale of some repute. I can't remember the name, but what's important is while I will hardly be the only stranger in town, I apparently look too much like my birth father to escape notice for long.

Therefore, I made sure to grab a cap and my big sunglasses in my attempt to stay incognito for as long as possible.

What I find, when I locate a parking place and stroll down the street until I reach the town square, is Magnolia Bloom is quaint. Arbois has been in existence in some form since the 1200s, so it is amusing people believe the shops around the square are old. Still, it does remind me of home in the sense of community in the air as I walk the sidewalks and window-shop. Like Magnolia Bloom, my home has remade itself into a tourist destination on top of retaining its dedication to our local vineyards and cheeses. The need for economic survival is the same all around the world.

I come to a stop, naturally, when I see the etching on the glass for the Magnolia Bloom Gallery. It is legitimately impossible for me to not press on the door and enter the cool respite of the small space nestled next to the Magnolia Bloom Emporium, which was my original destination.

"Hello, and welcome. Come in and stay awhile."

I pull off my glasses and spot a slender man standing behind a counter. He drops a polishing rag and comes toward me.

"Is there something I can show you?"

"I do not know. I have only been here for a short time and did not know there was a gallery here."

"By your accent, you must be Juliette Laurant."

I lift an eyebrow, but add a smile. "Must I be?"

He laughs and holds out his hand. "Emmett Everson, proprietor and cousin to Traycee Everson, new friend to Kiki."

"The chain of… ah… information makes sense now."

"It's gossip, Ms. Laurant, pure and simple."

"Call me Juliette."

"Then you'll call me Emmett. I'm thrilled you've come in, but I'm afraid our work will be a little provincial for your taste."

I make my way around, unsurprised to find Remington bronzes on display and other Western artists I do not know, but as I round the corner to the final wall, I stop. I wave a hand at a small frame. "Is that Rikki Wright?"

He's clearly surprised. "I thought you were a restorationist. You know photographers?"

"Not all, of course, but she has been featured in a number of articles of about up-and-coming female artists, and that is a passion of mine."

"I'm still impressed. Your reputation precedes you."

I laugh, something I've decided must no longer surprise me. It's happened too often since I've come to this charming place. "Now I have a chance to use one of my new colloquialisms. You are pulling my leg. I think you performed an internet search when you learned who I was through your family grapevine."

Emmett has the grace to look chagrined. "Guilty as charged. Still, you do have quite a presence in the art world."

"I disagree. Not in the art world, but in a small corner perhaps, and interesting to very few people."

"Count me as one of the few, then."

I look around at the gallery and see Emmett has made a significant effort to meet the needs of his clientele, yet raise the exposure of new talent and showcase masterpieces, all in a small space.

"I love your concept. My sister and I maintain a gallery and storefront in Paris, so I know the challenges of meeting your foot traffic and maintaining your own vision."

"Thank you. So, is there anything I can do for you? I could be wrong, but I'm guessing you're not here to buy a reproduction of *Bronco Buster*."

"No offense to Mr. Remington, but no, that's not on my list this trip. I did not come in with any purpose, actually. I am window-shopping, and I'm constitutionally incapable of skipping an art gallery."

"I hear you. Drives my partner crazy when we're on vacation."

"What I might ask you for is your recommendation on where to buy some authentic cowboy boots."

"I'd be happy to."

Emmett lets out a sigh of delight as a broad man who looks like he could carry a car engine instead of a vase of roses comes in from the back and eyes him suspiciously.

"What did I miss?"

Emmett puts his arm around the newcomer's waist and uses his other hand to gesture between us.

"Juliette, this is my partner, Wyatt. Wyatt, this is the art restorer I told you was at the castle. She's here taking care of the trove they found by Gavina MacInnes."

"Wyatt." I add a nod. "It's a pleasure to meet you."

Wyatt steps from Emmett's embrace and moves to shake my hand. Both men look at me for a long moment, expectation evident on both of their faces. The moment stretches until I feel a blush heat my cheeks but I have no idea why I'm disconcerted.

"I'm sorry, but I seem to be missing a beat. You appear to be waiting for me to say something?"

The men look at each other, and both start laughing. Emmett waves his hand before I grow more uncomfortable. "I'm sorry, it's you are the first person in the entire—and I mean *entire*—time Wyatt and I have been together who hasn't made a football joke when we introduce each other."

My frown deepens as much as my confusion. "Football? But... this is an art gallery."

Both men laugh louder and Wyatt pats my arm to break the unease. "If you hang around here long enough to become a Dallas Cowboys fan, you'll get it, but until then, don't worry about it." He turns to Emmett and changes the subject, for which I'm grateful. "Came down to see how things are going. Town's hopping today."

"Big wedding at the castle. Had some early traffic, but mostly looky-loos."

"Too bad." Wyatt moves toward the rear entrance, giving me a little salute with two fingers. "Nice to meet you, Juliette. Hope to see you around." He turns to Wyatt, and his lips curve into a more personal tilt. "See you at home. I'm fixing catfish."

"I won't be late. Promise."

Emmett returns his attention to me and my previous question. "If you want boots, we need to go to Henry's over on Second. He's got new and a selection of the most amazing restored Western footwear you can imagine. I think it would please you to no end, considering."

I raise my eyebrows, intrigued. "I didn't know there was a market for restored cowboy boots."

"Darlin', you have no idea what you're in for. We can go in about an hour. I close at five, but Henry likes to catch the late crowd, especially if they've walked the square and have had a few wine samples before they find him."

"We?"

"You don't think I'm going to let a fellow connoisseur shop alone, do you? Girl, I've already got the stereotype cornered on gay, Black art dealer, so we might as well make it official that I'm your new fashion BFF."

And there it is. Amusement again. Coming from deep inside me. It feels so warm and real, I wonder where it's been all my life.

"I'm only sorry I cannot be your French stereotype, as I do not smoke. I can, however, be your arrogant wine snob. Would that suffice to round out our new partnership?"

"Perfect! Now, you go next door and tell Traycee to fix you up with some bling jeans and a top worthy of Tidy's. We'll get you Bloomian'd before sundown."

"I'm sor—"

"Translation: I'm going to make a Southerner out of you, and we're going to go dancing at Tidy's. I'll tell Wyatt to wait on the catfish. Trust me."

And strangely, I do. This is another thing completely and utterly unlike me. Rory, and now Emmett, have broken the speed record for breaching my barriers. Not completely, I'm sure, but certainly they have scaled walls I have kept secure for a long time.

Then memory hits me of my intention to fly under the radar. "I appreciate this, Emmett, but I don't know if it's a good idea for me to go dancing."

"Why, because people will see you and know you're David Broder's daughter?"

He notes my stricken expression, but not meanly. "Girl, you've been here almost two weeks. More than enough time for word to get around. As to keeping who you are a secret, that bird's flown the nest. If you don't want to go, I get it, but if you think people 'round here haven't already put two and two together, you're wrong. Now, I'm not trying to push you into anything, but not going to Tidy's while you're here is almost against the law. Unless you're part of the big shindig at the castle this evening?"

My denial is automatic. "I'm not connected to the event, although I'd help Kiki if I could. I'm afraid I'd merely be more in the way than of assistance."

"Then it's settled. We'll get you boot-scootin' by sundown. Now, go." Emmett makes a shooing motion toward the door. "Traycee will take care of you, and I'll be by to get you in an hour. There's little chance you'll run into any of the Broders today."

"Why, pray tell?"

He stops for a second and adjusts a beautiful bronze sculpture by Philippe Pasqua. "Like the MacInneses, they've invested a lot in this town, but David and his family don't spend a lot of time downtown or at country dance halls. I see his grandson Jake the most. Nice guy, so don't worry. This'll be fun."

I'm a bit bewildered to find myself obeying, and he is correct. His cousin is delightful, and Traycee has me gasping with amusement as she has me try on pair after pair of blue jeans embellished with the most astonishing array of crystals and beads. Then we turn to tops I would not have chosen for myself in a thousand years. By the time Emmett shows up, with Wyatt in tow as promised, I'm arrayed in a white cotton top with drop shoulders, little puffed sleeves, and the hem tied in a style called Daisy Duke over the waistband of my new dark indigo jeans. The peacock design up the right leg is nothing short of eye-popping.

Traycee waves us off as we leave for Henry's, and I have to admit I'm having an amazing time. I feel like a country Cinderella.

Only, my ball is going to happen on a wooden dance floor lit by neon beer signs.

And that is fine with me.

A pang hits me, and I struggle to put aside the disappointment my sister isn't here to experience all of this with me. Noelle would have bought out Traycee's entire selection of jeans and bling, and she'd be in heaven dancing in the limelight.

This will be the first time I'll be there alone.

13
KIKI

BY THE TIME five o'clock rolls around, I'm ready to pull the carefully hot-ironed curls Tara managed to style into my mop straight out of my head. I don't, though, because Tara and Traycee threatened me within an inch of my life if I disturbed all their hard work. I had to call off my plan for some exercise with Harville this morning, texting him at five thirty about a pipe leak in the first-floor bathroom closest to the chapel, and it was all hands on deck while we attended to the crisis.

At least things were resolved, and I was able to take a deep breath at noon. When I went to my suite to take a shower, I realized my next dilemma and sent an SOS to Traycee. I don't have a single dressy-dress, and on top of the bathroom debacle, it was clear neither Mina nor Fina would be in any shape to save me from yet another evening of stand-in duty with the Glassmans. Traycee and Tara arrived like a cavalry of stylists, bringing over dress, hair, and makeup artillery from the store and the salon.

In less than two hours, I find myself in a forest-green knit dress hitting above my knees, and low heels in deference to how much running I might be doing. My hair hangs in soft ringlets, and my makeup is subtle but beautiful. The truth is, I've never looked this chic, and there's no way I'll be able to recreate it on my own in the future.

Not that I'll need to. I'm not going to let Mina or Fina ever get sick again.

How I'll manage such a crazy vow, I'm not exactly sure, but I'm damned determined…

At least I have hope this evening will go off without too much drama, as Bridezilla seems to have fully morphed into Bambi Bride, all blushes and kindness with enough wedding-day jitters to make her seem human. I'm like Harville. If I didn't see the transformation myself, I would not believe it.

Speaking of Harville, he's entering the kitchen, looking quite dapper in his suit. He stops in his tracks, literally, and I know my cheeks are now a brilliant red instead of Peony Pink by Kat Von D.

"Wow."

"Hey, SP. Ready for the big night?"

He squints at me and puts his hands on his hips. "This is going to be a thing with you, isn't it?"

"What?" I ask innocently, though I'm secretly thrilled I redirected him from further blush-inducing compliments. "You don't think Sexy Pastor fits? I do."

"I don't think it's the moniker I'm going for. If I was going for one. Which I'm not."

"It's a call sign, and you don't get to pick. Your sign's given to you. You have no say in it."

He gives me a look letting me know my Southern pastor has a sense of humor of his own. "So I get to pick yours?"

"Not today. One call sign a week. It's in the rule books."

"You made that up."

"Absolutely, but we don't have time to argue. The horde is assembling."

"Prepare for payback."

"Pastor! I'm ashamed."

"You don't get to play the pastor card only when it suits you."

I realize he's trying to stay in the lighthearted mode we've established, but I take a closer look, and there's tension around his mouth he's trying to hide.

"Hey, what's up? You look a little tense."

He closes his eyes and takes a deep breath. After a long moment, his shoulders drop a bit. "It's nothing I can't handle. I have an… aggressive church member who is making things a little uncomfortable around the office."

I want to make him smile again, so I try to find my inner stand-up comedian. "Are the troublemaker's initials DB?"

"I shouldn't say, but yes."

A memory surges of my last meeting at the church and how the queen bee of troublemakers gave me my own moment of grief. "Delores has you in her crosshairs, huh?"

His smile disappears, and he runs a hand over his jaw. "She and my wi—Madison were once best friends, and she's now decided to have righteous indignation on my behalf, which includes a sense of… entitlement where the church office is concerned. It was bad enough when Madison decided she wanted to be Brené Brown and things became tense when the congregation wasn't interested in being her adoring throng. Delores isn't making it any better right now."

"I'm sorry, SP. You shouldn't be so hot. This is all your fault."

He tips his head in my direction. "I never imagined you were quite this devious, Kiki MacInnes."

"You clearly don't know me yet."

"Apparently."

My watch beeps, and we both check our wrists.

"Show time." I wave him ahead of me, but he holds back to defer to me.

"Ladies first."

I don't know where this side of me has come from, but I cut him a grin. "Have we established I'm a lady?"

"Just a smart aleck so far, but go with it for now."

"Yes, sir."

I lead the way and hear him mutter, "I'm not sure if it doesn't scare me more when you comply."

I chuckle all the way down the hall, only to be met by Mrs. Momzilla Councilwoman Glassman.

"Where the hell have you been? Wynona is melting down, and for some reason I can't figure out, she's asking for you."

I immediately switch off humor mode and dive right back into PAO Major MacInnes. The very thing I don't want to be anymore.

"It's all right, Mrs. Glassman. I'm here now. I'll see what I can do."

So much for an easy night hanging around in the background.

Something beyond my control has me slowing and reaching for the door handle to the chapel as I pass by. I intended to give it a little pull, to be sure...

The pull turns into a tug. Then a yank.

I close my eyes and force myself to breathe while it feels like every molecule of oxygen has left the building.

This can't be happening. It can't.

Apparently, it can.

All I can do is whisper a word of thanks it's still too early to enter the chapel, anyway. The folks already here are either gathered around the cocktail tables in the foyer, or are in the pub even farther down in the North Turret. Either way, no one but me seems to be aware we've been locked out of the one room in the entire building I need entry to.

With little choice, I get my feet moving and step into the conference-room-turned-bride's-lounge. I personally oversaw the removal of the table and chairs, then arranged the sofas, each comfy cushion done in soft, neutral prints. I made sure the plethora of mirrors are spaced so everyone needing to primp and preen has a spot to do so. I didn't realize how much of this job includes being a furniture wrangler, but there you go.

Momzilla has followed me into the room, closing in with stiff I-mean-business steps. Another perfect blond is sitting beside the bride-to-be. It seems I'm not done with surprises for the evening, because I was sure I'd arrive to find a sobbing and distraught Wynona wailing into a handkerchief or tissue.

Dry-eyed Wynona looks up when I softly clear my throat, and

while she might not be crying, her gaze does have a miles-away quality, making me even more frightened than the tears I was anticipating.

"I don't know why she wanted you." Momzilla's hands land on her hips, and her bitch wings flare. "But you need to talk some sense into her."

I don't know why she wanted me, either. She certainly should have asked for Harville, or Fina, or Mina, but she didn't, and Mom's climbing my nerves like kudzu on a telephone pole.

I pull my neutral PAO expression, which somehow makes people feel I'm agreeing with them. It's a good thing we humans haven't mastered telepathy. "Why don't you give us a minute? Okay, Wynona?"

She turns when she hears her name, and her nod is absent, but visible.

Mom and the other woman—I assume she's the maid of honor—share a look, but they walk out, leaving me and my unasked-for charge in the quiet. I sit next to her and let the strains of a country singer's plaintive but hopeful ballad play in the background. It incongruent thoughts strikes me that the singer is none other than my cousin Ally, the MacInnes family music star, but I put the odd thought away.

When the song ends, I take it as a sign to speak, hoping my cousin was mystically sending me some MacInnes mojo I well and truly need right now. I keep my voice modulated, soothing, the voice I used with full-of-themselves generals on a tear or freshly minted LTs shaking in their shiny shoes.

"What can I do for you, Wynona?"

"You need to call the pastor and the caterer and all those folks you've been working with and tell them it's off. The wedding's off."

From decades of training, I reveal absolutely nothing, as if this declaration is no big deal. Nothing more consequential than she's decided to wear her flats for the ceremony rather than her four-inch Jimmy Choos.

"Okay. Can I ask why?"

"I've ruined everything. Everything. I thought it was all behind me, but I guess I have to accept it'll never be over."

"I see." I angle a bit more toward her and open my hand, but don't touch her. "Would you tell me about it? Maybe I can help."

Why the holy hell I said that, I will never know. The last thing I need to be doing is making any kind of promise, no matter how vague, when I'm neck-deep in a situation I've never been in before. Maudlin drunk? Check. Weepy barely post-teen bride? Nope.

"When I was sixteen, I was completely self-absorbed and thought I was the shit."

Okay. No big surprise there, so I employ my superpower. I stay silent.

"I thought my mother was the most controlling bitch on the planet who only cared about her political career."

Again, having met Momzilla, no big revelation.

"So I started dating the worst loser in school."

I'm still waiting for the part where she isn't reciting the script for the most stereotypical rich-girl-acts-out drama ever imagined. This is where she tells me she sexted him and now she regrets it.

"So he told me to send him nudes."

Man, I should be a writer.

"A guy I was sort of friends with walks up behind me in the stands at cheerleader practice—"

Of course.

"—and sees over my shoulder what I'm doing and stops me."

Okay. Plot twist.

"So, anyway, Brad and I…"

Naturally, his name is Brad.

"We became pretty tight. Dated for the rest of the year. Got sort of serious."

I keep my cape on, and the silence stretches. I finally break. "This is where the *but* comes in."

Wynona studies her perfectly manicured thumbnail. "Listen, I liked Brad. He was a good friend, and he stopped me from making a really bad decision."

"But..."

"But I tended to party pretty hard back then, and Brad was always there. Always had my back. Saved me from drunk-dialing old boyfriends."

Something pings in my brain. "By oh-so-kindly taking your phone from you." I put a hand on Wynona's arm. "And he downloaded your photo album onto his account. Accidentally, I'm sure."

"Yeah. Something like that."

I take a deep breath and plunge in. "Sweetie, I get those weren't your finest hours, but stupid teenage hijinks aren't really worth calling off your wedding."

"Unless your fiancé is the pastor's son of the biggest church in Fort Worth and on the path to taking over as senior pastor someday. And Brad has texted, saying he'll post the pics if you go through with the wedding."

I feel my frown carve tracks between my eyes. "Why does Brad care? It sounds like you broke up a long time ago."

"Yeah, but he's never stopped thinking it's his job to protect me. I was never serious about anyone at this level until I met Stanford. I know you might not believe me, but I'm not kidding. I've never been in love like this."

My attempt to rub out the grooves doesn't work. "So talk to Stanford. It'll be awkward, but better now than—"

"No, it'll ruin everything. You said today is supposed to be wonderful, the first of the best days of our lives, or some such. It's not supposed to be a day of shame and threats and my fiancé finding out I'm a skank. Not exactly the right start to being a preacher's wife."

Of course, Harville's face pops into my mind along with the details Fina and Mina have shared with me about his soon-to-be ex. Seems this church stuff isn't as boring as I've always thought. I give an internal wince, because I don't mean to be trite. The pain I've seen in his eyes is real and deep, as is the fear and worry I watch build in Wynona's.

I look up at the ceiling, hoping for a magical chyron to appear and scroll advice to me like a ticker tape on the wall.

No such luck.

I have zero guidance about being a preacher's wife or sexting pictures or douchebag blackmailers.

"So what does Brad want, other than waiting until the literal eleventh hour to stop your wedding?"

"He wants me to give him a chance to prove to me he's the right one."

"Brilliant plan. Extortion is the perfect start of a sail-off-into-the-sunset moment."

Wynona chokes a laugh and really looks at me for the first time. "You're pretty funny, you know?"

"You're the second person today to say so, but I have to be honest, humor's never been my strong suit."

"Maybe, but I appreciate it."

"Glad to help, but let's get back to your situation. We both know Brad's a douche canoe, but we don't know if his threat is the desperate bluster of a pathetic incel, or if he'll really try to hurt you."

"Incel?"

"Involuntary celibate. A loser who thinks a woman is somehow his, or owes him something. Your basic controlling ass on steroids."

"He didn't start out that way, but yeah, I guess it fits. The answer to your question is, I don't really know."

"Then we're back to square one. Most important question is, do you love Stanford?"

She looks at me, and tears fill her eyes. She doesn't even try to save her makeup and lets them spill down her cheeks. "I love him so much I can't breathe, but I can't ruin his future. He can get over being left at the altar. It can even be part of a great story for him down the line somewhere. Pictures of his naked wife all over the internet?"

"Hang on. We're missing a step. Don't you think he deserves a chance to weigh in here?"

"I don't want him to know. Ever. I don't want him to be disgusted when he looks at me instead of giving me that look that makes me want to melt. You know?"

No, I don't. I've never seen that look in a man's eyes. Lust? Sure, even in my own. But a love so deep I want to melt?

I push away the wistfulness trying to sneak into the moment and stay focused on the current dilemma. "Wynona, I'm going to lay this out for you. You can't change what you did as a teenager. It was dumb to take the photos in the first place. In fact, it was *really* dumb."

She lifts an eyebrow. "Thanks?"

I let my lip twitch, and since I can't pull out any psychology or theology, I revert to plain old 12-step tenets. "Lies cannot thrive in the light. They need the dark, and they need fear. If you love Stanford as much as you say you do, give him a chance. Don't let someone else carve your future. You take the chisel and be your own Michelangelo."

I close my eyes, but keep myself from groaning. I'd just offered the worst, most tortured metaphor I could possibly have used, but give me a break. This is not my skill set.

She looks at the phone clutched in her hand, then at me, then back at her device. "How'd you get so smart? You're not that old."

I cough. "Thanks, but let's say I've made my own bonehead moves landing me a little ahead of you."

Her hands start to tremble. "I'm scared."

I wrap my fingers around hers and squeeze. "It would be bizarre if you weren't, but courage is feeling the fear and doing the thing anyway. And the thing you need to do is talk to Stanford. Now. And if it all goes south, I'll be right here. I'll take care of everything. I'll even lend you a pair of sneakers so you can be a runaway bride and maybe get a movie deal out of it."

She leans over, putting her head on my shoulder. "I'm really glad those dumb doors didn't open last night. I never would connected with you."

Hmmm…

"It was humidity and old wood, but hey, let's not get distracted. I'll go get Stanford, okay?"

As if we conjured him, there's a quick knock at the door, and the young man himself pokes into the room. "Hey, Wyn. Your mom's knocking back soda and Jack a little too fast out here. You might want to—"

I stand and wave him into the room. "Stanford, could you come in here for a minute?"

He hesitates, but moves all the way in. "Uh, sure."

"I'll go talk to Mom. Wynona needs to—"

"Don't go!" She looks at me, her eyes a little wild.

The glance I cut her contains a full dose of understanding, but I hold firm. "Tell him. You don't need me."

Stanford moves closer to the couch, but comes to an abrupt halt. "Tell me what?"

She pats the space on her other side and I make my exit, happy to hear her beginning salvo is, "First of all, I love you…"

The door closes, cutting off the rest of her confession, but she started well. I hope the conversation ends on the same note.

Mom is indeed a couple of Jacks down when I hit the bar. I give the slice-throat sign to Jeremy when she lifts her hand in the universal signal for one more.

"Mrs. Glassman, I need you to listen to me. We're either going to have a crazy-beautiful wedding in about two hours, or your daughter is going to need you like she's never needed you before."

"I beg your pardon?"

Momzilla isn't begging anything.

"I don't want to overstep," as I completely overstep, "but I hope you'll come with me, and we can chat while Wynona and Stanford are talking."

Whatever woo-woo is going on today holds, and instead of ripping my head off and handing it to me, Momzilla follows me back to the comfortable sitting area outside of the chapel. A few more people have joined, including two young ladies holding aloft garment bags in one hand and enormous makeup kits in the other. I intercept them before they hit the ready room.

"Hi there, I'm Kiki, your liaison this evening. Wynona needs a minute before y'all join her in there. Why don't you put your stuff down and help yourself to the sodas and seltzer water right over there?"

They give me quizzical looks, but the girls join the young men they clearly know already tossing back Dr Pepper and chowing on the nut mix.

I glare at the chapel and have to call on all my don't-do-it, white-knuckle strength to keep from bounding over there and making those doors open if I have to Hulk them apart with the adrenaline coursing through me right now.

Mrs. Glassman joins the younger set, and thankfully, there's nothing with alcohol on the setup. My tension level notches down a tenth of a percent when Mrs. G puts a hand on the arm of one of the boys who hasn't quite grown into his size-thirteen shoes and starts talking.

Leaving me to shift my gaze from the chapel to the prep room and back again about eight thousand times. I swear, if one or the other doesn't open—

Wynona and Stanford appear, and tension drains from me so fast I go lightheaded. The pretty blond is nestled against his shoulder, and as I watch, he plants a long kiss against her hairline. Her mascara is completely gone, but her eyes are shining.

With joy.

The two attendants see their target and run over, squealing, oblivious to what has gone on.

Wynona pulls Stanford down for a kiss and shoos him back to his buddies. She says something to her mini gang and comes over to me.

I'm hardly surprised when I get a second stuffing-squeezing from her, but I'm so damned happy the crisis has been averted, I don't care.

I hold up a finger. "Not a word. You're welcome. Now go, get beautified, and get ready to have one of those best days."

She moves away, but something jars my memory. "Wynona, wait."

She stops, and I reach into my pocket, pulling out what I nearly forgot. I hold it out to her. "This is for you. It's a piece of lace made by the descendants of Alyssa MacInnes, and we give one to every bride marrying in the chapel. I hope you'll carry it with you today and know generations of MacInnes women are here with you and Stanford on this special day."

Her eyes fill with fresh tears, but these don't fall. "I'll cherish it forever."

She leaves this time, and as if drawn by a magnet, my eyes shift to the chapel, where the doors are ever so slightly ajar.

"It's coincidence." I whisper the words, but put some force into them.

The deep voice I've been desperate to hear interrupts my mantra-on-repeat.

Nothing weird is happening.

Nothing weird is happening.

Nothing weird is—

"I understand there's been a little drama while I was talking to Papa Glassman."

So that's where he's been…

"All taken care of. Want to help me give the chapel a last once-over?"

"Happy to." He stops me with a gentle hand on my arm. "Are you all right?"

No, truth be told. If I'd had even a second's thought about could-have-beens with a sexy pastor—and I hadn't—this little episode from *Days of Our Lives* would have been a vivid slap in the face. It's a stark warning to keep my head on straight around my new compatriot. He can be a friend, and that's that. He's a pastor. And a wounded one. And *the* last male on planet Earth I need to get involved with.

I'm ten times the mess Wynona is… was… so there'll be no forehead kisses and last-minute smooches before a walk down a silk-runnered aisle for me.

Ever.

14
FINA

It's a good bet Mina and I prayed harder Friday night and all day Saturday than we've ever prayed. When I got to my side of the duplex, thanks to Harville's help, I grabbed all the medicine I thought we'd need and went over to my sister's.

Next thing I know, there's a knock at the door, and I open it to a distraught CT Nelson. I don't have the strength to fight him as he orders me to bed in the guest room and starts playing the best nurse I've ever seen. I want to tease him for sleeping on the couch, but at the moment, I couldn't care less if he slept in the bathtub.

I awakened in a panic, needing to check on Kiki, but he assured me he texted with her, and other than a momentary breakdown by the bride, everything went off perfectly. I finally fell into a coma, knowing the party was in full swing, and we're in the clear.

Now it appears I've lost an entire day. It's Sunday morning, the sky is overcast and threatening some much-needed rain, and I think maybe, maybe, I'm going to live. I feel weak as a kitten, but I manage to slip on one of Mina's robes and shuffle into the living room to find her snuggled against CT on the couch, where they're watching *Meet the Press*.

"Hello, you two. CT, thank you for being a lifesaver."

Mina wiggles her fingers at me in hello, and CT eases out of her embrace.

"You sit down, and I'll get you some toast and tea. Mina managed to keep it down, so maybe y'all are in the clear."

"Sweet baby Jesus, I hope so." I melt into the recliner and tuck my legs underneath me, eyeing my sister. "You feeling okay?"

"Better now." Her voice is a little croaky, but mine is, too. Our throats are undoubtedly a little raw from the past thirty-six hours. "How'd the wedding go?"

I check my texts and confirm CT's report. "According to Kiki, Councilwoman Glassman is threatening to give us a bonus."

My sister snorts. "I'll believe it when I see the check." She pauses and wrinkles her nose. "I take it back. I'll believe it when the check clears."

I rest against the cushion. "I really don't expect to get one, or care if we do. I'm just glad our girl's baptism by fire hasn't singed her."

"Maybe, maybe not, but at least we can put a big giant X on the calendar tomorrow."

"Amen."

My erstwhile nurse and chef hands me a cup of sweet-smelling tea and two slices of perfectly browned toast.

"It's almond decaf. Should be pretty easy on your stomach."

"Thank you, again. I really—"

"We're family now, or close enough for government work, so hush."

I take a bite of toast to stop myself from arguing. I know he means well, but I'm not used to taking orders. It's always the other way around. However, my still-pale twin is looking at her intended with an expression bordering on beatific, so I'll let this one slide.

Besides, any retort I might have made is interrupted by a knock at the door.

CT once more takes charge, and I suppress another touch of irritation. I truly appreciate his kindness, but I hope I can escape to my duplex and leave the happy couple alone in short order.

"Hey, CT. Surprised to see you here."

He steps aside so my nephew can come in. Trey's soft gray Polo has a few rain splatters on it, and as he shuts the door behind him, a roll of thunder echoes across the sky.

"Hey, sweetie." I can't help but smile as he presses a kiss to my temple and then moves to pull his mother into his arms. That boy, man now and long has been, is the reason my life changed course so many years ago. I've never regretted it. I've never second-guessed staying to keep my sister and Trey as safe as I could inside a nightmare. I've kept sadness at what I gave up tucked away in the corner of my mind, but never regret.

After all the usual chitchat, Trey takes a cup of coffee from CT, and we're all seated around Mina's coffee table, the TV now silenced.

"What brings you over?" I ask, since he seems reluctant to reveal the reason for his surprise visit. Trey isn't a stranger around here, but neither is he particularly prone to stopping by unannounced.

"I was at the castle, stealing a biscuit from Mrs. Greene, when Kiki told me you two were sick. I stopped by your place first, but figured you had to be here when your place was empty."

Trey has keys to both our doors, so no surprise here.

"I'm sure glad you're here, but you still haven't said why. I don't need a reason, of course. Just curious."

"I've been needing to stop by, and I didn't want to wait any longer. Not with the wedding around the corner." He looks at his mother and gives her the smile that makes her melt. Then it slips. "But I figured I was dillydallying and needed to get this done. I know you're going to be upset."

"Spit it out, son." CT's voice is gentle, but firm.

"Momma, do you remember Mason Norris?"

"Sure, I do. You two were tight as ticks all through high school, but then you went on to Rice and he went to Baylor, I think, and y'all kinda lost touch."

"Bullseye, but thanks to social media, we revived our friendship a few years ago." He takes a sip of his coffee and looks into the dark cup long enough to make us all fidget. "Thing is, Mason's taking over his daddy's law firm in Lubbock and wants me to come on as a partner.

It's a good opportunity for me. The panhandle isn't exactly the far side of the moon, but it's not five minutes away, either."

"Congratulations, son." CT stands and offers his hand, which Trey accepts.

"Thank you." When CT moves out of the way, Trey meets his mother's eyes. "I hope you're happy for me, too, Momma."

Mina is blinking rapidly, and my heart goes out to my twin. "Of course I'm happy for you, sweetheart. This is… wonderful news."

We all stifle our responses to her blatant lie, and it brings a little color to her pale cheeks.

"Well, it is." Her tone is defensive, but her voice isn't strong. "I'm stunned, is all."

Trey looks at me, and I smile at the young man I claimed as mine, too, when he came into this world and bellowed indignantly at everyone in the delivery room. I held Mina's hand through all eighteen hours of labor, and I was the second human being to hold him. Well, third if you count the doctor.

"I'm happy for you, Trey. I know we don't sit in each other's back pocket, but I will dearly miss having you a phone call away."

"I'll still be a phone call away. A little longer-distance call away, is all." He gives me his cheeky smile, and I wrinkle my nose at him.

Mina asks the obvious question. "When are you moving?"

"This isn't a kiss and goodbye, of course. I have to sell my practice here, and it'll take more'n a New York minute, but I hope to be settled in before year's end. I figured since you and CT are gonna be in Italy most of December anyway, that made sense."

A pain pierces my heart when his statement sinks in. Momma's been talking about the Grannies doing a cruise over Christmas this year. Mina and CT will be on their honeymoon in Europe. And now my only nephew will be five hundred miles away.

And I'll be here. Alone.

I'm a veritable heel for feeling like everyone is abandoning me. It's selfish, and I need to get myself together. Everything in the world isn't about me.

I have the utterly childish thought to call up Brian Steele, and we'll have our own little orphan Christmas this year. It's not the end of the world.

So I congratulate Trey, and the boys move into the kitchen to make a heartier man-breakfast.

And Mina and I look at each other while matching tears escape down both of our cheeks.

15

KIKI

THE WEATHER DIDN'T COOPERATE on Sunday, so it's six in the morning on Monday before Harville and I are finally following through on our plan for a run. The castle has a small gym, and I made do on the treadmill, but I'm so happy to be outside I don't mind it's still an hour to sunrise. I'm already stretched out by the time he arrives at the bleachers of Magnolia Bloom High School.

I wait until we've exchanged greetings, and he's stretched before I take off my jogging suit. The weather is a perfect sixty-nine degrees with low humidity, so I need the coverage while I sit still, but certainly not while running. He does the same thing, and we both click on our head lamps and set off at a slow, easy pace. As we pass the halfway point of the first mile, he looks over at me.

"I thought you said you were a baby jogger."

"I think I said beginner, and I am. I only started running a couple of years ago out of desperation. I'm sure my technique sucks, but it's all I've got right now. I much prefer lifting to running."

"I'm with you on the gym over the track, and your technique is fine. Your torso is tall, your ears are in line with your shoulders, your gaze is forward, you're striking with the ball of your foot. Pretty solid form for someone who isn't serious."

"I didn't say I wasn't serious, and I think I mentioned I worked on an Air Force base, so I had plenty of advice thrown at me by dudes in amazing shape. Most of it unsolicited."

"Oops. I'll shut up."

I stumble for a step. "I didn't mean you, honestly. Thank you for the affirmation. I'm glad I'm not totally mucking this up." I cut him a glance to bring back our newly established humor. "Even if you do fit the dude-in-amazing-shape category."

This time, he bobbles a step, then he gives me the smile I'm becoming accustomed to. "Thanks."

"I have commissioned myself to be your PCO, that's personal compliments officer, since it appears people are too afraid to flirt with you."

Another stumble. "You're flirting with me?"

"Only as substitute teacher until you find some hottie to date."

"Kiki, you're using a whole lot of words not usually used in the same sentence with a small-town Southern pastor."

"Then it seems I got here just in time, then, doesn't it? Besides, this is what friends are for."

"I—"

"Shhh. We're getting to the place where I can't jog and talk at the same time. Save it for when we're done."

I see he doesn't believe me, but I'm not kidding. We've passed the mile mark, and if I'm going to make it another two before I fall down and die, I have to conserve my oxygen.

I end up calling the run at two and a half. It's not nearly as long as I want to get back to, but for today, it's good enough.

We're doing a cool-down walk when the sun begins to make its appearance. It's enough we can shut off our headgear and return to the stands to slip back into our tracksuits as it doesn't take long for the cool breeze to chill our sweaty skin. Or mine, anyway.

"Do you have time for coffee?" I wipe my forehead with my gym towel and put it back in my bag.

"Absolutely. Want to go to The Bagelry, and then we can watch the sunrise from the park? It will be our first official friendship breakfast."

"Excellent plan. I'll meet you there."

The city park comprises the greenspace surrounded by the buildings in the square's perimeter. It takes literal minutes to drive from the school to downtown, and it's early enough for there to be plenty of parking spaces in front of the town's new eatery. We all hope the enterprise makes it, as it's nice to have a place to go early in the morning for coffee and a pastry.

Harville starts to get huffy when I beat him to the credit card machine after we give our orders at the counter.

"You will not—"

"Yes, I will. Here's the first rule of our new friendship. Instead of haggling over money, we take turns. I'm buying today. You buy next time."

I can tell he's not happy about it. "I don't want to argue in public, so I'll let you win this one. For now."

The sun's up by the time we take our goodies across the street to one of the picnic benches placed around the grassy area parched for rain. Yesterday's shower wasn't nearly enough to solve our recent drought problem.

I've barely had time to take one glorious before Harville stiffens like he's been shot in the back.

"What is it? What's wrong?"

That's when I see Delores Bainbridge standing at the door to The Bagelry, staring lasers at us from across the street. She lets the look linger, then goes inside.

I feel Harville's distress like it's my own.

"Hey, what's up? You look like we've been caught in flagrante delicto, not sharing bagel."

"I'm not so sure she won't intimate exactly that."

I may not have a lot of friends, but I'm loyal to a fault to those I claim. "Now wait one minute. First, why can't you have coffee with a friend out in the wide open? And second, if she does say something so monumentally stupid, she deserves a major smackdown."

He smiles sheepishly, an expression I've seen before and yet doesn't get tiresome at all. "Of course, you're right. I don't mean to be ridiculous. I've just never…"

"Been single, at least around here?"

"I'm technically not single yet. I have an appointment this afternoon with Trey to sign the decree, and then it'll be entered in a couple of days by Madison and her lawyer."

I reach across the table and grab his fingers in a grip I hope conveys my support, my concern. I feel him tense, but Delores Bainbridge can kiss my butt. I'm not going to modify my behavior for her or anyone else.

"I'm sorry. I really am."

"You don't have to take on my troubles, you know."

"I'm not. I'm hoping we'll be the embodiment of the aphorism 'a burden shared is a burden halved.'"

He covers my fingers with his and squeezes. "I appreciate it. I knew this was going to get sticky, because people don't like others moving outside their proscribed boxes. I've never liked being treated like I'm some kind of icon of perfection. Half the town wants to treat me like I'm a broken glass, and the other half thinks it's helping to tell me my almost-ex is sleeping her way across the Southwest like she's trying for a Guinness world record."

"Ouch, but the good news is, you can talk to me about it, because I'm not a member of your flock, so there's no chain-of-command issues."

The words are barely out of my mouth when heat scorches my cheeks. *Holy Freudian slip, Batman!* I force the thought away before I dive down a rabbit hole of self-recrimination and despair. Luckily, Harville is lost in his own thoughts and has no way to know what the hell just happened in my brain.

"The truth is, I was willing to try to fix us. Go to counseling. Whatever it might have taken, but she didn't give me the chance."

"You—"

"Hold up. That sounded really whiny and self-indulgent. I promise you I was not without fault in our relationship failing. We'd been coming to this for a long time, but didn't expect it to end in such a nuclear meltdown."

"And everyone and their brother thinks they know how a pastor's marriage should work."

"Brother, sister, mother, cousin…"

"It's like doing your marriage in a fishbowl, like a celebrity or something."

"Or something. I've been trying to quietly ride this out. I love this congregation, and I don't want to be a source of conflict. I truly don't wish Madison ill. I'm hurt and angry, sure, but what I see in her behavior says she's a lot more lost than I am."

"Damn, Harville, you need to spend at least a week reveling in her misery, or you really aren't human, despite your claim to the contrary."

His smile is sad and amused at the same time. "Oh, I've had more than a few thoughts deserving time in a confessional, but in the end, it's not who I am. Maybe I'm a fool or too naïve to live, but I can't bathe in the acid of hatred and bitterness. I've counseled too many people caught in that hell, so no, thank you."

"It doesn't take a genius to realize you don't want to be fodder for the gossip mill, either."

"That, too."

"So what's the deal with Delores?"

"My dilemma is, she does a fine job as office administrator, and I have no basis to fire her. If I did, it would cause all kinds of drama, even if she's getting a touch inappropriate by deciding she's my personal keeper. I don't need one, and I never asked her to step into such a role by word or action."

"Come on, surely you see she's vying to be the next Mrs. Pastor."

He blushes, and it's so sweet. "I'm not stupid, Kiki. Just uncomfortable."

As if she's summoned our attention, both of our eyes are drawn back to The Bagelry as Delores leaves with a bag in her arms, but her focus is entirely on us.

We jerk forward again, and his smile matches mine. "Oops."

He snorts softly and takes a bite from his now-cold kolach. "I didn't mean to make you uncomfortable."

"You didn't. I don't have anything to hide from Queen Bee over there, and if she buzzes around me, she might get swatted."

"I thought you were shy and avoided the spotlight."

"I am, but I don't take it well when someone tries to bully me. Since I'm fine hanging around in the background, most people don't pay attention to me. Which suits me fine. But me not liking the limelight doesn't mean I'm a marshmallow."

"Sounds like there's a story there."

"Oh, there is, but I'm not ready to share. I will, but today is Getting to Know Harville Day. I'll take my turn later."

"As long as you promise."

"I do."

But I'd like to have his friendship for a little while longer before he looks at me with repugnance instead of flashing those dimples and letting me see the light twinkling in his eyes.

We finish our breakfast and crumple our napkins into the empty bag. "And thus ends our first friendship breakfast."

He taps the edge of his Styrofoam cup against mine and takes his last swallow. "I'll drink to that."

We go our separate ways, and as I wend my way back to the castle and the mountain of work awaiting me, a thought hits me. When I'm ready and I tell him the truth about my past, even if I lose his respect, he'll keep anything I say in confidence.

I've never had someone to trust like him. Not Traycee. Not even Paige. I've never had a safety net.

So, I'll enjoy my time as SP's new BFF.

For as long as it lasts.

16

JULIETTE

It's easy to lose track of days in my profession. While Noelle has many times accused me of being a workaholic, I don't have a classic office schedule. I'm as prone to work for days in a row with only catnaps when I'm immersed in a project, then need a break to get myself back in order. Which means, when I receive a text from Rory asking me to lunch, I have to check the calendar to realize how quickly October is passing. I didn't make it to the dance hall with Emmett, deciding after our shopping I wasn't quite ready. He understood, and I've been so lost in continuing my work on the paintings, time passed unnoticed.

It's not a surprise when there's a knock at the door at ten, as Rory is never late. What is interesting and unexpected is my sudden wish I'd done more than put on a dash of mascara and a bit of tinted moisturizer.

I am not a vain woman, but neither am I coy. I have dated and been sought after by some handsome and wealthy men. And, to be honest, a few women. I am in the art world, after all, and we are all—how had Gavina put it in Violet's journal?—a squirrely bag of nuts. I have had dinners at the finest restaurants in Paris, Vienna, and Prague. I have flown on private jets so luxurious it makes one's mouth water.

While some of these events were interesting and sometimes enervating, I don't recall my pulse ever racing. Not like this. Not as I hurry across a concrete floor in a barn, albeit a nice one, and open the door to a quiet, redheaded man with a country accent and Southern manners who probably has never sat in first class, much less seen a Gulfstream G6.

My thoughts are not meant to disparage Rory. In fact, they are quite the opposite. I have never been one to be impressed by wealth. I have had a lovely lifestyle, thanks to myriad blessings, but money for the sake of money has been nonexistent on my list of desires in a companion. My contacts at Sotheby's alone put me in the orbit of the upper echelon of the art world, and yet not one of those members of the self-important elite have made me feel the same rich, warm contentment as a country man from Texas.

This man, who chases after a little minx of a lamb with a mama bear's ferocity in protecting her cub, makes me want to sigh every time the image crosses my mind.

"Salut." I gesture my lunch companion inside.

"Mornin'. You look mighty spiffy."

I look down at the more subdued of the jeans I purchased from Traycee. These are white with a subtle sprinkle of blue stones down the right leg... *subtle* as far as blinged jeans go. I added a light, long-sleeved white shirt over my cobalt tank top and feel I'm the epitome of casual.

"I have begun my transformation into an honorary Texan." I raise my foot and lift the hem of my jeans to reveal the boots I bought during my trip with Emmett.

"Those are right pretty."

"I had no idea there was such a thing as restored boots. Considering what I do, this makes my heart happy. It seems a shame my jeans cover the hand-painting on this shaft."

"Henry does have an eye for pretty things."

Then I grasp he's looking at me as if I'm the interesting object. He realizes he must have revealed his inner thoughts, because he blushes a fiery red and looks away, clearing his throat.

I am not afraid of attraction or passion. While intrigued, I'm not afraid of the unexpected speed it has all happened. I *am* afraid of losing it when I have to go home.

I can only assume this all can be laid at the feet of my world being upended by Paige's visit and the rift forming between Noelle and me. How else can I explain my behavior so disparate from my normal mode? In the past, I might have made a concerted effort to get back in my lane, as the expression goes.

That inclination feels decidedly unappealing today.

My manners finally reappear, thankfully. "Thank you. Let me get my bag."

This gives us both a moment to regain our composure before we start our jaunt downtown. He has promised to give me a guided tour of the vendors on the side streets, which, he has said, "Need some love, too."

I lock the barn behind us, and he escorts me out with his now-expected quiet valor, and I mock-frown when I don't see a little black nose riding along.

"We do not have a companion with us today?"

Rory smiles. "I'm afraid not. The shops downtown are becoming more accepting of dogs, but they draw the line at livestock. And, in their defense, the law is clear on domestic companions."

I settle in and wait until he is behind the wheel before I continue. "Makes sense, I suppose, but I must insist we apply for an exemption for Lulu. She has quickly become more than mere livestock, to me, anyway."

His chuckle is deep and warm, and a matching heat spreads through my chest and other more intimate parts.

"That stinker is about to drive me to drink. I've seen a lamb mope when they're being weaned, but not to go riding in a pickup. She looked at me like I was abandoning her, for criminy's sake."

"Then we must get her after we have our sojourn into town to make it up to her."

Rory looks at me for a long moment, his smile starting slow and building until his eyes crinkle. "I guess I'm a little bit slow on the uptake, because I never thought to add a lamb to my pickup game."

My mouth mimics his until my eyes squint, too. "Do you have an established pickup game, Monsieur Campbell? You didn't strike me as the type."

He starts the truck and points it down the road toward the front property gates, his only answer a lift of his right eyebrow.

Delight bubbles through me. Maybe it is my own fault, a response to my personality, but people are often serious around me. Rory does not seem so inclined, and the fizzle in my bloodstream turns into effervescence.

"Would you mind if we rolled down the windows?" I ask, because the weather has turned delightfully cooler.

Again, I am delivered the raised eyebrow. "Happy to oblige. I'm just not used to ladies risking their hairdos."

"Which again opens my line of questioning of how often do you have ladies with risky coiffures in your truck?"

"Not so often, if I'm honest, and never one as pretty as you."

I have an instinctive tendency to discount flattery, as I am always trying to discern the angle behind the words. I'm not foolish. I know I am reasonably attractive, but for the first time in a long time, I hope the words are truthful.

"Merci." I cover the surprise heating my cheeks by lowering my window and letting in a cool breeze. Of course it ruffles my short hair, but a pixie cut does not require tremendous upkeep, so I'm not bothered. There are days my entire hair routine involves ruffling my fingers through my dark strands and letting it go.

The short drive into town does not give us much time for banter, and quickly Rory turns from chauffeur to tour guide. I already know the town center is more a rectangle than a square, but those are semantics. The longer north and south sides contain vendors. The east end comprises the city government complex and the library, while the west end has a law office, doctors' offices, a pharmacy, and surprisingly, a microbrewery. Rory promises to take me there after we have lunch.

We transition to the sidewalk, walking side by side in easy camaraderie. "I'm more of a wine person, but I am open to trying new things."

"Bunny West has a pretty good line going."

I stop in my tracks. "You are having fun at my expense."

He frowns. "About what?"

"The brewery is run by a woman named Bunny."

"You're the last person I'd expect to have sexist stereotypes, but the short story is Bunny got the brewery in her divorce. While the over-under was betting she'd sell it or shut it down to spite John West, who is best described as the south end of a northbound donkey, she didn't. Instead, she's turned it into one of the draws making Magnolia Bloom into a shopping destination."

We move again toward our goal. Rory has promised me everything from bagels to burgers to pizza, but today is reserved for Vivann's. Apparently, it is the major favorite of the locals.

"Kiki was speaking of another town—I'm sorry I do not recall the name—but your chamber of commerce is quite determined to similarly revitalize the economy with tourism."

"It's a work in progress."

"I'm glad for you. The town is charming."

"It's no Paris."

I shrug, the action seeming common between us. "I would be the last to deny there is endless charm in the City of Lights, but I and many like me become frustrated the only city in my country people know is Paris. It is like how it angers those who think New York City is all of New York. Or if I only knew of Dallas here in Texas."

He holds up his hands. "I didn't mean to touch a nerve."

"You didn't, really. Just an observation."

I raise a hand to Emmett as we pass the gallery. He returns the gesture, and we move one storefront down. Rory and I both stop when Traycee steps into the display area and drops the costumes in her hand, waving at us to come inside.

"Hi. Y'all off to lunch?"

"Trying to beat the rush. How's it going?" Rory, of course, has removed his hat. I find this dance between him and his Stetson fascinating.

"More costumes to unpack than a box of Cracker Jack has peanuts, but we'll get it done. What are you two going as for the festivities?"

Rory looks at me, but I demur. "I don't know if I'll still be here, and Halloween is not a thing in France in general. Certainly it has caught on in some places, but nowhere to the degree it has in America."

Traycee gives me an arch glance. "Girl, it may not be there, but here? You better get a costume now to cover your bases. If you wait until the last minute, you're gonna have to be a Ninja Turtle."

Both she and Rory are amused by my confusion. "Pardon?"

Traycee takes pity on me and looks behind herself, digging in a big box until she turns back to hand me a package. The picture indeed shows a turtle standing upright, wearing a blue mask, and holding two swords.

This does not ease my bemusement.

"I'll explain it over lunch." Rory takes the package and tosses it back in Traycee's box of items waiting for display.

"If you want a suggestion, I have a perfect idea for you two. I heard about the lamb y'all carried out to Spring Valley."

Rory nods in understanding. I merely deepen into my puzzlement.

Traycee explains, "There's three types of communication in this town. Telegraph. Telephone." She looks at Rory, and they finish together, "Tell-A-Grannie."

"Mamaw Ida is one of the Grannies," Rory adds. "They're a force of nature in this town, and you can bet good money if you want to know a secret about anyone, past or present, they'll have the skinny."

This news clarifies, in an oblique way, one point nagging me. "I see now why my belief no one knew about me caused you such amusement. These Grannies miss nothing."

Rory's expression is indulgent and amused. "Pretty much. They're harmless and are all sweet as pecan pie, but at the same time, I wouldn't cross 'em. They love this town and the people in it and are ferocious in protecting Magnolia Bloom. They may all be in their seventies and eighties, but I'd put money on their dice in a heartbeat."

Traycee picks up the dialogue. "What I was saying is, I got a couple of things in that are perfect. I went retro this year when I was ordering, and my Gram would say the angels were watching out for you."

She hurries to a rack of hanging costumes and is back before Rory and I can begin to discuss whether I might be here for the celebration.

The hanger Rory takes from her has an orange plaid shirt, a white vest with black cowhide splotches, and an exaggerated holster. I know even before she reveals it that she is going to hand me a pink dress with a bonnet and a plastic shepherd's crook.

"I'm sorry to disappoint you both, but *Toy Story* was probably as big in France as here. My papa loves the whole series."

"Then you'll be a perfect Bo. Rory already has a brown hat and, of course, jeans and boots. I can get you a blond wig, too."

"Mais non. I am not opposed to being a shepherdess, but I draw the line at a hot, itchy wig." I turn and give Rory a smile. "What do you say? If I am still here, shall we attend as Woody and Bo Peep?"

His grin lights up his entire being. "I can't think of anything I'd rather do. Besides, we have the perfect sidekick."

"You'd let me take Lulu?"

"I think if she heard about this through the sheep grapevine and we didn't take her along, she'd stage a revolt of the whole flock."

Traycee joins in our laughter, and I find myself leaving with a sack containing a pink dress with a polka-dotted skirt and a wide-brimmed bonnet, but no crook. Rory assures me he will lend me the real thing.

We're still chuckling over our costumes when Vivann's daughter, who I now know as Jillian, brings us our orders. I'm taking my first bite of a beautifully presented strawberry pecan salad when I feel a coldness on my neck, and tension rises in my veins like I've taken an antihistamine.

I look around the room and put my fork on the plate before I drop it.

It's him.

My biological father.

I have done several internet searches, as would be expected, and I confess the first time I saw him, standing with his seemingly perfect family, my heart lurched. I'm not sure why. I had a marvelous childhood. My parents have always, and still do, love me with a ferocity assuring me every day I am precious in their eyes and in their hearts. This isn't about a wound, more a missing piece. I could have lived my life without ever knowing this information, but now I have the opportunity to learn, and the flood of questions is not unreasonable.

And now I'm looking across a quaint restaurant in a charming town in a place I never imagined visiting, and I'm digging into memories and questions I thought were neatly packed away. Maybe I was foolish not to take Noelle's route of absolute determination to keep this door closed.

It's clear the rumor mill has reached David Broder, because there are a multitude of emotions playing across his face, but shock isn't one. A touch of surprise, no doubt exactly like the expression on mine. Neither one of us could have thought this would happen today, or we'd both have been better prepared.

What I see in him is sadness and pain and loss. Possibly regret. His wife's expression is harder to read. Her eyes hold pain, too, but I know even less about her than I do about David, so I don't know if it's discomfort for her husband, for herself, or concern for her children and grandchildren.

The wife stands, breaking the tense seconds, and he hastily rises. He gives me a small tip of his chin and escorts her away. I appreciate the acknowledgment, but I'm not sure what it means. Is it *I see you. Now go away?* Is it *I see you and will talk to you later?*

Rory touches my arm, drawing my attention to him. "Are you all right?"

His tone is the one I expect from him, the quiet, warm one simply saying, *I'm here.*

"I am fine. Perplexed, perhaps. Emmett said while we were shopping that the Broders don't come into town a lot."

"Not often, but not never. The Broders are a huge part of this town, like the MacInneses. If I had to guess, they're here for some meeting or other for the new hospital they're building. As fast as we're growing, we've needed one for years, and the Broders love Magnolia Bloom as much as the MacInnes side, so it's not like they're a celebrity sighting or something. They probably come into town a lot, and no one thinks a thing about it."

"I understand. I simply wasn't prepared."

Rory takes a bite of his salad and chews for a moment. "There are some things I'm not sure you could ever be prepared for. Theory versus reality. It's like knowing I'm going to lose lambs every season, but it still gets to me."

My heart squeezes. "You have to have a certain level of pragmatism, or you could not do your job, but I'm glad you care."

"This estate has a damned good reputation in all our animal husbandry, but this isn't for the faint-hearted." He waves a hand between us. "I didn't mean to start talking about me. Are you going to be okay?"

He eyes the empty doorway, and even though David Broder and his wife are long gone, I am touched by his concern. "I'll be fine. I was about to ask you to try on your costume with me when we get back so I can send a text to my sister. She'll think it's hilarious."

Or she would have in the past. Now? I stuff down the thought, worried she'll mock me and I'm afraid that might break me.

"I'd be delighted."

"Maybe another time. I'm finding both my enthusiasm and appetite have waned."

"I'll take you home, then." He signals Jillian for the check, and it's a matter of minutes before we're on our way back to the property.

And then it's only a few more before I'm pouring myself back into my work so I don't have to look into the hollow pit in my stomach that was briefly filled with silliness.

17
KIKI

THE THING about being insanely busy is time passes without me really noticing. I accept that might not be good for everyone, but it is for me. My almost daily run with Harville has become sacred to me. So much so I've barely gotten over to the garage and worked on my project car languishing in the bay. Today, the morning is dark and quiet, the temperature crisp and cool, the air sweet and clean as I take deep breaths and stretch. These rare few weeks of a Texas autumn are precious, as priceless as the time I spend with him.

And as fleeting. I don't like the days ticking by, the evil watchman in my mind constantly tapping against the glass as if to say, *Time's up*. The aching sadness trying to rise promises me one little hit would take the edge off, make this ache go away.

Which is a giant warning klaxon. I've put in extra meetings to fight the siren song and sent texts to Traycee, hoping she'd go with me. She's gone along a couple of times, but bowed out the rest. It's been an exercise in staying in my own recovery lane to not hover over her. I call, check in, either drive or ride shotgun to meetings she's willing to attend, but otherwise stay out of her business.

I worry about her.

I share my concerns with Harville as we stretch on our oh dark thirty Halloween run. Turns out, one, small-town pastors are crazy-busy, and two, the more modern branch of the American Presbyterians are not categorically opposed to Halloween.

Who knew?

St. Andrew's is having a Fall Festival Craft Show and Celebration today to serve the members of the congregation who do have an objection to the classic American party, and I admire Harville's nonjudgmental way of serving all the members of his congregation. He plans to join me in the Fun Run later this afternoon and spend the evening at the castle for the events planned there.

I wish my pulse wasn't so giddy at the prospect. There's been safety in the brevity of our regular time spent together. Just enough time to enrich a friendship, but not let myself get too invested. I haven't dared. We either run or work out most mornings, stop by any of the various eateries in town for a quick coffee or breakfast, catch up on what's happening at the castle or the church, then go on about our days.

It's been utterly lovely to feel seen. To be heard.

"What's up?" Harville folds his jacket with the neatness I've come to expect from him, another of his facets I appreciate. "You're a thousand miles away."

"I'm worried about Traycee and Bethanie. Then I start to panic with all I have to do before this evening. I've been here three months, and it feels like twenty seconds one day and ten years the next. Fina is losing her mind, because even though she's about to get Mina and CT off on their pre-wedding trip, she's obsessing about the dude arriving from Denmark. I have to confess I don't know why she's so bent—"

"You need to take a breath before you faint from lack of oxygen."

"Can't argue with you there."

We start the first steps of our run, although this time we've packed our outerwear into our cars and are running the trails around Broder Springs. The area reminds me of Barton Springs in Austin, as I spent many an hour on the bank of that piece of wonderland in college. Broder Springs, though, is a hot spring, not merely a natural spring, although technically it's both.

Over the years, the Broder family has developed the surrounding park and made access to the springs easier, manicured two multipurpose fields, and created an oasis outside of town. Once Harville and I established a comfort level with my skill, the move from the boring quarter-mile track to the trails was an easy jump.

It's a chilly sixty right now, so we're both eager to get moving. A dip in the springs when we're done would be nice, but neither of us has time today.

We slip into our easy rhythm and let the sound of our footfalls be our only interruption for a good fifteen minutes. Finally, my shoulders seem to be easing away from my ears.

"Now let's back up, and you start with why you're worried about Traycee and Bethanie."

"Not them as a unit, but I haven't heard a peep from Bethanie, and CT says she's managing to make it to work, but doesn't seem any better. As for Traycee, I don't want to judge or betray a confidence, so all I can share is she feels more distant over these past weeks. We talk every couple of days, but I'm hoping she's merely stressed from being a retailer at the beginning of the holiday season."

"It can't be easy for someone as empathetic as you to stay connected but not attached."

I chew on the thought for a moment. "I never considered myself empathetic, but the more work I do on getting healthy, the more I see it applies. Military minds think the word is synonymous with weak, and I was nothing if not hard-core military for a long time. I know it's not true now, or I'm learning from my shelves groaning with books by Anne Lamott, Pema Chödrön, Brené Brown, Thich Nhat Hanh, and so many more." I take a much-needed breath. We're almost at the stop-talking point. "Scares me a lot."

"Logical."

It is no surprise he recognizes my waning oxygen levels and doesn't ask for the rest of the details from my stream-of-consciousness list until we're done, back in our tracksuits, and sitting on the back patio of the Coffee Hut, another venue on the square. Steam is rising from our matching flat whites. I take a sip with relish, making up for lost time after so many years in the military, and plan on trying up every fancy coffee on the planet with all possible speed.

"So tell me what else is up."

"Nope. You already have the skinny on Fina, Mina, and CT, so it's your turn. And if you're learning to read me, I'm learning to interpret what's behind this übercalm facade of yours. Your energy is a little low. Is it Delores the Diva? What's happening in SP Land?"

His pretend frown includes a big dose of exasperation, but I think there's a little piece of my friend who doesn't mind his Sexy Pastor moniker. It's cute he still blushes, though.

"Things are hectic, but nothing new there, so… boring. As to the diva, she was doing better, but the closer it's gotten to today, she's ramping up, it seems."

"What's significant about Halloween to her?"

"Not Halloween, per se. I don't understand how she could possibly know, because I don't talk about it, but Trey says he has the file-marked copy of the decree from the court. I pick it up today, so it's done. I'm free."

I reach over and rub my hand down his arm, stopping to squeeze his wrist. "I'm really sorry."

He looks at my fingers for a long moment before putting his own on top. "Thanks, but the truth is, I'm glad it's over. Official. Signed and sealed, as it were." He pulls his bottom lip between his teeth, and it seems his breathing goes shallow before his dimples peek out at me. "You know one of the sucky things about being a preacher?"

The bottom falls out of my stomach at his touch and his sweet, vulnerable expression. "Can't say I have much experience there."

"I'll spare you the dramatic pause. People are afraid to touch me. Us. Now, there's a really valid reason why those in pastoral work are careful to keep boundaries in place, and they may seem higher than necessary, but—"

"But you get a lot of wounded people who might read more into an innocent touch than is there."

Like my gut is trying to read too much into the last two minutes.

"No. I mean, yes, there's absolutely a need to watch for mixed signals. But more, people need me to not be human. Or rather, I'm supposed to be extra-human, I guess, not inhuman."

He pulls his hand away and rests it on his thigh. We're sitting close enough that I can use the table as a shield when I reach over and thread my fingers with his. Not to hide because I have any shame, but out of deference to what he's said.

"Then let me be clear. I'm asking you to simply be Harville when we're together. Not Holy Harville or Venerable Magnolia Bloomian Harville, or any other prefix Harville. Just be my friend, and I'll be yours."

He freezes the instant my arm brushes his thigh, but after a moment, his grip is so tight it makes me gasp a little.

I squeeze back. "I know what it's like to be starved for affection. You know a little about my family. Paige, I think. Violet. But I carried our system of stoicism to an extreme in my career." I jiggle our joined hands. "This is a little new to me, so don't make fun, okay?"

I try to make my voice light, but he apparently hears the fear trying to claw its way up my throat.

"Never." His voice is warm and sincere, and he covers our joined knuckles with his other hand. "And thank you."

"You're welcome." I'm now absurdly glad I gave in to the urge to do this, to reach out both literally and metaphorically.

We let go, and I hope he feels a little lighter, like I do, as we drain the last of our cups. I figure since I'm on a roll, I should keep going. "This might be really weird, but would you like me to go with you to Trey's this morning? I know you're a big boy and all, but I'd be happy to keep playing sidekick, if you want."

"Well, I am wearing black, and you are wearing red."

It takes me a hot minute to get what he means, and it finally sinks home his athletic wear is indeed all Batman black and my top Robin red. I snort.

"That was... awful."

"Yeah, I really woulda been good at the dad-joke thing."

Pain slices through me like lightning through a darkened sky. The loss, the hurt bruises his gentle face and squeezes my heart in a vise. I get him concealing his emotions, reactions, and anything remotely seen as negative is his norm, but it's so grossly unfair he thinks he can't show his true self.

He really is a great guy. Self-aware without being emo. Intelligent without being egotistical. Funny and nerdy, without being wimpy.

I stuff that last one down ferociously. I have never, for a second, considered SP wimpy. I get to see him in T-shirts and shorts most mornings, so I can do the whole under-oath thing that the dude is seriously healthy-lady-parts-appealing.

And now is the time to put the high-pressure brakes on such dangerous trains of thought.

Thankfully, he seems to have taken my silence as giving him time to think, not an interlude of me mentally gawking at him.

"I appreciate your offer, but I'm okay. Just need to get this last item off the list."

"If you're sure, I'll go get some work done and see you at the church this afternoon. I've promised Traycee I'll walk all the booths with her, so you go do pastor things, then I'll meet you at the starting line for the Fun Run."

"Deal."

Despite the time it's taken for our jog and morning brew, it's still early, and downtown Magnolia Bloom feels asleep. For an instant, the world on the brink of awakening quiets even more, and I'm caught in his eyes.

It's fleeting. A matter of seconds.

But every bit of me coming alive after decades of being numb and shuttered responds to the wounded part of him continuing to show up, be kind, be… available.

At the same time, we both realize what's happened and jump apart like crossed jumper cables. Our matching, strained smiles hold us as we bus the table, but by the time we say goodbye, the moment has passed.

We head to our respective cars.

Excellent metaphor, that.

18
FINA

It's all I can do not to crawl back into bed after my trip to Dallas to drop Mina and CT off for their flight. By this time tomorrow, they'll be snuggled together in a luxury car as they do an iconic train trip across the Canadian Rockies.

Next thing is meeting with the Jensen Pharmaceuticals rep later this morning. I tell my pulse to cool it. It's just a rep. As it is, they're cutting things close. They still have time, if barely, to do a reset if we're not right for them. They get any closer to Christmas week, and they'd be hard-pressed to pull off such a big event. I don't know about Denmark's event market, but Christmas isn't a holiday you wait for the last minute to set.

I'm almost at the kitchen door when a car pulls in, and to my surprise, Ranelle gets out.

"Good morning. Of course I'm happy to see you, but what are you doing here?"

"These are the cookie packets Traycee said she'd provide for the party. She's cranky this morning, so I said I'd bring them over."

Ranelle moves to her trunk and takes out a huge plastic bin. Her biceps bulge, so I run my finger over the impressive muscle.

"Looks like someone's been hitting the gym with Quinton."

There's no way to hide her delight at the compliment. "If I don't, I'll never see him. He and his new business partner, Hunter, are there all the time."

"I haven't been in yet, and I feel guilty. They've been open how long now?"

"Almost two years, but of all the things I'd expect of you, being a gym rat isn't one of them, so don't worry."

"I don't have any brain space left to allot, so let's leave it at you look amazing, and I'm jealous."

I move closer and take one of the little burlap bags with a scarecrow holding a sign emblazoned with the Emporium logo. The edges of a napkin peek out of the opening, and the sweet scent of cookies escapes, which makes my empty stomach grumble.

"These are adorable."

Ranelle manages the container while I shut her trunk before escorting her inside.

"They better be. Traycee is on this eco-friendly kick, so we've been baking for the last three days, then stayed up to pack every one of these devils last night. She didn't want any plastic, so no early prep, which means about losing our minds to get these to you fresh."

"That's awfully sweet of her, on several levels, but I see her marketing genius all over these."

"Actually, Traycee dropped the ball a little, and these are all Suzanne Steele's doing."

I'm immediately reminded of my spur-of-the-moment offer to have her wedding here at the castle and nearly groan. "She's a sweetheart, and I'm glad she's found a place at the Emporium."

"With her crushing social anxiety, it's stunning she applied in the first place, but she's climbed a mountain since she started. It's been a joy to watch her grow."

I haven't put any thought into this future event, but I make a mental note to talk with Kiki about making sure the chapel is decorated to feel warm and cocooning. Some events call for bright and airy, but Suzanne is going to need warm neutrals and additional wall hangings to make the space close down rather than open up. We've developed a number of nifty tricks over the years to customize the relatively small space for each event.

Later, Fina. Put it on the list for later.

Ranelle puts the box down as I shut the door and block out the gloriously cool wind. She turns and plants her hands on her hips. "Check one off my to-dos, but I've added one to yours. Can I put these out for you?"

"No, but thank you. The table's already set up in the foyer, and it won't take but a minute to stage. They'll go like hotcakes."

"I hope so. I near burned my eyebrows off opening and shutting the oven, so it'd better be worth it."

I hear worry behind her banter and wave toward the table. "Do you have five minutes for a cup of coffee?"

She reads her watch and starts to say no, then relents. "Sounds lovely."

I pour us both a cup from the industrial decanter and wait until she's doctored hers to her preference before I look at her over the rim of my mug. "What's the matter? You're smiling, but your shoulders are all tensed up."

"I'm worried about Traycee, is all. Momma and I do what we can, but we have our own lives and have to make sure we're not interfering too much."

"Your momma is the lead Grannie, and you're trying to tell me she's not interfering?"

"Fair point. She more than me, but the thing is, Traycee is working herself to a nub, and so is Tara. She's gonna wear her fingers to the bone doing hair, and her last nail tech quit, so she's pulling double duty."

I feel instant sympathy. "The only good day in retail is yesterday."

"Lord, you speak the truth." She takes a long sip and sighs. "I don't know what I was thinking having five babies, much less having them all so close together. They may be adults, but they all give me gray hair. You're lucky you don't have all this worry."

She's busy stirring another dollop of cream into her cup, so she misses the pain lancing through me. I know she didn't say it to hurt me, but it's a statement I've gotten many times over the decades. I'm good at hiding the feeling someone's got their hand around my heart and is squeezing tight.

I provide myself further cover by fetching the coffee carafe and topping off our cups.

Kiki, bless her, saves me from my desperate search for a new conversation topic by coming into the room and aiming straight for me.

"Don't put that away." She takes the top off of her travel mug and holds it out. "Refill on lane one, please."

"Yes, ma'am." I carefully fill the steamy liquid to the rim.

"Good morning, Ranelle." Kiki tips her cup in a hello. "You ready for the festivities?"

"Absolutely. You?"

"Can't wait. This is my first Halloween ever at the castle. I've been here for lots of Thanksgivings and Christmases, but not Spooky Day."

"You make sure you have some fun because I know the two of you are nigh on to frazzled by now."

To my surprise, Kiki laughs. "Crazy thing? It's all pretty much ready. We've hired a bunch of the older kids from the youth group to man the event and refill punch and snack stations. Other than a little overseeing, it's going to be a fun night."

"Good to hear."

Kiki turns toward the door. "No rest for the wicked and all. I hope I see you this evening, Ranelle."

"Me, too."

She hesitates, but being Kiki, I'm not surprised when she asks, "Is Traycee going to come?"

Ranelle looks at me, then Kiki, a sad note in her eyes. "I think so. I hope so. I'm worried about her."

Kiki's nod is small. "I am, too. I keep calling and texting, often enough so she knows I'm here but not smothering her. I hope reaches out soon."

"You're a doll for caring. I appreciate you so much."

After giving each of us a wave, Kiki leaves and Ranelle is only a moment behind her out the door. When my phone pings not two minutes later, it's Kiki, telling me she's received the alert our site visitor is almost here. I post back telling her I'll take care of it and move to the front steps, putting on my most neutral, welcoming game face.

When the limousine pulls up, I'm impressed the company would pay for black car service for their employee.

And then my heart stops.

The long body unfolding from the back seat isn't some stunning, blond woman, all Scandinavian cheekbones and enviable bone structure.

It's a man. And no generic one.

It's Anders Jensen.

My flight instinct kicks in, and it takes every ounce of my thirty years in this business to stay put, pretending to be calm when I'm so lightheaded sparkles dance in my vision. I use the seconds it takes him to climb the stairs and drop his suitcase on the landing to suck in desperate oxygen.

"I was hoping it would be you meeting me."

His voice is deep. Much deeper than a teenage boy's and fitting for a man who's seen as many winters as I have. He's not much taller than when we'd said goodbye. That isn't so surprising, but how handsome he's become steals my breath. Time has been exceptionally kind to him, although there's probably genetics involved as much as a clear devotion to an exercise routine.

Mature and confident are definite turn-ons.

His slacks are custom-made of a gray wool so dark it could almost be black, but is the perfect shade to draw out the weft threads of his also custom-made dress shirt of arctic white with blue accent threads and stitching.

Who wears white to travel internationally?

I mean, seriously.

I search madly and find my voice. "I didn't know you were coming personally."

His eyes, which thankfully have enough crinkle lines to appease my vanity, squinch a bit. "I was afraid if I said I would be here myself, you might not see me."

He takes a step closer, into my personal space. He fills every available centimeter of my field of vision as I crane my neck. It's all I can do not to step back. He's not trying to intimidate me. I've had plenty of men try.

This is much more intimate.

"Do you think I'm a coward?" The words come out more softly, more hurt than I intended.

"No, but you never answered any of my letters, so I assumed…"

I viciously thrust away the geyser of agony and regret trying to roll over me like a tidal wave that's had years upon years to sweep across the ocean of my memory and build speed and depth.

No, I didn't answer. What would have been the point? And to answer, I would have had to open them. I knew the cost of my decision and wanted to cauterize the wound quickly.

"Welcome to Castle MacInnes," I say brightly, cutting off both his line of dialogue and my train of thought. "You can leave your bag, and I'll have a porter take it to your room. Come inside, and let me show you around."

"If it's changed as little as you have, I won't need much of a tour."

My heart trips, but thankfully my feet don't. "Aren't you sweet?" I look down at my tablet as if checking for the event notes… as if I don't have them memorized. "It looks like we'll be having a hundred and twenty-five guests, most of whom are couples. Between the rooms here, the RVs we have scheduled, and space in town, we have everyone covered. Most of your couples have another couple they want to room with, which makes things so much easier. I—"

Anders puts out a hand, and the instant his fingers touch my forearm, the words stop like a shut-off faucet.

"Fina."

I close my eyes against his voice. The velvet stroke of my name. It's a long moment before I can open them again and meet his gaze.

"You look beautiful. More beautiful than I imagined."

I could repeat those words verbatim, if I could get my throat to work. He is beautiful. Handsome in the easy style of a man comfortable in his own skin. Confident. Just the right amount of cocky.

And it's not like I haven't gone down the internet rabbit hole a thousand times since I found out exactly who booked the event. I've sat mooning over pictures of him like a teenage girl with an issue of whatever is today's version of *Teen Beat*. I knew exactly what he'd look like when I set eyes on him, except the real-life version is a thousand times more powerful.

I swallow enough times to get some moisture into my mouth. "Thank you. You haven't changed at all."

"A sweet lie, but I appreciate the sentiment." He holds the door for me to precede him inside. "Is there somewhere we can go have coffee?"

We both know how foolish the question is, but my pulse ridiculously and determinedly won't calm.

"Sure. Let's go to the family kitchen on the second floor. The big kitchen is heating up with preparations for tonight."

His mouth quirks up on one side, and I realize at the last second we used to sneak into the second-floor space many times while he was here. His host family at the time was living in Manor Three, and with Momma being chief cook back then, I had unlimited access to the castle.

Coke floats. Ice cream sundaes. Toaster pockets with pepperoni and cheese burning our mouths every single time.

Which didn't stop the epic make-out sessions. If there's one thing a castle provides, it's endless places for hormonal teenagers to hide and do all the things they're forbidden to do.

I busy myself with the simple tasks of putting the kettle on and preparing the French press, unable to stop the trembling in my hands despite my every effort. In the way that he did even as a teenage boy, he leans against the sink with his hands behind him, his energy calm, his eyes following me, his expression a mixture of bemused and enthralled.

It unsettled me back then, but I can be forgiven, since I was a teenager myself, just entering womanhood, naïve in the feelings ginned by hormones and newness and lust.

I have none of those excuses now. I'm a fully mature woman staring at my sixtieth birthday in two months. I'm no giddy girl, no doe-eyed virgin.

I scold myself with an inner *snap out it*, rinse my hands, and lean my own hip against the edge of the counter a few feet away, hoping I manage at least a semblance of the same nonchalance.

"So, how are you? It's good to see you. A surprise, but good." I'm grateful my voice oozes a confidence I don't feel.

"I'm well, and I will confess when I had this idea and sprang it on my assistant, I almost changed my mind. Each year, we do a big event, but we only do something this extravagant every few years."

I stare at the electric kettle, begging it to hurry. "We don't get many events from overseas. Individuals and couples, of course. But groups this size are rare, except for the games. We had five thousand this year."

I bite the inside of my bottom lip to stop myself from babbling. I've never been prone to it.

The water starts bubbling, and he watches me with the same patience he had decades ago. It's unnerving, but I keep at my task until we're seated at the table, my watch counting down from four minutes before we can pour.

I decide to say what's on my mind, because there's no sense in acting like such a ninnyhammer. I meet his eyes, steeling myself not to get lost in the rich, blue pools that captivated me then and apparently have not lost their power.

"Anders, why are you here? You're insanely wealthy, and your company is respected around the world. You could take your people anywhere. Why here? Why now?"

He braces his forearm on the table as he presses closer and reaches out with his other hand to trace a fingertip down my cheek.

It nearly undoes me right there, melting me.

Destroying me.

"Because on the night of the ball, it will be forty years to the day I kissed the woman who owned my heart goodbye."

"I was a girl, not a woman. And you had to leave."

"And you had to stay."

I close my eyes, swaying in my seat, feeling like I'm the heroine in some movie, except this isn't a movie. It isn't fiction. It's real. It's my real life and my real heart pumping so hard I swear the organ has relocated between my ears.

"All true. You were a student, and your time was up."

"I tried to talk to you. I learned from my friend here what happened with Mina, but I never understood why you wouldn't answer my letters."

I study my nails, unable to hold his gaze despite my best attempts. "There wasn't any point, really. You were headed off to university, as I was. More importantly, there was quite literally a world between us. All it would have done was make me wish for things I could never, ever have. It was easier to shut things down."

"Was it? For you? It wasn't for me. Yes, I was a boy, but both my parents and grandparents met at ages not much different from ours then, and they stayed together for life, so I don't accept we were too young."

I think about my own parents. I miss my father every single day. He and Momma met when she was fifteen. He was sixteen. And while their marriage wasn't perfect, they loved each other madly until he died much too young.

"You haven't answered the question. You know I looked you up as soon as I figured out who was coming. Your private life is amazing, as far as the internet is concerned."

"I'll satisfy your curiosity. I did go to college and graduate school. I took over my father's company and am proud of what it has become. I married when I was thirty. Divorced at forty. I have two children, a boy and a girl, each of whom I adore. I have two grandchildren and one due in February. I work too hard, to keep myself occupied."

I can certainly relate to that.

He continues, never taking his eyes from me. His hand traces down my arm to capture my wrist so I'll meet his gaze.

"When I turned sixty a few months ago, a friend of mine who claims to be a witch but who I generally label a fun kind of crazy, told me I had one chance left at happiness, and it was entirely up to me if I chose to risk my very comfortable existence for an amazing future."

The air leaves the room. It's a damned good thing I'm sitting, or I'd be one with the floor.

"So you flew five thousand miles and assumed I'd be here? Waiting?"

"Not waiting. For me specifically. But this is the thing about the internet and having a lot of money at my disposal. I knew... I know you aren't married."

"That doesn't mean I'm available."

"This is true, but the one insurmountable obstacle isn't in our way."

Our way. Do *we* have a way?

The timer dings, and he reaches for the French press. It's such a stupid, simple movement, but my entire being is fixated on watching the plunger slowly slide down inside the glass.

"May I?" He gestures to the handle of the carafe.

"Please."

He pours, and I take a moment to spoon some sugar into my cup, adding a bit of creamer.

"You still like a milkshake more than a cup of coffee, I see."

Okay, more than a bit...

"I've never learned to drink it black. Not like Kiki."

A rustle at the door captures our attention, and I'm not sure if I'm relieved or annoyed.

"What's this about me?" Kiki breezes in, stopping to kiss my cheek, then offering her hand to Anders.

"Mr. Jensen, it's a pleasure. I'm Kiki. I've been corresponding with your assistant."

"First, you are forbidden from calling me mister. It's Anders. And

Erik is now a big fan of yours, saying this could have been one of the most arduous events he's ever scheduled, but you've made it as easy as skating on polished ice. You'll get to meet him in December."

"Wonderful." Kiki turns to me, and I'm grateful for the moment's reprieve from Anders's arctic-blue eyes. "I'm off to peruse the booths with Traycee. Is there anything I can do before I leave?"

I know I shouldn't accept her offer. Taking the coward's way out is something I rarely indulge in, but today has been a special day as far as my nerves are concerned.

"Would you show Anders to his room? I need to do a few things at my place before tonight."

I keep my eyes laser-focused on Kiki. Her surprise is obvious, but she doesn't hesitate.

"Sure. My pleasure." She turns to him and beams the lovely smile coming to her more naturally these days, a fact making me ridiculously happy.

"It's down the long hall, and I'm sure the porters have already put your bag inside. We're not full tonight, but we do have quite a few folks who've booked rooms so they don't have to leave after the festivities, which is always a good thing. Did you bring a costume? If you don't have one, we have tons you can choose from."

Anders looks at me, but I've already risen and am walking toward the door. "I'm glad you've arrived safely. I'll see you around the party this evening, and we'll go over your event tomorrow after the dust has settled."

I escape before he can argue, but I hear him speaking politely to Kiki, as I know he would. Or as I assumed he would, as I can't image an Anders Jensen who would morph into an arrogant jerk.

At least on that level, I seem to be correct.

But what Anders Jensen wants from me after forty years is too big for me to dig into, especially after the gut punch of seeing him. Add him touching me even on the most innocent of levels, and my equilibrium has gone completely off-line.

I've got to have space. I've got to have some oxygen. I've got to find a way to endure seeing him again, being with him again.

Because even these few minutes have nearly destroyed me.

No matter how innocent his intentions, I can't do this. If I risk reaching for this thread of hope he's offering, only for him to decide he's made a mistake, I will be destroyed.

I can't survive losing him a second time.

19
KIKI

"It was really weird," I tell Traycee as we accept our little paper boat of Frito pie topped with shredded cheese from Grannie Lorraine manning the Ladies Auxiliary booth and claim a space at one of the picnic tables.

Kids are running everywhere. The amazing sunshine and cool temperature have brought out everyone within a fifty-mile radius, it seems, and the general chaos is delightful and invigorating.

"Doesn't sound like Fina at all."

"I know. She was so flustered, and for an older guy, this Anders Jensen dude is seriously hot. But that doesn't seem like enough to disturb our deep-waters Fina."

Just as obvious as Fina's slip off her normal balance beam is Traycee's nervous fidgeting with her plastic fork and caloric-nightmare lunch.

I won't play games with her. We're friends and companions in a similar journey, and she deserves my real attention. "So, you want to tell me what's up? And don't say nothing. We both know what lies do to our program."

After taking a listless bite and a much longer drink of soda, she sighs. "I thought Vern and I were going to be different. He started out gung ho about me getting sober, but..."

"Let me see if I can recite a few lines. 'Why aren't you fun anymore?' 'Does this mean we never get to party again?' 'I didn't think this would be so boring.' I'm sure I'm missing some."

Her laugh is short and a bit wistful. "Were you hiding behind the curtains last night?"

"Nah, just hanging around meetings."

She gives me her trademarked wrinkled nose and narrowed eyes. "Subtle."

"I know, right?"

Traycee throws her fork onto the table and sits back, rolling her head in slow circles. I wish I could help. Old Kiki wants to jump in and fix this, but new Kiki knows the only thing I can do is be here for her. I can't change what's happening in her life, and I can't make her choose wisely. She's barely six months sober, and the patina of early hope and happy internal monologues of *I've got it this time!* have faded.

"You know you're in the danger zone, right?" I hand her the napkin that blew over to my side of the boards. "You're at the point where it hits us that sobriety is forever."

"It's scary."

"More, it's often overwhelming. Add in you're not prioritizing any 'you time.'"

"It's high retail season—" She cuts herself off when I give her a Spock brow. "Yeah, yeah."

"Want to go to a meeting? I can skip the run, and we can find one online, or there has to be something in Atlanta or Texarkana."

She waves off my offer. "You're a doll, but I'm okay. Maybe tomorrow after church."

"Let me know. I'll go with you anytime."

Tears fill her gorgeous gray-green eyes, and she dashes them away with her rescued napkin. "Now look what you've done. It took me thirty minutes to get this makeup perfect."

I hand over the last clean square we anchored with a salt shaker.

"It's one of my superpowers." I take a deep breath to keep my own tears from forming.

You can't fix this, Kiki.

Traycee sucks in her own lungful of oxygen, and I'm only the tiniest bit mollified. Whatever's up with her hasn't changed and isn't going to be resolved this afternoon.

"You getting ready for the Fun Run?" She's back to her normal, affable self, which isn't necessarily a good thing.

"As I can be. I left my bag in Harville's office so I won't have to go back to the castle to change."

One of those perfectly penciled brows lifts dramatically. "Oh, really? We now have premium-level rights and privileges with handsome Harville, do we?"

I jostle her with my elbow as we walk to the trash cans. "It's not like that."

'Then do tell. What *is* it like?"

"We've become a lot closer. We work out and jog in the early mornings—"

"On purpose? You crazy."

"So I've been told. We started working out at your father's gym a few days a week. He goes every day, I think. I'm not so dedicated, but he's become a friend."

"Mmmm-hmmm."

I roll my eyes. "Friend. Just friend. His own life is a little sticky, and he doesn't need the mess that's still me, so it's nice not to have any pressure."

"That won't last long."

"It's lasted this long." I try to keep defensiveness out of my voice. I don't want to reveal my own doubts. Not about Harville. He's every bit the gentleman when we're together. It's my own thoughts straying into Lascivious Land giving me pause.

"It's lasted this long because he wasn't divorced. But now he is. The decree is signed, sealed, and filed. And all teasing aside, he's one handsome man, and you're a beautiful woman, and you like each other."

"I—"

"Hey, if you get to play pseudosponsor with me, I get to do it for you, too. Be careful. I might not be as far along as you, but I already know how quickly things can get screwed up in the romance department."

"There is no rom—"

"Girl, you play games with yourself if you want to, but you're gonna lose."

"Now wait a second. Men and women can be friends without being intimate."

"Absolutely. I have guy friends, and there's zero danger there. But I also don't look at them across a room like they're a white chocolate brownie fresh out of the oven."

"I do not—"

"Not often, but I've seen it."

She has?

Well, shit.

I dust my hands together as we've reached the edge of the walkway to the church. "We both have places to be, so we'll pick this back up on a drive to a meeting."

Traycee sends me a you-don't-fool-me frown. "Yes, ma'am. We'll both take turns under the klieg lights until we each confess."

"Will I see you at the castle tonight?"

"Of course. Momma took over the cookie packets from the store this morning, and I told Fina I'd do a round of chaperoning the kids from seven to eight."

Fina explained that in the early hours, we have tons of teenagers and younger kids on the grounds. The haunted house through one of the big barns is a perennial favorite, and dancing in the big ballroom is always a riot. But we're not foolish. Even though the adults have access to alcohol from the cash bar, where masks are required to be removed and showing IDs is nonnegotiable, we aren't crazy enough to think our intrepid youth aren't trying to find ways to make their punch a little punchier.

I was a teenager once. A million years go. And I was a pro before I needed a full-sized bra.

At the last second, I remember a question. "What are you wearing?"

"I'm Cruella de Vil. I've talked Tyrell's girls into coming as puppies. I figure if I have to be Auntie Traycee all evening, it might as well be cute."

"Can't wait to see it."

"What about you?"

I start laughing. "Harville is coming as Batman. I understand he tends to do the superhero thing most years. I'm going to dress up as Robin."

She nails me with a look. "Sure. Just friends."

She walks away before I can retort, and I stuff down a surge of irritation at her blatant teasing. I get it, but this is an area where she doesn't know me yet. When I was in the service, all my friends were guys. I didn't plan it, it happened. And I told her the truth. I didn't sleep with every dude I palled around with.

I open the door, glad I get to bypass Dragon Delores, because a) it's Saturday, and b) Harville and I have given each other permission where he pops over to the castle when he has a second and can come by my office, and I can do the same. The difference is, I have no threshold guardian at the castle giving him the stink eye.

The halls are quiet, and the peace is one of the things I love about the church, even though I'm not big on the whole organized religion thing.

I open his door just as there's a chorus of "Amen."

Heat burns my cheeks scarlet. "I am so sorry." My words come out in a horrified blather as I stumble backward.

Harville stands, waving me in. "Nothing to be sorry about. Please, come in. I'd like to introduce someone."

With their faces up, I can see the other gentleman in the room is the youth director, Isaac Shale, who is a doll and helps explain why the roster of younger members is going gangbusters. A recent graduate from TCU, he's in his first year at seminary. He's young and bright and full of hopes and dreams.

I envy him, and I'm so happy for Harville and the church and that he's chosen St. Andrew's to start his journey. His grin's as big as his heart as he holds out his hand, which I take immediately. He reminds me of a big ol' puppy, and I wonder if I ever had a smidgeon of his youthful exuberance and wide-eyed optimism.

The quick and easy answer is no.

The other person present is a lovely, dark-skinned woman who radiates kindness from her small frame.

Harville waves a hand in the petite woman's direction. "This is Maya Kamaka. She's agreed to join our team as associate pastor."

I step into the room and take her outstretched hand. "Welcome to Magnolia Bloom. I'm Kiki MacInnes, and if there's anything I can do for you, please let me know. You'll learn nothing in this town is more than a few minutes away."

Harville nods in my direction, but he's looking at Maya. "Kiki is the manager of the castle. You'll find out all about the MacInneses in short order."

"But not today," I interject, wanting the focus off of me. "When will you be moving?"

"In two weeks. I was taking care of my mother, who passed last month, so I can change directions pretty quickly."

"I'm so sorry for your loss."

"Thank you. It's been a long journey." She brightens, and her smile returns to full wattage. "I'm so ready to be out of the cold, and if I never have to do another Portland winter, I'll be fine."

"Oregon or Maine?"

"Neither. North Dakota. I'm Polynesian, and the cold about did me in."

"You'll appreciate Magnolia Bloom, then. We get cold enough so we can all gripe about it, but other than a few snow days a year, we're pretty temperate."

"I grew up on a tiny Hawaiian island you've never heard of called Niihau, so I can take the heat. I'll miss the beach, though."

"It's not the same, but we have an awesome hot spring not far from here."

"And the lake."

"Which is pretty awesome, too."

Maya picks up a briefcase from beside her chair. "This has been lovely, but I think a nap is calling my name before the party tonight."

I lift an eyebrow. "Are you coming to the castle?"

"I wouldn't dream of missing it."

"If you need a costume, come a little early. We have a whole closet of things you can borrow, if you'd like."

"If I can't make it to the Emporium, which these two were also telling me about, I'll do that."

We take care of all the usual goodbyes, and then it's just Harville, smiling at me.

"I'm really sorry I interrupted." I can't help myself. Everyone was gracious, but I still feel awkward.

"You came in as we literally finished praying. It was hardly an interruption."

"I was coming to grab my bag to change for the run. You still in?"

"Of course. Wouldn't dream of letting you hold me chickening out over my head."

He tosses me my bag from behind his desk and grabs his own, then we're walking side by side down the wide hallway to the public restrooms.

"I wouldn't do such a thing." I try to put affront into my voice, but I'm not sure I succeed.

"This is a church, you know. Lying is frowned upon."

I push open the door to the ladies' room and toss him a look over my shoulder. "Then I'll save all further retorts until we're not on holy ground."

He gives me the smile lifting the right side of his mouth a little higher than the left, making one dimple make an appearance. I have to swallow a catch in my pulse.

"Good plan."

The door shuts behind me, and I press my hot back to the cool tile. I'm a little off-kilter from Traycee's teasing. There is nothing wrong with noticing Harville is a good-looking man. I've had good-looking friends before.

There's nothing more to it. Nothing.

These past weeks have been lovely. Proof I can stay the course of my recovery and make new friends. With things being super busy at work, staying on top of my program, and getting back in shape, my nerves are a normal part of getting healthy again.

That's all.

Really.

Nothing more.

I push away from the wall, certain it's about to crumble as easily as my excuses, and step to the padded bench to change into my gear.

20

JULIETTE

I WAS HONEST WITH RORY. Halloween isn't a thing in France outside of Paris. There are plenty of parties, if one is inclined in that direction, but we're known to embrace the spooky or outrageous during Carnival, and Halloween is generally reserved for All Saints' Day events. Usually the chaos of bodies and noise would be disconcerting, but maybe it's having Lulu as my emotional support lamb and Rory as my guide making it all less intimidating.

I crack up when he arrives at my door to escort me to the castle, all starched and pressed and handsome. Lulu is quite pleased with herself as well, bouncing beside him, her fleece white and a big pink bow around her neck.

I scratch under her chin. "You got a bath, pretty girl. You look beautiful."

"As does her shepherdess." Rory hands me the crook he's brought along. "Now you're perfect."

Traycee was right. While I feel a bit absurd as Bo Peep, Rory looks utterly adorable as a redheaded Woody.

I am not known for spontaneity, but before I can stop myself, I put the crook on the large counter and move in front of him, taking the edges of his faux cowhide vest into my hands. "Thank you for being a wonderful companion. You have made my time here amazing."

Before he can get the shocked look off his face, I pull him toward me and kiss him. I'm unsurprised to learn his lips are soft and sweet, and I might have startled him, but he doesn't hesitate. His arms slip around me, and he pulls me fully against him, completely willing to see where this moment is going to go.

A jealous *baaa* and a headbutt mean it doesn't go far. We arch away from each other, laugh, and move apart.

I give Lulu another scratch. "So this is how it's going to be, is it? We have a fluffy chaperone now?"

"She's not a chaperone. She's just jealous. And I have to say I didn't see that coming, but you're welcome to come again anytime."

My smile is instant and easy and new and delightful. "I've never felt this way before." My confession catches us both by surprise, and I feel my cheeks flush. "I mean, in a lot of ways, all of this is so new to me. I've been spontaneous and—"

"Happy?"

I pause and study the wall for a moment. "Yes. I mean, it's not like my life was misery before I came here. It wasn't. I was fulfilled and challenged. I have a wonderful family."

"All of that's exterior, but for the first time, I can truly say I understand what you mean. Before you came, if someone asked me if I was happy, I'd'a said yes. I have my kids, and I love what I do. I have a crazy family all mixed in with the MacInnes lot. A town I love."

"And all of that is exterior."

He smiles at my serving his words back to him.

"Exactly. My marriage wasn't evil, but it wasn't good for either of us. We got Kaden and Lilith out of it. So I don't regret it, but I don't miss it."

I take a moment to gather my crook and hat and turn down the lights so only the nightlight is left. The sun is not down yet, but the room has gone into dark shadow as I move next to him.

"I don't want you to say you no longer consider your life happy," I say softly as we walk toward the door.

He stops and slips his hands up the backs of my arms. "I'm not unhappy. I've just been shown what I'm missing."

He leans forward and kisses me. I press in and smile against his mouth. Miss Jealous squeezes between our legs, and we both laugh.

"I'm not exactly sure where this is going." I don't want to break the glow of our moment, but the words spurt out without permission.

"Right now, where it's going is to the castle for too much sugar and too much dancing. We'll figure the rest out later."

I can't argue with his logic, and then we're at the party, Kiki rushing toward us.

"Y'all are adorable. You'd win the costume contest hands down if you weren't disqualified."

Kiki is too busy petting Lulu to see my frown. "I don't understand."

"I didn't think to tell you." She pats Rory on the arm. "Looking good there, Woody."

"Hard not to when you've got Bo Peep for a date."

Kiki meets my eyes and clarifies the rule stating estate employees and family are ineligible for the prizes. "It's only fair."

A warmth pierces through me.

Family.

She said it so easily. So naturally. So nonchalantly. Stating a fact.

I have *family*.

I mean, I've always had family, but now I have more family. People quite different from my placid maman and papa. As my grand-mère was. Incredible, wonderful people who love me and gave me a blessed childhood.

But life in a small town on a quaint vineyard in northern France feels as if it is on another planet compared to this boisterous bunch.

And I find I love both options equally.

I'm not given any more time to ruminate, because I hear Kiki gasp. I turn toward the grand staircase and watch Fina float down from the second floor. She's wearing a dress from the Tudor period. The low and wide neckline exposes most of her shoulders. The dark fabric makes her pale skin glow. I'm used to her hair being up, but the pearl-studded headpiece is the perfect touch to bring all the attention to her beautiful features.

"My goodness." Rory's words are a mere breath, and I have to agree.

"She is as regal as a queen." I can easily picture her on a canvas I've been given to restore, as she looks as though she's stepped out of a time portal from the court of Henry VIII.

Kiki's eyes widen in wonder. "I know she always comes in Renaissance garb, but… *wow*."

We don't have time to gawk any more as she joins our little troop.

"Good evening, everyone. You all look lovely."

Lulu bounds over to her, and we all laugh. Fina is gracious. "And you, too, Lulu."

With the lamb placated with another scratch, the mood returns to the jovial tenor of before.

Kiki wiggles her hand at Fina. "You look amazing."

"Thank you, sweetheart. I needed a little false courage tonight, so I picked out one of my favorite outfits. I haven't worn it in years, but I only had to loosen the laces in the back an inch or so, thank goodness."

We all chuckle, as she expects us to, and Rory and I move away to claim some punch and supervise the group of girls who have spied Lulu and are all on the floor around her, lavishing her with attention. A man comes up in a Batman costume, talking to Kiki, who is dressed as Robin. I thought that odd until Rory tells me the man is the kind pastor I've spoken with a few times. It appears the faux superhero has formed a close friendship with my cousin.

Knowing what I know now about Kiki, I am glad for her.

I look around the room and see Thomas and his partner, Monroe. They are dressed as salt and pepper shakers. Cute.

I hear some delighted cries and turn to see Paige and Zachary coming into the room. Kiki flies across the floor and is hugging her sister stronger than a sumo wrestler. Zachary is dressed in an exaggerated zoot suit, and Paige is his sexy moll. She looks wonderful and is positively glowing.

When someone pulls Kiki away, Paige makes a beeline for me.

"Juliette, you look amazing."

"As do you." We share the French greeting, and it pleases me to no end to kiss her cheek.

"You, too, Rory. Sorry." Paige winces.

Rory's teasing smile stirs a contentment in me. I've never been a woman who sees her value in her date or partner, but tonight I'm inordinately glad he's mine. "I know I'm invisible standing next to this goddess."

"Good answer." Paige gives him a pat on the arm.

The Lulu-adoring throng of girls leaves, and Rory and Zachary move off to chat. Paige turns back to me, her voice soft and concerned. "How are you? How's everything going?"

My smile should reassure her. "It has been wonderful. I have two canvases cleaned and am beginning restoration on the most damaged one this week."

Paige gives me a teasing smile. "I don't mean the paintings, although, I mean, of course I want to know. I mean, how are *you*?"

"I am very well. I have not spoken with David yet, if that is what you are wondering. I saw him and his wife across the diner, but we have not pursued anything yet."

She puts a hand on my arm. "You know I'm a phone call away if you need me. If I can be any help at all."

"Yes, and you are sweet. I'm sure the time is drawing to an inevitable moment when I shall meet with him, but I'm still learning about Gavina and Violet. You shared so much of what you know of her, being so close. And I thank you."

"This has been an interesting year for all of us, I think."

"Indeed." I wave toward Fina, who is lost in conversation with a blond man much taller than the King Henry he is portraying. "I think there's something interesting there."

Paige follows my direction and gives a soft whistle. "Wow. Fina looks stunning, and the man's certainly inside her personal zone."

"Indeed. Kiki said they are having an event in December with his company from Denmark, and if I had to guess ancestry, he looks Nordic to me."

"Hmm… With Mina out of the picture for a while, you'll have to get all the deets and text me."

Deets? Ah, details.

"Are you not staying?"

"Just tonight and tomorrow. We've got a lot of balls in the air. Zach is going to step back and do consulting with his company, I'm going to retire from the law firm, we're going to downsize our crazy-big house and buy a motor home, and then we're going to travel for a while."

"I'm so happy for you."

"Yeah, my friend Kase, whom you haven't gotten to meet, was going to sell her cosmetics company, but now she's decided she's going to expand instead, so I'm going to become a partner with her and start a new adventure for myself as well."

"That is a lot of change at one time, mon amie."

"Indeed, but I can't wait. I need this time with Zach, and then I'll be more than ready for my second career."

"I shall extend your offer back to you. I have some experience in being a businesswoman, so if I can be of service, I shall be honored."

"Good deal. I accept. Now, it's time to get something to drink and hit the dance floor."

I watch Paige float back into her husband's arms, and the warm feeling I've been experiencing grows even bigger. I do not know, nor do I want to know, all the details, but what could have ended in sadness appears to be blossoming into a renewed love affair, and I could not be happier for her.

I've never thought I'd be so connected to so many people. Paige and Zach brought me into this delightful community. Kiki has treated me like a beloved cousin from the time she set eyes on me. Fina, finally accepting we are only ten years apart, has stopped treating me like another child of the family and more of an equal.

And with her being a twin, we have had plenty to talk about as she has strolled the estate with me or shared a meal. We don't see each other every day, which is fine. She is incredibly busy, and I am often engrossed in Gavina's paintings, but the time we do spend together has given me a lot of information about this family. In many ways, she and Mina are adopted MacInneses, providing yet another similarity between us.

Rory reappears with a fresh drink, and we move into the throng, and for the first time in my life, I feel…

Light.

And I like it.

21
KIKI

THE PARTY HAS BEEN a tremendous success, which I'm told is not unusual, but when most of the younger crowd leaves and the energy level drops at least enough to change the noise from a cacophony to a decibel level less likely to damage my hearing, I'm ready for a break. I'm not surprised when Harville joins me on the back portico, the sounds of the dancing behind us loud but muted.

"I saw you leave. I figured you'd reached max with the people and the noise. I'm surprised you lasted this long."

We descend the stairs together, and he pulls off his headpiece, breathing in the cold, fresh breeze. I force myself to look away when he scrubs his hands through his hair, a bit matted and sweaty from his costume, and ends up with a messy and mouthwatering look I have to think he has no idea he's achieved.

"This is the last year I do a full mask."

I keep to myself that if this is what he ends up looking like, it's not a bad choice at all.

I clear my throat and look around to distract myself. "Did you know Fina and Violet took care of this garden until a few years ago?"

He looks around the formal garden, the moonlight augmenting the light of the torches spaced at perfect intervals to create a scene out of a Hollywood blockbuster.

"I didn't, but no surprise."

It's one of the many things I'd learned since I'd come home. "It appears Fina loves digging in the dirt and getting sweaty and messy, which seems out of character for the always proper, always neat, always put-together Fina. She's been really closed down since we lost Violet, which is understandable, but the gardener told me she won't even come out here and sit anymore."

"It may be too hard without her friend." His deep voice is soft and understanding.

"I'm sure you're right. She's working extra hard to keep up her persona, so I worry about her." Believe me, I know about keeping up a persona.

"I do, as well, but she has never been as amenable to talking to me as Violet was. I don't press, of course, because I didn't know if it was because I'm a man or her natural reticence."

"Me, either. Or rather, I try to press gently, when she'll let me, and it seems she and Juliette are growing closer. Which I love."

"Rory seems to be spending quite a bit of time with a certain Bo Peep, too."

We smile at each other.

"I don't know Rory well, although we talk often when I get his reports on the flocks. He's seems a good man."

"He is." Harville gestures to a bench, and he gallantly extends his cape around me against the chilly wind. Luckily, it's a gentle one, but it still bites. "I spoke with Paige and Zach. It was good to see them."

"It's been a mini-family reunion. I was surprised to see her. She usually gives me a little notice, but she wanted to surprise me." I reach under my collar and pull out a necklace. "She brought me this."

There's just enough light for him to see the pendant. "That's the cairngorm Violet left with me. I gave it to Paige a few months ago."

"She and I went for a walk, and she told me about how she met one of our many relatives in Scotland and learned some interesting details about our aunt Alyssa, Alisdair's sister. She promised to tell me more later, but the short version is, she believes I'm supposed to have this since I'm the chatelaine. Temporarily, at least."

He cocks his head at me, his frown visible in the dim light. "Temporarily? Are you leaving?"

"I don't know what the future holds, so I don't have plans. I'm in a comfortable place right now, but I've learned it never lasts."

When his silence starts to make me nervous, I shift so I can look at him. "Why are you so quiet all of a sudden?"

"I suppose I'm taken aback. I didn't know you were thinking of going away."

"I said I'm not planning on it, but history has shown me not to get too comfortable in one place. I didn't mean to upset you."

He chuffs a laugh. "There's nothing to apologize for, and the last thing I want to do is put my expectations on you."

I want to smile and cry at the same time. I want to smile at the sweet look in his eyes and cry at the inevitable place this all ends. "You know, sometimes you're too nice."

This time, his expression contains a shot of irony. "Oh, there are plenty of times I'm not."

"I've never seen it."

"There's been no cause to show you."

If the sudden tension in his muscles is an indicator, now might be the time for revelations.

"We've had this discussion, I believe. You get to be human around me. Not perfect. Not a saint."

"What you get tonight is on fire."

His arm slides from behind my shoulders so he can move, shift, make space for his hands to come between us and frame my neck and my jaw with warm, strong fingers. I should tell him no.

Don't do this.

Don't change this.

Don't change us.

Because if you want me like I want you, we're going to go to a place that will leave us both destroyed.

But I don't. I can't. I can't stop him. I can't breathe. I can't do anything but beg him.

"Please. Kiss me."

"I've been waiting forever for you to ask."

His words are whispered against my lips, and then we're too busy exploring for words to interrupt. It's all about sensation. His mouth whispering against mine. My tongue seeking his. My hands sliding over his chest to clutch his shoulders. One of his hands sweeps behind my head so he can tilt my face to an even better angle for our connection.

I'm afraid I'm going to melt the iron bench underneath me as my pulse thunders in my ears. I want to tear his clothes off, remove the fabric hampering my need to touch him, feel—

"And then Rory said—oh, damn."

My brain is a swirling mass of confusion as Harville wrenches himself away from me. I try to jump to my feet, but he won't let me.

"No. I'm not ashamed."

He holds my hand, and we both stand slowly, not at all like chastened teenagers. I turn to my very embarrassed great-uncle and Monroe.

"Hi, Uncle T, Monroe."

He smiles at me. "Well, this tops the awkward column." He nods to my rather disheveled Batman. "Harville."

"Thomas."

I look at Monroe. "You're gonna have to pipe up in here, too, you know."

His smile is actually quite devilish, which I wasn't expecting. "Doesn't look like a whole lot of talking was going on."

I'm grateful for the darkness, although my cheeks are probably traffic-light red.

Monroe puts a hand on my arm. "Ain't nothing for you to be embarrassed about, girl. This spot is perfect for romancin'. Why do you think Thomas and I walk home this way most times?"

I choke on a reply. Monroe isn't known for saying much, but when he does, it's usually profound or funny. Sometimes both.

Harville adds to the humor. "Should we vacate the bench, then?"

Thomas's laugh is the deep rumble I've loved my whole life, and have not heard nearly enough. "Not tonight, but thank you. It's a little too cold for these bones. Come spring, though, we may have to set a schedule if you're gonna make this a habit." T winks at Harville. "I highly recommend it."

Come spring. Would I be here? Or if I am here, would there be any chance what's happening won't immolate like dry brush sparked by heat lightning?

I put up a hand. "Okay, boys, enough. I've reached my tolerance for public embarrassment, so let's all get along to our respective destinations."

Uncle T's chest rumbles again, and he gathers me into the bear mountain of his arms.

"Come see me, girl, you hear? I've been giving you space, but it's time."

He releases me into Monroe's much-less-massive embrace while moving over to Harville.

"I know what a man looks like when he's in love," Monroe says to me. "Don't be afraid."

I hiccough. "Afraid? I'm terrified."

"Then saddle up and ride the storm anyway."

"It's too soon, Monroe. I don't know—"

"Better too soon than too late, girl. Trust me. I almost lost the best thing that ever happened to me because I was scared."

I nod, not necessarily because I agree, but because these are the most words I've ever heard Monroe say, and he's saying them to me.

T and Monroe move on, and Harville and I return to the castle. It's not merely that the moment's been broken. I'm starting to shiver so hard from the cold, my teeth are chattering.

Turns out, Harville is a damn fine dancer, and after a two-step, a jitterbug, and a West Coast swing, I'm more than warmed up enough to need a fresh cup of punch.

Harville has to leave around midnight, and I'm both sad and glad.

My head needs him to go away so I can think straight for longer than five seconds…

And my heart needs him to go away so we can shore ourselves up against any more nonsense.

22

FINA

The smell of the barn hits me almost as hard as seeing Anders in his velvet doublet. During our SCA years, we were more medieval than Renaissance, but the regal Tudor style suits him well. Still, the scents of hay, sweet feed, pine oil, and of course, warm, happy horses returns me to those days in an instant. As far as the barn goes, decades have not changed Brian's hand in keeping everything in showcase condition, even during the hard years when we had to stretch baking soda and lime to keep odors down but budgets intact.

Anders and I spoke little on our walk over from the castle. I swore I wasn't going to give in to him, yet here I am, back in the barn that has changed little in the last forty years, except for the different curious noses poking into the breezeway from the stalls. I stop at the third gate down.

"This is the granddaughter of Texas Sunset."

"I remember her. She was incredibly sweet, until someone tried to outrace her."

"I remember you riding her hell-bent for leather."

"And we won."

I rub my hand down Honeysuckle's velvet nose. "This girl has her grandmother's sweetness, but not her competitiveness. We could only allow trained riders on Sunset, but Honeysuckle's happiest when she's doing a slow walk around the paddock with some of our therapy kids."

Anders joins me, stroking Honey's blaze with the gentlest of touches. She eyes him with bright curiosity and pushes at his hand with her nose.

"Sorry, girl. No treats for you this evening. I'll bring some tomorrow, though." He looks over the chestnut ears at me. "Do you still ride?"

"Not much these days. Once Violet got sick, there didn't seem to be time to breathe, much less go riding."

"You miss it."

It's a statement, not a question. And of course he's right.

"I hope to get back to it once the holidays are over."

Honey snuffles, and we give her a pat before moving away. "She's an attention hound like her mother."

We traverse the barn, giving soft rubs to the interested noses, respecting those clearly not interested in being touched. Anders had a way with horses back then and clearly hasn't lost it.

"Do you ride much?"

I can't stop a flood of memories of him in the saddle. Cocky, fearless, a master horseman who respected his mounts. I'm a good equestrian, but Anders was a natural, riding with a brazen, breathtaking confidence.

"When I get to my property, yes, which isn't nearly often enough, and part of what I'm wanting to change. I'm tired of working so hard. I want to slow down. Enjoy life more."

"Sounds lovely."

A barn cat appears from the dark recesses of the building to wend her way between Anders's long legs, and I roll my eyes at the feline. I don't have to check to know it's a girl. Four decades ago, any female, human or otherwise, was always drawn to him like magnets.

I certainly had to count myself in that column.

"I wish you had answered my letters. I could have come back."

"When? In the summers? You had a future to attend to. I had things I had to do here. You couldn't stay. I couldn't go. End of story."

"I could have helped. You and Mina."

I don't want to hurt his feelings, but he's avoiding the truth. "You're romanticizing the past. You were a kid starting college. Your parents would never have allowed you to get involved in Mina's mess of a life, and by extension, mine."

"You don't know that. If I'd known—"

"It wouldn't have made any difference." I brush past him and move toward the entrance, my steps agitated.

"I wish I could believe that."

"We can't change the past, so the bigger question is why? Why here? Why now?" I stop and hold on to a beam for support. "Why me?"

"Because I've never stopped thinking about you. And—"

A soft moan makes us both jerk around.

"Did you hear something?"

"Back here."

We race toward the sound, and I cry out when I see Brian on the floor beside his chair. Anders beats me to the prone figure and looks at me.

"Call 911."

I've already dialed Allen Sanford, our volunteer ambulance driver and EMT. There's no time to explain that Magnolia Bloom isn't part of the 911 system because we have no structure to support it. Thankfully, Allen is in town and is on his way before I hang up.

I go to my knees beside Brian and put my hand on his wrist. I know the basics of first aid, but I can tell his pulse is faint and thready, and his breathing is erratic, punctuated by low, short moans.

"Our local EMT will be here in ten minutes, and that's if Allen drives like a man possessed." I put my hand over Brian's balled fist. "Hold on, Brian. Please, hold on."

Anders reaches over and clasps my shoulder in a comforting grip. I'm grateful he doesn't offer platitudes, telling me everything will be okay. It's clear from Brian's pallor and moans he's far from okay, and I feel more helpless than I've ever felt in my life. I have zero medical training, but logic says he's had a stroke or a heart attack. And the outcome of either is not particularly optimistic for a man in his seventies.

I don't know what Anders does, but I spend the next agonizing minutes praying, something I confess I don't often do, but now seems a good time to start.

The barn door slams open, and Allen comes running in with Eddie, his volunteer sidekick, a gurney between them with supply boxes piled on top. Anders and I get out of the way.

Allen and Eddie are both former combat medics and darn good men to boot. Eddie is on the phone to the hospital in Atlanta while Allen does all the things I've seen on television a hundred times. Except this time it's real, and it's got me so scared I'm shaking in Anders's arms.

I've texted Kiki, Harville, and Thomas. I wait on calling Suzanne and her mother until the triage is finished.

I send another note to Kiki, telling her to let Nellie, our lead vet, know. And also Dex, Brian's assistant.

Who else? Think, Fina!

Of course, Rory. Where is my brain?

I can't call Mina. Or rather, I won't call unless the news is dire. She can't do anything from the Canadian Rockies, so it can wait until we know more.

Strong hands clasp both my shoulders, and I'm pulled into a warm, strong, heady embrace. "I'm so sorry, Fina. What can I do?"

My nose brushes against his broad chest. "Nothing. Just stay with me."

"Of course."

"I've called everyone I can think of—"

Allen calls to me. "Fina, we're taking him to Christus. They have the closest trauma unit."

"Of course. We'll be right behind you."

By the time Eddie and Allen are pulling away in the older but lovingly restored ambulance the city pays to keep running, Kiki is running up to me with Rory, Juliette, Paige, and Zach right behind. Thomas's truck skids to a stop, with Nellie and Dex rounding out the crowd. I give them the little information I have, and we're all frustrated it's not enough.

"Nellie, you and Dex make a plan with Rory. You know all the rotations a thousand times better than I do. I'll keep you all on speed dial and let you know what's up as soon as I get to Atlanta."

Kiki moves in and puts a hand on my arm. "Fina, you're not going to Atlanta alone."

Thomas joins in while Monroe, bless him, stays out of the fray but is clearly poised to help. "I'll drive. The Suburban can hold eight of us. Kiki, take Fina to her place so she can change and get a bag. We'll meet up in the kitchen and get on the road as soon as everyone's gathered."

Anders steps up. "I'll take Fina, Kiki. We'll be there momentarily. It won't take me but a second to grab my bag. I haven't even unpacked yet."

"You don't have to—" I shut up immediately when I see the look in his eyes.

Everyone moves like a coordinated military unit, with Kiki leaving me and Anders the golf cart. He drives us to my duplex, then helps me out of my garb and waits as I race around and put on jeans and a tunic, dragging a brush through my hair and twisting it and jamming a comb in to keep it up. I slam the brush, an extra set of clothes, underwear, my toothbrush and toothpaste, some lotion, and a light jacket into the overnight bag and zip it shut with shaking fingers.

Anders takes it from me, and we're bumping along the path in the golf cart until we hit the main road and are soon back in the kitchen.

"I'll be right back." Anders kisses my forehead and races out of the room, headed for the back stairs with sure direction. I suppose even though it's been four decades, he hasn't forgotten his way around the castle.

The Suburban is stuffed with Thomas, Monroe, Anders, me, Kiki, Rory, and Juliette. Paige and Zach stay to supervise the rest of the night's events, and Harville is on the way to support Suzanne and her mother, bless him. He'll follow along as soon as he can. We endure the drive in silence, and the thought strikes me how grateful I am to have hands to hold. I take Kiki's in one and Anders's in the other.

And just hang on.

As is the sad truth in an emergency, there's nothing to do but sit on hard chairs and drink bad coffee. We all embrace and move away, then come together for more hugs as the hours drag on. Suzanne is a wreck. Her mother is more in control, but Brian's sister has his quiet and stoic nature, so nothing surprising there. Harville is a pillar. A rock of peace and comfort, visiting with each of us, praying with those who wish it, holding the space of acceptance and warmth for those who don't.

It's coming up on five o'clock in the morning before a weary doctor comes in, taking a scrub cap off. Then she says the words making tears flood my eyes.

"I'm so sorry."

Bits of the rest of her words register as I burrow into Anders's shirt.

Aneurysm. If it hadn't ruptured. Too long without treatment. Did the best we could.

Suzanne swallows a howl of pain. She was so close to Brian. Much closer to him than to her mother. Harville is holding her, stroking her back, not trying to shush her anguish.

Then we're all back in the Suburban again, except for Kiki, who's waiting with Harville as he takes care of Suzanne and her mother, helping with details and paperwork before they can leave the hospital.

The rest of us are all coffee'd out by the time we reconvene in the kitchen for a final round of kissed cheeks.

Then each weary body leaves for their respective abode. Anders won't hear of me taking the car to my place alone, and I don't have the strength to say no. And I don't have the strength to argue when he moves straight back to my bedroom, lies down, and pulls me beside him, my head finding the perfect hollow in his shoulder.

He holds me. Lets me cry.

And lets me sleep.

23
KIKI

With the bizarre quiet that falls after a tragedy resolves, I'm lost in every movement Harville makes. Each adjustment to his driving. How he scans the road with the same diligence he seems to give everything he does. So it surprises me when he yanks at the top of his shirt after we drop Suzanne and her mother off at their place. I feel his anger. Not something I expected.

"Are you okay?" I put my hand on his arm as tension radiates off of him.

"I've been in the clergy for a long time. This is what I do, what I've been trained for, but tonight I just feel like for the first time I failed. That all I had to offer is so… banal."

I struggle for words. I despise platitudes, but the things coming to me in quick succession can only be labeled trite. I close my eyes and beg whatever powers might be out there to give me the words, plead to let me say the right thing.

We're almost at the back of the castle, so I wait until he's pulled in next to the kitchen door and shut off the car. I walk around to his side where he's shut his door and back him up against the side panel, pressing my lower body into him so my forearms can rest on his chest and my hands clutch his shirt by his shoulders.

"Do you know what I saw all through the long hours of last night and this morning?"

He slowly shakes his head.

"I saw a man who never stopped giving. You went to every single person there, spoke to each of us. You held hands. You offered tissues and cups of coffee and, when the moments were right, said something anecdotal to make everyone give watery laughs. You prayed with them and comforted them, and you made them feel like they weren't alone, hadn't been abandoned. I get it that everyone has a crisis-of-confidence moment, so of course this only makes me adore you more. But good gracious, Harville. There's literally nothing more you could have done."

He starts to deny my words, so I use his shirt in my fists to jostle him. "You gave and you gave and you gave. And they took and they took and they took. And no one gave back to you."

"That's not true—"

"It is. Humans are incredibly selfish in moments of shock and grief. It's human nature. I'm not saying anyone was bad. I'm saying the street only went one way last night, and you were giving to a whole lot of people from a well I think is a little low right now. You've had your own series of blows, and I think last night emptied your bucket."

He reaches his arms over mine to take my face in his hands, running the pads of his thumbs over my cheeks in a whisper stroke of gentleness. "It's too bad I don't wear a clerical collar. I'd give it to you."

I cough. "If only you knew how sweetly absurd that statement is, but we'll let it slide on the excuse of exhaustion."

I don't resist an iota when he pulls me against his chest. I let my arms slide around him, and I hold him tightly, my nose buried in the hollow of his throat. We just breathe as the sun finally makes its way into the sky, and I think for a second we're both going to fall asleep standing there.

I smile when his lips press to my forehead before he sets me away. I stroke his cheek this time, uselessly trying to brush away the fatigue pulling at his eyes. "Go get some sleep. Maybe we can talk later?"

He takes a peek at his watch. "No sleep for a while."

Then it strikes me. It's Sunday, and he has services barely an hour from now.

"Oh, Harville, I'm so sorry. I should have left with Fina and the rest instead of making you drag me home."

He takes my hand and kisses my palm. "I'm so glad you stayed with me. Thank you."

"You're welcome." My whisper holds more than the simple words, but I can't dig into them right now, and I think he's too tired, too.

"I'll call you this evening. Maybe we can have dinner."

"I'd like that. Be careful driving into town. You're about done in."

"This isn't my first all-nighter, but thank you. Now go hit the hay."

"Yes, sir."

He bends down as if it's the most natural thing in the world and kisses me. I lean in, for despite my confused brain and emotions, I'm not about to deny myself these few seconds of connection with him.

I give him a jaunty salute as he drives away, feeling like I'm wearing lead sneakers by the time I make it to my suite. I send quick texts to Fina, Paige, and Juliette so they won't worry, then manage a blisteringly hot shower.

When I climb into bed and wrap myself in my blankets, my only regret is it's not Harville's arms cocooning me in warmth.

I don't bother Harville when I wake up six hours later, other than to text him to let him know I'm thinking about him. He probably needs some time alone. What I need is a meeting. There's been too much emotional upheaval these last few days, and it would be too easy to convince myself I have too much to do, it's no big deal to wait until tomorrow… Except it gets easier and easier for tomorrow to never come.

I call Traycee, and my heart lurches when she brushes me off, saying she's too busy to get away. I don't press, other than to say I wish she'd change her mind, that the work will be there when she gets back, but when she gets peevish, I know it's time to let it go. I'm not her sponsor, and I'm not her counselor. Even if I were, I don't have the power to make anyone do what they don't want to do, no matter how much I know they need to.

I talk at the meeting for the first time in a long time, but something has loosened inside me enough to let the words come again. The dread hanging out in the back of my brain is far from gone. It's a monster, lurking, resting. Waiting. Trying to steal the teeny-tiny flame of hope reaching out to catch some oxygen. Talking puts the terror back in the cage, but the gate isn't latched.

The meeting's about half over when the door opens, and my heart jumps. I know if I don't go catch her, she'll bolt, so I slide over to the newcomer.

"Hi, Bethanie." I whisper the greeting out of respect for the others in the room. "Would you like to come sit by me?"

She hesitates, clutching the straps of her purse like they're lifelines, but she takes the seat next to me, so score one. I keep my attention on the rest of the speakers, knowing how desperately she's trying to appear invisible. When the meeting is over, I introduce her to a couple of the people hanging around and finally walk with her to our cars. I wait until she opens her door so she feels she has a shield between us.

"I'm really glad you came. I hope you'll keep coming back."

"I don't know." She throws her purse onto the passenger seat and threads and unthreads her scarf around her fingers. "I'm not sure this is for me."

"It's a little weird at first. The language and, for me, the God thing."

She looks startled. "Really?"

"Really. So if you have any questions, call me, okay? Or if you need someone to come to a meeting with you later this week, I'm here."

"But you've already been to one." She gestures at the church behind me.

"Never hurts to get in some extras. I'd be happy to join you."

She looks at the concrete, then starts to get into her car. I wait, and eventually she meets my eyes. "You're really sweet. I don't deserve it."

"You absolutely deserve it. Let me be your personal ice cream truck for a while, but instead of rocky road, I'll offer you scoops of be-nice-to-yourself with some it's-going-to-be-all-right sprinkles."

Her laugh sounds rusty before she looks away again. "I can see why my dad likes you."

"Your dad rocks." I wait until she looks back one last time. "And he loves you, Bethanie. A lot."

Tears fill her eyes, and it's all I can do to hold my place. "He's something else I don't deserve."

"Stick with me, kid." She winces at my very bad Bogart impression. "I'll convince you you're awesome." She gives me the full eye roll. "Eventually."

She can't take any more, and I know it.

"Drive safely, and call me if you want."

I don't wait for an answer. I slip into my own car and take off, waving out my open window.

Harville is delighted with the news when we're having a late dinner at the castle a few hours later. I asked Fina, Anders, Rory, and Juliette to join us, but they all declined, so it's him and me for store-bought lasagna and a bagged salad. I've never mastered cooking for one, so in my book, this is gourmet.

He doesn't tease me as he digs in.

"I'm so glad to hear this."

"Maybe, but I shouldn't have said her name. I wasn't thinking, and I breached her anonymity, so consider this pastor-client confidentiality."

"I don't think that's exactly what it's called, but don't worry. I hope she tells CT soon, though, because it would ease his heart."

"She probably won't for a while. She doesn't trust the process, me, anything yet."

He takes a drink of his tea and then smiles at me over the rim. "You really are incredible, you know?"

I give a little cough. "Huh? It's boxed lasagna."

"Not the food, silly. I'm talking about how caring you are."

"There's not a whole lot of people who would ascribe caring to me. She's kinda shown up and surprised me since I put down the bottle."

"I like her. A lot. And I've been thinking about what Traycee asked me a few weeks back. About starting a meeting at St. Andrew's."

"It would be good for her, but I don't think she's ready to take on the responsibility."

"What about you?"

The bite of noodles in my mouth turns to plaster, but I manage to get it down. "I don't want to take it on right now. I've got enough on my plate, and if I revert back to my old habit of doing too much, it's not going to end pretty."

"I certainly won't push you, but if you ever decide to, let me know. We tried holding some church-sponsored recovery meetings a couple of years ago, but it did not go well."

I frown at him. "Seems strange, knowing you."

"It wasn't me. It was my ex-wife's project, and even though my gut warned me, I didn't want to stop something I hoped would serve the community well."

"Can I ask what happened?"

"Ego run amok."

"Ah. Sorry."

"I keep telling you churches are buildings with flawed people inside. No matter what face you wear on Sunday morning, the real one's with you the other six days of the week."

I put my fork down and fold my hands under my chin. "I've refused all offers of gossip about you, you know."

His smile has a tinge of bitterness at the edges. "Rather hard to do in a small town."

"I've lived on military bases most of my life. I know all about the power and danger of the small-town mentality. Even though I tried to stay outside it, I know your wife cheated and left, which has to be worse for someone in the ministry."

"More salacious for some minds, maybe, but not worse than anyone else going through it. In my case, I knew on the honeymoon I'd made a bad mistake. My pastor had counseled me for months not to marry her, but my hormones were in charge of the decision back then. But once it was done, I was determined to make it work."

"Kinda takes two to tango." I pick up my fork and start sorting the tomatoes and croutons in my salad. "I'm sorry if I took the conversation in an awkward direction."

"I thought we agreed there would be no sorries between us. Friendship rule number one."

"I think alternating credit cards was rule number one, but okay."

I pulverize a crouton and blurt out what his mini confession caused to jump into my brain. "I've never had sex sober, so I have no idea what it's like to be completely caught up in someone you fall in love with."

"Never?"

I shake my head. "I started drinking in junior high, but I didn't start having sex until high school, surprisingly. By then, if I wasn't drunk, I was high. I've done a lot of work these last couple of years. I know all the blah-blah-blah. I was trying to find connection. I needed to feel wanted."

"Still sucks."

There aren't enough words to express the understatement. "Definitely."

I want so badly to tell him the rest. Tell him all of it. Get it out now.

He takes my fork away from me and wiggles my wrist until I look at him. "News flash. I know you're an alcoholic. You've never hidden that, and second news flash, you're not the first addict I've ever known."

"Yeah, well, I guess I figured you should know how screwed up your new friend is."

"I like her. Just as she is."

"Thanks, Fred Rogers."

He strokes the inside of my wrist, watching my pulse jump under the pad of his thumb. "Rest assured, my thoughts about you are decidedly not proper for PBS."

I swallow, mesmerized by watching him watching me. I've told him the second-worst thing about me, and he hasn't run. Do I dare let a flicker of hope take life?

Bringing my hand up, he presses his lips to my madly thrashing pulse. "I'd better get out of here."

I want to tell him he doesn't have to go. We both know my suite is a few yards down the hall, but I have enough guilt still clawing through me keep me from adding *defiling a minister* to my list.

He takes a deep breath, sits back, and puts his napkin on the table. "From a box or not, dinner was delicious. Thank you."

I grab the lifeline with both hands. "Of course. You've already told me you don't eat when you get super tired, so I was worried about you today."

"I got a good nap after church. Put off a few meetings. I'm almost good as new."

"Is there anything I can do to help with Brian's funeral?"

"No, but you're sweet to ask. I talked with Suzanne before I came over, and we'll have services on Tuesday."

"I didn't know Brian well. On a surface level, of course, like so many people on the estate. And I learned he and Violet were an item all these years, but they kept it totally on the QT."

"It was a known secret. Everyone respected their privacy, which might seem a little shocking in a small town."

"Completely shocking."

"I think it's because everyone felt like they were in on the mystery. Makes us feel special."

"Interesting twist."

"Add in the Grannies, who had a soft spot for Violet. Everyone knows better than to get on the Grannies' bad side."

I bark a laugh, doing a mental roll call of the octogenarian roster. Traycee's Gran, Emma. Mina and Fina's mom Eunice. Lorraine from the Ladies Auxiliary. Rory's Mamaw Ida, and her sisters Myra and Willie. Nina Goodson's grandmother, Mabel. I know there's more, but my memory won't cough up any more names.

"You know, I think the Secret Service is missing out on some prime candidates right here in Magnolia Bloom."

"I think if they'd extend the age limit, you'd be right."

My smile falters as the air in the room goes warm and heady, and the look in his eyes heats up.

"I'd better go."

I don't want him to. But I need him to. "Probably."

"Forecast is for rain tomorrow. Meet at the gym at six?"

I nod, because my throat is tight.

He gives me another one of those I-can't-stop-myself kisses.

And I can't stop myself, either.

I reach over and lace my fingers behind his neck and kiss him back with everything I'm worth until we break apart. We press our foreheads together, and I'm gratified his breathing is as ragged as mine.

"I'd better go."

"So you said."

"I did, didn't I?"

"Yeah. And you should."

"Darn it."

"Language, Pastor."

"Very funny."

We hold hands the ten feet from the table to the doorway. I stop, thinking it might be a bad idea if I follow him all the way to his car.

"Drive safely."

He gives me a little grunt.

And walks away.

24

JULIETTE

I SLEPT FITFULLY after Rory delivered me back to my little apartment above the barn. I asked him if he wanted to stay, and his regret he had to say no was a lovely consolation prize. I had the option to get into my bed and rest. He had to be at the offices in the big barn to meet with the team to form a plan. It would be hours before he saw a pillow today, if at all.

But we kissed for a long, long time before he forced himself to leave.

It's turned out that those kisses have become precious, because as each day has rolled on, he's been too busy to spend much time with me. The Juliette of old wouldn't have wasted a second's thought about days between visits. In my entire life, I've never lost precious work time daydreaming about a lover.

Yet now I find myself with my scalpel hovering over the corner of the canvas where I'm harvesting repair threads, and the clock provides irrefutable evidence I've been frozen there for large swaths of minutes. I can't train my mind away from thinking about a ginger shepherd or wondering when he's going to appear, hopefully with a black-faced and white-fleeced companion.

I have refrained from visiting him around the property, as I am apparently too much of a distraction at a time of year when he's insanely busy. There are lots of sales being finalized and winter barns and shelters being inspected. Just as I don't ask Rory to listen to the minutiae of my job, he keeps the details of what he does to a minimum. Suffice it to say, animal husbandry is a time- and labor-intensive job with no set schedule. During lambing, he might be out all night, and all the hours are filled with concern and hard physical labor.

It has added up to several long days since the loss of Brian, and we're all meeting up in the castle kitchen in a few hours to go to the funeral together.

Together. Family.

The soft knock I've been anticipating comes at the door. I hurry across the cold concrete and pull the door open.

"Bonjour."

His smile is tired, and sad, but brightens after I move in to kiss him.

And not on the cheek.

"Bonjour, ma'am."

I lead him into the cavernous room and aim straight for the coffeepot. With a sigh of thanks, he takes the cup I pour, and we settle at the little table in the bubble of warmth provided by the ceramic heater diligently working a few feet away. He's dressed for the funeral happening in a few hours, as am I. I almost feel guilty we're delaying our walk up to the castle, but I have become miserly with my minutes with him.

"I'm worried about you." Rory looks around the space, which is bright from the proliferation of windows.

"I'm fine. Like you, I dress for my environment, and one of the last things Brian did for me was bring me these space heaters so I'm able to control the temperature of my workspace nicely."

"You can't blame me for worrying."

"I can't?"

"Nope. I've got you figured out. When you get into what you're doing, you don't eat and hardly sleep and neglect yourself."

I raise an eyebrow. "I recognize another person in this room who fits that description."

The curse of being redheaded means his blush cannot be hidden from my amused eyes.

"Yeah, yeah."

Any additional teasing is interrupted by a knock at the door. We look at each other questioningly, but I rise to answer the summons.

It's a familiar delivery truck, and I've come to know the route drivers by name.

"Bonjour, Timothy."

"Ma'am. Can you sign here?"

I usually don't have to provide a signature for the items I've ordered, so now my curiosity goes into overdrive as I do as requested and take the letter-sized package. Timothy tugs at the brim of his cap and jogs back to his van, leaving me to close the door, rip open the seal, and remove a sheaf of papers as I return to Rory.

"What's up?"

I shrug. "I do not know, other than this is from Sotheby's."

It's impossible to miss the distinct and elegant logo at the top of the cover letter.

I scan the contents, then go back to the beginning and reread. I drop the pages to the table and look at Rory.

"It's from Sotheby's."

"I think you clarified it as such."

"They are the largest and most respected art auction and sales house in the world."

"Even this little hick sheepherder knows that."

I give him a teasing frown. "You are not a hick."

"So what does fancy-pants Sotheby's want?"

"To offer me an interview for an entirely new division they are considering forming, in response to my recent CV."

"Well, that's exciting."

"Except I did not submit one. I am a consultant for Sotheby's already and quite content with my connection to them."

"Then how—"

"My sister, it appears, has been meddling."

"I thought you two were at outs."

"We are. It has been too long since we've spoken about anything more than the needs of our business."

"Which hurts you. Bothers you."

"In some ways, yes, but distance has provided me time to examine my relationship with my twin. I've had to acknowledge I have been content to let Noelle handle the endless details of the retail side of our ventures, which freed me to stay absorbed in the work I love. We have been a good team, until recently. I love her and believe she thinks she is doing the right thing to preserve our fates and fortunes, but the longer I'm away, the more I like it."

"You don't seem like the under-the-thumb type to me."

"I bear responsibility in creating my own mess because I despise the paperwork and the calls and the mountain of office work required in running a business. Noelle thrives on all of it. She adores being the boss and setting the schedules and approving catalogs and campaigns. That is what made us such a good team."

"And now things are changing."

"Some things have changed irreparably, and I think Noelle is panicking. In her mind, I should have returned to Paris weeks ago, and apparently she thinks she's casting out an irresistible lure to bring me home."

Rory plays with the handle of his mug, studies the cooling contents, and finally looks at me. "Is she?"

I flip through the pages behind the letter and grasp the top notes of the offer. I might as well have written the job description for myself. Sotheby's has numerous dedicated directors overseeing specific types of art, but this would be a position to curate women artists through history. The challenge would be my specialty is canvas. I would have a steep learning curve to add photography, sculpture, and other textiles.

My eyes scan a listing for additional staff, so I wouldn't be doing this alone, but I'd have no time for anything except this undertaking.

So why am I not dancing around the room? Isn't this the literal manifestation of what I've wanted for decades? I would be a director, a respected voice deciding which artists are given a place in the spotlight. I would have the opportunity to celebrate women who, since the dawn of history, have been grossly underrepresented. How can I turn down such a phenomenal opportunity?

Our watches beep simultaneously, and my mental musings must wait as I move around the room, shutting off lights and heaters. Rory helps me drape the sheet over my table, pausing before he lets go of his side as he takes in the new masterpiece.

"She really was incredible. You don't have to have a lick of talent with a paintbrush to see that."

"Naturally, I agree."

This piece has Gavina's love sitting on an iron chair, and I'm fairly certain, if we could find Gavina's sketches, it was staged on the back balcony of the castle. The beautiful woman is pitched slightly forward, her arm on a table barely in the composition, her delicate chin resting on her knuckles. She has a thousand-yard stare, her mouth neutral. Not happy, for certain, but not pinched or angry. Just contemplative.

Like most great art, the magnificence isn't in the pose. There are millions of pictures and who knows how many portraits of individuals staged identically, so that is not what makes me cry as I bend close to the canvas to remove dirt and dust and old varnish, or in the countless hours I've used to reweave, thread by thread, a tear in the upper corner.

Rory pulls the door shut behind us, bringing my attention back to him. We've decided to walk to the castle because the day is glorious. The air is crisp, humidity is negligible, and the wind is light, enough to ruffle Rory's hair, in need of another trim, and mine, which is getting long enough to need more than a scrub with a towel and a finger-combing to get it out of my eyes. I make a mental note to call Kiki's friend's sister. On top of needing a haircut, it'll be another excellent excuse to go into town.

We talk about the paintings, about how tied Rory's family has been to the MacInneses through the past five generations, about Magnolia Bloom. About the joys of small towns and villages. About the disadvantages.

About death.

By the time the group has gathered and then dispersed into vehicles for our caravan to the church, my mind is not as settled as I hoped.

In fact, it's in even more of a whirl than I imagined it could be because I'm barely through shaking hands and kissing cheeks in the vestibule of St. Andrew's when the one person I've been keeping off my mental checklist walks in.

My birth father.

I'm not prepared. I didn't give a thought to him being here, but should not be surprised. I grew up in a tiny village and know well how weddings and funerals gather people together who rarely see each other.

Or in this case, never.

I can't count the momentary eye contact we made at Vivann's. I thought he'd make a gesture to reach out to me, but as the days went on, I let it go. Maybe he's waiting for me to initiate contact? If so, time has passed, and each day I decide I'm not ready.

Apparently, it is being decided for me today, although there is no requirement that we converse. I make the first move, stepping toward him and offering my hand.

"Bonjour. I am Juliette Laurant, although I'm sure you know."

He takes my hand in his, covering it with his free hand before releasing me. "I'm so very happy to finally speak to you."

A moment of uncharacteristic snark threatens, and I nearly say, *Really? That does not seem true.* Instead, I say, "I'm sure you agree today isn't the time for more than a hello, but we should talk soon."

"I'm happy to meet with you anytime."

"Why don't you come to the first big barn behind the castle? It's an event space, not an animal space."

"I've been there many times. Is later this afternoon too soon?"

"Not at all. We are having a family dinner after the services, but five o'clock should be convenient."

It feels so odd to be discussing the meeting as if we're doing nothing more than planning coffee, but what option is there? Now is not the time to talk of anything deeper.

"Five it is."

He walks with me up the aisle until I move to the right and take my seat with the family, and he pivots left, toward the other gathered attendees, but sits alone.

Which strikes me as interesting.

And sad...

25
KIKI

Juliette slides into the pew to sit beside me.

"Where's Rory?" I'm ashamed I have an instant of jealousy at Juliette's building relationship with him. I am thrilled for her, without a doubt, but there's a piece of me a little green with envy.

"He's in the back. He couldn't be persuaded to sit with us. He's terribly shy sometimes."

I nudge her shoulder and smile. "You'll have to tell me more."

She has a distinct twinkle in her eye.

I grasp her outstretched hand as I scan the backs of the people sitting in the rows in front of us. Brian's blood family has all come to pay their respects, and that's no small number of Steeles. With his four brothers and one sister, a small army fills the pews, plus half a regiment of employees from Steele Feed and Supply behind the MacInnes contingent. With assorted cousins added in, the church is about to burst.

It's yet another amazing testament to this family, created by Evajean and Alisdair so many years ago. The bonds on this estate and throughout the town are cemented by common love and history.

Harville comes in through a side door and moves to the front row, shaking hands with all the Steeles, and my breath whooshes out of me.

I've never seen him in his vestments. I've seen him in a range of attire, from shorts and T-shirts to what I call his uniform of slacks and button-down shirts, even full suits like his officiation of Wynona's wedding, but that's quite different than the picture before me.

He seems to feel my laser focus and looks over at me, giving me a mere hint of the dimples now precious to me. I smile back, bemused by what I feel. Of course he's invited me to church, but I'm not drawn to organized religion, and some part of me did not want this reminder of the gulf between us.

I've held tightly to my Harville. Plain, average citizen Harville.

Something inside me didn't want to see him in his official capacity, his chosen vocation, the very thing bricking me upside the head as a detail we cannot overcome.

Someone behind me puts a hand on my shoulder and squeezes. I welcome the distraction and turn slightly to acknowledge Uncle T and Monroe, who've taken seats beside Fina and our Nordic client, which surprises me to no end that he's still here. Then Paige and Zach slip in with Mina and CT. Harville takes the pulpit, and the service begins, and I can't take my eyes off of him.

He's everything I imagined he'd be. Gentle. Calm. Reassuring.

And he's everything I can't have. A man of the cloth. A beloved and respected public figure.

I've kept Colonel Sassman from my thoughts with rigid determination, but here he comes, barreling in from the corner, reminding me decisions have consequences. He certainly gets a share of the guilt pie, but in the end, I'm the one who made the choices, acted on them, and have to pay the piper.

When the service is over, and I'm standing at the back of the sanctuary, I'm a bundle of hot nerves doing everything I can to avoid Harville. I need a few more minutes to get myself in check.

I feel someone come up behind me and turn, hoping to snuggle into an awesome Uncle T embrace, but I pull up sharply. If there's one thing I can be sure Demon Delores doesn't want to give me, it's a hug.

"He is such a wonderful counselor."

I wonder if she knows how openly her eyes are devouring Harville, still busy at the front of the room.

"He certainly is." What am I supposed to do? Argue? Even if that was my first inclination.

"I'm praying he finds a compatible wife soon, someone who understands the ministry and supports his mission."

"Or husband."

I feel her start and hide my smile.

"It's hard for someone of his gifts to be unequally yoked." Points to Delores for hanging on to that bone.

I might not be religious, but I have enough memory of Bible study as a kid to get the reference. Doesn't mean I'm going to bite on the shiny lure Delores is casting out. Especially since there's truth in the statement, even if her intention and delivery suck swamp water.

"Hmm."

"I'm sure you can understand."

I look at her, employing the time-tested MacInnes Busybody Defense System.

I stay silent.

It takes a moment, but it works, and Delores makes some noise about needing to check on the Steele family and all but stalks away.

I wish I could say my success makes me feel better, but though I didn't respond, her barb hit home. Harville does need someone who understands him and supports him. I need someone who understands and can forgive the past tearing behind me like a tornado about to touch down.

Thing is, the woman exists who can fit the bill for him.

My dating site would be only a barrage of swipe lefts.

I make it back to the castle with the family crowd, but beg off from the luncheon with a headache compounded by a heartache chaser.

I put on some thermals under my jeans and grab my puffy coat, slipping down the turret stairs to wend my way to the gardens. I'm afraid if I stay on the balcony, someone might come looking for me.

But someone does come looking for me. I'm not lost in the whirlwind of my own making for more than fifteen minutes before Uncle T's massive shadow falls over me.

"I thought I saw a little mouse out here. Thought I'd come investigate."

I scoot over to make room on the bench.

"You shouldn't be out in the cold."

"What, an old man like me? I'm fragile all of a sudden?"

He lays his arm across the back of the bench, and I scooch under his warm, outstretched arm. "If you catch a cold, Monroe's gonna come take a stripe out of my hide."

"Nah, he'll cluck and mother hen and make me drink chicken soup."

"It's good to be loved so much you'll drink soup when you despise chicken."

"I'm fairly certain he knows. Surprised you do."

"I may not have been here as much as I should have over the years, but I'm not completely unobservant."

His lips brush my hairline. "You're too hypervigilant. And too sensitive."

"Now who's being the Mrs. Kravitz of Castle MacInnes?"

A chuckle rumbles in his chest. "Isn't that reference a little before your time?"

"Hey, I grew up on Nick at Nite and the oldies are the besties. I just wish I could wiggle my nose and magically make things better."

I look out over the ornamental kale and cabbage, winter honeysuckle, and all the other plants I couldn't name if my life depended on it. I know Violet and Fina did most of this work, creating the exquisite beauty in every hedge, every part of the miniature maze. I don't consider myself much like my aunt Violet, but in this I feel a kinship with her. Out here, everything follows orders. Obeys. Is kept rigidly manicured. Proof that if you abide by the rules, beauty can thrive.

Or so I always needed to believe. Tried to incorporate into my own life, except for the little alcohol and drug thing.

"So are we gonna keep making jokes until I turn into a Popsicle, or are you gonna tell me what's going on? I'm thinking you picking this particular place isn't a coincidence."

"Nothing like getting caught necking by your uncle and his husband to make things awkward."

"Monroe thought it was sweet. He's happy for you. He likes the preacher."

"Do you?"

"Absolutely. Harville is a gentleman and a scholar, and one of the most decent people I've ever met."

"Great. More evidence he's frickin' perfect."

"I don't recall saying he's perfect. I'm fairly sure he's a human being and a healthy young man."

"All true, but the last thing he needs in his life is the mess that is me."

"Come on now. You're not trying to say he's somehow a saint and can't be with a mere mortal?"

There's no sense in playing games with Uncle T, so I spill it all out in one giant puke of a paragraph. "So when he finds out I had an affair with a married man and my superior officer, he won't have anything to do with me anymore. He might still be willing to be my friend, but if we take this any further, I'd hurt him more than I can bear."

"Don't you think he's the one who gets to decide?"

"But—"

"Look, kiddo, I know a hell of a lot about guilt, and you have to trust me on this. If your feelings for him are what they appear to be, you have got to forgive yourself for what you did in the past and give him the chance to do it, too."

"Even if he thinks he can let it go for now, it would eventually come back and cause an unbridgeable rift." I clench my fists inside my jacket pockets, but my fingers still feel cold.

"So now you're a crystal-ball reader, as well as a smartass, and can tell the future?"

"Paige is the smartass. I'm just smart."

"You're damn sure kin and kindred. And you're both my girls. The kids I wish Monroe and I could have had."

I stretch up so I can kiss his cheek. "That would've been pretty awesome."

"At least Paige's Aiden is getting what could never be for me, but we're not talking about my great-great-nephew right now." He pauses and huffs, his breath coming out white in the cold air. "Damn, I'm ancient."

"I think the world of Aiden, and I'm more than thrilled he and Chen adopted the adorable Marceau, but the advances in social justice aren't what's got me whirling. I've got this vise around my heart after losing Brian, and I wasn't especially close to him. If I lost you—"

"Sweetie, you're gonna lose me. Not today, I hope, but the impending loss makes it more imperative for you listen to your wise old uncle."

"I appreciate it, Uncle T. I really do. But if Harville was anything other than a preacher, maybe we could get around it, but my past will come back and bite me on the ass. It always does, and this is a small town. I'm not sure when, but it's inevitable, and I can't embarrass him. I just can't."

"It's clear you're going to be as stubborn as your aunt Violet about this, so I'll let it go for now."

I snuggle in closer, and he puts his tree trunk of an arm more firmly around me. "I love you, you know."

"Never doubted it for a second."

We sit in the cold but brilliant sunlight for a few more minutes, then take our chilly bones back inside. We arrive in time to join in the dessert course, and by the time I've scraped up the last crumb of my apple pie, I'm smiling again. Monroe winks at me from across the table, and I wink back. Some heat flushes my cheek, but he's a dear man, and I guess he deserves to tease me a little.

Fina passes a pitcher of tea down the table. "Did anyone besides me see who was at the back of the church?"

I answer. "You mean Alyssa? I guess she goes by Ally now, but yeah, I tried to reach her, but she jetted before I could get back there." My brain has been so busy since then, I forgot about seeing my cousin until Fina's words brought her back to mind.

Heads bob around the table, but Fina picks up the thread. "I'm a little surprised she came, but then again, not at all. When the ABCs were here, Ally was always Brian's shadow."

I move in to explain when I see Juliette's confusion. "Evajean and Alisdair had seven children, six of whom lived. Ally and her two sisters are descendants of the second son. Ally's mom was told she couldn't have children, and when she got pregnant with her, they thought she was a miracle baby. Then Bailey was born just under eleven months later, so they figured out real quick the doctor was wrong. But she caught all kinds of grief when Cammie was born ten months after Bailey."

"Three children born within twenty months? Goodness."

"Yeah, she said it was like having triplets. We call them the ABCs. Anyway, Ally became a country music star, Bailey's a doctor, and Cammie's a lawyer. An entire family of overachievers."

Fina takes over to add, "I guess we'll find out soon enough why Ally's here."

I listen to the conversation floating around the table, all the touches and joking and banter. I might not know how this Harville situation is going to work out, but I've gotten one thing clear.

Love is a helluva thing.

26

FINA

"Mina is exactly the way I remember her." Anders takes the seating plan and menu for the feast and settles into the corner of the couch at the center of the seating area in my office. I've retreated behind my desk.

"She's reverted to her former self in a lot of ways, which is great. For a long time, she was lost and locked inside herself, but that all happened after—"

I cut myself off. Of course it all happened after he left, but it sounds like he skipped off like a check runner, when in truth his time as an exchange student simply ran its course.

I try to pretend the moment didn't just turn awkward. "She was in a horribly abusive marriage, but she's come out the other side of it now. CT's a terrific guy, and I'm utterly happy for her."

"I'm sorry for the history, but I'm delighted for her. She seems blissful."

"She was certainly surprised to see you."

"She didn't know about the Yule Ball?"

"Yes, but she's been a little flighty lately and hasn't kept up on all the little details like she used to. Kiki has been in charge of your event almost from the first email, so even I didn't figure it out right away."

He dives his attention back into the folders, and I quit pretending I'm doing anything but drinking in every angle of him as he gives his attention to the notes and spreadsheets and seating plans Kiki and I have drawn up.

He looks up and realizes I'm watching. "Why do you keep staring at me? Don't get me wrong, I like it, but do I have spinach in my teeth?"

"No, I was thinking that you look like—"

"Peter Andersson."

"I don't even know who that is."

"Swedish actor. Dragon tattoo movies. I don't think I look remotely like him, but it's happened a few times."

"I'll take your word for it, but I think you look like Bruce Willis in *Armageddon*."

You'd think I'd told him Santa Claus is real.

Yup. Same aw-shucks, Boy Scout grin.

"Truly? Awesome."

"Don't get a big head about it."

I mean, it's not like I've watched every Bruce Willis more than once. Or that I think bald men are hella sexy. Or that right now I'm picturing Anders Jensen without his shirt and wearing Ray-Bans beside a pool.

He shifts the papers to the seat beside him and glides over to park his hip on the edge of my desk. "Can I get a little bit of a big head about it?"

It's such a smooth move I'm seeing spots before I realize I need to take a breath. I sit up straighter, but it doesn't help me feel one tiny bit more in control of whatever's happened to the oxygen in the room.

I clear my throat and grab my pen and pad off the desk. I cross my legs to give myself something to brace the notebook on. "So, does everything look good on those preliminary sheets?"

Anders takes my shield and sword and tosses them back where they were. With equal confidence, he swivels around so my legs are between his. He rests his palms on the desk, but somehow I don't think he needs the support of my desktop as much as I need my chair to stop me from sliding into a puddle on my chair mat.

My neck is craned back to look at him, and there is absolutely zero chance he doesn't know his moves aren't sexy as hell.

"Everything looks amazing."

His voice is husky and deep, and his eyes are locked with mine, so there's no chance of misinterpretation.

Taking my hands, he pulls me to my feet and then into the V of his thighs. He is a thousand times more handsome as a mature man than the boy ever was. Of course young Anders was stunning, all long blond hair and still forming muscles. This Anders has—my, oh, my—grown into his muscles and has the lines and planes earned from a life full of both laughter and tears.

"I've missed you."

He locks his hands behind my back, but I'm not trying to escape. Not yet.

I brace my hands on his chest and lean in, resting my cheek on his shoulder for a long minute.

"It's been forty years."

"I've missed you for all of them."

I finally find the strength to look deep into the eyes of the only lover who ever mattered to me.

"I've missed you, too, but that doesn't explain all this." I point at the event details we've been discussing.

"A friend of mine, my best friend, died a few months ago."

"I'm so sorry."

He plants a kiss on my temple before continuing. "He was a marathoner. Worked out like a demon. Was in better shape at sixty than we were at thirty." He looks over my shoulder, but I know he's not seeing the painting hanging behind me. "Dropped dead. In the gym."

"I—"

"We're not kids, Fina. Our teenage years are long behind us, but we're not half in our graves, either. The incident scared me so badly I went to my doctor the next week to have tests run, and my doctor says I'm in great shape."

I can't stop a smile. "I could have told you and saved you the trouble."

His lips quirk, and he drops a kiss on my nose. "I don't know about your medical file, but you are just as gorgeous as you were at Pennsic when we danced the branle du chandelier."

"Get much chance to do the candlestick dance these days?"

"Not much, but I've never forgotten it."

"I've never forgotten you were wearing a short houppelande. Green velvet with yellow satin trim. You caught a lot of grief from your buddies."

"I wasn't trying to get *my buddies* to look at my legs."

"You certainly had more than this fair maiden enthralled."

Anders reaches behind me and eases the decorative comb holding my twist in place. I'm gratified his breath is as short as mine as he uses both hands to fan my hair out over my shoulders.

"I seem to remember that was the last night you could claim to be a maiden."

"I seem to remember that, too."

He combs his fingers through my long strands and brings a small handful to his nose, inhaling. "I love your hair. You still use vanilla shampoo. And lavender."

I've used the shampoo he loved for forty years. Brands had to change a few times, but those two essences have always been in my bathroom.

His long fingers move to frame my face until he has me in the tenderest of traps.

He pulls me closer, but it doesn't take much urging. Our mouths meet, and the years melt away, only this time there's no teenage fumbling, no innocent ignorance. He's a man who's grown confident in his maturity, and I'm a woman who's learned what she likes and wants. Or what I wanted until I shut everything down inside me because no one I've been with has come close to this.

My lips part for him as an eagerness I thought had disappeared springs to life. With the first whisper of his mouth against mine, I'm alive. Gentle exploration becomes a fury, a fusion of need and desire and desperation. Kisses turn to a bruising melding, and our hands tangle as I unbutton his shirt, and he pulls off my tunic, separating only long enough to get the job done, and then he's unhooking my bra as I'm yanking his shirttail free so I can get the damned thing out of my way.

His skin is hot, his chest hair rough against my hands and then my nipples as he hauls me against him so every possible inch of our bodies meet in our desperate and urgent need to connect. Then we're on the couch, though I have no memory of moving, and all the fabric is gone between us.

I welcome him to me, my body remembering every touch. This time, though, the uncertain hands of the boy have been replaced by those of a man who knows how to please a woman, how to get her hot and ready and begging for him.

He doesn't make me beg for long.

But he does make me cry his name more than once before the sun goes down, leaving only darkness outside the windows and the sound of our ragged breathing as we recover. At the moment, Anders is seated but stretched back, and I'm splayed out on the length of the sofa with my head on his thigh, his hand cupping one of my breasts.

Eventually I sit up, my muscles weak as I rise, looking around for my clothes. I'm not embarrassed. Well, only a little. He hasn't given me any time to be shy.

About anything.

When we're both dressed, he pulls me back into his arms. "Come to my room. Stay with me."

I look at him, at this man who's always had the ability to persuade me to do, persuade me to want, everything he wants.

We move down the hall to his much more comfortable king-sized bed.

And proceed to find out how many more positions we can manage on the expanded space.

27

KIKI

"We did legs last time. Chest today, birthday girl?"

I shut the trunk of my car so I can see Harville. "Sounds good, birthday boy."

I want to call him SP, but something has shifted between us, and while he is absolutely still Sexy Pastor in my book, I can't tease him about it right now. We spent the rest of the week after losing Brian being super busy and ended up seeing each other only on the trails or at the gym, but we made a promise to spend our mutual birthday together. Our plan starts this morning with a workout.

Then it's breakfast, and since the weather has held nicely, we're going to the hot spring. We're letting ourselves play hooky until noon, then it's to our respective offices until five, at which point I'll go change, and he'll pick me up for a drive into Texarkana for sushi.

My language goes from genteel Southern lady to drunken sailor by the time I do the last frickin' bench press, incline fly, and skull crusher. I normally like chest day. Apparently, today is not that day.

I do manage to swear internally, though, in deference to my workout partner.

I'm almost in tears by the time I manage to struggle into my maillot, and I nearly moan orgasmically when we reach the hot spring and

I submerge myself, staying under until my lungs threaten a revolt. My arms hurt so badly I'm afraid Harville will have to haul me out of the water because I'm not sure I have the grip strength to hold on to the rail right now.

Then again, being lifted into those rather impressive arms kept hidden by his proper button-down shirts might not be a bad thing.

Stop it! Mind back in the friend lane, missy.

I know, technically, since we've kissed that's pretty silly to hope for, but I'm rather desperately trying to make myself believe I can.

I swim as close to the source of the spring as common sense will allow and float for a minute, letting the heat and the natural minerals in the water do their magic.

Long, strong arms pull me back to a broad chest, and I rest against the wall of muscle I feel privileged to be one of the few to see. Soft lips kiss my ear.

"You all right?"

I give him a side-eye. "You lied to me."

"What?"

"You said I'd get my form back in no time. I think I'm broken."

He kisses the curve of my neck and *mmmmms* against my skin, the vibration intoxicating as it ripples across my shoulders. "I'll put you back together."

I close my eyes again, clenching them even though he can't see me. At least I don't think he can see what has to be pain in my eyes. I can blame the water on the tears escaping, but not the ache of knowing I'm storing up birthday memories to hold me for a good, long time.

I straighten, and he lets me go. I twist around to splash him. "Come on. I'll race you to the steps."

I call on every ounce of determination I have left and swim with all my might, even though I know I have no chance of beating him. I ignore the outcries of my pecs and biceps, promising myself I'll bathe in lidocaine cream when I get home.

When we reach the steps, Harville hauls me into his lap, and I snuggle into his chest, the water a warm blanket around us. We're far enough from the fountainhead for the temperature here to be deliciously decadent rather than roast-your-skin hot.

"What's up?" He stops me from answering when he kisses me, and I'm wondering why I'm so surprised he's so damned good at it.

"Kinda hard to talk when you're sticking your tongue down my throat."

"Sorry."

"I wasn't complaining, just noting the disconnect."

"I'll behave."

I sigh dramatically. "If you must."

"So, spill. Is it Traycee?"

I grab on to the excuse like it's a life buoy. "Partly. It's killing me she won't call me, and she hasn't gone to a meeting in three weeks now. I'm scared. But on an upbeat note, Bethanie has gone to two meetings without me, so good news there."

"You're triceps aren't broken. It's your too-kind heart."

"Says the undercover Arnold Schwarzenegger."

He snorts and actually rolls his eyes, not a move I usually associate with him. "Hardly."

"You know, if you did a shirtless Sunday sermon once a month, St. Andrew's would be, like, a megachurch by Easter."

"I don't think the presbytery would approve that build-the-flock campaign."

"Well, I think it's a great idea."

"I'll put it on the spreadsheet."

"Um-hmmm."

Our birthday or not, I have to put it out there. "You know we have to cut this out, right?"

He pulls back, his brow furrowing. "We do?"

I reach up to stroke his jaw. "Because if this goes any further, we're both gonna get really hurt."

"Why can't it go any further?"

I wiggle to sit up straighter, but I don't relinquish my comfy seat. "Because you and I have different rules about relationships, and I've been reminded you need someone in your life who supports your ministry."

The frown turns fierce. "I'm assuming this has to do with the little sideline tackle from Delores at Brian's funeral and why you avoided me for three days afterward."

"Yeah, but she's not wrong. You do deserve someone who can be your partner."

"And why, pray tell, can that not be you?"

"Because I'm not a Presbyterian. At best, I'm an agnostic."

"And you don't support what I do?"

I stroke the cheek I've had more than one very hot dream about. "I do. Completely. I think you're an amazing pastor. You're good and decent and everything I think a minister should be, especially in times like today."

"It seems many people mock anything smacking of decency these days."

"Which is why you're needed more than ever. You, personally, in little old Magnolia Bloom, give people hope that there are genuine, kind people in the world. You've actually restored my faith, no pun intended. I got pretty soured on organized religion for most of my life. But even though I believe you're the real deal doesn't change that I can't pretend to be what I'm not."

"I think we need to table this discussion for later."

I pinch the rueful dimple that's made an appearance. "You really have a hard time taking a compliment, don't you?"

"Hello, Pot. My name's Kettle."

"Ha-ha. Stick to sermons, not stand-up, buddy."

"You started this, and I think we have a birthday to celebrate, and we're going to leave all additional serious matters until tomorrow."

"So now I call you Scarlett instead of Harville?"

"Sure, if that's what it takes."

Then he closes the admittedly small distance between our mouths and makes me forget all the things I'm supposed to be thinking, all the reasons I need to remind myself this isn't a good idea.

Because right now, this seems like a very good idea.

We're both heaving like bellows when we hear the distant sound of voices and know our time alone at the spring is done.

"You may have to walk in front of me until we get to our towels." His voice is a low growl, and I choke on a laugh.

"Terribly racy there, Pastor Harville."

"My soul may have a higher calling, but my body has moved quite firmly into the carnal zone."

"Firmly, huh?"

I wiggle, even though I know I shouldn't be mean.

"And you need to stop."

He sets me away, and we climb out of our momentary sanctuary. We end up making it to our towels before the young couple is close enough to witness anything un-minister-y. We return their wave, and when he kisses me one last time after I've gotten in the car, I'm glad I'm sitting down, because I think all my muscles are officially mush.

He puts a knuckle under my chin. "I believe in miracles, and I'm not going to let you get away. We'll find our path."

"Harville—"

He stops me with supreme effectiveness by kissing me breathless again.

When he stops, I struggle to keep myself from grinning like I've gotten into the nitrous oxide at the dentist's office. "Who knew ministers were such hotties?"

"I can't speak for anyone else, but this one has some serious motivation to up his moves."

"Pastor's got game. I like it."

"Good. Now, let's get to breakfast, then you're going to the castle, and I'm going to my office. I'll be by to pick you up at five for dinner."

"Yes, sir."

He slips on his Ray-Bans, and I just about melt right there in his car.

28
JULIETTE

I AM IMMENSELY grateful the intensity of my work allows me to become so engrossed that I lose track of time. As the clock has ticked forward on Friday, I have made excellent progress on Gavina's painting, and it takes a moment for me to register it when there is a thump at my door.

When I open the door, there is my Lulu, only my little girl isn't quite so little any more.

The sound of a car engine rather than a diesel truck tells me my visitor isn't Rory, so my invited guest has arrived, and despite all my self-talk, my stomach clenches.

David Broder gets out of an expensive sedan, wearing black slacks and a beautifully crafted cable-knit sweater. He moves forward, taking his sunglasses off and smiling tentatively, looking curiously at Lulu, who's gone to attention at my side like some kind of woolly guard dog. If David were Rory, she'd be bounding over to him like a supersized rabbit, but she's stock-still beside me, and although I don't know how she sees anything with the soft strands of wool constantly in her eyes, I feel she's staring at him. Judging him.

Not unlike myself.

He's tall. Undeniably handsome. His hair is silver. Expensively cut. And he's nervous.

Good. I shouldn't be the only one.

He moves closer and holds out his hand. "Hello again."

"David." I accept his hand, giving a half-second's thought to how awkward this moment is. "My birth mother called you Ephraim in her diaries."

His smile is small and sad. "She thought the name Ephraim was exotic, although it's not an uncommon name."

I step back and make space for him to come inside. "Please, join me."

He looks around as he enters, his eyes lighting on the massive worktable I've covered with a sheet. Not to hide anything from him, but out of habit to keep the space neat and dust off the paintings.

"Would you care for some coffee?"

He takes in the small kitchen area tucked into the corner, which includes a counter, sink, microwave, and refrigerator. "Thank you, yes."

I had already put the kettle on, anticipating the social niceties, and it's not long before we're sitting at the small table and looking at each other, both of us feeling uncertain.

"It's lovely to see you, Juliette."

David holds my eyes for a moment, then looks down to pay inordinate attention to stirring cream into his cup.

I jump to my feet and pull a small box from the refrigerator. I bought the confections earlier this morning and nearly forgot them.

David raises an eyebrow when he sees the contents. "Madeleines?"

"From the new bakery. These have a fig compote."

He goes still. "Fig?"

"I'm sorry, do you not like—"

"Figs are my favorite fruit in the world."

I take a sharp breath. It is exceptionally rare to find someone who shares my love of this particular little treat. Genetic or coincidence?

Does it matter?

He helps himself, but I'm not ready to eat anything. "Did my mother like them?"

He coughs on a crumb, taking a drink of coffee to clear his throat. "I honestly don't know."

Interesting. You could ask Papa, and in a split second, he could tell you Maman's favorite foods, both savory and sweet, in order of preference.

David clears his throat again. "I didn't know about you and your sister."

I nod. "I know. Violet was clear in her diaries. You wanted her to abort us."

"She told me she did."

"She told you she took care of everything."

His fingers are agitated as he twists his cup on its coaster. "I was a self-centered bastard then, but I want to believe if she'd told me she kept you, I'd—"

"I don't think you get to rewrite history in your mind to make yourself feel better. I am sure Violet was not a perfect person, and her diaries are of course colored through her lens, but you were happy for her to be an invisible, convenient piece of your life."

"She shouldn't have—"

I hold up a hand. "Are you about to say she shouldn't have let Maman and Papa adopt us? You'd rather Noelle and I didn't exist rather than make you uncomfortable?"

I am not sure my voice rose, but Lulu moves closer and presses her weight against my left hip. I comb the tufts away from her beautiful black eyes and give her a scratch. I'm not sure if I'm somehow trying to reassure the lamb or myself.

"No, that's not it." He runs both hands over his head before wrapping them around his mug. "I wish she'd brought you back."

"You wish her to have gone through the torture of giving us up, then yank us away from Maman and Papa, who are utterly amazing parents, once you decided to stop thinking with your penis and grow up?"

It's a long moment before he meets my eyes. "I'm not really sure what I wish. I didn't know you and Noelle existed until a few weeks ago. I've done nothing but think about what a miserable excuse for a human being I was back then, and I desperately want to believe I might have done things differently, but the truth is, I probably wouldn't have. Then."

He slams back the last of his coffee and sets the cup down. Hard. Then he stares out the huge windows for a long time. "I have three great children and seven wonderful grandkids. I've had a very good life. I love my wife." His voice cracks. "But your mother was the love of my life, and I was pathologically narcissistic back then. I destroyed something amazing, something rare and precious."

Lulu shifts, her hooves making a clacking sound on the concrete. He looks at her, still clearly confused as to why a sheep is guarding my side, but pulls in his thoughts.

I watch him struggle for words and try to parse all the emotions swirling through me. I've always had a hole inside me. Not something huge and destroying, as some adoptees feel. Just a… missing piece. Or maybe a snag I wanted smoothed by an emery board of information.

I could have gone the rest of my life without knowing about him, or Violet, but now, after meeting David, it's like I've filled in a divot with fresh soil. I'm patting it down, and I'm ready for grass or wildflowers or some other appropriate living thing to come in and take root. Make something new.

"I wish I could have known her, but I do not regret my life. I have amazing parents and had a wonderful childhood."

"I'm glad. Still, I wish I could go back and change the past. Be there for her. For you."

"I don't need you as a father. I have a father who was there for me."

I don't mean to be cruel, but I also have no obligation to make this easy on him.

"I know you don't need me, but I'm hoping we can get to know each other. Maybe Noelle—"

"Put no hope in ever knowing her. We might be twins, but we are very different, especially in this regard."

"I don't deserve to get to know you, so I won't be greedy."

He's correct, of course. He doesn't deserve to know me, or Noelle, but while my momentary schadenfreude doesn't make me proud of myself, one of my favorite German words perfectly fits the situation. I might not be typical where relationships are concerned, but I'm hardly abnormal. If I weren't conflicted, I wouldn't be human.

I change the subject, as we've both poked the wound enough for the moment, and ask about his family, his factory, his place in Magnolia Bloom. I learn Broder Vanity has made much more than lingerie over the decades. During the world wars, they retooled to make parachutes. During Vietnam and some of the Gulf conflicts, they partially restructured to make uniforms and, surprisingly, backpacks and duffel bags. Those government contracts are a big reason Magnolia Bloom survived many tough years, as the factory is the largest employer in the area, with the MacInnes estate coming in an important second place.

The estate and the lovely people on it have already changed me. I had no idea what to expect when I decided to visit the wilds of East Texas, but now I can't imagine not having this wonderfully bizarre and eclectic mix of people in my life.

Yet the ache comes back hard and fast as David continues to tell me about the Broder family plans to soon build a small hospital with an emergency room in Magnolia Bloom. His pride in his grandson Jacob, who will be overseeing the project, is clear in every word. I can't help but wonder if such a facility were available now whether it would have made any difference for Brian Steele, but I push that aside.

By the time I escort him out of the barn, I'm emotionally done. We shake hands again, as awkwardly as the first time, and I agree to come tour the factory next week, and hopefully join his family for a luncheon or dinner soon. His shoulders are sloped as he walks away, but I don't try to alleviate whatever he's feeling. Not only is it not my job, it's not my place. He might be responsible in the strictest sense for my existence, but we are far from being connected.

We may never be, and I didn't realize until now how sad that might make me.

The sound of a diesel engine comes down the road as David's Mercedes disappears, and Lulu races out the door like a canine escapee. I want to laugh as Rory scolds his ovine Houdini, but I can't.

Rory takes one glance my way and jogs over. Without a single word, he engulfs me in his long arms, pulling me against a chest more muscular than his slight build would suggest.

"Hey, you. What's wrong?"

I rub my nose against the hard plane of his shoulder. Why do we try to pretend nothing is wrong when something clearly is?

Humans are so confusing.

"I talked with David Broder. I'm feeling… torn."

"Wanna tell me about it?"

To my shock, I do, but I realize what I want first is much more primal.

I lock eyes with him, letting my hands roam the planes of his chest, over his shoulders, up his neck, and through the soft, red hair definitely needing to see a barber… but I like it. I like that he cares about himself but is not vain. I like that he attends to important things with quiet diligence. I like that he's just… Rory.

I press into him and kiss him, our mouths slow at first, then diving into a hungry, hard, insistent need.

"Do you have time to stay awhile?"

Another thing I like about him is he never plays coy. "I have all the time in the world."

Which is not true, and I simply don't care.

Taking his hand, I lead the way inside, making sure our not-so-little troublemaker is locked downstairs as we make our way to the little apartment above the barn I now feel is entirely mine.

I've never become lovers with a man in such a short time. I've never been able to feel drawn or connected to anyone until I've had time to get to know them. In so many ways, Rory has done all the things I once thought impossible in terms of my relationships. I assume it's because he is simply quiet and kind and filled with gentleness.

I will think about it later.

For now, my fingers are too busy unbuttoning his plaid shirt, and his are yanking my sweater off.

Then our mouths are too busy exploring the new landscapes of skin available to worry about philosophy anytime soon.

29
KIKI

As the pretend world of twelfth-century England swirls around me, I'm grateful to sit for a moment. It seems time has been in fast-forward since Halloween. Before I could grasp it, Thanksgiving came, and we had a perfect day from top to bottom getting Mina and CT married.

The tiny family chapel in the West Tower was perfect for the ceremony. I love the main chapel where most events are held, but the public is never allowed in the small space. It's not because the stained glass in the windows is priceless, but because it's completely reserved for family. It's where every MacInnes baby is christened. It's where the family gathers during times of heartbreak and joy.

Harville stood with his back to the section of stone between two of the famed windows, wearing a suit and his simply embroidered stole. Mina and CT held hands and were completely lost in each other's eyes. There was enough room for Fina and Anders, Fina and Mina's mother, Trey, me, Paige and Zach, Juliette and Rory, and CT's daughters. All the rest of the friends and family were gathered in the ballroom for the big reception.

I saw tears in Fina's eyes when Harville presented Mr. and Mrs.

CT Nelson. I think she believes her look in Anders Jensen's direction was surreptitious, but I saw deep, anguished longing.

Harville brings me out of my reverie when he joins me in the back corner at one of the smaller round tables I've claimed in the near darkness.

"Hi, you." He leans over and gives me a quick kiss.

I put my hand on his chest. "What is wrong with you? There's a hundred people here."

"None of whom know me, and even if they do, we're in the darkest corner, hiding like teenagers."

I hear the teasing in his voice, but I chose the spot for exactly that reason. The darkness, not the teenager thing. By the nature of the beast, I've been impossibly busy today and the recipient of a lot of compliments about how incredible the castle looks with all the Christmas decorations in place. The entire castle staff as well as Fina and I needed a regiment of masseuses for the cramps coming on after our grand finale transformation into all things holly, pinecone, and red and green… and no small amount of Scottish blue and white.

I force my thoughts back to the memory of standing in the grand entryway and looking up, literally catching my breath at the winter wonderland we created. Every barking muscle was worth it.

"Come back."

I try to clear my head, but it's hard. "Old habits. When things get uncomfortable, distract."

"Where'd you go?"

"I was thinking about how amazing the castle looks. I'm about done in from all the work to get it done so Mina's wedding would be perfect, and the gardeners and grounds crew all deserve big giant medals, or big raises, for all the outside work. I like driving around and coming in through the front to feel like I'm stepping back in time. It's magical."

"Do you rub Penny's nose?"

I snort a little. "Every time. I think I might have made one side of her snout uneven."

"She'll forgive you."

Ouch. He had no way to know his words are a gut-punch reminder that, sure, the stone dragon might absolve any number of sins, but that wasn't going to extend t0—

"Dance with me."

I look at the hand he holds out to me, the hand of the man I have oh-so-unfortunately fallen face first in love with. The man who has no idea—

"Quit thinking and come dance with me."

I force all the crazy, mixed-up thoughts back into the corner and stand on legs a little wobbly, not from fatigue, but from the replay my brain is doing.

The man I've fallen face first in love with.

The easy waltz lets me get my bearings as I'm shown, once again, my sexy pastor is a good dancer. It surprised me to find I'm pretty decent myself, now that I'm doing it sober. We segue into a West Coast swing leaving us both a little out of breath, then end with a slow rumba we're dangerously close to turning into a classic in-place, side-to-side prom dance.

I know I'm wearing a stupid grin as he goes to grab us servings of punch. The cucumber mint recipe isn't too sweet, and we both need the hydration and the cooling.

I'm almost ready when he takes my hand and kisses my knuckles, looking deep into my eyes.

"Kiki, I—"

"Excuse me, are you Rebecca MacInnes?"

I look over his shoulder at the middle-aged man who looks like he's more comfortable in a biker bar, his jeans and boots jarring against the backdrop of renaissance pageantry. I drop Harville's hand and pull back instinctively, every nerve going on red alert.

"Yes?"

He hands me an envelope. "You've been served."

Without another word, he pivots and walks away, not making a scene, but a lot of eyes follow him nonetheless.

Nausea climbs my throat at the plain manila envelope. My hands tremble as I open the package as carefully as if it were booby-trapped. In a way, I suppose it is.

"What is it?" Harville's voice is full of concern and care and all the things I desperately love about him. Things I can now officially declare as over. I can read the basics in the light cast from the candles on the table.

"It's a subpoena to appear at a deposition in the divorce trial of Colonel Sassman."

"Who?"

I lick my lips, shame covering me like I've been doused in cold water. "The superior officer I had an affair with in Alaska, who was with me when I had the DUI costing me my career."

I knew it would happen eventually, but despair still overwhelms as I look out over the ballroom and see such happiness all around me. Fina and Anders and Juliette and Rory are all on the dance floor, all sending out waves of happiness and connection. For about ten seconds, I had that. I had an incredible man look at me with hunger, with a desire not influenced by any man-made substances.

He reaches for me, but I pull away. There's no point trying to soft-serve anything now.

"I was involved with him for a year. This was no one-night stand I can blame on my copious use of alcohol. On so many levels, everything about what I did was wrong, not only legally but certainly morally. The only reason I was allowed to separate honorably—insert ironic laugh here—is because his family is extremely wealthy and powerful. I did not ask, but they intervened, and my DUI was reduced to running a red light and swept completely under the rug. I was given the... opportunity to separate so nothing got out about the affair that might damage Sassman's future political ambitions. Apparently, his hope has come unmoored."

"But—"

I stand and back away, grabbing my shawl off my chair, clutching it to my stomach like a shield.

"There aren't any buts, Harville. I was going to tell you about the disaster that was my life culminating in a nuclear detonation in Alaska. I just wanted a friend who didn't know what a monster of a human being I am." Tears slide down my nose as I take another step away. "For a little while."

I turn and run, ignoring his call to wait.

Kicking off my shoes, I grab them in my trembling hands and run for all I'm worth to my suite, grab my keys and purse, and then pound down the turret steps and out the back. I hear steps crunch on the gravel behind me, but whatever delayed Harville has given me enough time to get to my car, start the engine, and race away.

I drive aimlessly, clutching the cairngorm necklace I rarely take off. I'm coming up on a neon sign when the stone goes hot in my hand, and I find myself pulling into the parking lot of a dive bar on the outskirts of Atlanta. With the car stopped, I look at the smoky stone in confusion. This isn't the first time it's heated against my skin, and I've tried to pay attention when it's happened, but I find it a little odd that Paige's—or rather, Alyssa's—magical stone would lead an alcoholic to a bar.

Ignoring the twinkle lights and animatronic Santa and sleigh on the small bit of grass, I walk through the wooden door to an unexpected interior. I presumed to be assaulted by various levels of dust, dirt, and stale beer, but instead I find it older and scarred, but clean. As I couldn't give a good goddamn about the décor, only the labels behind the bar, I put the surprise aside.

For a Friday night, the place is dead. Maybe it's not late enough, but whatever the reason, it's me, the bartender, and a jukebox.

I sit on the stool at the end with my back to the wall. I never saw combat, but I served with lots who did, and it's a habit I picked up from them, so… not surprising. I spent a lot of time in bars of varying degrees of respectability, making the pretense of security somehow logical in my fuzzy brain.

The bartender walks over to me, flipping a towel over his shoulder, and I almost snort at the level of stereotype going on.

"You're a bit overdressed for this place." He braces both hands on the bar, his expression open but not in the gross come-on kind of way. "Runaway bride?"

"No, period-themed Christmas party." I put my purse on the counter and try to nip the conversation in the bud. "Vodka, neat. House is fine."

The man straightens and walks down to the center of the bar, but I'm too busy picking at a cuticle to notice much more.

Except when he returns, he puts a normal glass with clear liquid in it, bubbles happily chasing each other to the top.

"That's not vodka." I look up and frown.

"It appears you're both smart and pretty."

I snort. "You need some work on your pickup lines there, buddy."

"You're one-for-one. My name is Buddy."

I tilt my head and give him a full, "Come on."

He takes out his wallet and hands me his driver's license. "Buddy Gene Autry."

"Okay, now I know this is fake. Gene Autry? Really?"

"Yup. I have a sister named—"

"Don't tell me. Loretta Lynn Autry."

"Close. Loretta Gayle." He wipes down the already pristinely clean bar in front of me. "So, you still active duty?"

I look around, wondering how I'm being punked. I had no plan to stop, much less this place of all places, so no film crew could have arrived before me.

"All my vets come to this end of the bar. Right there in particular."

"I thought only jarheads were so predictable."

"I can usually pick out a fellow Marine in about ten seconds. My gut says you're either a swabbie or a zoomie, and my mama says I'm half witch."

"Wouldn't that be half warlock?"

"If you're being picky, I suppose."

"I haven't heard 'zoomie' in ages."

"I'm old enough to be your daddy, so we'll call it a generation gap."

I push the soda closer to his hand. "I don't think you're collecting Social Security yet, and this still isn't vodka."

"You listen to country music?"

I pause, frowning at the non sequitur. "Sometimes."

"You like Kenny Chesney?"

"Well enough, I guess."

"Ever listen to the song *The Good Stuff*?"

"Can you just get right to the CliffsNotes?"

Buddy gives the bar another wipe, then throws the towel back over his shoulder. "Guy walks into a bar to drown his sorrows. Fight with his old lady. Bartender gives him a glass of milk and tells him about diving into a bottle when he lost his wife and how he finally found the good stuff, and it wasn't whiskey."

"That sounds familiar, though I don't know why you're playing Dr. Phil. I'm not here because of a fight."

Buddy shifts so his hip is against the industrial ice machine to his left. "Hmm. My Spidey sense is off, it appears. Why don't you tell me about it while I try to find the Tito's?"

I pull the glass back and take a sip of the lemon-lime bubbles. "Do you always extort your patrons?"

"Only the ones who go to meetings on Tuesdays in Atlanta and recently got a new chip."

My eyes jerk to Buddy's, and it takes me a minute to put it together. I made the Tuesday meeting only a few times. Wednesdays or Sundays are my regular days.

"Of all the gin joints in all the towns," I mutter under my breath.

"Maybe the angels directed you to mine."

The door opens, and a trio of men come in, offering a hello to Buddy but heading straight for the pool tables.

"Excuse me a sec." Buddy moves to the taps and expertly draws a pitcher of Bud Light and takes it and three mugs to the guys racking up for their first game.

"Isn't the reformed-alcoholic bartender stretching credulity a bit much?" I don't mean to be a bitch, but I don't have a lot of space right now for being a good girl.

"You might be surprised at how many bartenders don't drink. Owning a bar can be some pretty successful aversion therapy. In my case, I've managed to cultivate a clientele generally coming in to play pool, watch a football game, or shoot the shit for a while. The dirtbags opt for the place about two miles on down, which is fine with me."

"I appreciate the chitchat and all, but you're not my sponsor or my therapist, so why don't you be my bartender and find that bottle?"

"If that's what you really want." He reaches under the counter, pulls out a quart of Tito's, and sets a tumbler in front of me. "But is it?"

I look at the familiar beige label with the bronze metallic stripe across the bottom.

"Yeah, it really, really is." But I don't reach for it.

"Is it gonna fix anything?"

"Have we begun the rhetorical-questions part of the evening?"

"Yup."

So I tell my new friend Buddy the short version of the story. It's not like there's any reason not to. He listens patiently as I spill the ugly truth, taking my glass to top it off with fresh soda and putting it between me and the bottle.

"Subtle."

Buddy nods. "That's my middle name."

"Your middle name is Gene."

My phone buzzes for at least the tenth time, and I pull it out of my purse. Whatever has happened, I have no excuse for being a heartless jerk all night long.

I read through his texts and sniff back a tear.

SP (as I have him in my call list): Please tell me you're okay.

Me: I'm not okay, but I'm not hurt or in a ditch somewhere. I need some space. I'm sorry.

I turn my phone off and toss it away.

Buddy comes back from delivering more drinks to the pool players and a quartet of guys who've also come in and staked their claim on a table by the big screen TV.

"So don't you think the sexy pastor gets a say in this?"

"Were you hiding in the bridal salon while I was talking to Wynona?" I suppose his statement isn't that odd, but still, it's a little weird to have my words thrown back at me almost verbatim.

"Pardon?"

I give him the abridged version of my bridezilla turning into a blushing bride.

"So you can give good advice, but you're now going to explain why you're terminally unique."

I give him a huff and take another sip of soda. "You're a pain in the ass, you know?"

He uses a handheld dispenser to make himself a cola, and I decide not to tease him when he tips in cherry juice from a Costco-sized jar of maraschinos.

Apparently his middle name should be *Patient*, instead of *Gene* or *Subtle*, because he just stands there and lets the silence linger. When he eventually puts his glass next to mine, he offers, "I might not be *your* sponsor, but I am *a* sponsor."

I pull out a five-dollar bill from my purse and push it across the bar. "I should get back."

I stand and put my wrap around me. It's not nearly enough against the mid-December wind, but I only have to get back to my car.

"There's a twenty-four-hour package store on the other side of Atlanta. Turn left out of the parking lot."

I frown. "What kind of sponsor are you?"

"One who's been around awhile and one who relapsed pretty spectacularly before I got serious. If you need to go that route, you might as well get it over with. Just don't drink until you get home. That's all I ask."

My keys are hard and cold in my hand. "Been there. Got the refrigerator magnet." I step away, then turn back. "Thanks."

He puts the Tito's back under the bar and reracks the tumbler. Then he tosses a business card at me with an expert flick of his wrist.

"Call me if you need to talk."

I put the card in my purse and hitch the strap back on my shoulder. The clack of pool balls covers my heel taps as I walk out, the cold air slapping me after the warmth of Buddy's place.

I get in my car and drive to the exit, sitting at the edge of the asphalt for a long time. With a sigh and the way clear, I press the accelerator and turn right.

30
FINA

"I swear there's nothing sexier than a man seeing a beautiful woman in his dress shirt."

I know I blush, but I stay put in the doorway where I've been watching him. I thought he fell asleep, needing a nap after our relentless drive to know every inch of each other's skin. Clearly, I was wrong.

I picked up his shirt from the chair and put it on to have his scent against my skin despite the insanely expensive kimono-inspired robe lying right next to his classic white button-down. The gift was sweet, and even I know enough about Carine Gilson to appreciate the thought and the expense of the lingerie, but no matter how sexy and sensual the pale rose silk is, the swish of his oxford weave feels a thousand times more intimate.

And I'm vain enough to admit the classic shirttail hem shows off my legs.

"You can't have it back yet."

"You can keep it. For now."

The low growl in his throat makes my blush heat. I wonder where this teasing vixen has come from whose words keep popping out of my mouth when I'm with him.

We haven't had that much time together since he's come back into my life like an unexpected storm. He arrived on Halloween and sidled up next to every atom in my body. Even with the sadness of losing Brian, it has been a whirlwind of reconnection and lots and lots of sex crammed into his visit. He came back for Mina's wedding, and now we've brazenly snuck out of the Yule Ball, assuaging our consciences that everyone is having too good a time to notice. Besides, we've promised each other we'll get back in time for the feast. People might notice if we aren't at the head table, but we have a little time. Which we intend to use wisely.

I had no idea I missed it so much—all of *it*. Flirting, dancing, acting like a couple. Finding out I'm quite comfortable with the term *wanton*.

Or rather, I had no idea I was able to push lock away this part of me so completely, stuffing it down with a ferocity making the escape startling to both of us.

"You are so incredibly beautiful."

The words are whispered, but I hear them. More, my soul hears them.

I push away from the doorframe and try to do my best sexy-cat crawl onto the bed and on top of him, enjoying every hot inch of his skin sliding against mine as I settle my thighs on each side of his hips.

"Mmmm... that's nice."

His hands move to my backside, and he shifts me to exactly where he wants me. The warm scent of sex and skin and sleep are a heavenly perfume as I lie on him, my head naturally finding the perfect spot under his chin, the sound of his quickly increasing heartbeat under my ear.

I am more than happy to let nature take her course, and by the time Anders joins me in a hot shower, every muscle in my body is weak and utterly content. I eventually stopped counting the times I've orgasmed and accept I'm happy to leave the top number limitless.

Anders takes over the sexy lean against the bathroom wall as he watches me brush out my hair. I didn't give a second's thought to playing coy last night when he asked me to stay with him, so I came prepared with everything I'd need for several days.

The rest of tonight will be taken up by the ball, then tomorrow we'll have a family breakfast. Then he has to go home.

Which is as it should be, but I'm finding I have a selfish streak inside me I never knew about. All I want is to grab Anders's hand and drag him away, run to where no one can talk to him, or to me, or do anything to interrupt my education in how amazing sex can be at fifty-nine. I had no idea, but I'm quite willing to continue my intense and dedicated study and more than willing to let Anders continue to be my teacher.

I turn off the dryer and meet his eyes in the mirror. "If you keep looking at me like that, we're going to be late for the feast."

As if my words are an invitation, he moves behind me and wraps his arms around my waist, pulling me back against the undeniable evidence of his choice of our next activity. Burying his face in my neck, he uses one hand to sweep away the heavy length of my hair to kiss my spine. "I'm hungry, but not for chicken."

He lets me turn around, and I wrap my hands around his neck as he lifts me onto the counter, and it's the most natural thing in the world to wrap my legs around him and welcome him back.

As his mouth takes mine, a throaty laugh escapes, and he pulls back so he can see me.

"I'm amusing you?"

"In every wonderful—oh, nice—way."

Words aren't possible after that. Then we have to take another shower. And I have to dry my hair again.

I put the brush down and start my practiced twist only to find my hands stilled by his.

"Leave it down."

I have an anxious clench in my stomach. I never wear my hair loose.

"I don't—"

"Please. For me."

I put the decorative clip on the counter and let it all fall. He runs his fingers through the heavy strands, from my crown to where they end in the middle of my back.

"I want to do this every day for the rest of our lives."

I freeze, looking at him, but his attention is on my shoulders as he pulls my hair forward into a cascade down my chest.

"Anders, this has been wonderful and all, but—"

"And it's just the beginning."

"I don't think we should get ahead of ourselves. I mean—"

"I finally have you again. I'm not letting you go."

My feminist ire gets heated. "I think I have a little to say about this."

He stops his playing and looks at me, surprised. "Of course. I just thought things were wonderful."

"They are, but you seem to be making assumptions about a future we haven't begun to discuss."

His fingers still. "Do you not want a future? An us?"

Do I? After all this time, do I want the complication of having someone in my life, demanding my time? There are moments I'm jealous of Mina and the joy she has found, but at others I get vastly irritated every one of her decisions is preceded with, *Let me call and talk to CT*. What happened to making a decision and doing what she wants?

I put one hand on his chest and stroke his cheek with the other. "I'm overwhelmed at the moment. Give me some time, okay?"

He kisses me, a long, slow melding of our mouths making both of our blood pressures start to rise and our hands wander to body parts conveniently exposed.

And we're going to be very late.

31
KIKI

THE YULE BALL is still in full swing when I make my way back to the castle. I hope Fina is dancing her slippers off with her handsome Scandinavian. I have my fingers crossed she'll get a happy ending like Mina has, but Fina's keeping her feelings close to the vest. That's her nature, but it feels deeper, like she's afraid, but I hope I'm projecting.

On a whim, I drive up the long entryway to the front of the castle and park. I scramble for the jacket I needed back at Buddy's but left in my minuscule back seat. Maybe a quick chat with Penny will help leaving behind the first place I've felt connected again less horrible.

I get out, shrugging into the anorak jacket that had saved my bacon in Alaska, and pull up the hood before shoving my fingers into the gloves waiting in the pockets. The chill of the fabric quickly warms, and I almost look around to see if anyone's watching my silly mission.

The fountain's dry because we've had a few days below freezing, but Penny seems unperturbed by the chill. She rests her chin on her front leg, her wings splayed as though she's just flown in, gotten settled, and is about to furl them around her. I've always held this fantasy that if I could snuggle up next to her, she'd wrap those beautiful wings around me in a cocoon of beauty and strength, and for a hot second, I'd feel… safe.

I settle on the stone wall, removing my gloves so I can feel her cold nose as I stroke it.

"Hi, Penny. I've missed you. I think I'll miss you more this time when I leave, because for a brief minute, I thought this would be home."

I wish she could answer me. I wonder if she'll miss me or if she watches the centuries of the comings and goings of the humans around here in amusement. Or exasperation.

And I wonder if she can see my tears as my words echo in my brain. Searching my pockets delivers a sad, crumpled tissue, but it's enough to keep me from looking like a toddler after a tantrum.

"There you are."

His voice comes from behind me, and I glare at Penny, feeling a little betrayed.

"How'd you know I was here?" I ask without turning around, because I know who's there.

"I had this feeling all of a sudden. I was skulking about the back parking lot, to be honest, watching for your car. Then I had this urge to say hi to Penny."

"You should go home. It has to be almost midnight."

"Close, I think. I wasn't really watching the time."

Harville moves around me to sit on the ledge, facing me but reaching over to stroke behind Penny's ear.

"I don't need a watcher, or a babysitter."

"I'm not trying to be either. I'm trying to be your friend."

"There's the problem, but with everything blowing up in my face, there's no use pretending anymore. I don't want to just be your friend. This has all happened so fast, and I've tried to get a handle on it, but at least the good thing from the evening's events is I haven't shamed you publicly."

"You wouldn't have shamed me."

I close my eyes, trying to will the tears to recede. "I can never outrace the shadow of the things I've done, and I refuse to let you bear any damage on my behalf."

He's so quiet I eventually open my eyes, half expecting him to be gone.

"No member of the clergy is ever glad someone has made poor decisions. What you've endured breaks my heart, but all the things in your past, no matter how dark or poorly chosen, brought you here. And I can't be sad about that."

"You have no idea what I've—"

"Done? You told me."

I grip the edge of the fountain, the concrete cutting into my fingers. "After what you've gone through with your divorce, you're saying it doesn't bother you I had an affair with a man I knew was married? I can't dilute it, deny it, or deflect it."

"Would you do it again?"

"No. I can look back at my choices while I was headfirst in the deep end of a bottle of vodka with a lot of clarity now, but my alcoholism does not excuse my behavior."

"I know enough people battling addiction to know the person they were before is nothing like the person they are now. Those who truly deal with their problems and do their level best to make amends are far, far better people than they were before. You've been through hell, Kiki, and came out of it like a phoenix or, if you want another analogy, purified in the crucible."

"I appreciate the absolution. I really do, and I can deal with what people think of me. The problem is I would damage my family." My voice catches, and it's hard for me to finish. "I would damage you."

"I'm hurt you think I'm so fragile."

I'm stunned a laugh escapes. "I've thought of a ton of words for you. Amazing. Kind. Intelligent. Funny. Sexy as all get-out. Fragile wasn't ever a consideration for the list."

"Then believe that I'm strong enough to deal with any blowback from what happens. You don't even know if the news will reach here."

"Oh, it will, because people like Delores will go looking for it." I shift on the stone, the cold leaching into my thighs. "Do you know a fish will rarely outgrow its tank?"

He frowns. "No, but I'm feeling there's an analogy you're going for here."

"I've been in a fish tank all my life. I've swum in other people's expectations for me." I clench my fingers again, determined to say it all. "This is going to sound really, really stupid, but part of the reason I let things go down the wrong path with the guy in Alaska is because it was so forbidden. Added to the fact I already felt I was irredeemable, it was the perfect storm for me to excuse my behavior to myself."

"I get it. You made some bad choices, but I also get you aren't that person anymore. Moreover, you want to be a better person because you've looked into the darkness and don't want to live there ever again."

I stand and back away, struggling to put literal and metaphorical distance between us. "What you don't understand is I love you, and I won't let you sacrifice your vocation because of me."

I execute an about-face, but he stops me.

"Kiki, please don't run."

"I'm not running. I'm slowly and deliberately walking away. You might have counseled addicts, but you've never lived with one, and in this arena, I know more than you do. If you pursue a relationship with me, it's going to hurt you, and I cannot allow that."

I follow through this time, walking into the foyer and past the porters we've assigned to stay until the last guests have made it to their rooms. If I could see past the tears in my eyes, I'd probably be able to address them by name, but it's all I can do to make it up the stairs and push my way into my apartment, fall onto my bed…

And cry.

32
JULIETTE

THE WEDDING WAS LOVELY, the reception beautiful. Afterward, I enjoyed learning more about American Thanksgiving. Then the Yule Ball was a second delightful chance to dress up in costume, although we had to leave Lulu out. I've spent more nights than not in Rory's arms.

So why am I so out of sorts?

It's not because he had to leave my bed so early. He has help, of course, but he's in charge of the sheep, and he's already warned me that there is nothing more intrusive on a relationship than animals and children. Thankfully, we have to worry only about one of the two.

The door opens, and I look up, expecting to see him coming back for something he left behind, or maybe even an extra good-morning kiss.

Instead, I find myself looking at my sister's angry face.

I'm taken aback, but I manage to regain some composure. "What are you doing here?"

"I heard from Terrance at Sotheby's. He says you're not answering about the position."

"And you flew eight thousand kilometers to tell me something I am aware of?"

"I—

Baaa.

Noelle stops her advance into the room and stares at my new companion, who Rory and I have decided is mine, whether I think I have any say in it or not.

"Why is there a sheep in here?"

"Her name is Lulu, she's a serial escapee from one of the flocks on the estate, and she has decided I'm her human."

"I'm sure there's a fascinating story there, but I decided there was no use trying to talk to you over the phone, so I came over."

I wave to the small table and busy myself making us tea. I'm the coffee drinker of the two of us. Noelle won't touch it.

She's stirring in a small spoon of sugar when I restart the conversation. "This is where you tell me why you flew all the way from Paris to Dallas, rented a car, and arrived here without first sending so much as a text. I might not have been here, you know."

"What communication we have had has made it fairly clear you aren't leaving anytime soon."

I let my look linger between us.

She frowns and drinks her tea. "And I might have had to hand-deliver a purchase to a buyer in Dallas, and since my flight was already paid for by the client, I decided to spend the money on a car to come talk some sense into you."

Now that makes more sense. We have any number of high-end clients who pay the exorbitant cost for Noelle to hand-carry their purchases directly to them. Because of it, she's seen about every country on this planet, while leaving me blissfully behind to do my work.

I suck in a deep breath and try to get my reactions, pinging in every conceivable direction, under control.

"I've missed you." Apparently, my confession surprises her, because it's a long moment before she responds.

"I've missed you, too."

"If you'd talk to me, you'd know how much I want, still want, to share all of this with you." I wave a hand around the beautiful workspace I've claimed, but include the wider estate in the gesture.

"I've been waiting for you to get over the honeymoon phase and get back to work."

I'm afraid my frown is going to cause a permanent indentation between my brows. "I have been working. I sent you pictures of the paintings I'm restoring."

"Yes, but these aren't works we can put in our gallery. You're giving away weeks and weeks of work for free, and the store can't afford that."

I stare at her, beyond confused. Noelle and I have been insanely, ridiculously lucky. Yes, we work hard, but we somehow hit a niche from the very beginning and have the most amazing, loyal customers anyone could ask for.

"You've spent our entire lives playing Chicken Little. I review our financials every week, more if things are busy. We spent decades building a reputation for finding breathtaking artwork in many modalities, leaving us both financially comfortable in an industry known for being capricious at best. The truth is, neither one of us has to work a day again if we don't want to."

She pulls back as though I've slapped her. "We're too young to retire."

"I didn't say I want to. I said we don't have to work at the breakneck speed we've maintained for twenty years."

"But this is finally the position you've always wanted, to be able to showcase women artists from all over the world."

"You keep seeing these events as happening right now, but you don't see I've been hungry for something different for a long time. You haven't heard one word about how I love it here. You dismiss this all as a lark. There was a time when this position at Sotheby's would have been a dream come true, but every time I think about it, all that comes up for me is why I don't want it, not why I do."

I can tell she wants to deny my words, but she remains rigid. "I should get going then, as this is pointless."

"So you're just going to leave? Not meet any of our family while you're here?"

"My family is in Arbois. It pains me you've forgotten and would continue to hurt Maman and Papa—"

Anger roils up in me and spews out before I can contain it. "Enough! If you've been talking to our parents, you would know I speak to them often. Maman has said she hopes I find what I need here and that she and Papa know my love for them is not threatened. This is your issue, Noelle, not our parents', and it's time you stopped using them to try to bully me into doing what you want."

Her mouth moves, but no sound comes out. Her response is to grab her purse off the table and storm out, leaving me and Lulu looking at the door with sad eyes.

I do the only thing I can do, which is dive into my work to distract my tear-filled heart. It's where Rory finds me when he stops by a few hours later.

I wasn't aware how much I've come to depend on his daily visits, which turn into nights together, but it's the connection I feel with him filling my soul right now, more than the sex... good as it is.

"Hey, you okay?" He runs his hand down my back, holding me close as I launch myself into his arms.

He has no idea how different this behavior is for me, to seek out physical connection and comfort when I'm upset. I'll tell him sometime. For now, I want his gentle embrace.

Lulu moves in and forces herself between our thighs, determined to be an inseparable part of our trio. We share an indulgent laugh, but don't let go.

"My sister came by."

"I heard. She confused the heck out of the secretary at the castle because she thought Noelle was you and didn't understand why you were asking for directions to find yourself."

I can understand their confusion, as I've dealt with it my entire life. I wish I could claim a franc for every time someone started talking to me, sure I was Noelle, only to be embarrassed and confused when I had to clarify.

"With my hair getting long, I can see the problem. You normally can tell us apart by my short style, but right now, we truly do look like mirror images."

"Do you want to come to my place? I'll fix us some dinner, and you can tell me all about it?"

I have learned Rory is a good cook, and I've enjoyed more than a few evenings at his table. His son, Kaden, often joins us, his daughter, Lilith, a time or two, as well. The younger Campbell is very much his father's son, although his hair is a darker russet brown than Rory's vibrant red. Temperamentally, though, they are much the same, and I enjoy the son's quiet nature almost as much as the father's. Still, I'm never sad when he bids us good-night and leaves me with the more mature Campbell and an empty house.

By the time we make the drive to his small home on the other side of the property and put Lulu in the fenced backyard, I've gone from upset to deeply sad. I give inordinate attention to the salad I've been tasked with preparing while Rory puts spiced rice into hollowed tomato and bell pepper shells and pops them into the oven.

While they cook, I try to explain my complicated relationship with my sibling.

"I love my sister. We are so close in so many ways, but this is the first time I have utterly defied her, and neither one of us is quite sure where to go now."

"Don't be mad at me, but she seems a little bossy."

I chuckle, the sound wry. "It would be silly for me to deny it, but I must be honest and tell you I didn't mind for a long time. Noelle has this restless, endless energy, and she is a whirlwind of brilliant ideas and plans for our ventures. It's why we've been so successful. It allows me to stay back in my shop and do what I love just as much. Unlike siblings who fight because they both want to be the boss, we've been happy with Noelle as the brains of our operation."

"You don't exactly have a deficit in the intelligence department."

"Of course not. I merely mean our disparate styles served us perfectly. We never fought, because we were each doing the piece we did well, and our partnership ran like a Swiss watch."

"And now you're threatening it."

"Nothing has ever had the power to claim my attention away from work." I take a sip of the crisp wine he's poured for us and look at him over the rim. "Until you."

His smile is so Rory. Slow and sweet and eye-crinkling. "I like that." He clinks his glass against mine. "I never thought I'd catch the eye of a woman as stunning as you. You take my breath away and I have to admit you are way out of my league."

I choke on my pinot and have to clear my throat. "I've never been described quite so touchingly. Details about me usually include a question of whether I'm a savant or on the spectrum because my social skills can be rather… awkward."

"That seems awfully harsh."

I shrug. "Noelle is so much my opposite and has all the energy and vivacity our clientele wants. Most people leave me alone, and I've been quite content. Being here, meeting this whole new family, has been amazing, and I find I like being more social. It makes no sense, but I don't feel like such an odd duck here."

"I'm glad. I keep praying that whatever's happening is enough to keep you here. I don't want you to leave."

I slowly turn the stem of my glass between my fingers. "Is that our only option? Me staying here?"

He takes a long time to answer, which I appreciate more than most people might. "I don't know. I've never had a thought to leaving the estate. Leaving Texas."

"You know we have sheep in France. And my home is mere kilometers from the source of Lulu's bloodline."

He glances out the sliding glass door to where Lulu is contentedly munching on grass in the backyard. "I know. And I'm not necessarily opposed. I never had a reason to even consider it."

With the comfort I've grown so accustomed to, we finish our dinner in the quiet of our own minds. It's such a treasure to be able to be with someone like this. No need for idle chatter, although that's fine when it happens.

But Rory is simply… peace.

And now I've met David and answered those questions. And I'm close to being done with Gavina's paintings. And now my sister has reminded me I have a business and a home waiting for me…

I have to decide what I want. What is right for me.

And I'm not sure I know how to do that.

33
FINA

My body's numb as I kill time, waiting for Anders to be done with his meetings. My mind replays the evening of the Yule Ball, which was everything I imagined and more. I was glad when Anders had to leave the dais to mingle with the crowd as it gave me a chance to process the flood of memories overwhelming me. My vantage point from the queen's chair and the flicker of torches created the perfect ambience as well as the distance I needed to sort through my whirling thoughts. Although Anders and I were never the "royals" at any events we attended all those years ago, we sat beside each other at many a feast, both above and below the salt. Tonight had been equally as magical.

The decorations were perfection, not only because the castle is always jaw-dropping in opulence at Christmastime, but the candles turned the ballroom into a medieval fantasy the likes I'd never attended. And I attended a lot of SCA events back in the day.

It was as if Anders and I were kids again, in so many ways, but this was so much better, so much richer, so much more than two teenagers groping in the dark, completely uncertain of their own bodies.

Anders lavished me with attention, and we had a ball—no pun intended—playing King Henry the Second and Eleanor of Aquitaine.

He looked mouthwatering in his tunic and hose, and my bliaut was intricately embroidered blue silk, the ornamental girdle soft yellow, and my belt bright gold. All of it a perfect foil for my white velvet cape. I know velvet had not been invented at our pretend time period, but doubt anyone else would have such obscure knowledge of medieval fabric and fashion. In that spirit, I honored Anders's request and left my hair loose and long under my coronet, forgoing the barbette credited to Eleanor.

His employees were all delightful, and even though he had to spend a good amount of time playing host, the rest was spent at my side on the dais, or in each other's arms on the dance floor. We did a bit of period dancing, but it quickly devolved into modern music, but we were certainly willing to roll with the anachronism.

I hate to admit it, but I've had a sense of tension ever since the night of the Yule Ball ended. Anders extended his stay these extra two days, and we had some kind of silent agreement not to talk about anything serious, but he's about to go home, and the feeling of the other shoe about to drop has expanded my thoughts to bursting.

I try to deflect my discomfort by reminding myself I've spent more time here in his room than in my own duplex this past week, and I don't have a single regret.

"What are you smiling at?" His words jar me out of the past, his tone carrying his own curiosity and amusement.

"Just thinking you haven't lost your touch. I think you had me out of my chemise and hose faster than I can ever remember."

"Hopefully there haven't been too many others as anxious as me to get you naked."

I cut him a terse look. "You don't think I've been celibate and pining for you all these decades, do you?"

"No, but I have been doing a lot of thinking about making disrobing you my favorite new game moving forward."

There it is. That going-forward shoe. And it feels like a size-twelve steel-toed work boot.

I can't hide my distress, and my anxious fingers have slowed while unbuttoning his shirt.

He uses a gentle knuckle to raise my chin. "What is it? Why do you freeze up every time I start talking about the future?"

"Because I've been enjoying our time together and savoring every second, but we both know it's going to end again. I don't want to waste a precious moment of this."

"Why does it have to end? We aren't teenagers anymore. I'm not an exchange student with no choices but to go home."

"No, you're an unfathomably wealthy businessman who has no choice but to go home and tend to his company."

"But this time you can go with me."

"Oh, I can? You mean because I'm just a business manager in a little Podunk town in East Texas, there's no reason I won't hightail it out on your fancy jet?"

"That's not—"

"I have family here, Anders. My mother is here, and she's starting to get a little frail. Mina's here. My MacInnes family. I have a job here, a life here."

"I understand, but you always wanted to travel, see the world. We can do that now."

"If Violet were still here, and Mina weren't married and gallivanting all across the globe, then maybe I could say yes, but Violet's gone, and Mina is going to be busy with her new life."

"So you're expected to give up your entire life for your job? Your happiness doesn't finally deserve priority?"

Hot tears flood my eyes. "Please don't do this to me. Not now. Maybe we can talk about this after—"

"No. I tried to reach you forty years ago, and you didn't even read my letters. So I'll be clear and up front this time." He takes my hands and kisses each palm. "Fina, I love you. I've loved you since I was seventeen. I think we have a lot of good years left to spend together, but I'm not waiting any longer. I want to marry you. I want you to gallivant with me and see all the places we talked about as starry-eyed teenagers."

He lets go of my hands and steps back, running an agitated hand over his head to cup the back of his neck.

"I'm stepping down as CEO of the company. I've got some smaller ventures I've wanted to play with for a long time, and I'm putting them in motion. I'm done with eighty-hour workweeks and million-air-mile credits. I want to spend my remaining years with you. I love you, Fina."

I close my eyes, but despite my best efforts, a tear slips down my cheek. I open them again and try to smile. "I love you, Anders. I've never stopped. But there isn't an easy solution to this."

He stands and moves over to the suitcase almost ready to be closed sitting on the caddy. He drops something inside my watery eyes can't make out, then latches it shut.

"I'm not asking you to walk out the door with me today, but I am telling you this. I'm not waiting forty more years. I have to go home today, but I'll have my pilot come back and stay at the airfield until noon on the twenty-third. If you want me, all you have to do is call, and he'll wait for you. If you don't, he'll return home so he can spend Christmas with his family."

"Wait. You're leaving a jet waiting for me?"

"Yes. And if you decide to join me, I'll be at my house until Christmas evening. Then I'm off early the next morning to Australia for six weeks and then New Zealand for a month. I'm not sure where I'm going from there."

"You're walking away from your career?"

"In a way. I'll consult, and like I said, I have other irons in the fire. I want time for me now. And I want you to join me."

I watch as he hefts his suitcase and drapes his blazer over his arm. I'm frozen on the bed. He's leaving. He's leaving… again.

"I thought… We have the rest of the day—"

"It's best if I go. I've said all I can say. Shown you in every way I know how that I love you. It's up to you now."

And then he's gone.

If I thought I knew what a broken heart was forty years ago, the agony crushing me now proves how innocent I was.

34
KIKI

Even though the stained glass in the castle's family chapel isn't well lit in the morning hours since the windows face west, it's still a stunning place to sit in silence while trying to make sense of the world. Each window is an exquisite piece of art commissioned by Evajean and then Gavina. I know absolutely nothing about art, so I know only that one window is by an Irish artist named Sarah Purser and one is by Mary Lowndes because I had to have all of the artwork reevaluated for insurance when I first came on board. I did a dive down an internet rabbit trail when they piqued my interest. Today, I look at each masterpiece on display, and I'm stunned to be surrounded, almost literally, by such beauty.

I've never been much of one for churches or chapels, and I sure can't explain what has brought me up here. I started to go down to the mechanic's bay, where my project car sits neglected, deciding I might as well do something useful and start the deconstruction process if I'm going to play insomnia roulette and lose. Instead, I find myself in one of the padded chairs in this place that has listened to the prayers of every generation of MacInnes women.

If I were the fanciful sort, I'd say I can feel the legends who came before me, sense their presence, their power, their perseverance, but one thing I've never been accused of being is imaginative. I've always been a nose-to-the-grindstone kind of gal. All I seem to be able to do lately is bury myself under a mountain of work, or naval-gaze and ponder what I'm going to do.

The truth is, I'm lost, and while I've won the vodka battle since my embarrassment in front of Harville, I know I have to shore up my defenses because this isn't going to get any easier. I've been counting the days, needing to get through the holiday, as I don't want to disrupt anyone's lives any more than I already will by leaving, but today is the twenty-third. After the Christmas Eve dinner tomorrow, I can make my escape.

The chapel door opens, startling me, and Fina jumps as well.

"I'm sorry, dear. I didn't know you were in here. I mean, I was looking for you, but I didn't think to find you until later."

"No apology necessary. It's not a place I'm known to visit, if I'm being truthful, but I couldn't stop myself this morning."

Fina starts to turn away. "I'll let you be, then."

"Please don't go. There's room for both of us."

She sighs as she joins me, settling into the chair beside me. "I understand now why they say sleep deprivation is dangerous. I can't seem to get two thoughts to come together."

She says that while I rub my eyes, so all I can do is laugh. "I'm with you." I settle my hands on my lap. "So what brings you here at this hour of the morning? Shouldn't you still be snuggled in bed with a certain handsome courtier?"

She blushes so prettily I want to tease, not out of meanness but out of sheer joy to see her so happy, but then I see a deep sadness in her eyes, and my heart constricts.

"My handsome faux king has left."

"Is he coming back?"

"I don't think so."

"Oh, Fina, I'm sorry."

She pats my leg and changes the subject. "How did the deposition go?"

Pain slices through me, with a stiff embarrassment chaser. I know she's asking out of kindness, but it still hurts to think about it. I told Fina about everything because she deserved to know what might blow up around us.

"Trey was amazing. He arranged for it all to be by videoconference, and in the end, it wasn't as awful as I expected. I didn't enjoy it, by any stretch, but it was survivable."

"He's such a good man, and not just because he's my nephew."

"As the expression goes, the apple doesn't fall far from the tree, so I have to agree with you. He made a rough day as good as it could be."

And he had. Trey might be a small-town attorney, but that doesn't diminish his skill, intelligence, or dedication to the law, and I'm grateful I had such a bulldog in my corner.

"I'm glad it's over for you, though."

"'Glad' doesn't begin to cover it. What surprised me the most was almost all the questions were about very specific days and events, a lot of which I had zero involvement with. I was expecting something really personal and humiliating, and in the end, it was kind of... sterile." I huff a laugh. "That's not a complaint, mind you. Just unexpected."

Fina grows quiet and does a long study of her fingernails, enough to make me nervous.

"Honey, I'm so happy to hear it went well, and it makes me really uncomfortable with what I need to tell you."

All my nerves go rigid as a startled porcupine. "Give it to me straight. It'll be easier on me. On both of us, I bet."

"I won't diddle-daddle. Delores Bainbridge is causing trouble for Harville. She's sent letters to the senior members of the church and asked for a vote of confidence."

"She... *what?*"

"She's said she wants an investigation into whether Harville is a suitable shepherd to the flock when his behavior is publicly improper."

I try to clear my confusion. "She found out about the deposition?" I squeeze my eyes shut, then open them to see if anything is clearer. "That doesn't seem possible."

"She didn't mention the lawsuit, but she mentioned you and Harville and the hot spring."

I laugh. I have to. "Come on, Fina. This has to be a joke. It's the 2020s, for the love of Pete, and he kissed me. It's not like we were having wild sex on the steps."

"I know this sounds utterly ridiculous. It is utterly ridiculous. The thing about the Presbyterian Church is, it's extremely egalitarian, and any member can bring any issue before the presbytery at any time."

I fidget in my seat, but realize what I'm doing and stop. "What's her goal? I can't imagine a pastor's going to get recalled because he kissed a woman in public. Jesus, should I start sewing a scarlet A on my tops this morning?"

Fina lifts a what-can-you-do? shoulder. "The thing is, I can't believe she thinks anything major will come of this. I think she's trying to embarrass Harville because he asked her to resign her position in the church office more than inflict any real damage."

"Ooof. I didn't know."

"Harville is a terrific pastor, and he usually has good staff around him, but Delores went from a mild pain in the ass to a busybody on steroids after Madison left."

"It's pretty obvious she wanted to be the next Mrs. Pastor of St. Andrew's."

"She didn't take it lightly that he never showed the slightest interest in her."

I burst off the seat and pace around before forcing myself to sit back down. "My brain can't sort this out. It sounds like a horrendously bad screenplay. What does Delores possibly conceive could happen in her favor from all this?"

"I think she somehow feels scorned, which is bizarre."

"Wait, how do you know all this?"

"Let's just say the church secretary is best friends with Lorraine Pepperdine's daughter, and Lorraine is—"

"One of the Grannies."

"Yup. Fastest mode of information transmission in three counties.

Which is why I can tell you the senior staff is meeting at three o'clock this afternoon."

I rub my brow ridge, trying to stave off a headache, then look back at Fina. "I thought the Grannies were off on a Christmas cruise."

"They leave tomorrow."

"Ah, well, thanks for telling me. I'll go into town and talk to Harville. Maybe we can smooth this over before I leave."

Fina starts visibly. "Leave? What do you mean?"

Blood heats my cheeks as I realize the many conversations I've had with Fina about how it would be better if I left Magnolia Bloom happened only in my mind.

"I didn't mean that to come out so baldly. I've been practicing almost nonstop in my head how to tell you for the last two days."

If blood rushed to my face, it has raced away from hers. "Kiki, please, please tell me you're not leaving."

"Not today. I wouldn't do that to you. But we've gotten all the big events done, and Christmas Eve dinner is a walk in the park by comparison. It'll be quiet for a while. The historical data says we have steady but small bookings until at least March."

"True, but I can't do this by myself."

"Mina's back, isn't she?"

"They got in late last night."

I realize she's stiff, and she's shaking. I put a hand on her arm, my alarm bells going off like mad. "Are you okay?"

She takes several long breaths, but everything seems obviously strained. I don't have to be a trained body-language expert to know she's stressed out.

"I'm fine. I was taken by surprise, is all." She gets up from the seat, all of her usual grace lacking. "I'll let you get back to what you're doing. We'll talk later."

I stand and follow her, determined to get to the bottom of this, but she cuts me off. "Before I forget, your cousin Ally came by my office yesterday and talked to me for a bit. She wants to know if it's okay if she uses Brian's little house and barn out by the lake for a while."

I frown. "Okay…"

"You have the final okay on housing assignments."

"I do?"

She nods. "Violet, Mina, and I had meetings to discuss any transitions, but things have been a little crazy these last weeks."

"Months, truth be told. The easy answer is, if you think it's fine, I certainly have no objection."

"Great, I'll let her know."

"Fina, hold up a minute. When you came in here, you said you were looking for me but didn't expect to find me here, so why are you here? Do you need some meditation time? Because you look wound tighter than a tick."

"No. I'm fine." Her denial is too quick and too sharp.

"Forgive me if I call bullshit. You don't seem fine."

She sighs and lets go of the door. "It's just I have a lot on my mind, about Anders. The last thing I want, though, is to pile any of my issues on your shoulders. You have enough to deal with."

I point with a stern finger at the chairs we vacated. "Sit. Now." To my surprise, she does. "So, what's the problem?"

She's silent for a long time before she heaves another long sigh. "Anders has basically given me an ultimatum." She looks at her watch. "But it doesn't matter. Time's up anyway."

"Time's up for what?"

"For me to join him in Copenhagen, to see where this renewed connection could go. Twelve o'clock was my cutoff."

"Noon? In like, two hours?"

"Two hours, two days, it doesn't matter. His pilot leaves at noon, with or without me. Then he's leaving for two months for a trip across Australia and New Zealand."

I sit back, blinking rapidly. "Wow. That sounds like the plot of a Hallmark movie."

She snuffles, and I reach across the seat to snag her a tissue. "Yeah, except in those movies, there's always a happy ending."

I wait until she's wiped her eyes and taken a long breath. "So explain to me why you're hesitating, even for a second."

She looks at her lap and starts shredding the tissue. "I—"

The door opens again, and to my delighted surprise, Mina rushes in. Fina jumps to her feet like a fire has been lit under her seat. "What are you doing here?"

Mina grabs her twin in a hug and then me. "What a fine way to greet your sister."

Fina shuts her eyes, and I swear she counts to five. "Can we save the chitchat for later? You got into town in the wee hours of the morning, so honestly, what are you doing here? Is something wrong?"

"Not with me." Mina pats my cheek. "Hello, lovely. How are you doing?"

I'm confused, but don't want to add to the taut energy in the room. "I'm okay. Or I will be."

Mina, as if she saw me mere seconds ago, points to the chairs. "Now, you two, sit." She pulls one over so we're an imperfect triangle.

Fina holds up a hand. "Wait a dadgum minute before we go one step further. First, I find Kiki here in the chapel, which is honestly the last place in this castle I expected." She winces and gives me an apologetic grimace. "Sorry, honey."

"No sorries. I'm sure it was a shock. It was a bit of a surprise to me, to be honest. I felt… compelled. It's totally weird."

Mina's smile is blinding. "It's nothing of the sort. I've been telling you for months, sister. The magic is coming back."

I stop myself from rolling my eyes or in any way indicating my doubt. Mina is so earnest, I can't be mean.

"Now, this little come-to-Jesus meeting is now in session." Mina folds her hands in her lap like a schoolteacher about to give a lesson. "You, sister, are being an idiot. Get your butt up, get your keys, and drive to that airfield and fly to Anders."

"How do you—"

We all lock eyes and say in unison, "The Grannies."

Mina gives a sharp up-and-down bob of her chin. "That's right. Anders's pilot was staying at the Rise and Bloom, and it seems he and Nina had quite a nice chat over dinner last night."

Fina fills me in. "Nina is Mabel Goodson's granddaughter."

I don't need to ask to know Mabel is one of the infamous Grannies.

"All the ins and outs aren't important," Mina says. "What is? You are being a *damn* fool."

Fina's chin goes up, challenge in her eyes. "I am not. I cannot leave the castle with no one in charge."

Clearly affronted, Mina rears back. "What am I? Chopped liver?"

"No, but you've got a new life ahead of you, and Kiki thinks she needs to move on, so I can't go. Not now. Maybe I can talk to Anders when he gets back from New Zealand. I'll have to see how everything sorts out."

"All you do is sort and plan and think and manage. For once in your life, Serafina Greene, jump off the cliff and fly."

The cairngorm on the necklace around my neck grows warm, and before I can stop myself, I add my two cents. "She's right, Fina. It's time for you to stop putting yourself last. I'm not running out the door. I promise you, no matter what happens with Harville, I won't leave Mina in a lurch."

"But—"

Mina's frown threatens to burn the tapestries off the wall. "When did I ever once tell you I was leaving my job here at the castle? Sure, I might not be able to work as many hours as we have all these years, but by golly, we've put in enough endless days. Kiki and I can handle things until we get more people on board. We've needed to for a long time now."

"But—"

"It's time for you to stop saying *but* and get your *butt* out of your chair. We're gonna break the land-speed record to get you to a certain private airfield if it's the last thing I do."

Fina's face goes white. "I can't. I haven't packed—"

"Packed, schmacked. Anders Jensen can afford to buy you a hundred wardrobes. I'll bet dimes to doughnuts he's got plenty of guest toothbrushes at his house, too. All you need is your passport and some gumption. Now, come on."

She stands and marches toward the door.

I put my hand on Fina's knee. "You need to go. Now. Call that pilot and tell him you're coming, and we'll ask the castle angels keep you off the Highway Patrol's radar."

"But—"

"Last time, Fina. No more buts. *Go.*"

Her legs are wobbly as she rises, then she sucks in a deep breath and straightens her shoulders.

Mina holds the door. "Come on, sister. We've got a plane to catch."

Fina squeezes me, and I squeeze back. "Go find your happiness, Fina. It's your turn."

She kisses my cheek, and Mina blows one to me from the hall.

Then I'm alone again.

It's a long time before I realize I've been standing there, staring at the door. I'm not sure exactly what just happened. At least Mina's explanation of the all-knowing Grannies makes more sense than any magical woo-woo, although there's a little part of me that wanted, for a second, to think it was real.

My watch says I have time to get cleaned up and get into town to talk to Harville before he does anything foolish in response to Delores's accusations. If I leave, the problem is solved. I won't let his tenure as pastor of his church suffer because of me. He doesn't deserve it. His congregants don't deserve it. The town doesn't deserve it.

But Harville does deserve to hear my decision straight from me. It's been a long stretch of days since my world crashed and burned around me, and he's been patient long enough.

I accept the consequences of my choices, even if it means breaking my own heart.

35
JULIETTE

It's farther to David Broder's house than I realized. Rory is driving us to a Hanukah luncheon his family is hosting, and while I don't need Rory to come with me, it's wonderful he agreed. The only thing missing in the truck is my little black-faced angel, who wasn't part of the invitation.

"Did Noelle ever text you back or call?"

My heart is sad to have to tell him no. "She hasn't responded, and I told her about the invitation as soon as I received it. I know it's not easy to fly from Paris to Dallas at the drop of a hat, but I hoped she'd thaw enough to come."

My mind goes to a line from Violet's journal seared to my heart. *Take care of each other. And please, somewhere in your tiny, perfect hearts, remember me.*

Rory takes my hand and kisses my knuckles. "I'm sorry, baby. I wanted that, too."

I look at the man who came out of—I laugh at myself—left field and has taken over my life. Well, not life, really, but heart certainly. My days are nothing short of blissful as I do the work I was born to do, restoring truly magnificent art and giving it a chance to shine once again, and my nights are filled with everything from movies and popcorn, holding hands on the couch, or having to lock Lulu in the barn so she'll leave us alone while we make love for hours at a time.

How it has all come to this, I truly do not understand, but I'm almost afraid it's a dream, and I'll somehow wake up in my apartment to the sounds of busy Parisians going about their day. So far, though, each morning I've awakened, most recently and often, in the arms of the man confidently driving his big truck toward a rather stunning mansion ahead of us.

I rub my hand down his arm and twine our fingers back together. "I'm glad you're with me." I use my free hand to indicate the house. "Have you been here?"

"Several times. The Broders have some pretty elegant soirees up there, and they host half the town every year or so. I don't go all the time, as fancy parties aren't at the top of my to-do list, but I can clean up enough not to embarrass anybody now and then."

Just as he is now *cleaned up* in fine wool pants, a pristinely white dress shirt, tie, and tailored blazer. I play-punch him on the shoulder. "Stop that."

"Nothin' to stop. I have no airs to put on, or need to. I'm a sheepherder, and I'm a damn good one. I can hold my own in about any conversation, unless you want to start talking about Sartre. I never could get my brain around his stuff."

Now I know he's teasing. We've spent many an evening discussing art and philosophy over glasses of wine, so while I accept he is no philosophical devotee, he studied more than herd and land management when he was in college, and his reading library is not completely filled with Western novels and thrillers.

"Don't play the hick with me, sir. I know better."

"Yeah, but don't let it get out. Don't want folks around here thinking I'm bigger than my britches."

I laugh, as he intends. His use of slang is magnified the more he tries to be self-deprecating. We don't have time for any additional teasing because we've arrived, and he's turning off the engine and assisting me out of the car.

Not that I need assisting. It's simply one of the elements of Southern manners I quite enjoy.

Holding Rory's hand as we walk up the long walkway helps ease my nerves. I'm not prone to them, but I'm going into a situation I have no preparation for. I've been in the finest salons of the world, so it's not the rather dramatic wealth on display intimidating me. It's meeting Mrs. Broder for the first time, and David's children. He has assured me his entire family wants to meet me, but I cannot help but be disconcerted.

Those feelings fade quickly as the door opens, and David invites us in. It's oddly comforting to see some trepidation in his eyes as he kisses my cheek and shakes Rory's hand. Neither of us has time to dwell on these feelings long, because the foyer becomes a melee of people, all wanting to either shake my hand or hug me, with equal welcome being given to Rory, albeit with less hugging. If I feared snobbery from the Broder clan, I'm delighted that if it exits, it's hidden exceptionally well.

Soon, I find myself completely lost with all the names thrown at me. I think I remember only his grandson Jacob, who has told me quite insistently he goes by Jake, because clearly the young man is a duplicate of his grandfather at a young age. On that alone, I can see why Violet fell for her Ephraim, all those years ago.

The thing is, my eye casts across the room to where Rory is talking with the woman I know is Mrs. Broder, the last person I have yet to meet. He is perfectly at ease, his smile, now a permanent part of my heart, creasing the mouth I love to kiss. I have never judged a man by his looks, my lovers ranging from French actors whose names are screamed by adoring fans, to bistro servers who will never be called good-looking. Rory is in the middle. He is, without question, absolutely handsome. But he's not a pretty man.

Which I have no objections with.

He sees me looking, and Mrs. Broder turns to follow his gaze. I can see her take a deep breath before she moves toward me. I step in as well, as I do not wish for her to think I'm waiting for her to approach. She reaches out a delicate hand, and I shake it. There is warmth and firmness in her grip, and I'm touched she does not try to pull away quickly.

"Mrs. Broder. It is… good to meet you."

Her mouth wavers for a second before firming into sincerity. "Please, you must call me Zivah. Welcome to our home."

She pulls me in and kisses my cheek. I admit I'm stunned, but also deeply touched. I return the greeting. "Thank you, Zivah. I'm delighted to be here."

And finally, I am. I know I'll never be an intimate part of this family, but I also have no need to be. Just meeting them, knowing that even deep wounds can heal, is enough.

A dulcet chime rings out, and David goes to the front door again while Zivah and I chat about some of the amazing art she has in her foyer. David has obviously told her what I do for a living, and she seems delighted to be able to speak to some of the deeper aspects of the pieces she has clearly spent a lot of time choosing.

We're discussing the Vincent Glinsky reclining nude sculpture when I hear a voice I instantly recognize. I do a slow turn and find my sister shaking David's hand, then Jake's hand, then excusing herself to come toward me.

"Oh, my," Zivah breathes when Noelle reaches us. "You truly are twins."

I don't want to say anything untoward to Noelle in front of Zivah, so I make the introductions and wait until the normal chitchat is finished and Zivah excuses herself, saying she needs to check on the luncheon.

I look at my sister, my stomach a knot. "I didn't know you were coming."

She shrugs one shoulder, a move she often uses. "I didn't either until the last minute. I stayed in Dallas last night to be sure this is what I wanted. That way, I could have left if I needed to."

A young boy who is clearly one of the great-grandsons comes up and offers us each a champagne flute filled with what I assume is a mimosa. We accept with our thanks and move through the room and out onto a small balcony.

I take a fortifying sip. "Did you meet Rory?"

"The redhead? Yes, I did."

My gut clenches, despite my determination not to overreact. "What does your tone mean?"

"It means nothing." Her words are blithe, but her intent is not. I know my sister, and she knows I know.

"You might as well say what you've come to say."

She takes a breath, and I give her credit for trying to get her temper under control. It seems when we were born she got all the fight genes, and I got all the flight ones.

"I've practiced what I want to say a thousand times, and yet all I can say right now is you've dated artists, musicians, lawyers, doctors. Some millionaires. One a billionaire! And you're choosing this?"

She doesn't have to point to Rory, who's still chatting with the Broder sons, to let me know exactly who she means.

I know my sadness has to reflect in my eyes in an equal dose with affronted anger. "I'm ashamed to hear such nonsense from you. I've never judged a man, or woman for that matter, by their titles or their bank accounts and certainly never their looks. I didn't think you did, either."

She blushes an angry red. "I don't mean I believe you have to marry someone who is wealthy, but honestly, what do you see in him?"

"I don't know... Kindness? Gentleness? Humor? Companionship?"

This time, she gives me more of a smirk. "All quaint, but I suppose these are the 2020s. It's as acceptable now for a man to find a sugar mama."

I draw back as if she's struck me. "I cannot express my disappointment, my shame, at what you're saying. I know we've had our differences, that we're hardly mirrors of each other except in appearance. But this is too far, even for you."

Her cheeks burn even brighter now, but I see remorse shadowing her eyes. "I'm sorry. I'm afraid for you. What can this man offer you?"

"Why do you think he has to offer me anything? Or what if all he has to offer is love, and that's more than enough?" I give her a hard look, the coldest I think I ever have in our entire lives. "Or what if you're simply jealous I no longer need you to control my every move?"

"You certainly didn't mind our arrangement for almost fifty years."

"True. You were bossy from the moment you came out of the womb."

We both take sharp breaths and long drinks from our stems.

It's then that Rory meets my eyes from all the way inside the house. It's a moment, but it's enough, and I'm fortified.

More, I'm happy.

"Noelle, I love you. You're my sister and truly half of me. I will admit I spent most of our lives letting you be the conductor. I never wanted to do the things you do so brilliantly. But the time has come when I want something different, and I know this change is massive and sudden. For that, I'm sorry. But I do not apologize for knowing, for the first time, exactly what I want to do with my life."

"I still do not understand how you can give up a dream position at Sotheby's. Of Paris, for goodness sake."

I put my free hand on her arm, giving it a squeeze. I try to lighten my tone, but I need her to hear me. "I'm not ready to give it up, which you'd know if you'd read my texts. I'm talking with the director about how the position might work remotely. I find I don't want a position that would literally take all my waking hours, no matter how much it would satisfy the artist in me. Not long ago, I wouldn't have hesitated to say yes. Now I'm suggesting a narrower focus for the position, which I can do much of from here, then fly to Paris when I need to. This is the modern world, you know."

She looks stricken, and something finally shifts completely inside me. I put my flute down, take hers and set it aside, then take her hands in mine.

"I know you are scared you are losing me. You are not. Yes, I have a new vision, and it is very different from our lives before. But nothing changes my love for you. You are half my heart, and I will never be more than a video chat or flight away."

Tears spill down her cheeks, and her fingers tremble before she pulls them away, but only so she can pull me into her arms. My tears fall as freely as weeks upon weeks of distance from her fade.

With the barriers torn down, we can't seem to talk fast enough, and before we're close to finished, Rory is walking toward us, his face more reserved than I've ever seen. I don't like it, this sense that he's uncertain.

I gesture him closer and make a formal introduction to my testy twin, but Noelle being Noelle, now that she's decided everything will be okay, gives him a Texas-sized hug, making the genuine joy return to the man who owns me body and soul.

Love has come to me unexpectedly, which is why I cannot stop marveling at it.

As Rory wraps his strong arms around me and chats with my restored sister, my world is complete. I have no doubt this luncheon will be lovely. I'll learn lots of nice things about the Broders, and I look forward to learning more as the years roll on.

But the only one I truly want kisses my temple and tells me it's time.

He doesn't realize it, but he's right.

It is time.

For me.

Oh, and Mom? I didn't get to know you, but I promise you, somewhere in my heart, I'll always remember you, and Noelle and I will take care of each other. Always.

36
KIKI

I CAN'T QUITE BELIEVE how calm I am as I drive into town. I've timed it so I'm a good thirty minutes early. Partly because I'm a chickenshit. I want to be there early enough to say what I need to say, but not leave enough time for a long discussion. Harville has enough to do today.

I park in the front and hurry in. There's a notice on the glass saying the office staff is off until after Christmas, but the door opens when I tug. So far, so good.

I hurry toward Harville's office, stopping when I near his voice coming from the conference room I've passed during my visits to the church.

"Thank you all for coming early. Pastor Kamaka wants to get on the road to her family for the holiday, and I can only apologize I've asked you here at all."

There are murmurs of other voices, and panic floods me. I thought I had more time. This isn't how this is supposed to go.

"I'll get right to the point. In recent weeks, a congregant has become increasingly displeased with my leadership and has elected to bring their concerns before you, as is their right. My reason for this informal meeting is to make clear to each of you as ministers, elders, and deacons of this church where I stand."

Someone says something, but they are too far away for me to make out the words.

"Thank you. I appreciate your support before I even begin, but we must never discount the concerns of any of our members."

He's incorrect. I want to offer a discount of my fist to Delores Bainbridge's mouth, and if that's wrong, too bad.

"This won't take long because what I have to tell you is quite simple. I love this church. I love this flock. I love being here and being part of a wonderful community. But my vocation does not demand I sacrifice all of me. I'm not asked to be a martyr, nor are any of you. We are to be servants. Those are different things. I am not going to give in to a demand, a ransom, an extortion. I am human and fallible, but no one, not even any of you here, has the right to tell me who I can love."

My heart stops right there. I want to bust in and tell him to stop. That's not what he's supposed to be saying.

"I am in love with a very special woman. I was completely unprepared for it to happen, either so quickly or completely, but I am telling you my behavior with her has never been improper. It is the 2020s. Kissing someone in public is hardly lascivious, so I will not apologize for it. You do need to know that she does not share our affiliation to the church, but there are no rules stating our partners must. I don't know what the future holds, but if you decide my pursuit of my affection is at odds with the running of this church, then I will resign. No matter how much I love it here, I love her more. If you don't agree with my decision, then I will make any transition to a new pastor as painless as possible. But I will leave. Thank you all for listening."

It seems every other voice in the room starts talking at once, but I can't make out individual words. I press my back to the wall and slide down, my legs too unsteady to hold me. I hug my knees to my chest for long, long minutes, then I force myself to stand. I look to the outer door, everything inside me screaming at me to run. *Run! Now!*

It takes all my strength, but I don't. Clenching my fists, I take the few steps to the conference room door, and Harville's head whips up as he looks at me. I'm caught in the fierceness of his blue eyes, his face firmly set. He's not angry.

He's determined. Unmovable.

He looks down the long table and says, "If you all will excuse me, I need to step outside for a minute and give you time to talk."

I wait until we're in his office, the door shut, before I launch myself into his arms. I clutch his shirt in my fists and try to shake him. "You weren't supposed to do that."

My words are muffled against his chest, but he obviously hears me.

"I wasn't supposed to do what? Tell the truth?"

I arch back. "I came early to talk sense into you because I was afraid this very thing would happen."

I don't try to stop him when he bends and claims my mouth in a searing kiss. I've missed his touch so desperately, although I've denied it to myself for the long days we haven't seen each other.

"I'm glad you heard. I'm glad I didn't know you were there, because now you can never doubt my sincerity."

"I've never doubted you, even for a second. But what's between us is too new. We don't even know if it will last, and you're putting your position with the church on the line." My chest constricts, and I can hardly finish. "For me."

"And I won't take back a single word."

In one smooth move, he shifts and takes a seat in one of the guest chairs, pulling me onto his lap. I probably should fight him, but I can't. Moreover, I don't want to.

Pressing me to his shoulder, he kisses the top of my head before resting his cheek on my hair.

"My vow to be of service here is not one of blind obedience, nor subjugation to any one person's belief about how I should behave. What kind of leader would I be if, by example, I showed my congregation I'd throw away the greatest blessing of my life to accede to such a ridiculous demand? That would turn me into a bitter subjugate rather than a willing servant."

"But there are rules you have to follow, rules you agreed to."

"Of course, but my partner is not required to be a member of the church. Pastors aren't puppets. At least this one isn't."

"This is all very noble, but it's not going to stop gossip and rumors. People can hurt you."

"Gossip and rumors are cancers, and the only way to defeat them is to refuse to give them fuel. I will not live my life bent and swayed by every person who might get put out with me. If my leadership doesn't serve this community, then it's time for me to move on."

He tips my chin up and kisses me, then wipes the tears from my eyes with his thumbs. "You fill the empty places inside me. You made me see how alone I've been, for a long time. This church fills a piece of me, yes. But you fill my soul."

"You're barely divorced. This is all too soon."

His *hmmm* is short and dry and sad. "My marriage was over a long time ago, but I was holding on, hoping somehow a miracle would happen." He strokes my hair away from my eyes with those long, capable, gentle fingers. "The thing is, my prayer was answered. Just not how I imagined it would be."

I sniffle, the tears coming again. "I can't be the reason you lose this church. I can't."

He pulls back so I can see his eyes, even though mine are watery again.

"You can't unbreak a glass or unring a bell. I can't unknow how much I love you, how much I need you."

I snuggle into his chest and rest, absorbing all he's said, relishing the feel of his strength as he holds me against him. I breathe in the faint, crisp scent of his cologne, holding my breath so I can infuse it into my lungs.

"You chose me."

I don't realize I spoke the words aloud until his chest rumbles against my ear. "Of course I did."

I lift my head this time so he can see my eyes. "You don't understand. In my entire life, no one has ever chosen me, fought for me, claimed me."

"Then let me make it clear. I want to claim you forever, Kiki

MacInnes. I want you to be my wife. I want you to be the mother of my children, if that's what you want, too. I want you to be my partner. Forever. Please say you'll take a chance on a really imperfect man who loves you, body and soul."

I stroke my fingers down his jaw to his chin. "Only if you're willing to take a chance on a flagrantly flawed, recovering alcoholic with a whole cargo plane of baggage."

"I can handle it. We can handle it."

"I love you, Harville. I can't believe of all the men I could have fallen in love with, it's with a small-town pastor. The odds in Vegas have to be astronomical on this hand."

"Don't expect me to say I'm sorry."

"I'd appreciate it if you didn't."

"You still haven't said yes."

I hold the feeling, deep and strong, for a long, precious moment. Not to torture him, but to simply let the warmth expand inside me, open all the places that have been locked down for so long. I'm scared. Scared to death. But I'm more scared of not finding out if forever is as wonderful as this moment right now.

"Yes." I tip his chin down and reach up to punctuate my answer. "Yes today, and yes forever."

Our kisses grow from tender and full of commitment to raw and full of desire. I finally pull away, gasping.

"I think you'd better get back to your meeting."

His breathing is equally ragged as he rests his forehead against mine. "I think that would be a good idea."

"Can I see you later?"

"I'm going to be really late tonight. I have several families who've asked to meet with me, and the truth is, I've been keeping myself busy so I could survive each day without you in it. Now I wish I'd said no to a few of the requests coming across my desk."

"Tomorrow, then? For Christmas Eve dinner at the castle?"

"Wouldn't miss it."

I move in for one last, searing kiss, then make him let me up.

"Finish what you've got to do. I'll go home and count the hours until tomorrow."

He's clearly reluctant to obey, which makes my heart happy, but he does, leaving me alone in his sanctum.

I turn in a slow circle, wondering, despite our rosy hopes, how this will all work out. As I hesitate, the cairngorm heats up against my skin, and I know this is right.

He's right.

We're right.

The castle magic doesn't promise you won't have hard times, but it does promise you'll have the strength to make it through them.

I close my fingers around the stone and press it against my heart.

I'll just have to have faith.

37
KIKI

I KNOW, intellectually, that the turkey, fixings, vegetables, and rolls I've consumed are not particularly unique or special, but each bite tasted like ambrosia. And as perfect as the food has been, the decorations are even better. From our plaid tablecloth, to the green runner. To the candelabras with every red candle lit. To the wreaths hung on the walls. To one of the small, but numerous, Christmas trees in almost every room. This particular one is adorned in light blue and white and everything Scottish.

I look around the huge table and do a silent roll call. Mina and CT, who look like they're about to eat each other.

Juliette, who's snuggled in the curve of Rory's arm. They're laughing at something Trey just told them.

My cousin Ally is also at the far end of the table, joining in on the jokes, even though there's a sadness baked deep in her eyes. We haven't had time to catch up yet, but we will.

Now that I'm home to stay.

I pull my thoughts back in and give CT's daughters a wave. I'm especially happy to see Bethanie practically glowing from her announcement she's gotten her one-month chip.

Paige and Zach are about as wrapped up in each other as CT and Mina, and they're getting a lot of grief from their kids. I'm beyond excited to see Ainsley and Aiden again and meet their kiddos.

We all miss Fina, but she's called and texted, making sure we all know she got to Copenhagen hale and hearty. Turns out, not only was the plane waiting for her at the airfield, Anders was, too. He fibbed when he said he'd go home. Instead, he took care of a lot of US business while he hoped for a Christmas miracle.

It seems there's a lot of those happening this year.

Harville shakes my hand, the one he's been holding under the tablecloth practically the whole evening.

"Where are you?"

"I'm here," I assure him. "I'm very much here. I'm looking around and seeing how much I have to be thankful for."

Paige and Ainsley slip away from the table, returning with an enormous pie in each hand, and all our attention is taken with making ourselves miserable.

It's not until a couple of hours later, as Harville and I are snuggled together on one of the couches in the family room, watching the Hallmark channel on the big screen, that I realize how perfect this day has been. Every single thing, from food, to family, to the enormous Douglas fir in the center of the room nearly touching the top of the vaulted ceiling. The lights twinkle, the bulbs glow, and the ornaments dance a bit when the heater kicks on and creates a breeze.

And I'd finally faced the armory, showing Harville the six generations of MacInneses... especially the portraits of Evajean and Alisdair who, thankfully, seem at peace in their frames.

I toss off our lap blanket so I can reach the package I stashed behind our seats earlier this morning. The box is small but perfectly wrapped by Traycee herself. I stopped by the Emporium after I left the church and was gratified to find her there. We talked a bit, and I told her I was still here, if she was ready. When she was ready. She started crying, but didn't make any promises. That's a good thing. Better no promise than a lie.

"Christmas isn't until tomorrow, you know." He doesn't, however, give the gift back.

"I know, but I've always loved Christmas Eve more. I used to sit and look at the tree and the lights for hours, holding the anticipation around me like the best blanket ever."

"Then it's only fair I give you this." He reaches from his end of the couch and comes back with a box not unlike the size of mine.

"Sneaky. I didn't see you bring that in."

"Maybe SP also stands for Sneaky Pastor."

"Oooh, I like it." I scooch back over against him and cover us again. "Before you open that, though, I need to tell you something."

"What?" He fits his arm around me, and I wonder how he intends to open his present in this position, but I stay on target.

"We better get married fast, because my resistance to you is pretty much nonexistent. Still, I refuse to add leading you into temptation to my penance list."

"Too late. Already led and bought real estate." He kisses me to let me know he's closed escrow on a pretty large plot. "You should know I wasn't a virgin when I got married, and we didn't wait for our wedding night, either. I'm hardly a paragon of virtue here."

"Maybe not, but I'm not budging on this one, Preacher Man." I have to pause for another round of pure kissing indulgence. By the time I push him away, my good intentions are strained with the desire to throw them out the window, but I'm determined to finish my thought. "It's because I respect the rules you play by, and I've bent or broken enough of them to date to have no need to ask you to bend yours. If you think it's silly in this day and age, too old-fashioned—"

"I think it's wonderful." He shifts in his seat, giving me a wry smile. "Just a little uncomfortable."

"You're not the only one." My tone is wry but conveys I'm just as frustrated.

"If you ever decide to come to a service, you'll never hear me say sex is bad. I happen to think it's one of the greatest gifts we've been given, to be able to join so completely with another person. It's not the be-all and end-all of human existence, but when it's with the right partner, it is amazing."

I pause, his words striking a sore spot. "Is that going to be a problem?"

He shakes his head in confusion. "Sex? I hardly think so."

"No, me coming—or rather, not coming—to services?"

He moves so he can take my hands in his. "Listen to me, but more, hear me. You do not have to hold the same beliefs as I do. As long as we respect each other, we can find a path through anything." He stops for a long moment. "Do you know how I can tell within two minutes if a couple I'm counseling is going to make it?"

"Do tell."

"If they are kind to each other. If there is kindness and respect between two people, almost anything can be overcome, navigated."

My lower lip trembles. "Do you really believe that? Honestly?"

"With every fiber of my being."

"Then I think we'll be okay."

Round whatever this is of lips and tongue and teeth and hands tells me he's having as hard a time convincing himself to agree to our temporary moratorium on what we both want more than oxygen at the moment. He leans back against the couch and moans. "I'll tell you this. You're gonna have to make an honest man of me, and quick."

A chyron running across the bottom of the TV screen catches my eye and makes me squeal with happiness. I scramble off the couch, grabbing his hand and pulling him to his feet. "Come on. Hurry! Grab the blanket."

Clearly confused, he nonetheless obeys as I half drag him the long distance to the doors to the balcony. Sure enough, the weatherman is right.

Snow is falling.

Little, light flakes, to be sure, but I'll take them. White Christmases aren't unheard of here. The information scrolling across the screen said the last one was in 2012, but I don't care about statistics. What I care about is, I'm standing on a balcony. Of an honest-to-goodness castle. And snow is falling on Christmas Eve.

Most of all, I'm in the arms of, honestly, the last man on earth I could have imagined falling in love with. He's standing behind me, his arms wrapped around me, and a blanket warms us both.

The flurries probably wouldn't impress someone used to snow, but to me, watching the white bits flutter to the ground is another one of those miracles I never believed in.

I realize in our haste—well, my haste—we've forgotten our presents, but I've already gotten mine. The best one I could ever have asked for. I've been forgiven and am loved for being exactly who I am, pretty places, ugly faults, and all.

But so much more than that, I've forgiven myself. And I may be starting to love me a little bit, too.

A trill of flute notes comes from my back pocket and Harville leans away so I can pull out my phone and a chuckle tickles my ear.

"Is that *Kung Fu Fighting?*"

I nod, but can't laugh with him. "Very good, eighties boy. It is indeed."

I'm not surprised he hears the tension in my voice as I check my texts and his arm slips around my shoulders in comfort and support. "Bad news?"

"Yes and no. Let's get in out of the cold and I'll explain."

We return to the couch but instead of snuggling back in the blanket, I'm searching for my socks and shoes. "It's Traycee. The song is an inside joke between us, but the point is, I promised her I'd always let her calls come through. She relapsed weeks ago when Vern left her, but had been keeping up a false front. She's making an outcry, and I need to be there for her. She's ready to go to rehab, and I'll make some calls, but I doubt I can find her a bed tonight. It'll probably take all day tomorrow to get her a spot. I'm sorry."

I type a reply to Traycee to tell her I'm on my way.

Harville hands me my elusive left boot and waits until I've tied the laces before pulling me close. "Let's make a pact right to never say we're sorry when we're doing the things we feel are part of our mission. Sometimes it's going to suck being married to me. I can unfortunately promise that."

I kiss him long and slow, melding into the heat of him. The love of him.

"I guess we're kind of spiritual first responders and it's no nine-to-five gig."

His basso laugh vibrates against my chest, rippling all the way to the bottom of my soul, filling me. Completing me. "Good way to put it, but the important thing is, we have a lifetime of holidays to share."

I flail a hand toward my apartment. "I've got to get my coat and get going."

"I know. Do you want me to come with you?"

And there it is. That instant dive into giving, into support, into what-do-you-need, not what's-interrupting-me.

I put my forehead against his chest, shaking my head as laughter bubbles up despite the sadness of the moment.

"What's funny?" His tone is clearly confused, which only makes me laugh harder.

I swipe my thumbs over the dimples that are at least the third most amazing thing about him. "I'm gonna need you to not be quite so perfect, okay? I need some deep, dark confession pretty soon or I don't think I'll be able to stand you."

His mouth opens and shuts and then he tilts his head, his eyes squinting. "I can guarantee I'm not perfect. I haven't had the opportunity to prove it yet, but it'll come, I promise."

"Good, because I can't be the only broken one in this relationship."

He goes completely still, in his Harville way, and waits until I look up and meet his eyes. "You're not broken, Kiki. Not anymore. And when some cracks show up in the future, I'll be here with gold to fill them in. Just be prepared to do the same for me."

"Deal."

Our kiss this time borders on sacred and I fight the old voices, the mocking ones in the back of my head trying to downplay this moment that feels nothing short of enchanted. I know they'll never be silenced completely, but I have a very tall, very dark, very sexy defense system now. And I plan on employing him at every available opportunity.

I pull away and we go our separate ways, him to his home as there's no need for him to hang around the castle all night, and me to my suite as I throw on a coat and head down the back stairs and out into the cold.

I look around the grounds stretching far away to the banks of the lake and see nothing but ghostly shadows on the cold ground. The night is still but for the lightest wafts of snow still drifting down, sound blanketed by the flakes.

I take a moment to let my car heat up, and realize Mina's right. The magic is back at Castle MacInnes. The miracles are back.

I reverse out of my parking spot and head down the road, a smile that just might be permanent on my lips.

I'm living proof.

MAGNOLIA BLOOM, in order

Springtime in Magnolia Bloom
(Coming March 2021)
Mistletoe and Magnolia (Book 2)
Return to Magnolia Bloom (Book 1)
Welcome to Magnolia Bloom (Origin novella)

Please sign up for my newsletter at PaulaAdler.com to receive my next free novella, updates, and information on all future releases. You can find my author pages at all the usual places: Amazon, Goodreads, BookBub, Facebook

ABOUT THE AUTHOR

Paula Adler is a born and raised Texan with a traveling soul. If she's not writing, she's out SCUBA diving or dancing. She's doing her dream… one book at a time. For more information, please visit https://www.PaulaAdler.com

Made in the USA
Middletown, DE
19 September 2021